DEATH
BENEFIT

ALSO BY ROBIN COOK

DEATH

BENEFIT

ROBIN COOK

**Doubleday Large Print
Home Library Edition**

G. P. PUTNAM'S SONS

New York

This Large Print Edition, prepared especially for Doubleday Large Print Home Library, contains the complete, unabridged text of the original Publisher's Edition.

PUTNAM

G. P. PUTNAM'S SONS
Publishers Since 1838
Published by the Penguin Group
Penguin Group (USA) Inc., 375 Hudson Street, New York, New York 10014, USA

Penguin Books Ltd, Registered Offices: 80 Strand, London WC2R 0RL, England

ISBN 978-1-61793-493-3

Printed in the United States of America

This is a work of fiction. Names, characters, places, and incidents either are the product of the author's imagination or are used fictitiously, and any resemblance to actual persons, living or dead, businesses, companies, events, or locales is entirely coincidental.

While the author has made every effort to provide accurate telephone numbers and Internet addresses at the time of publication, neither the publisher nor the author assumes any responsibility for errors, or for changes that occur after publication. Further, the publisher does not have any control over and does not assume any responsibility for author or third-party websites or their content.

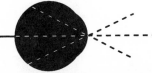

**This Large Print Book carries the
Seal of Approval of N.A.V.H.**

To all the foster children

ACKNOWLEDGMENTS

A writer needs a lot of friends: At least this writer does. These are the friends that don't mind fielding a call, often out of the blue, and being asked a question of fact or preference, or being willing to read an outline or character study and lend an opinion. You all know who you are, and thanks. Of course there's always Joe Cox, who knows more about law and business than I'll ever know, and Mark Flowenbaum, a real forensic pathologist. And, of course, there's Jean Reeds Cook, who is a great reader and doesn't allow me any slack. Thank you all.

DEATH
BENEFIT

PROLOGUE

Prek Vllasi touched his right forefinger to the scar on his upper lip, where the cleft had been crudely repaired when he was an infant. It was something he did without thinking many times each day, more often when he was under pressure. Right now, standing in a filthy room on the tenth floor of a derelict Soviet-era tower block in the Russian city of Krasnoyarsk, he was getting more nervous by the minute.

Prek checked his watch again and looked over at Genti Hajdini. Genti was leaning against a foldout table, periodically yawning as he worked on a fingernail with his pocketknife. Every time he saw Genti, Prek was slightly taken aback by the straight lines of his lieutenant's beaky nose. From this angle, it looked more like the sharp end of a hatchet. Yes, he was sure the Chechens were coming, Genti had just told him for the tenth time. Good people back home in Albania had vouched for this outfit. Even though he could feel it, Prek checked the Makarov pistol stuck in his belt at the small of his back. The Puma bag containing 500,000 euros was on the floor. Genti had brought the guns and money hidden in a truckload of Turkish fruit he'd driven deep into Russia. No wonder he was tired.

There was nothing else to do but wait.

It was freezing—the temperature had topped out at twenty below and the sun would be gone in an hour and a half. Outside, the sky was the same dirty color as the buildings and the ground. Prek started pacing around the large room, what must once have been a communal area in the apartment block that sat just outside town. Prek was a meticulous man; he'd read up about Krasnoyarsk. Forty miles or so down the Yenisei River was the town of Zheleznogorsk, better known by its old Soviet name, Krasnoyarsk-26. This was a closed city, home to factories handling God-knows-what exotic and dangerous materials to make God-knows-which agents of destruction. Weapons-grade plutonium had been produced in three nuclear reactors there, the last of which had just recently closed. For years the Soviets simply dumped the radioactive waste from the nuclear plants straight into the river until they thought better of it and drilled hundreds of wells to pump the deadly sludge underground. Prek knew there was as much radioactivity as a hundred Chernobyls humming away in the caverns around here, another reason he'd be happy to get out of this place.

Quietly, two men walked in. Wiry and rugged-looking, they wore identical black overcoats. Genti looked up.

"Artur? Nikolai?"

One of them stepped forward until he

was ten feet from Prek. "I'm Artur," he said, and gestured back to his companion. "That's Nikolai."

Prek looked back and across to Genti, who nodded. These were the names he had been given: Artur Zakoyev and Nikolai Dudaev.

"This is a lot of money you're asking for," Prek said in Russian.

"This stuff isn't easy to get," said Artur. "If it's easy to get, why do you need us? What do you want this for, anyway? You making a big boom somewhere?" Artur grinned. He was referring to the fact that the substance could be used to make triggers for nuclear weapons.

Prek winced. He'd seen better teeth on a mule.

"What we do with it is our business," said Prek. "How do we even know it's genuine? It needs to be good, not some old shit you had lying around in a warehouse."

"You have to trust us. That's why you pay us. You have the money?"

Prek looked down at the bag and kicked it toward Artur. Prek glanced at Nikolai standing behind his boss and to his right. *That's the second time he's looked at his watch*, Prek said to himself. Artur stepped forward and went down on his haunches, his hands in front of him. Everyone knew the drill: they kept their hands down and in plain sight by their sides. Artur unzipped the bag and pulled out a brick of hundred-euro notes and flicked through it with his thumb. Prek saw Nikolai glance at his watch again.

He's waiting for someone, thought Prek. He looked at Genti, who was watching Artur counting money. *He's waiting for someone and they're late.*

"Now you have to trust me," said Prek. He was in a hurry. "The money's all there so I'll take the merchandise."

Artur stood up and held up his hands.

"Okay, okay." His right arm still aloft as if he were taking an oath, Artur reached into his right coat pocket with his left hand and pulled out a small object. Prek rocked forward and back on his heels—he'd had no time to react but he knew Genti could shoot both Chechens in the head in a second. This wasn't a gun—it was a small aluminum vial about three inches long and an inch around. Prek moved forward, took the vial, and put it in his pants pocket. Nikolai said something Prek didn't understand and without another word, the Chechens turned and were gone, Artur clutching the bag with the money.

"Come on," Prek said in Albanian.

When he reached the doorway, he turned left, the opposite direction to the way they'd come in and where the Chechens were now headed.

"The car's back there," Genti said, but Prek was running now, heading to a stairway on the far side of the building. They could hear loud voices echoing up from the other stairway and the sound of hobnail boots on cement. This was who the Chechens were expecting, and it wasn't the chamber of commerce coming to thank the Albanians for their business. Fortunately, Russian timekeeping hadn't gotten any better since the fall of Communism.

Guns drawn, Prek and Genti raced down the stairs. Prek saw parked police cars and black vans ahead, doors hanging open. He turned and ran around the back of the building, Genti following close behind. The Chechens were in front of them, running toward a solitary car parked in the corner of a walled-in courtyard. *Fucking ama-teurs.* Prek saw the opportunity.

The Chechens jumped in the car, Artur throwing it into reverse and backing up and around so the car faced forward. Before Artur could get it into drive, Prek and Genti were on the car, firing into the windshield three times each. Artur was hit and thrown back into his seat, his foot pushing onto the accelerator so the engine raced in neutral. Prek and Genti pulled open the doors and dragged the Chechens out. Artur was dead, his head blown open. Nikolai had been shot twice in the neck, blood bubbling out of his airway as his life ebbed away. Prek slammed the car into drive and took off, looking for another road out of the complex. Prek's heart was threatening to break out of his rib cage and he cursed loudly. He was sitting on glass and he had to lean forward so his head didn't come into contact with whatever of Artur's gray matter was splattered on the headrest behind him.

"What happened?" he yelled.

"They sold us out," said Genti. "There . . ." He pointed ahead to a track off the service road leading away from the apartment complex. He knew they wouldn't last five minutes on a highway in a car with no windshield before being spotted.

"Hey . . ." Genti said as Prek slowed down on the unpaved road. Prek looked over and Genti turned his head to look in the backseat. Though streaked with blood, the Puma bag sat perfectly safe. Prek banged on the steering wheel and turned to Genti and both men laughed long and hard.

PART I

1.

COLUMBIA UNIVERSITY MEDICAL CENTER
NEW YORK CITY
FEBRUARY 28, 2011, 7:23 A.M.

The girl, twelve, awakens with a start.
She's lying on a thin mattress on a low,
narrow bed and circling around her is
a pack of girls. They're older—sixteen,
seventeen—and as they shuffle along,
they're staring down at her with obviously sinister intentions. Some are sup-
pressing giggles, others are smiling, but
these smiles aren't signs of happiness,

they're smiles of anticipation. It's still nighttime. There are other cots in the long room and the girl knows the other occupants are awake but they won't move to help her because they know what's about to happen.

Transfixed with terror, the girl is unable to react as the mob falls upon her. As she's being dragged off the bed she sees her chief tormentor, the ringleader's face twisted in a manic grimace. Still, she knows better than to scream for help. Somewhere in the dormitory, there's suddenly a loud banging sound. And again.

Pia Grazdani, twenty-six, woke up in a panic and a cold sweat, unsure for a second of where she was. She breathed out with relief when she realized she was safe and in her dorm room at Columbia University Medical Center. Someone was banging on the door.

Taking another deep breath, Pia leaped out of bed in her flannel pajamas, took three quick strides to the door, flipped the dead bolt, and pulled it open. As she expected, it was George, her fellow fourth-year medical student.

"Pia, do you know what time it is? This isn't a day you want to be late." His tone was not as strident as the syntax suggested. At six-one, George Wilson had seven inches on Pia, but somehow he always felt smaller when he was in her presence. As he explained it to himself, she had what he called a tough, plucky personality and could at times be rather volatile.

Pia held the door open and George took a couple of steps into the small dorm room. Pia let the door close and turned and hurried past George, pulling her pajama top over her head as she did so. George looked at Pia's bare back, at the cut of her shoulder blades framing her flawless olive-brown skin. She stood in front of her low dresser and pulled out some clothes for the day. As she did so she caught George's stare in the mirror.

"Sorry, George, I couldn't sleep and then when I could sleep I was dreaming. You go ahead, I'll catch up with you later today."

With that said, Afrodita Pia Grazdani turned her full attention to getting ready. When she pulled down her pajama pants, George turned his head and looked out the window. He would have preferred to watch her but was afraid to do so. Instead he concentrated on the dramatic view that he and the other medical students had learned to take for granted. He could see the giant George Washington Bridge connecting Manhattan with New Jersey. Its usual morning rush-hour traffic was at a standstill in both directions.

"It's okay, Pia," said George, "I'll wait." Then, searching for something to say, he added, "I guess you still haven't figured out how to use that alarm clock I bought for you. I can't get you up every day—you've got to do something about being on time. You could always use the alarm on your cell phone if you'd prefer."

George stopped talking. He'd turned his attention back to the room and was immediately transfixed by the sight of Pia brushing her jet-black hair. He felt an immediate crushing sadness. The few times Pia and George had slept together, four exactly, Pia had asked George to leave before he fell asleep. And each time she'd stood at that same dresser with her back to him brushing her hair, just as she was doing now. Over the course of time George had become painfully aware they hadn't truly slept together at all those four precious times, they'd just had sex: Wham bam thank you ma'am, in reverse.

George was athletically inclined and good-looking in a preppy, stereotypical fashion with an unruly shock of blond hair and a ready smile. During his Ivy League college days it had drifted back to him that many preppy women found him to be a "hunk." There had never been a shortage of willing girlfriends. But George had set his sights early in life on becoming a doctor and did not want to become involved. As a consequence, George's romantic life had been a string of one-night stands and short flings with little emotional commitment. He'd hurt people, he knew, especially now that the tables had been turned and he was the "hurtee" rather than the "hurter." With Pia it was completely different. She truly didn't seem to care, and it drove him crazy. Numerous times he had told himself to forget her, that she was damaged goods, but he couldn't. Instead he'd become obsessed to an extent. George desperately wanted to have a romantic relationship with this woman, but he had no idea what she wanted and why it hadn't happened. He'd been trying during three and a half years of medical school.

"Come on, what are you waiting for?" Pia barked when she popped out of her tiny bathroom still applying a pale lipstick that was more for lip protection than color. She grabbed her medical student white coat, pulled it on, and draped her medical center ID around her neck. She held open the door behind her as if she were the one waiting.

Emotionally flummoxed, as per usual, George awakened from what could have been considered a petit mal seizure and followed her out through the door. He had to practically run to catch up to her as she hurried down the hall toward the elevators.

Pia continued to walk quickly as they made their way out of the dorm and turned right toward the medical center complex. Columbia University Medical Center lies in Washington Heights on Broadway as it runs north along upper Manhattan's spine. Even at this time of the morning, the place was busy. The more purposeful people in the varying-length white coats making their way along 168th Street were the doctors, students, and staff of the hospitals and research facilities. The patients and their relatives who were arriving were more hesitant, trying to figure out where they needed to be and clearly apprehensive of why they were there and what the day might bring.

George turned up the collar of his jacket against the sharp wind that came off the Hudson River and was funneled into 168th Street by the curve of Haven Avenue. Tomorrow, it would be March, the month in which any day the temperature might be in the sixties or it could snow. At that moment it wasn't particularly cold, but the wind was a reminder that winter still had some kick.

George and Pia were heading for different buildings to start their fourth-year month of elective. Fourth year of medical school was a series of monthlong rotations in various specialties, which included an elective period where the individual students could choose something of their particular interest. That month Pia was to do research, as she'd done during her month of elective in her third year. George was to work in radiology, as he too had done the

previous year. These choices were particularly apropos since three weeks earlier,
George, Pia, and the rest of the class of
2011 had learned the results of the residency matching program. Both Pia and
George had been awarded positions there
at Columbia University Medical Center,
thanks to their superb academic records
and strong faculty recommendations: Pia in
internal medicine and George in radiology.
By special dispensation, Pia would also
be starting a concurrent Ph.D. program in
molecular genetics, which would allow her
to continue her lab work while fulfilling
her requirements as a medical resident.

Awaiting Pia that morning at the William
Black Medical Research Building was the
noted molecular geneticist Dr. Tobias Rothman, winner of both a Nobel Prize and a
Lasker Award. In addition to being known
for his accomplishments, Dr. Rothman was
even better known around the medical
center for being a difficult person to work
with, thanks to his renowned total lack of
social graces. Rothman did not suffer fools.
In fact Rothman did not suffer anyone except his long-term research assistant, Dr.
Junichi Yamamoto. Originally Rothman's

reputation had made George nervous for Pia when she started her third-year elective in the man's lab, but his concern had been tempered by his personal knowledge that she herself was a handful. From direct experience he knew that she could be counted on to hold her own in most any situation. As it had turned out, to everyone's surprise, even Pia's, she had gotten along famously with the famed and feared researcher. In fact it had been Rothman's suggestion that Pia do a Ph.D. program at Columbia with her practical work taking place in his lab. Until Pia had come along, Rothman had never mentored anyone. For a while it had been a major point of gossip in the entire medical center as people wildly hypothesized what on earth was going on between the exotically attractive medical student and the universally disliked but respected curmudgeon who was the center's major research celebrity.

"Pia! Wait up!" George called out. In her typically self-absorbed fashion, Pia had gotten ahead of George in the crowd. Dodging the phalanxes of medical students in their white coats who were all converging on the Black building, George scuttled ahead to catch Pia just before she entered the building. He pulled her aside. Pia looked up at George with her big brown eyes wide open, as if surprised to see George, whom she was supposed to be walking with.

"Do you want to have lunch? It's the first day, so they might go easy on us. I know for me it's probably going to get crazy after today."

"I don't know, George. Rothman's . . . Rothman's, you know . . ."

"Rothman's an asocial asshole, that's what I know."

"Let's not argue! I know what you and just about everyone else thinks, but the man's been good to me. I don't know what he has in mind for me today or for the month, for that matter. What I do know is that I can't make plans to meet for lunch before I find out what the day is going to bring."

"I can tell you what most people think he has in mind for you."

"Oh, please!" Pia snapped. "Let's not get into that again. I've told you time and again the man's never made one advance or off-color comment in my presence. What he is is a genius who believes he's surrounded by morons, and he might be right, at least comparatively. All he's interested in is his work, and I'm interested in it too. I'm well aware of his asocial reputation, but I'm lucky that he tolerates me. I can't wait to get in there. If I have a moment as the day progresses, I'll call your cell."

For a brief second George saw red. All at once his brain was flooded with unreasonable jealousy of the prick Rothman. Everybody hated the guy and here was the woman he was romantically obsessed with essentially telling him to bug off and that she couldn't wait to rendezvous with the aged sourball instead of planning to get together for what might be the last lunch of the month. George sucked in a lungful of air while he regarded Pia's obviously scornful look. In a flash he wondered anew what the hell he was doing continuing to pursue this woman when she seemed to be merely tolerating his company.

Instinctively George knew he shouldn't put so much importance on whether or not she would make plans to meet for lunch, but he couldn't help it. It was just another episode in a long list of episodes. The last time they had made love, which was the way George wanted to think about the "hookup," as she called it, George had tried to be open about how her dismissing him made him feel. Her response then, as it was now about lunch, was to get irritated. Of course, after he left her room, instead of feeling good about making his feelings known, he'd worried himself sick that he'd scared her off for good. But he hadn't. Instead, a couple of days later, George had received a surprising note from Pia in his mailbox. "Maybe you should call Sheila Brown." It included a cell phone number. George called Sheila Brown and had one of the oddest phone conversations of his life. He was to learn more about Pia's past in that one conversation than she had ever shared with him.

"Hi, my name is George Wilson. Pia Grazdani asked me to call you."

"Hello, George. Pia told me you would be calling. I was Pia's caseworker and her therapist for some time. Pia told me it was okay to talk to you."

"Oh, er, okay . . ." Caseworker? Whatever George had been expecting, it wasn't this.

"I know it's extremely unusual for a

therapist to talk to a stranger about one of her patients, but Pia asked me to speak with you."

Therapist? This was going to be interesting.

"Normally I wouldn't be speaking to you as I am since it's against any number of rules of my profession, but Pia persuaded me to do so. If I can help Pia emerge from what she faced in her upbringing, I'm willing to do most anything within reason.

"I worked with Pia for years, since she grew up in foster care, including a stint in what used to be called a reform school. As a result, let us say that she's always found it very hard to form any meaningful relationships. Trust is an issue. She didn't tell me much about you, but I find the fact that she asked me to talk with you very encouraging. I think she wants you to know something about her, but she can't tell you herself. So she asked the person who she believes knows her best to do it. Pia has different ideas about privacy and attachment than most people."

That George knew from painful experience.

Without going into specific details, Sheila

encouraged George to "keep trying" with Pia because it was her opinion he would be "good" for her. Sheila concluded by giving him her office number to have in addition to her cell phone number in case he ever wanted to call back. George never did, and despite Sheila's disclaimers, he questioned the professionalism of the conversation. At the same time he appreciated the information. He never brought up the issue directly with Pia by saying that he knew she'd been through foster care but rather tried to get her to open up about her childhood in general. Unfortunately she always responded that it was something she did not want to discuss. It was a no-go zone. That was okay with George; he set it aside and didn't think about it. He was giving her as much time as she needed.

George let out the lungful of air with pursed lips. The slight delay gave him a chance to collect himself and not blurt out something he'd regret later. He even tried to mask the fact that he was upset.

"Well, I hope your day goes as well as can be expected," he said finally. "I know you can handle yourself, Pia. But I still don't know how you can stand to work with him."

"I don't need to get along with him, George. It's not kindergarten. If he tolerates me and I learn from him and he can help my career, that's all I ask. We're grown-ups—we don't have to be friends."

She'd used that line before, and George had to wonder, was she talking about Rothman or about him? George's worry that Pia was going to abandon him resurfaced.

"Okay!" George said simply, while holding up his hands in mock surrender. "Sorry to even mention it."

"Stop apologizing!" Pia said sharply, looking at her watch. "You sound nerdy when you apologize. Now I really am going to be late."

Pia hurried away. George asked himself what time Pia might have gotten up had he not gone to her room to wake her. He couldn't help but notice that she'd not bothered to thank him, much less make a commitment to have lunch. Unfortunately it all was irritatingly pro forma.

Pia showed her ID to the security guard with all the other students who were mostly first- and second-year heading off to their eight o'clock lecture. Instead of following them she took the elevator to the four-teenth floor of the Black Research Building and headed for Rothman's sizable labora-tory. He commanded the most space of any researcher in the entire center. As soon as she went through the anonymous-looking metal door and entered the suite, she could sense that the lab's day was already in full swing. The three research technicians, Panjit Singh, Nina Brockhurst, and Mariana Herrera, were loitering around the lab's communal coffeepot having al-ready calibrated all the instrumentation that needed to be done on a daily basis. Rothman, fastidious about what he ate and drank, kept a Nespresso machine in his office that only he and Dr. Junichi Yama-moto, his senior associate, were allowed to use.

"Morning, Miss Grazdani," said Marsha Langman, Rothman's secretary, from be-hind her desk. One overdefined eyebrow was raised as she looked at the clock on the wall opposite. "You don't want to make this a habit."

Pia followed the woman's line of vision and glanced at the clock. The second hand had just ticked past vertical: it was 7:49. Pia stopped and half turned toward Rothman's ultraloyal retainer-cum-secretary for the inevitable reprimand.

"You know he likes everyone to be early," Marsha said in an accusatory tone.

"I'm not late," said Pia. Students were supposed to begin lectures and other activities at eight unless they had been on call the night before for specific rotations that required it.

"Ah, but you aren't early either. Let's not start the month off on the wrong foot. And I should warn you, you'll be having some company in your office. There's a man from maintenance in there trying to find a problem in the wiring. The security system is down."

"How long's that going to take?"

Marsha, a middle-aged African-American woman in a lab coat her position didn't call for, made a face that said, *How would I know?*

Pia was exasperated. There was barely room for her in what was generously described as an office.

"Is the chief going to have time for me this morning?" Pia was one of the handful of people who didn't reflexively kowtow to

Rothman and wait for him to come to them. As Pia asked the question she turned to fully face Marsha. The research technicians were quiet. Pia wondered if they'd timed their coffee run for her predictably not-quite-early arrival and were eavesdropping for any possible gossip.

"You know how pressed for time he always is," Marsha said. "He's being pressured to finish his most current salmonella typhi experiment with Dr. Yamamoto. We have to e-mail the manuscript to *The Lancet* in the next day or so."

Marsha always talked as if she were actively involved in the research. It was part of her strategy of erecting barriers and building sand traps for those wanting time with Rothman. She watched over him like a killer guard dog.

"He's been in since six"—"in" being the biosafety level-3 lab, frequently referred to as BSL-3, where the work on the salmonella strains was being done. "I'll see if I can get word to him that you want to speak to him."

"Thank you," Pia said, her eyes betraying irritation. "Getting word" to Rothman meant flipping a switch and talking to him by intercom. Hating to waste time and having finished the last project he had assigned to her, Pia needed to see Rothman to find out what she was going to be doing that month. And now there was some workman in her office to complicate things.

Pia was fortunate to have an office at all. Few of the other people in the lab had such a privilege. When Rothman's chief technician was fired after getting into an argument with Rothman over some picayune detail of lab procedure, his successor, Arthur Spaulding, took an office nearer the biosafety level-3 area, and Pia took over Spaulding's broom closet. Pia saw that her office door was ajar, and she bristled. There were sensitive files in there, even if only a handful of people on the planet would understand what they meant. As she entered she saw that her bench area that also served as her desk was occupied—an electrical blueprint was laid out on the flat surface and there were tools and wires strewn on top. In the corner of the tiny, windowless room was a stepladder with a human form standing on the top platform, head and shoulders hidden up inside the dropped ceiling. Three panels had been taken down and stacked against the wall.

"Excuse me!" Pia called out. When there was no response, she called louder, "Hey, you up there!"

Pia's sharp words caused the man to flinch and hit his head on a pipe up in the ceiling. The man let out an indistinct curse and slowly emerged from the ceiling. After taking one look at Pia, he climbed down from the stepladder. He was about forty-five with grayish stubble and salt-and-pepper hair, wearing dark blue coveralls. His forehead was deeply lined, and he had the sunken cheeks and pale complexion of a lifelong smoker. His body was thin but muscular. His security tag read "Vance Goslin."

"How long are you going to be?" Pia demanded. She had her arms akimbo.

Goslin was struck immediately by Pia's remarkable and exotic beauty, her glowing, flawless skin, her full lips, and, perhaps most of all, her huge dark eyes. Adding to her allure was her apparent confidence and forthrightness. In Goslin's world, girls who looked like Pia acted significantly differently. He was more than casually attracted to her. He was intrigued.

"Depends when I find the problem," he said. He pointed to two areas on the blueprints lying on the bench. He had a distinct accent that Pia thought she recognized, especially given the name Goslin. "If the problem is here, it's easy to fix. If the problem is there, it's harder, but one way or the other we'll get it done. It might even be done by tonight."

Goslin nodded as he finished talking, eagerly continuing to scan Pia's shapely body as he'd done while he'd been talking. He did it overtly, as if it were a matter of right. Eventually his gaze alighted on Pia's hospital ID. "Grazdani," he voiced, raising his eyebrows questioningly. "Now, that's an unusual name."

Pia didn't respond, making him think she might be hard of hearing.

"Your name is unusual. Is it Italian?" he said, raising his voice. He had assumed a wry smile as if he knew Grazdani was not Italian. It was his way of flirting.

"No, it isn't Italian. And why are you shouting?"

Pia had talked about her Albanian heritage maybe twice in her life and she wasn't about to do it now with this person. There were thousands of Albanians in New York City, and Pia remembered enough of the language to recognize an Albanian accent when she heard it. Once when she was ordering a slice of pizza, two young men behind the counter started a frank appraisal of her physical attributes in their language before Pia asked them in English if they wanted her to talk to the manager about their rudeness.

"Actually I'd guess Albanian," Goslin said, the smile continuing. "I'm of Albanian descent, and I have a lot of Albanian friends here in New York. They work in maintenance like me. We've kinda taken over the business. . . ."

Pia wasn't listening. It was barely an hour since she'd been dreaming about one childhood nightmare and now this man was reminding her of another—her father—which added to her growing irritation. Even though she was offering nothing to this maintenance worker that he could take as encouragement, he was still talking, trying to engage her in conversation.

"So where are you from?" he asked. His eyes narrowed and head tilted, as if he were about to make a guess. Such a situation was not uncommon for Pia. Many people, particularly men, tried to guess her genealogy from her appearance, usually coming up with such suggestions as Greek, Lebanese, or even Iranian, but she wasn't going to play the game with this guy even though he'd been correct about her name. Her father was indeed Albanian, although her mother was Italian.

"I'm American," Pia said. "Hurry up with what you're doing! I'm going to need my office sooner rather than later."

"And what do you do?" Goslin asked, vainly trying to keep the conversation going.

Pia didn't answer. She walked out of the room, pausing only to pick out a couple of files she thought she might need.

To the surprise of the lab technicians, who had moved from the coffee nook to their respective individual benches, Rothman suddenly emerged from the biosafety unit. This was a surprise because everyone expected that he would be closeted in there for the day, as had been the case for the last several weeks. As a stickler for rules, he had gone through the airlock and removed his protective lab garb and donned his street clothes. Without a lab coat on, he resembled a gentleman banker more than a research scientist coming from working with extraordinarily deadly typhoid-causing salmonella. Although asocial to a fault, he was a careful dresser, a disconnect as it suggested he cared what other people thought. But he didn't. The clothes were purely for him and the ensemble was the same day after day: conservative three-button Italian suit, pressed white shirt, dark blue tie with matching pocket square, and black penny loafers. He was not a tall man, but he projected well and appeared taller than he was. Moving quickly, he was an intimidating figure with martially erect posture and an expression that did not encourage conversation. His dark brown hair was cut conservatively to match his suit. His almost invisible rimless titanium glasses were his only concession to current fashion.

As Rothman strode toward his private office, the eyes of the technicians followed him. It was immediately apparent to all of them what had brought Rothman out of the biosafety unit. Catching sight of Pia, he had motioned for her to follow him. As the office door closed, the lab technicians exchanged knowing looks with a tinge of collective jealousy. All of them knew that with the pressure of the upcoming *Lancet* article, Rothman would never have left the biosafety unit specifically to talk to them. In their minds Pia was a kind of teacher's pet made worse by her not being all that friendly. Similar to Rothman, she was always too busy for small talk and kept to herself. On top of that, they all thought she was a bit too good-looking to be a medical student and thought captiously she would have been better suited to playing one on TV. Pia was an enigma to the laboratory staff, made more interesting by the gossip that had it she was going to be a nun.

If the lab technicians had had the opportunity to view the scene inside Rothman's office, they might not have felt any jealousy whatsoever. It appeared more like Rothman and Pia were engaged in an arcane ritual, rather than having an actual conversation. Neither looked at the other throughout the entire, brief encounter. After

Rothman told her he wanted her to edit the current salmonella study for *The Lancet* that day, he picked up one of two copies of the paper from his desk, which he was now studying intently. Pia appeared equally distracted, her arms crossed, looking at her feet. The uninitiated might sense a social ineptness on both sides as the awkward silence extended; a clinical psychologist, given enough time, might talk more in diagnostically precise language.

Finally Rothman, half standing, leaned over his desk and handed a copy of the *Lancet* paper to Pia. "Make sure this is up to snuff. I'll want it by morning. Tomorrow we'll talk again about what you will be doing for the month." He still did not look at her. "Let me say that I know you have always been more interested in my stem cell work than my salmonella work, and I'm fine with that. You've earned it, considering you finally know something practical about genetics rather than the garbage they taught you in class. And one other thing: Two fourth-year students have been foisted on me for a month of elective by the damn dean. So I want you to give some thought to what they can do while they're here. It's not going to be easy. I'm sure they'll be worthless."

"Where are they and how can I meet them?"

"They are supposed to start tomorrow. Dr. Yamamoto will introduce you. The main thing is that I don't want them tying up a lot of Junichi's time as he seems to enjoy that kind of crap. I need him to concentrate on our work."

"I can't do anything with that maintenance man in my office."

"My understanding is that he'll be done sometime today. So, tomorrow then." Rothman was never much interested in the details of running his massive lab. Suddenly he was again absorbed in the *Lancet* manuscript.

Ignoring Rothman's dismissal, Pia said, "There is something I want to tell you. The residency matching results came in. I'm going to be here at Columbia doing a combined program getting a Ph.D. in cellular biology with you, as you so generously offered, and completing a residency in internal medicine. I hope you're pleased."

"Well, I'm not!" Rothman said with emotion, his infamous ire rising. "I'm disappointed. If I told you once I told you a dozen times that for you, doing an internal medicine residency would be a complete waste of time, just like it was for me. I think it is totally apparent that you, like me, are cut out for research, not clinical medicine. You should be here in the lab full-time! I said as much in my letter of recommendation for the Ph.D. program."

A level of tension hung in the air. For a few beats neither spoke, nor did they so much as exchange a glance.

"But I have the sisters to think of," Pia said. Pia's education had been partly underwritten by the Missionary Sisters of the Sacred Heart, an international religious order situated in Westchester County. Pia had fled to the order for emotional safety after aging out of foster care at age eighteen. Although initially Pia had thought briefly of joining the order as a nun, after finishing her high school equivalency and a portion of college at New York University, she had changed her mind. Consequently the relationship with the sisters, particularly the mother superior, had become more transactional. Although Pia would complete her medical training and still go to Africa to help with the organization's missionary work, she would not become a novitiate.

Although Pia had received full scholarships from New York University and Columbia Medical School, the Sisters' contribution had been considerable. She felt justifiably obligated. "I don't think I can renege on a plan I made ten years ago. Although I've come to agree with you that my personality is more suited to research, I think I have to go through with the original plan to become a doctor and, at least for a time, serve the order's needs."

A rush of mumbled profanity escaped from Rothman's lips. He shook his head in disbelief. "Here I am offering you a part in making medical history with my stem cell research, and I have to be concerned about a bunch of nuns in Westchester." He paused for a moment to collect his thoughts. "What kind of money are we talking about?"

"I don't know what you mean."

"Come on. Don't be obtuse. What do you think you owe them in dollars?"

"I'm not sure I can think of it in those terms."

"Let's not be difficult. Give me a figure however you want to create it."

Pia thought for a moment. It was not an easy task. She'd never put a figure on how the sisters had nurtured her and given her a sense of protection from the evils of her foster care experience. She shrugged. "I don't know. Maybe fifty thousand. Something like that."

"Done," Rothman said. "You'll get a loan from my bank to the tune of fifty thousand, and I'll cosign for it."

Pia found herself momentarily speechless. Never in her life had someone stood up for her financially, especially to the tune of fifty thousand dollars. She didn't know how to react. "I don't know what to say," she mumbled.

"Then don't say anything! We'll revisit this issue, but for today I want you to jump on this paper for *Lancet*. It needs another set of eyes and the statistics checked. I know you are a whiz with statistics."

Rothman got up from behind his desk. With his attention buried in the piece of paper he'd been intermittently studying, he walked out of his office. Pia was stunned. Rothman had just essentially lent her a large sum of money and asked for her help on a vitally important paper.

"Okay," Pia said to herself, "I've got work to do. Now I just have to get that man out of my work space." Following Rothman out through the door, she headed back to the lab bench where she had set up her temporary work space.

2.

CONVENT OF THE SISTERS OF
THE SACRED HEART
WESTCHESTER, NEW YORK
FEBRUARY 28, 2011, 7:20 P.M.

Armed with Dr. Rothman's pledge of financial support, Pia made an appointment
with the mother superior of the convent of
the Sisters of the Sacred Heart for that
same evening. It wasn't a meeting she
looked forward to. Pia recalled how years
before the mother superior had found her
as a teenager sitting on the convent wall

after getting into a fight with her foster family at the time, who lived a couple of miles away. She had brought Pia inside, and they had talked. The result was that Pia returned the very next weekend, with her family's permission, to help out in an unstructured fashion. The rest was history, culminating in Pia's decision, when she aged out of foster care, to join the convent with the idea of possibly becoming a novitiate.

Pia would be forever grateful for what the mother superior had done for her in the years following her moving in, especially as it was an enormous improvement on what she had experienced in the foster care system. Although it was, in reality, another institution, Pia had finally been at peace. She had found the mother superior to be sympathetic not only in helping her adjust to the convent's community living but also in helping her navigate the tempestuous waters in the real world beyond the tranquillity of the convent. It had been at the mother superior's insistence that Pia turned to academia and became a superior student rather than an adequate one. But obtaining her high school equivalency and attending college had allowed Pia to learn about herself to the extent of realizing that a nun's life was not for her. Instead she decided on a career in medicine, where she sensed she could excel and find equivalent peace. After all, during her entire tumultuous foster care experience, she had always viewed the doctor as the sine qua non of power and control of one's personal destiny. But the decision had had consequences, especially with regard to the mother superior.

About five years earlier Pia had made a similar appointment with the woman. It was then that Pia admitted that she was not going to become a sister but rather a doctor. It had been a difficult meeting as the mother superior had been obviously disappointed and made her feelings known. At the same time she had been encouraging about Pia's new career track and voiced how desperately doctors were needed at their missionary locations in East Africa. Now, as Pia walked into the mother superior's stark office, she knew she faced as difficult a situation as—and maybe even worse than—when she had decided against becoming a nun. The more she thought about her goals, the more she thought Rothman was right about her being uniquely qualified for medical research.

"Pia, my dear, it's a blessing to see you. We have all missed you. All the sisters ask about you day after day."

"And you, Reverend Mother."

Pia kept her eyes glued to her hands as they worked at each other in her lap. Her anxiety had peaked. She hoped it was not reflected in her voice. She had dressed simply in a black dress that broke at the knees and plain pumps. At first glance, the mother superior had looked the same as when she first met her ten years before. The uniform of the order helped with that. But Pia could tell that age was taking its toll. The mother superior had moved slowly when she walked around her desk to greet Pia. From Pia's perspective her hand had felt bonier and more delicate when she placed it on Pia's shoulder than on Pia's previous visit a month or so previously.

On the short train ride out of Manhattan, Pia had rehearsed what she was going to say. She wanted to be clear so there would be no misunderstanding. She was confident in her decision, more confident then than she'd been in Rothman's office, but she knew the mother superior had a talent for ignoring what someone was saying as she worked the conversation back to a position more in tune with her interests and opinions.

As the pleasantries continued, Pia's mind rapidly played over the extraordinary changes her life had taken since she arrived at the convent in what, at that moment, seemed like a previous life. She was now in her fourth year at Columbia Medical School, as amazing as that sounded even to her. She recalled how difficult it had been to convince Columbia to accept her. She remembered how she'd had to explain why, at age eighteen, she'd decided to join a Catholic African missionary order. Her experience at New York University had been a breeze. From the get-go the college admissions people were convinced, no questions asked, that Pia, as a young woman emancipated from foster care, would make a valuable addition to the rich tapestry of NYU undergraduate life.

Columbia, on the other hand, had expressed early concern about Pia's history

and its potential effects on her indepen-
dence and ability to empathize with patients. They didn't voice their concerns in
such a clear fashion, but Pia had gotten
the message, especially when she was
asked to undergo an interview by one of
the medical center's psychiatrists. Recognizing that she wouldn't have been asked to
do the interview if they weren't interested
in her, Pia had acquiesced. To her surprise, the interview turned out to be more
pleasant than she had feared. The psychiatrist had been well versed in the ineq-
uities of the New York foster care system
and seemed sympathetic when he learned
that she had been under its questionable
aegis from age six to eighteen. Unfortunately, she had never experienced an adoption
or even a final placement.

Although the psychiatrist did not have
access to her records by law, Pia was rather
open with him and explained her experiences, although she downplayed some
of the grittier elements. She fully admitted
that in retrospect she knew that she had
been abused and that she had had to grow
up without a nurturing presence in her life,
but she added that rather than hindering

her, she believed, her experiences would make her a better doctor. She also downplayed any symptoms she'd experienced such as her mild brush with an eating disorder as a teenager and the recurrent nightmares she still experienced.

As the interview had progressed, Pia's openness apparently won the day as the psychiatrist was equally open with her. He actually told her that he was impressed with how she had been able to cope and that he agreed with her that her experiences might make her a better doctor, especially if she became interested in a specialty like pediatrics. He told her that he was particularly impressed by her near perfect grade point average at NYU, her near perfect MCAT scores, and the fact that she had won acclaim as an actress with the NYU theater group. He said it was all indicative of her commitment to her goal of becoming a doctor and to the adjustment she had achieved to everyday life despite her history. He also told her that he would be strongly recommending her for admittance to the class of 2011.

After the psychiatric interview, Pia had been ecstatically hopeful that she would be accepted. But months later she found out that it had not been enough to convince the admissions committee. There had been a number of people who'd apparently demurred, thinking it was too big a risk despite the psychiatrist's recommendation. It took an unexpected last-ditch intervention by two people to carry the day. First, the mother superior offered to become involved and sent a flurry of carefully worded, beautifully argued, and persuasive e-mails. And the second person was Dr. Rothman, who, at the time, was sitting on the admissions committee for an obligatory three-year term. Pia found out about this surprising twist of events only years later, after working with Rothman during her third-year elective. He'd brought it up suddenly at one of their typically uncomfortable meetings. He admitted to her something that he said no one else knew: that he too had suffered through the New York State foster care system because he had been a difficult, hyperactive child. He said a diagnosis was not made until he was an adult, when he himself recognized he had Asperger's syndrome. Pia had been stunned and was still stunned. Respecting his confidence, she had told no one about the revelation.

"The last time you made a formal appointment to see me," the mother superior continued, "you had sad news for us here at the convent, saying you had decided against joining us by becoming a novitiate. My intuition tells me that you are here today for similar reasons. I hope that is not the case. We love you here at the convent and are very proud of you and your accomplishments."

Pia looked up briefly to engage the mother superior's unblinking stare, but she couldn't maintain it. Almost immediately she looked away, finding herself staring at the crucifix on the wall over the woman's shoulder, thinking of pain, sacrifice, and betrayal. Pia took a fortifying breath. As usual the mother superior was miles ahead of her, seemingly sensing what was coming. "I'm starting another month of research in Dr. Rothman's laboratory."

"He is a gifted man. The Lord has looked kindly on him."

"He is going to make history by personally ushering in regenerative medicine. His work with stem cells will be seminal. I want to be part of it."

"From my perspective, you already are. From what you have shared, he has taken to you. Not that I am surprised. How can I help?"

Pia looked back down at her hands. She felt a tinge of guilt after all that the mother superior had done for her, and here she was immediately offering to do more. "I believe I will want to do medical research full-time, meaning I don't think I want to go to Africa."

There, it's out, Pia thought. She felt immediate relief. For a few moments silence reigned in the room. Pia suddenly realized how cold it was. "I know this is a rather large change since I offered to go to Africa to repay you and the order for all the help you've given me over the years since I aged out of foster care."

"Your going to Africa was to be for you, not us," the mother superior said. "Pia, please don't be rash. I know I'm going to sound very old-fashioned, but is there a man involved? There must be—it is your burden to be so beautiful. I hope to God that Dr. Rothman is being honorable."

Pia suppressed a smile. The mother superior's suggestion was so far from reality as to warrant such a reaction. She and Rothman had trouble making eye contact much less something more intimate. "I can assure you that Dr. Rothman has been quintessentially honorable."

"God has limitless ways to test us," the mother superior continued.

"Reverend Mother, I don't believe God is testing me. This does not involve a man, I assure you. I have made my decision because it pleases me and because God has given me a facility for the work. But I would like to repay the convent. Thanks to Dr. Rothman's generosity, I have access to fifty thousand dollars. I would like to donate this money to the convent."

"I will be willing to accept any donation but not as repayment. For our services you do not owe us anything. After all, your presence was payment enough."

"It would please me to donate the money," Pia said.

"As you will. But I do have another request. I don't want you to forget us. I trust that you will still make it a point to visit us on occasion. If you forget us, that will be a betrayal."

Pia, who had been looking past the mother superior at the crucifix, was stopped short. Suddenly, her suit of armor was dented, and she looked down at her shoes, feeling young and small. *Betray. Betrayal.* When she first encountered the word "betray" in a novel when she was eleven, she looked it up in the school's big dictionary. The definition seemed just right. That's what her family had done, it had *betrayed* her. *Betrayal* was the tragedy that had stalked Pia ever since she was six, on the day when the police burst through the front door of the apartment she shared with her father and uncle and placed her in the clutches of the New York City foster care program.

3.

COLUMBIA UNIVERSITY MEDICAL CENTER
NEW YORK CITY
MARCH 1, 2011, 7:30 A.M.

She knows the man's important but she can't remember his name. The girl is standing in front of a long desk, wearing a plain, very loose-fitting, institutional gray shift with her shoulders slumped forward and her hands clasped in front of her, elbows tucked into her sides. Even sitting down, the man is very large, enormous, in fact, and he's leaning

forward, talking to her, not looking her in the eye but right at her chest. She can't make out what he's saying. She's been bad, she's misbehaved, she's going to need to be punished, that's all she knows.

She can hear him now. He's even bigger than he was before, telling her to stand up straight, to pull her shoulders back. Why is she wearing that shapeless garment? Pia remembers that she's fifteen or at most sixteen and this is the head of her school, and it's as if she's at the back of the room, watching this girl who is her but not her. He pushes his chair back and stands up. Coming around the desk, he approaches her with a cruel, lustful smile. "Pia . . ." he orders. "Pia . . ."

"Pia . . . Pia . . . !" Pia sat up in bed and breathed a deep sigh of relief. Her T-shirt was sticking to the sweat on her back as she stretched forward, listening to George calling to her from the other side of the door. She let him in and hurried to get dressed, vowing that she'd remember to set the alarm that night. Her internal clock used to wake her up at six without fail but the last couple of weeks she'd had trouble sleeping, suffering from a number of recurrent nightmares. She felt exhausted. She'd not had nearly enough sleep. After visiting with the mother superior, she'd gone back to Rothman's lab. By the time she'd gotten back to her dorm room and crawled into bed it had been 4:23 in the morning.

As she dressed, she found herself mulling over the meeting with the mother superior, and she shared some of it with George on the way to the medical center.

"I'm glad you went," George said as they walked in the crisp morning sunshine. "I mean, you were never going to join the order, and I can't see you in Africa doing whatever missionaries do nowadays. I've never known any nuns, but I can't imagine you're the nun type." From one of their four lovemaking events, an erotic image of a satiated Pia naked in bed flashed through his mind. He noticed Pia shoot him a look, and he cringed. Could she read his mind? It wasn't the first time George had this worry.

"I don't think becoming a nun and taking the vows would have been a problem for me, George. I'm not even saying I'll never do it. I've seen how life is at the convent, and it's very peaceful. It's different from the world out here. The sisters support each other. It's safe."

George immediately felt uncomfortable, like he was patronizing Pia. He couldn't blame her for wanting some security in her life with the little he knew of her childhood. But becoming a nun? It seemed extreme. "I guess what I mean is that it seems like a way of avoiding life. There are other ways of being safe besides going and hiding out in a convent."

"I don't think of becoming a nun as hiding. It's the opposite—they have to give all of themselves to the world they have chosen." *They don't betray each other either,* thought Pia to herself. They had reached the Black research building.

"Actually I think you'd be equivalently hiding if you end up spending your whole career working in there with Rothman," George said, indicating the building with a tilt of his head. His concept of medicine involved helping people directly, one-on-one, having an effect on the lives of people he could see and touch. As far as he was concerned, research was too cold and abstract and populated with asocial martinets like Rothman who were as welcoming and warm as a file full of algorithms.

"So, what about lunch today?" George said, changing the subject and ever hopeful. As he had feared, they hadn't met up for lunch the day before. In the three-plus years that George had known Pia, they'd never had an official lunch date. They had lunched together numerous times, but not as a planned event. During the first two years they had managed to have pretty much the same schedule so it just happened. But now that George was on a radiology elective and Pia was holed up in Rothman's lab, he knew that the chances they'd run into each other by accident were slim. But why he was bothering to ask her he had no idea, since he knew it wasn't going to happen. And why was he always so damned accommodating?

"Sorry, George, I can't make plans," she said. "Yesterday I had to spend the entire day and come back at night to work on one of Rothman's journal articles, and it still isn't done. On top of that I'll be meeting with him sometime to find out what he has in store for me for the entire month. I seriously doubt I'll even be getting lunch."

Pia was unhappy to see that the pesky maintenance man was still in her office. He was up the stepladder again, only facing a different direction this time. The day before, as she had worked on Rothman's paper on one of the benches out in the lab proper, she'd noticed that he'd left at twelve and didn't come back for four hours. At that rate she worried about him being there pestering her and keeping her from her cubbyhole for a week. Her office was small, but it was hers and she could leave her stuff spread out on the countertops, something she couldn't do in the main lab.

Pia made enough noise dropping her bag on her tool-littered desk to ensure Vance knew she was there and not particularly happy. "Hey, you up there," she called out.

Vance pulled his head down into the room and, seeing Pia, climbed down, smiling, rubbing his hands on a rag. "Ah, Miss Grazdani! How are you today? I missed you yesterday when I left."

"I noticed you took a four-hour lunch.

You should have told me you'd be away so long. I could have been working here in my office. Anyway, yesterday you thought you'd be finished. What's up? How long is this going to take?"

"The job is turning out to be more difficult than I had thought. All I can really say is that I'm trying my best. As soon as I figure out what the hell is wrong, I'll knock it right out and be outa here."

Pia merely sighed irritably and lifted her bag.

"Miss Pia, I've got a surprise for you. I made an extra sandwich today for lunch, one for me and one for you. How about joining me for a bite? I make a wicked pastrami sandwich on a ciabatta roll. What do you say?"

He was smiling again. Jesus, men were so predictable. Pia glowered: Was this guy suffering from delusions? She wasn't staying to find out nor did she want to encourage the man.

"Just hurry the hell up with the job. Please!" she snapped. As far as the sandwich offer was concerned, she didn't even want to acknowledge it.

Pia turned and stepped back into the

main lab. She put her bag on the bench area where she'd worked the previous day. But instead of jumping right in, she walked back to Marsha's desk to find out where their leader was that morning. To her surprise, she learned that Rothman was in his office and waiting for her. Pleased, Pia hurried in through the open door. Immediately she noticed he was dealing with the same maintenance inconvenience Overhead, a number of ceiling tiles were missing and spaghetti-like wires dangled from the holes. An assortment of tools dotted one of the countertops and a few were scattered on the floor. In the corner was a stepladder leaning against the wall and the security camera was missing from its mounting.

"Good morning, Dr. Rothman," Pia chirped. She never knew what to expect mood-wise but hoped for the best. "Marsha said you were expecting me."

"Miss Grazdani. How do you spell 'catheter'?" Rothman demanded, not even bothering to look up from the sheet of paper he was holding. She could tell it was part of the *Lancet* manuscript she'd worked on.

"C-A-T-H-E-T-E-R. Why?"

"Well, it seems you know how to spell it, so I'm wondering why you felt the need to make up an alternative version for my paper?"

Pia had worked on Rothman's article, making several suggestions for changes in structure and rewriting one whole section she found particularly opaque. Late last night she had been in a hurry to finish, and she hadn't run a spell check.

"One wonders what they taught you at NYU, if anything. There were several spelling errors and two grammatical ones."

From experience, Pia knew how Rothman worked. These jabs at her spelling and grammar almost certainly meant that he had accepted her structural changes. If you lived for compliments and praise, you'd starve to death working for Rothman. Rothman took good work for granted. If you weren't good, you didn't last long, so the only elements worth talking about were the minor faults. Rothman twisted in his seat to face his Mac and started pecking his way around the keyboard. Pia surmised he was adding her changes to the original manuscript. Pia took a seat without being asked. If she waited to be asked, she'd be standing all day.

Pia had enjoyed laboring over the *Lancet* piece. Scientific writing was something she enjoyed and seemed to have a facility for. Over the previous three years, Pia had collaborated with Rothman on his salmonella studies and had even got credit as one of the authors on several. It had been exciting work. Rothman was continuing his award-winning, landmark research that he had accomplished concerning salmonella virulence, a subject for which he'd won his Nobel and Lasker prizes. Virulence was the microorganism's ability to invade and kill its host cells, something salmonella was particularly good at. Over the years Rothman had found, classified, and defined the five pathogenicity "islands," or areas, in the salmonella genome that encoded for various virulence-related factors such as specific toxins and antibiotic resistance, both of which had contributed to salmonella being by far the largest cause of human food-borne illness in the world. Every year salmonella caused the mortality and morbidity of countless millions of people. Every year typhoid fever alone still killed upwards of half a million people, a situation Rothman had his sights on rectifying and was coming closer to each year.

Initially when Pia first joined Rothman's lab, she had been more interested in his newer area of research, namely stem cells, and had hoped to work with them. But he had had other ideas and wanted her to cut her teeth with his continuing salmonella work. As time passed she'd become as committed as he in the microbiological arena, fascinated by bacteria and viruses in general and salmonella in particular and the microscopic realm they inhabited. Soon she found herself reveling in the involved science while enjoying the thrill of working with one of the greatest minds on the subject. On a daily basis Pia had come to relish refining her knowledge of genetics so that she could one day make her own contribution to basic research. Gradually she had come to realize how exciting research could be and how well it fit with her personality.

Pia watched Rothman type away in front of her. The level of his concentration was truly remarkable. One minute he'd been talking with her, the next he was totally absorbed, as if she were no longer in his presence. Pia did not take any aspect of his behavior personally. After he'd confided about his Asperger's, she'd read about the syndrome and guessed that many aspects of his personality were dictated by it, even ignoring her as he was doing at that moment. Instead of being annoyed, she thought about the content of the article she'd rewritten. It was about studies that Rothman had been doing involving salmonella typhi grown in outer space on the orbiting International Space Station. Rothman had found that growing the bacteria in a zero-gravity environment made it enormously more virulent than control bacteria grown back on earth. It was Rothman's belief that the conditions in space somehow mimicked to a marked extent those present in the human ileum, triggering the bacteria to turn on the genes in the pathogenicity islands to produce effector proteins. Pia was one of the few people who knew that at that moment in the refrigerated storage facility inside the biosafety unit there were three strains of these enormously virulent, space-grown salmonella.

She also knew that what Rothman wanted to do was to figure out how zero gravity caused these changes with the hope of learning how to turn them off, not only in space but in the human ileum as well.

Although Pia had learned to be patient in Rothman's presence, she had her limits. After a few minutes had gone by Pia coughed lightly. She'd found by experience that coughing seemed to penetrate Rothman's concentration more than anything else. Almost immediately he peered around the screen of his Mac and pushed a box of tissues in her direction. He had a phobia about people coughing in his presence. He was, after all, a firm believer in the "germ" theory. Pia took one of the obligatory tissues.

"Right. Miss Grazdani, for this month's assignment . . ." He disappeared from her sight again. He resumed his two-finger typing but at least kept talking. She couldn't see his face but she preferred it that way, which he did too as both had trouble maintaining eye contact not only with each other but with everyone else as well. "I want to move you over into our induced stem cell work. You've done a knockout job with salmonella, but it's time you started in the other arena."

A smile of anticipation appeared on Pia's face. Rothman's words were music to her ears.

"We've been making breakthrough discoveries of late involving organogenesis."

Pia's heart picked up speed. It was the first time Rothman had talked to her about his stem cell work. She knew what organogenesis meant as the word was self-explanatory. It was now the cutting edge of stem cell research. It was the last hurdle before creating organs that could be transplanted into patients—organs like hearts, lungs, and kidneys. It thrilled her to think that Rothman was making enormous leaps forward. And the idea that she would become part of the effort gave her chills down her spine.

"At this stage our biggest problem is that tissue culture techniques and fluids have not kept up with the breakthroughs that we're making. Current tissue culture techniques were developed for sheets of cells, not solid organs. I'm sure you can gather what I mean. It relates to oxygenation and removing metabolic waste while maintaining acid base balance within extremely narrow parameters. It's been basically a combination of pushing the limits of biochemistry and engineering. We have come up with some impressive hardware breakthroughs, but the involved fluids have not kept pace. The problem that is now holding us back is the acid base balance. My guess is that the pH is varying too much. We can't figure out why. What I want you to do is to become a tissue culture fluid expert and figure out why we're having this pH problem. Got it?"

"I think so," Pia managed. She had learned that it was never a good ploy to question any of Rothman's directives. Anything and everything could be discussed again, but not on the spur of the moment.

"Good! Get to it! And when I finish making these changes in the manuscript, I'll see that Marsha gets you a copy for your final review. Now get out of here!"

Rothman's typing picked up pace, a few keystrokes followed by several frantic deletions. Pia kept her seat despite Rothman's final comment. She sensed that this was all the information she was going to get about her month's elective at the moment, and it wasn't much. Inwardly, she shuddered a little. She had expected to be working on some aspect of Rothman's salmonella research as she'd done in the past. Tissue culture was a new discipline for her and what she was being tasked to do sounded like an entire Ph.D. project, not a month's assignment. She was going to need a lot of help from Rothman and from the other technicians, especially Nina Brockhurst, whose job it was to take care of the physical plant of Rothman's organ-growing experiments, which would include the baths. In the past Nina had openly resented Pia, claiming Rothman played favorites with her. Pia had taken the situation in stride as she knew there was always intrigue when people were forced to work together, especially when the boss's signals were so hard to read.

But whatever the workload and her colleague's demeanor, Pia knew she was going to find the month fascinating. Even if the fluid bath assignment wasn't, on the face of it, very exciting in and of itself, it was still vital experience she would be gaining, learning the basic techniques for taking care of newly created organs, a key stepping-stone in the journey from studying organogenesis in mice to studying it in people. Most important, the work was in the stem cell arena: the place she believed she really wanted to be.

Pia coughed again, this time into the tissue that she had in her hand. Rothman's face reappeared around the side of his Mac. His expression was one of surprise that Pia was still there.

"I went to see the mother superior at the convent last night," she said. "I told her about my not wanting to go to Africa."

"Good," Rothman said simply. His face disappeared. The typing recommenced.

"She was nice about it, but I could tell she was not happy."

"That's her problem, not yours. You'll be doing a lot more of God's work here in my lab than going to any godforsaken part of Africa."

"She said she did not want to be repaid."

"Good for her. So don't."

"I think I should. Are you still willing to cosign for a fifty-thousand-dollar loan?"

"I am, but I think you're crazy. She doesn't want to be repaid, or so she says. Save your money."

"She used the word 'betrayal,'" Pia said. She knew she was distorting the reason the mother superior had chosen to use the word, but the fact that she had used it at all still bothered Pia.

Rothman gave a short, mocking laugh. "Betrayal! She's just trying to foist some Catholic guilt on you, Pia. For chrissake, pay her the money if you need to and be done with it. I'll have Marsha take care of it with my bank. As a fourth-year medical student, I'm sure your credit is adequate. Remember, it's your life, not the mother superior's. Now, get out of here and get to work."

Pia got up and left Rothman to his typing. Passing Marsha, she thought about hitting the library. Her initial plan was to read everything on tissue engineering that she could get her hands on. She had no doubt it was going to be an overwhelming amount of information.

4.

Having loaded up on books and printouts from a Google search in the library, Pia spent the morning reading, sitting deep in concentration at a bench area outside her windowless office. She'd been vaguely aware of the maintenance man doing his thing, but she had ignored him until he came up behind her. Disregarding the fact that she had her iPod buds in her ears, he had the nerve to tap her on the shoulder.

"Pia, darling dear. Want to reconsider my pastrami offer? You won't be disappointed."

"Not on your life," Pia said, with emphasis, hoping he'd get what she intended as a definitive message. He shrugged and smiled and gave a little silly wave as if Pia had been gracious rather than scathing. She was beginning to think that Vance was one of those men who reveled in rejection. Irritably, she repositioned her earplugs and went back to her reading. When she heard her name being called again, Pia was momentarily livid, wondering what she was going to have to do to get him to leave her alone. Tearing out her earpieces, she looked up to see Rothman's assistant, Dr. Yamamoto, standing in front of her flanked by a young man and woman in newly laundered, dazzlingly white lab coats.

"Miss Grazdani," Yamamoto said. He was a slight man with what appeared to be a kind of half-smile frozen on his face. "I would like to introduce our new students with us for the month."

Dr. Yamamoto was often held up within the medical center as a perfect example of how opposites attract. He was well liked, soft-spoken, considerate and communicative, always encouraging people to address him as Junichi: the positive to Rothman's negative. Also in contrast to Rothman, he was casually dressed as always, in a Hawaiian shirt beneath his wrinkled and not-too-clean lab coat. If there was one nod to his playful side, Yamamoto was said to be the originator of elaborate and brilliant practical jokes stemming from his graduate student days involving one particularly pompous medical student's expensive fool's errand to a "convention" in Geneva that never was. On the serious side, Dr. Yamamoto's most important characteristic was his complete and total devotion to Rothman and Rothman's work. What was accepted around the medical center was that Rothman was the brains and Yamamoto was the worker bee. They were yin and yang.

"Perhaps you know Lesley Wong and William McKinley," Yamamoto said.

"Like the president," the young man said. "But call me Will."

Will stepped forward, a big smile on his face, hand outstretched. Columbia University Medical School had about 640 students spread over four years of training. In general the first two years were primarily spent absorbing the science of medicine with progressively more and more time creatively devoted to introducing students to patients. The third year was the principal clinical year with the major attention devoted to internal medicine and surgery. The fourth year was mostly rotations in various clinical subspecialties combined with electives according to each student's personal interests. At Columbia the emphasis was on academic medicine. Lesley and Will were fourth-year students in Pia's class. Both thought they had a new interest in research, which was why they had been assigned to spend a month in Rothman's lab.

Pia took Will's outstretched hand and stood up.

"Pia. Grazdani." She noticed that Will was tall, even a little taller than George, who was above average. Like George, Will had blond, unruly hair.

"You're George's friend, right?" Will said.

"George? Yes, of course."

"Love George, great guy. I often play b-ball with him."

"I'm Lesley Wong," the woman said, shaking Pia's hand in turn.

For a moment there was an awkward silence. Pia briefly eyed the two students, realizing they had to be the students Rothman had briefly mentioned the day before and then never brought up again. He had said something about tasking her to come up with something for them to do, as if she wasn't going to be busy enough. One way or another it was going to be a burden of sorts.

Lesley and Will eyed Pia back. For their part, they weren't terribly excited about meeting her either. For them, finding out they had been assigned to Rothman's lab was the equivalent to being sent someplace in Dante's inferno. Rothman had the reputation of destroying every student's sense of self-confidence by making them feel stupid, which they invariably were in comparison to Rothman's encyclopedic knowledge. And they had heard about Pia as well. She too was known as being over-the-top smart and also strangely detached and had taken an early interest in research in addition to the regular curriculum. For most people being a medical student was demanding enough. Except for being tight with George Wilson, who was one of the more popular students in the class, a mark in her favor, Pia never had had the time or inclination to be particularly friendly with many of her classmates. And all that was on top of the gossip that she and Rothman had something going since she was the only person in the entire medical center that he got along with except for Dr. Yamamoto.

Lesley looked over at Will, but he was staring at Pia. When they'd received their assignment, Lesley had told Will that she'd sat next to Pia in a lab every day for a month the first year but she was sure Pia wouldn't remember. Lesley hadn't made up her mind if Pia was extremely focused on her work or just plain rude, although she thought it was the former. As for Will, he was excited to be finally matched with Pia—he'd wanted to be for three and a half years. He'd been sure to introduce himself to every woman in the student body he deemed attractive, but this was the closest he'd come to her.

"Okay. Introductions done," Yamamoto said. It hadn't been quite as awkward as he feared, and he was relieved. He could get down to business.

"If it's okay, we can go to my office. I'd like you to come as well, Pia. There are a couple of things we need to talk over and then we can all go take a look at the organ baths with Dr. Rothman."

Yamamoto beamed a smile and walked away, the two new students padding closely after him. Pia brought up the rear, reluctant to be leaving her reading but excited at the same time. Even though she had been working there for years, she had never seen the organ baths. Although she had spent more actual time with Dr. Yamamoto than she had with Rothman, she didn't feel she knew him as well. In her mind he was more complicated than Rothman. She thought of him as a kindly man but knew that in his own way, he was just as demanding as the chief. He suffered fools no more gladly, but his reprimands and corrections were delivered more politely and at lower volume. Pia had gathered from experience that the quieter Yamamoto spoke, the more important it was to listen.

"Okay, guys, find a seat."

The condition of Yamamoto's office in comparison with Rothman's was as different as the men's personalities. Yamamoto's looked like a typhoon had passed through it. Books, journals, files, documents, papers lay everywhere, including on each of the two seats in front of the desk. Visitors took it on faith that Yamamoto actually had a desk as every square inch was under paper, including a mountain of academic journals positioned so that a curious passerby couldn't see whether the doctor was sitting behind his desk or not.

"Just move those papers," Yamamoto said, as Pia and Lesley Wong gathered them up from the chairs but searched in vain for a free surface on which to put them down. Yamamoto gestured to the floor, a suggestion the women took. He leaned his posterior against the front of the desk and folded his arms. "You could get a chair from the lab," he suggested to Will.

"No problem," Will said. "I'll stand."

"I thought it appropriate for us to do a small review and go over some introductory material so you people can better appreciate what you're about to see,"

Yamamoto said. "You are in for a treat today. I've gotten special dispensation from Dr. Rothman to show you our organ bath program, which has been kept a secret of sorts up until now. It couldn't have been kept a complete secret as there are too many people working here, and we're here in a very public medical center. Since the professor and I are close to publication, secrecy is no longer the issue it was since the university has already seen to it that the appropriate patents have been applied for. At the same time, we would prefer that you keep what you see today to yourselves. Deal?"

All three students nodded.

"All right, let's start at the beginning. But I don't want to make this a boring monologue so help me out! Somebody tell me what a stem cell is."

The three students eyed one another. Will spoke up. "In simple terms it's an undifferentiated immature cell that has the potential of becoming a differentiated mature cell."

"Right on," Yamamoto said. "An example is a bone marrow stem that can become an adult blood cell. These cells are often called adult stem cells. What's a pluripotent stem cell?"

Lesley spoke up: "A stem cell that can turn into any of the three hundred or so types of cells that make up the body of a multicellular organism like a human."

"Right on again. You guys are making this easy for me."

Pia felt a wave of impatience wash over her. She was eager to see the organ bath unit. Had it been up to her, she would have preferred to forgo any review session.

"Up until four or five years ago, how were pluripotent stem cells obtained?"

"From blastocysts." Pia spoke up by reflex. She wanted this little talk over with.

"Right," Yamamoto said. "Blastocysts from fertilized eggs, meaning very early-stage embryos. Why was that a problem that led to serious delays in stem cell research?"

"Because it offended conservatively minded people," Pia said. "Particularly here in the United States, limitations were placed on what could and could not be done in stem cell research with government funds."

"Well said," Yamamoto commented. "Here's a harder question. Let's say that the research on embryonic stem cells had been allowed to proceed unimpeded. Can anyone say what the major problem would have been if the research had advanced to a point of using the stem cells to treat patients?"

None of the students moved.

"Let me give you a hint," Yamamoto said. "I'm referring to an immunological problem."

"Rejection!" Lesley called out, her eyes lighting up.

"Exactly. Rejection, meaning that any use of such embryological stem cells would have elicited some degree of rejection reaction. Some techniques would have reduced this problem but not completely eliminated it."

All three students nodded. Everything that Yamamoto was saying they had heard before. "Now, can anyone define 'induced pluripotent stem cells' in contrast to embryological stem cells? These are the cells that Dr. Rothman and I have been working with exclusively."

"They are pluripotent stem cells made from mature cells, usually a fibroblast and not egg cells," Pia explained. "They are 'induced' by particular proteins to revert back from being a mature fibroblast to being a stem cell."

"Exactly," Yamamoto said. "And isn't it a marvel that it works? For a long time one of the tenets of biological science was that cellular differentiation was a one-way street, meaning the process could never revert. But people should have known that this particular tenet was false. After all, it was known that certain animals could regrow body parts, like starfish and salamanders. Also cancer should have been a hint that the process of differentiation could go in the opposite direction, as many cancers are composed of immature cells that arise in organs populated by mature cells."

Pia found herself glancing at her watch and sitting up straighter in her seat. She wanted to speed up the review session but didn't know how. She inwardly groaned when Lesley piped up with a question: "How exactly are the cells changed back from mature to immature?"

"The same way that everything else is accomplished in the cell," Yamamoto said. "By switching on and off genes. Remember, every eukaryotic cell—that is, a cell with a nucleus—contains a copy of an organism's entire genome. Meaning that every nucleated cell has all the information necessary not only to build itself but to build the entire body. How this works is a process called gene expression, meaning the turning on and off of genes in a kind of molecular ballet. I know you learned all this in your genetics courses in college and during your first two years here at Columbia. Anyway, cellular maturation proceeds by a sequential switching on and off of the appropriate genes. It used to be thought that genes functioned by producing specific proteins, sorta one gene for one protein. But now we know it's far more complicated, as there are significantly fewer genes than originally thought. For the cell to go in the opposite direction of maturation, the sequence has to be reversed. Are you all with me so far?"

All three students nodded. Despite feeling impatient, even Pia was now finding Yamamoto's review fascinating. Like all other researchers, Pia was aware that biological science was unfolding its mysteries at an ever-increasing, mind-boggling speed. The nineteenth century had been chemistry, the twentieth physics. The twenty-first was undoubtedly going to be biology.

Yamamoto checked his own watch. As if answering Pia's hopes, he said, "We've got to move this along if we're going to catch Dr. Rothman in the organ bath unit. Let's go back to our discussion of stem cells. Now that we have the induced pluripotent type that are going to avoid immunological rejection problems and be more acceptable to religious conservatives, what is the first step toward making them useful to treat the patient who donated the fibroblast? Anybody?" Yamamoto glanced from face to face.

Will shrugged and offered, "Get them to mature again but into the kind of cell the patient needs."

"Thank you," Yamamoto said. "Indeed, that is exactly what most stem cell researchers have been busy doing for years: finding out how to regulate gene expression such that the stem cells mature into the kinds of cells that make up the body, like heart cells, kidney cells, liver cells, and so forth. Stem cell researchers have now gotten very good at this, including Dr. Rothman and myself. But here is where Dr. Rothman and I have separated ourselves from the pack and are about to usher in twenty-first-century regenerative medicine that's going to extend and improve the quality of life. We have been able to make virtual leaps in the ability to have these mature cells organize themselves into whole organs. In other words, we've managed to stumble on a host of structural genes and other transcriptional processes that are responsible for creating the lattice-like scaffolding that forms the basis of a three-dimensional organ. Once we had the structure, it was relatively easy to get it populated by the appropriate cells. It's a process called organogenesis. Take, for instance, a liver. Although we and others have been able to make hepatic cells for years, we have never been able to get them to organize themselves into a whole liver with collagen, nerves, and blood vessels, the whole deal. We can do it now. We're doing it with rapidly increasing efficiency. It's phenomenal."

"I assume you've been doing this with animal models?" Pia said.

"Of course! Mostly mice. The whole stem

cell field has extensive experience with the murine model."

"And you believe what you've been learning will be applicable to human cells?"

"We do, and not only on a theoretical basis. Concurrently we've been carrying on this research with human cells as well." Yamamoto held up his left arm and pulled his lab coat sleeve down with his right hand. Proudly he pointed to a number of inch-long scars of varying age along his forearm. "I've been the guinea pig for the source of human fibroblasts. Although most of our research is done with mice, we have some human organs functioning equally well, human organs that could be used to treat me if I needed one of them. You'll see in a few minutes. Any questions before we head over to the unit?"

Yamamoto looked at each of the students in turn and then paused. Finally he said, "Okay, let's make our visit. Hope you guys are ready. You are about to visit the future." He pushed himself up into a fully erect posture.

When the women started to replace the papers and journals they had removed from the chairs when they first arrived,

Yamamoto motioned for them not to bother. With Yamamoto in the lead, the group exited his office. They walked the length of the sizable lab since the organ bath unit was located at the far end on the opposite side from the biosafety unit. As they passed through the lab, some of the technicians looked up from their work and eyed them questioningly. Visitors to the organ bath unit were not common.

First they entered an anteroom where there were caps, gowns, booties, masks, and gloves. There was a similar room on the other side of the lab that guarded entrance into the biosafety unit, just as this room guarded the organ bath unit. Interestingly enough, the rationale was just the opposite. For the biosafety unit the gear was for protection of the visitors. With the organ bath unit it was called reverse precautions and was for protection of the contained specimens. It wasn't until everyone was suited up and had been checked by Yamamoto that they proceeded.

5.

Using a keypad, Dr. Yamamoto punched in a combination, unlocking a simple door. Although she wasn't trying, Pia noticed it was the same code used for the biosafety unit, an alphanumeric sequence that was the time and date of Rothman's birth. Yamamoto stepped aside and ushered the three students into a starkly modern, brightly lit room filled with the gentle, hypnotic sound of running water. Pia felt a slight breeze against her as she advanced. She knew that was evidence of the room having positive pressure, meaning air came out of the room, not in. That was the opposite of the biosafety room, where the laminar flow was into the room.

Stepping beyond the door, Pia shaded her eyes against the sharp bluish light that came from banks of recessed fiber-optic fixtures. She assumed the light had something to do with sterility in the room. Stopping with the others, she took in the scene before her. They had entered a large space painted bright white. Pia was puzzled as to how this lab fit in with the rest of Rothman's suite—it seemed larger than it feasibly could be. At the back of the room, a figure dressed in similar protective garb was hunched over a stainless-steel cart mounted on wheels, making some adjustments on a control panel. There were three rows of such carts and Pia counted thirty of them in all. Set atop each were clear rectangular Plexiglas aquarium-like containers of various sizes. Below were shelves holding various and sundry equipment.

Each also had an attached pole supporting a control panel with an LED display. One of the carts was a few feet to Pia's left and she moved over to take a closer look. Lesley and Will followed.

This was one of the organ-growing baths whose contained fluid was what Pia would be investigating for the month. She leaned over and peered into the container at a miniature translucent object suspended in the liquid by a kind of spiderweb that she was later to find out was made of the same material as real spiderwebs. As for the object itself, she could see it was connected by filament-thin lines to a central clamp where the lines were gathered. A thicker cable fed out of the bath and down into the body of the cart, where there was a boxy device with multiple readouts monitoring the conditions in the bath. An attached magnifying device on a movable arm was also connected to the cart. Pia maneuvered it into position so she could see the contained object better. Although it was not too much larger than a pine nut, its appearance was unmistakably that of a kidney, albeit a very tiny kidney. Most of the lines contained red fluid along one larger one that was clear. The red ones were presumably functioning as veins and arteries. The clear one was acting as the ureter to take away the urine the miniature organ was producing. To one side of the container was a jet, like one attached to a pool circulator, only in miniature. It was pulsating at a very rapid rate. Gentle eddies of liquid coursed around the container, causing the organ's surface to pulsate slightly.

"We find that we must keep the fluid in the baths in constant motion despite the organs being perfused internally. But it has to be carefully modulated. Occasionally the rigid bath sets up a wash that can disturb the organ." Yamamoto had stepped over to join the students. He noticed Pia straighten, looking down the length of the room.

"It's quite something, isn't it?" he said, speaking directly to her. "Of course, I see it every day, so I've come to take it all for granted."

"How are the organs started?" Pia asked.

"They are started in tissue culture dishes designed to mimic the mouse uterine environment in terms of temperature and with pulsation waves close to the normal mouse heart rate of around five hundred and fifty beats a minute. As I said earlier, the whole process, first in the tissue culture dishes and then in these organ baths, is a ballet of gene expression with a careful adherence to sequence and timing. It starts with an aliquot of induced pluripotent stem cells held in close proximity by spiderweb-like restraints. Remember, to form a whole organ we have to involve all three germ layers: ectoderm, mesoderm, and endoderm. Once the organ has reached a size that can be manipulated, it is moved into these baths to develop to its full extent."

"Are there other organs in here besides kidneys?" Will asked.

"Heavens yes," Yamamoto said. "We've got all the usual transplantable organs such as livers, pancreases, lungs, and hearts so far. The kidney program is the most advanced, since it was kidneys we started with. To prove we are on track with what we have been doing, we have already transplanted some organs back into the individual mice from which the fibroblasts were taken with complete and utter success. And let me share another leap forward that we are in the process of making.

We've found that carrying out organogenesis with multiple organs works even better than growing them singularly, meaning we have preparations in which the developing organs are helping each other, like the heart pumping the perfusing fluid and the kidneys removing waste."

"Do you think sometime in the future you could essentially make a whole new organism?" Pia asked with astonishment and not a little dismay.

"At the rate we're going, I see that as a definite possibility, although I can't imagine what the rationale would be."

Pia reflexively shuddered as she realized that Frankenstein, that nineteenth-century nightmare, could very well resurrect itself to haunt the twenty-first in a frighteningly more plausible fashion. If the Rothman-Yamamoto organogenesis worked well with kidneys, hearts, and pancreases, there was no reason it couldn't work just as well with brains.

"Where are the human organs?" Pia asked.

Yamamoto took a few steps down the kidney line and pointed into a larger Plexiglas container. "This is human, as you might expect considering the size. It's also one of the composite preparations with a human heart to do the kidney's internal profusion."

Pia stared into the bath, transfixed by what she was looking at. The kidney did look human, but the heart did not. She asked Yamamoto why.

"Good question. Since oxygenation of the perfusing fluid is being done by the oxygenator on the lower shelf, we did not need a four-chambered heart as two would do. So we altered the design of the heart."

Once again Pia was amazed. "You have that much control of the organo-genesis process to alter the overall three-dimensional architecture?"

"Absolutely. As I mentioned, once we made the original organogenesis break-throughs, our progress has been truly phe-nomenal and isn't slowing down."

The figure Pia had seen earlier finished what he was doing, stood upright, and came toward the group. As he neared, and despite the surgical mask, Pia was further surprised. She could tell it was Rothman. Wearing some kind of goggles with thick, tinted lenses, he made for an eerie figure, like the prototypical mad scientist in his lair. Pia knew that what Dr. Yamamoto had said outside was true—this truly was groundbreaking work. In the stem cell race to move from the promising hypothetical to the clinical, Rothman and Yamamoto had advanced much further than any other team in the world.

Rothman moved the goggles to the top of his head as he came to a stop. He looked at Yamamoto. "Have they been given a short introduction?"

"Yes, Doctor."

Rothman nodded. He knew he was going to have to show off his work to any number of interested biotech venture capitalists over the coming years, even though it wasn't something he enjoyed or found easy. Yamamoto had helped him prepare a script that he'd practiced again and again with his wife. The students were to be a kind of dress rehearsal.

"Welcome to Columbia University Organogenesis Laboratory," Rothman said. Yamamoto coughed gently into his hand. Rothman had trouble deviating even slightly from the prepared text.

"It is common knowledge that there are currently more than one hundred thousand people on waiting lists for organ transplants in this country, and these are people with end-stage disease. The list grows at a rate of about five hundred a month. Currently the same number of people, five hundred or so, die every month. On top of this grim statistic there are thousands upon thousands of additional patients who could benefit from an organ transplant even though they are not yet in a life-threatening situation. Obviously in the current environment the supply of viable organs from either a live donor or a recently deceased individual has not come close to keeping up with demand. Even for those patients lucky enough to receive an organ, the match is often far from optimal, meaning they are relegated to a life of immunosuppression with dire health consequences. What we are doing here, in a cost-conscious fashion, is to create organs which will simultaneously solve the supply problem and the immunological issue. This goal has not yet been reached, but we are making significant progress. At this stage we are looking for outside funding to ramp up production at multiple centers across the country.

"What you see in this row of baths are kidneys that have been created from stem cells derived from fibroblasts—connective tissue cells—of specific mice." Yamamoto tried to interrupt to say that Rothman was covering material that had already been mentioned, but he couldn't get Rothman's attention. Rothman was on a roll. "I wear these magnifying lenses so I can work with the lines, but take my word for it, each organ is hooked up to a pump that circulates a blood-like solution into the kidney's main artery and out its main vein. It's connected by a cannula, or thin tube, from its ureter to a port where its urine output can be sampled. That's one of the functions performed by the monitoring unit beneath the bath. All the data is collected in the mainframe so we can see how tiny fluctuations in conditions affect the kidney and its development.

"Each kidney will soon be implanted back into the same mouse that supplied the original fibroblasts. We've already done this twice with no rejection phenomena whatsoever." With his hand, Rothman gestured toward another group of baths. "These vessels contain pancreases, which have quite different needs than kidneys. Initially we had more difficulty getting the organogenesis process to start than we had with the kidneys, but those initial reverses have been solved, and we are now doing equally well. With the pancreases, we have had to be very careful about the integrity of the connections with the pancreatic duct since the pancreatic secretions contain digestive enzymes. Initially some of our preparations digested themselves."

"Have there been any problems with teratomas?" Pia asked. In contrast to the others, she did not feel intimidated by Rothman. She knew that teratomas, a kind of developmental tumor, were something feared by stem cell biologists.

For a moment Rothman faltered. He had not been expecting to be interrupted in his prepared remarks. Except for the sound of moving fluid emanating from all the organ baths, a brief silence reigned.

"No teratomas at all," Yamamoto said,

coming to his boss's aid. He was well aware of his boss's quirky personality.

As if he had forgotten the students' and Yamamoto's presence, Rothman's attention diverted to the appearance of a small blinking light accompanied by a pinging noise coming from the control panel of one of the baths. Without a second's thought or explanation, Rothman headed in its direction, slipping his goggles back on as he walked.

"That's an alarm that some aspect of the bath's parameters has started to change," Yamamoto explained.

The students watched him go. Lesley and Will were awed at having been in the famous researcher's presence and having survived without being belittled. Pia was impressed by the alarm: "What would have happened if no one had been in here to hear the alarm?"

"Not a problem," Yamamoto said. "All information is followed in real time by the university's mainframe, and Dr. Rothman and I have apps on our iPhones such that we would have been instantly alerted."

"Earlier Dr. Rothman talked to me about a problem with the tissue culture fluid," Pia said. "Was he referring to the fluid in these baths?"

"I'm sure he was," Yamamoto said. "We've been having a continuing problem maintaining the correct pH balance. Did he ask you to look into the problem? Because if he did, it would be a great help. It's not been a particularly big problem, but neither of us has had a chance to look into it. I know I'd feel a lot better if we could solve the issue."

"I'll give it my best," Pia said. "The problem is I'm starting at ground zero. I've had no experience whatsoever with tissue culture."

"That didn't seem to bother you in relation to salmonella," Yamamoto said.

Pia smiled behind her mask. She took Yamamoto's comment as a compliment. "What about Lesley and Will? Maybe it would be appropriate for them to give me a hand."

"That's a great idea," Yamamoto said. He looked at Lesley and Will. "How does that sound to you?"

Both students shrugged. "Sounds good," they said in unison.

As they left the organ bath unit, Pia

turned just before exiting. She looked back at Rothman tending to the bath. The pinging had stopped. Once again the thought of the mad scientist in his lair popped into her mind, and once again she shuddered. She'd visited the future in this room and was excited to become a part of it. At the same time she knew instinctively that there could be a dark side. Biological science was advancing almost too fast, and the problem with science is that it cannot be unlearned.

6.

GREENWICH, CONNECTICUT
MARCH 1, 2011, 3:30 P.M.

Edmund Mathews went to answer the front
door of his waterfront mansion in an extra-
exclusive enclave of the already-exclusive
Connecticut town of Greenwich. It was unusual that he was alone in the house, but
his wife, Alice, had gone to the city with a
girlfriend on a shopping expedition, and
the au pair, Ellen, wasn't back from school
with Darius yet. There was no gardener on
the grounds, no workman in the house,

nor were there any painters, decorators, deliverymen, mechanics, cooks, or anyone else anywhere on the property. The $10 million house was quiet and unattended, just the way Edmund liked it.

This will be Russell, Edmund thought. Edmund and his partner, Russell Lefevre, had decided to take this Tuesday off because their work was about to get crazy. This was going to be the last free day they would have in months, and it seemed like now he was losing some of his free afternoon. Russell had called a few minutes earlier, sounding upset, and said he wanted to come over immediately to talk about something important. Russell had a habit of insisting on talking about anything sensitive in person. Back at Morgan Stanley, when they worked together in asset-backed securities, their calls had been recorded in case either party misremembered the terms of a trade later on. Edmund doubted very much that anyone was listening in nowadays but the old habit lingered with Russell. He was a worrier and he always had been.

Edmund opened the door and greeted Russell. His partner was a tall, lithe man with a sweep of blond hair tinged with gray. He was wearing tennis whites with a sweater thrown over his shoulders. For a man who was usually quite a dandy, he looked thoroughly bedraggled. When he wasn't in a suit, Edmund preferred to wear old T-shirts and shorts, even in winter. He was thicker in the body than Russell, but not overweight, and he kept his hair short and neat with weekly trips to the barber in town.

Edmund could see that Russell had haphazardly parked his Aston Martin DB9 in the driveway and not over by any of the garages as Edmund preferred. The Aston Martin was a fine piece of automotive engineering but it was too ostentatious a machine for everyday use for Edmund's taste. The garish crimson paint job only exacerbated the feeling. Edmund preferred the in-your-face statement he made in his black Escalade, but for driving enjoyment, he loved nothing better than taking his Morgan runabout on the back roads deep into Connecticut. His true pride and joy he drove only rarely: in his garage was a Ferrari 250 GTO that had cost him millions back in the days when that didn't seem like such an extravagance.

"We've got a problem," Russell said as he entered the atrium.

"So I gather. Let's go into the kitchen," said Edmund, who preferred to keep business discussions out of the house if he could help it. This was going to be one of those days he didn't have any choice.

Russell and Edmund had both worked as derivative traders at Morgan Stanley. Edmund was one of the best traders there, agile and decisive and brilliantly able to find someone to take the other side of a position he was holding. He knew Russell had some limitations as a trader, but he had a quant's mind that could calculate risk quickly, and Edmund could rely on him to tell him if something he was planning was feasible. Russell had seen the potential for making money in CDOs—collateralized debt obligations—exotic financial products that took advantage of the subprime mortgage market to create apparently risk-free investments that could make billions in profits for the company and tens of millions for the traders. With property prices on their seemingly unstoppable upward curve, the investments were safe as houses, as people in the know liked to say.

Eventually it turned out that many of the executives at the brokerages selling CDOs and at the financial institutions here and in Germany and Japan and elsewhere who bought them were completely ignorant of what a CDO actually was. They knew what asset-backed securities were, but the assets here were mortgage bonds packaged together and sliced up and sold in bundles. Many of the individual loans the bonds were backed by were subprime loans that would never be paid off, and only a few loans needed to fail before the whole package defaulted. It was inevitable that this would happen.

When Russell explained to Edmund precisely what the subprime loan crisis was going to mean to CDOs and other financial products and for the system as a whole, Edmund was unnerved and excited at the same time. He immediately, and secretly, used his own money to short his own firm and made bets on the failure of other companies exposed to CDOs. He continued to sell the doomed bonds even when disaster was inevitable. He made staggering amounts of money and after a while he told Russell, a loyal company man who'd never dreamed of acting that way, what he was doing. As Edmund predicted, Russell wanted in, and Edmund gave him some of his action.

As the banking catastrophe unfolded there were many victims: investors who'd lost their money, shareholders who found their stocks worthless, countless workers who lost their jobs. Men like Edmund Mathews and Russell Lefevre were not among them. Amid a clamor that the bankers involved should go to jail, they left the firm with close to $100 million in compensation between them.

Edmund had enjoyed his first weekend of unemployment to some extent, taking Darius to soccer practice without bringing his BlackBerry, having dinner with Alice and another couple in town, reading the Sunday paper. But by 9:05 A.M. on that first Monday, he was bored stiff. In his home office, he had two screens showing Bloomberg and MSNBC and he noodled around, making minor trades for a few tens of thousands of dollars through his online account. At ten, he called Russell and suggested they get back in the game on their own.

.　.　.

Okay, Russell, what's the problem?" Edmund said, after handing Russell a glass of ice water. The men stood at either end of the island in the middle of the state-of-the-art kitchen. Edmund flipped Russell a place mat before he could put his water-beaded glass on the butcher block.

"I was playing tennis with Teddy Hill—"

"Teddy Hill? He's got to be sixty-five. I hope you went easy on the old boy."

"Ed, this is serious. I play with Teddy because he knows everyone, and he tells me things he hears. As he did today. When he told me, I practically ran off the court, left him standing there."

"Told you what, Russell?"

"We're being shorted big time."

Russell was right. This was serious.

When he called Russell during his first Monday of alleged freedom, Edmund found that Russell was as anxious as he was to get something going. Unbeknownst to Edmund, Russell needed to be earning. In 2008, he found himself personally long on real estate, owning a portfolio of properties in Florida and California suddenly worth a lot less than their outstanding mortgages.

When Russell had fixed his problem, he was low on cash and needed to leverage his severance money into something more substantial.

As they had done many times as part of a large corporate group, the two men took a weekend away to a hotel in Boca Raton to brainstorm. Before getting down to business, Russell insisted on going to the local mall to pick up some T-shirts for his four kids. Edmund waited for Russell outside the Gap and watched people passing by.

"Look at the people, Russell," Edmund said when his partner returned. "What do you see?"

"Families, strollers, couples, lots of old people. What's on your mind?"

"Right. Old people. It's Florida, famous for oranges and old people. What do old people have?"

"I dunno, high car insurance premiums?" Russell said.

"That," Edmund said, "but this generation also has lots and lots of life insurance."

And Edmund told Russell his idea. It was called "Life Settlement."

The partners figured they had stumbled

upon something big. Russell crunched numbers for weeks while Edmund discreetly got advice from his old contacts: lawyers, traders, bankers, ratings experts, and hedge fund managers. The idea was legal, and it was doable. And Russell said the numbers were watertight.

"The only way this doesn't work is if we have the Second Coming and Jesus stops people dying," Russell said.

"And we know that's not going to happen."

In early 2010, LifeDeals, Inc., was formed with Russell as CEO and Edmund chairman of the board. The start-up money was most of their $100 million take from the subprime debacle, and they used it to buy up life insurance policies from thousands and thousands of Americans desperate for cash. Edmund hired the most aggressive salesmen he knew and told them to hire even more hungry people to go out and pound pavement and buy policies for no more than 15 cents on the dollar. There were millions of Americans who needed money for long-term care, or to finance an operation when they didn't have medical coverage or, as was increasingly the case, even when they did, but the coverage wasn't adequate or the insurance company figured out a way not to pay. LifeDeals had to pay the balance of the premiums, but when the policyholder passed on, as they would as surely as night follows day, the payout was theirs.

Within six months, the LifeDeals board was confident enough to take the company public. Edmund and Russell held options that made them very wealthy once again, but they wanted capitalization to buy more policies. Edmund's favorite statistic was that there was more than $26 trillion in life insurance policies sloshing around out there for the taking. Their plan was to start securitizing the policies, aggregating them, and selling bonds. This time, the assets behind the securities were cast-iron, personally guaranteed by the grim reaper. And thousands of people every day were walking away from policies they had paid into for years because they couldn't afford the premiums. They were waiting to be picked off.

Edmund liked to think his company could someday be worth a trillion dollars.

Who is it?" Edmund asked.

"Teddy doesn't know. He heard it from a

friend who heard it from a friend. But he trusts the party. Swears it's true."

"It's just someone being a wiseass," said Edmund.

"No," said Russell. "It's a biggish bet. Whoever it is, they're sure we're going down the toilet."

"Well, we fucking well better find out who it is before we catch a cold."

Russell knew the implications as well as Edmund. They needed a large institutional investor to underwrite their securitized package, and if it was known on the street that LifeDeals was getting shorted, that partner would be very hard to find. Everyone remembered what happened in 2008.

"We need to start going through the 13Fs right away," Russell said, referencing the quarterly statements institutional investment managers had to file with the SEC outlining their holdings.

"And I need to start making some calls."

Russell had left Wall Street with more intact relationships than had Edmund, and he could easily plug into the rumor mill. It was, after all, a very small community. Edmund didn't need to say anything, both men knew what was at stake.

7.

Off by themselves, Pia, Lesley, and Will were sitting in the mostly empty hospital cafeteria nursing cups of postprandial tea and coffee. Seeing what Rothman and Yamamoto were working on had left each of them shell-shocked. As medical students, they were well aware from an academic standpoint what was being done in the lab and having seen it with their own eyes made it real and concrete. They'd been to the future, and it was difficult to absorb.

"I can't get over it," Lesley Wong said. "I'm still blown away. Growing organs from a patient's own stem cells. Something like that is going to revolutionize medicine."

"It's certainly going to revolutionize the care of degenerative disease," Pia said. "It's going to provide cures instead of just treating symptoms."

"Down the road we could grow our own organs and freeze 'em for when we need 'em," Will said. "Hey, I wonder how Columbia divides the cash on a medical breakthrough like this. This is going to be huge. Yamamoto said that the university has filed patents, but don't you think that Rothman and Yamamoto have to get some kind of cut? Don't you think, Pia?"

Pia had come with Lesley and Will not because she wanted company per se, but because she still felt unnerved by what she had seen and wanted to talk about it. After Dr. Yamamoto led them out of the inner lab with the organ baths that morning, they'd settled in a corner of the lab with the intention of discussing tissue culture fluid. Instead they couldn't stop talking about the progress Rothman had made in organogenesis. As interested as they were, they realized that reading books from the library and doing Web searches was fruitless. The textbooks on this stuff hadn't been written yet.

"You're asking the wrong person," Pia said, responding to Will's question about Rothman and Yamamoto getting a cut. "Money and I don't have much of a relationship."

"But he's gotta be looking at billions here. Doesn't he? I'm going to call my dad, he'll know someone who knows."

"Your dad?" Lesley said.

"Yeah, his broker is pretty well connected."

"I don't think you should be talking about any of this to others," Pia offered. "Particularly people outside the medical center. Remember what Yamamoto said. At least during this month while you're working there or until the key publication is released."

"You might be right," Will said. "But it can't be that much of a secret, as Yamamoto admitted. But certainly it's best not to get on Rothman's wrong side, especially with his reputation."

"I'm just pleased to be part of the scene," Lesley said. "I'd be happy just checking bath temperatures for the month."

"After all the terrible stories I've heard about Rothman's treatment of students, I was expecting the worst today," Will said. "But hell, he seemed very nice to us. Maybe he didn't know we were coming today or didn't know who we were?"

"He had to know who we were," Lesley said. "I think he was using us to practice showing off the progress they've been making. But whatever the reason, I don't care. I'm happy just to have been able to see it."

Inwardly, this was exactly what Pia was thinking. It had been a magical experience for her to visit Rothman's inner sanctum. It had been a long wait, but she didn't care. Nor did she feel any resentment that Lesley and Will had gotten to do it on the very first day of their elective. For Pia, it was as if she had entered a different physical dimension. The room, and what was happening inside it, seemed to belong to a realm quite apart from all that lay outside. What she remembered was a white space, glowing blue, like something from a science fiction movie.

"It was one of the most tantalizing experiences of medical school," Will said. "I loved it."

"Me too," Pia said. "I could have just stood there and watched baths all day."

"Hey, everybody," a voice announced. It was George Wilson, standing at the foot of the table, carrying a cafeteria tray. He'd just emerged from the food table line. "Is this a private party or can a tired radiology extern join you?"

The three students eyed each other. It was Will who spoke up: "If it isn't Mr. Wilson! Hello, George."

"Will, how's it going?" George said. He tried to conceal his displeasure at seeing McKinley sitting at a table with Pia.

"You know Lesley Wong," Will said, playing the host. "And Pia, of course."

"Lesley, hi, how are you? Pia, how was your day with Rothman?"

George was feeling extremely uncomfortable as he'd not yet been invited to sit down and so stood awkwardly next to the threesome's table. It was late, and he'd managed to get to the cafeteria just before it closed. The last person he expected to see there was Pia. The second-to-last person was Will McKinley, who usually held forth in the medical school dorm cafeteria chatting up all the women medical students.

"We were just talking about it," Pia said, unaware of George's discomfort. Social cues were not one of her strong points. "Lesley and Will are also spending their electives in Rothman's lab. And about the day? It was . . . let's say interesting."

"Crazy Rothman saves the world," Will said.

"What do you mean by that?" Pia said. There was a sharpness in her voice.

"Nothing, nothing," Will said, holding up his hands as if he expected Pia to attack him. "It's known you worship the guy—"

"I *respect* the guy—"

"Listen, it's fine, he's clearly some kind of crazy genius." The look on Pia's face persuaded Will that he might be better off changing the subject.

"What we were wondering," Will said, "is how much money Rothman stands to make if he finds investors to back him."

"You were wondering," Lesley said.

"Yes, I was wondering. There's got to be big money in this. Rothman's sitting on a gold mine. Don't you think, George?"

"I'm not exactly sure what you're talking about," George said. "But I can tell I'm interrupting a meeting here." He started to leave, but Will grabbed his jacket just above the elbow and restrained him. "Don't go! Take a seat!"

George glanced at Pia, and she motioned with her head for him to sit down, which he did, unsure if it was the right move.

8.

Edmund Mathews was back at his front door, and again it was Russell. This time Russell hadn't called ahead; he simply texted Edmund on his BlackBerry to say he was coming over. There was only one reason he'd come back. Edmund figured he must have found out who was shorting LifeDeals.

"Edmund. We need to talk."

"Tell me what you found out."

"I need a drink and so will you. Can you fix me a scotch?"

Edmund knew Russell liked the eighteen-year-old Talisker single malt he kept in the den, so he walked Russell over to the room and closed the door behind them. Edmund had been sitting in there reading some research and had started a fire in the grate. The room smelled slightly of smoke, and when Edmund opened the bottle, the peaty aroma of the whiskey added to the effect that they were in a Highland lodge.

"So what do you know?"

Edmund poured two drinks and handed one to Russell, who stared into the fire, an elbow leaning on the mantel.

"I'm a big boy, Russell, I've heard bad news before. Out with it!"

"Gloria Croft," Russell said, snatching a glance at Edmund, then throwing down all of his drink in one shot.

"Excuse me? I thought for a second you said Gloria Croft."

"I did. That's who it is, Edmund, Gloria freaking Croft. She's doing it plain as day through BigSkies."

"You've gotta be kidding me. You have *got* to be fucking *kidding* me!"

Edmund was yelling nearly at the top of his voice. This was why Russell had been concerned—he knew Edmund was going to flip out. There was a knock at the door, and Alice, Edmund's wife, popped her pretty blond head in.

"Oh, hi, Russell. Edmund, Darius is going to bed. . . ."

Alice took one look at her husband's face twisted in a rictus of unalloyed rage. She could see it would be a hopeless task to get anything out of him in this state.

"I'll say good night for you, then. Bye, Russell," Alice blurted, and withdrew, closing the door behind her.

The interlude cut short Edmund's tirade. He poured himself another drink and then one for Russell, closed his eyes for a second, and took a deep breath. Why did it have to be Gloria Croft? "You'd better tell me everything."

Russell sat down on a low padded stool by the fire. Edmund stayed standing.

"I made some calls. It only took two, actually. I called the guy who told Teddy Hill he heard about the shorting and the guy gave up his source. It was someone I'd met before, at some mortgage convention in Vegas. He runs this bullshit financial newsletter. He got it from the horse's mouth."

"The horse's ass, more like. Did he say why she's doing it?"

"Didn't say much. I think once he'd told me he thought better of it and got off the phone pretty quick. He got nervous. She's a big player. BigSkies has a lot of money."

Edmund was experiencing a less-than-pleasant sense of déjà vu. Through her hedge fund, BigSkies, Gloria Croft had taken huge positions betting on the failure of the CDOs issued by, among others, Edmund and Russell's desk. She'd taken the positions early, in 2006, when no one else was doing it and when it was cheap to do. Hundreds of thousands of dollars could turn into tens of millions. What she was indicating was that she thought the AAA-rated mortgage-backed bonds would fail and jeopardize the futures of Wall Street giants like Bear Stearns and Lehman Brothers. Almost no one agreed at the time: There was no chance their stock could go so low. But it did, and it went lower.

Russell and Edmund were quiet, Russell staring into the bottom of his glass, Edmund at the fire hissing and spitting in the grate. He held back the fire guard and popped another log into the flames.

"She's got some balls," Russell said finally.

"She does."

"This is different, though."

"You're right about that."

Russell and Edmund's thinking was following the same track. Sub-prime mortgages were a disaster; as assets, they were just terrible. In their "Life Settlement" paradigm, the debtors were the nation's largest insurance companies, some of the richest institutions in the country. The bottom line was solid, encapsulated in one of Edmund's favorite sayings of recent months: What are the insurance policy holders going to do, not die?

"So what is she doing?" Edmund said after another long pause. "It doesn't make sense. We know the numbers, right? We're solid all round. Actuarially, we did the worst case—people living a little longer for God knows what reason—and we've taken those tolerances into account. Unless she's shorting you and me personally. But she's too smart for that. Way too smart. There's gotta be something she sees in the numbers."

"If there was anything in the numbers, *I'd* have seen it," Russell said a little testily.

"I know that, Russell. She's seeing something that isn't there. It really doesn't matter why she's doing it, she's doing it and we might be left standing in the rain with our dicks in our hands. God *damn* it."

"So what do we do?"

"We have to talk to her, find out what she knows," Edmund said. "Try to talk some sense into her. When she understands what the upside is, perhaps we can help her out."

Edmund was talking about offering Gloria an inside track to invest in the company and share in the enormous windfall they were confident was coming.

"Maybe that's what she wants," Russell said. "She's sending up a smoke signal."

"She could call us on the telephone and ask," Edmund said. He thought for a second. "Let's call her right now."

"Now? It's after nine o'clock at night."

"Call her anyway. She's always working. I'm not sure I'll be able to get to sleep tonight unless we talk to her. Do you have her cell?"

"Yes, but why me?"

"You did business with her. And she's not going to take my call. Pure and simple."

Years back, Gloria had worked for Edmund as a humble analyst two jobs before she went out on her own. Edmund's desk was a boys' club and women had to be very thick-skinned to work there. This much Russell knew. There was more he didn't know, but the bottom line was that it hadn't ended well. Russell happened to have been present the last time Edmund had seen Gloria, when she walked out of a bar full of about-to-be-former traders where she'd gone to commiserate with one of her friends who had been fired. She was walking out because Edmund, who was very drunk, was yelling at her.

"You're the reason these people are out of work," Edmund had shouted. Many people would contend that it was the products Edmund sold that ruined the firms and caused people to be fired rather than the shortsellers who saw an opportunity.

But from Edmund's perspective, his own participation was purely short-term expedient. Gloria's role was more causative.

Russell scrolled through his BlackBerry for Gloria Croft's number. He dialed, and Gloria picked up after a couple of rings.

"Gloria, it's Russell Lefevre."

"Russell, how are you?" Gloria's voice was level and deliberate. She didn't act surprised in the slightest to hear Russell's voice despite the hour.

"Good, thank you. I trust you are too. Where are you? I hope you're not still in the office at this hour." Russell could hear background sounds that suggested she was.

"Just watching Asia open. I've been expecting your call. Is Edmund there with you? You can put me on speaker if you like."

"Hang on a second, Gloria."

As Edmund rolled his eyes, Russell fiddled with the buttons on his phone, then propped it up against the bottle of Talisker.

"Okay, Gloria," Russell said.

"Hello, Edmund. How are *you*?"

"Okay, Gloria," Edmund said, trying to sound carefree. He looked imploringly at Russell. This was his call, couldn't he just get on with it?

"Gloria, we'd like to get together with you," Russell interjected. "We have some things we'd like to discuss."

"What types of things, Russell?" Her voice was carefree, as if she were enjoying herself.

"Stop screwing around, Gloria," Edmund said, all lightness gone from his voice. "LifeDeals, as you know perfectly well."

"Ah, the same charming Edmund Mathews I remember so well. If you want to talk, you're welcome to come and see me at my office."

This was a power move, and Edmund was making a vigorous throat-slashing gesture with his right hand. He didn't want to go to her office and cede her the offensive.

"How about we meet for lunch?" Russell suggested. "You like Terrasini, I remember. And I haven't been there in a while. Would that work for you?" He was suggesting the excellent midtown Italian restaurant, long a financiers' favorite.

"Russell, I'm sorry, I'm booked solid. And I'm going out of town. It's here or it's nothing until next week."

"Hold on, Gloria."

Russell picked up the phone and quickly muted it, just in time.

"Jesus, who does she think she is?" The veins in Edmund's neck were bulging. It was as if Gloria were still working for him, and she were talking back to him.

"Edmund, she's got us over a barrel and she knows it. We need to know what she's looking at. I'll go, if you can't stand it."

"No, I'll go. Like some damned supplicant. She's going to pay for this. Somewhere down the road. And big-time."

For once, Edmund's curiosity had trumped his vanity. Russell got back on the line.

"Gloria, sorry about that. Any chance we can see you tomorrow?"

"How about nine o'clock?"

It was another raised middle finger as far as Edmund was concerned. Nine o'clock meant driving into Manhattan and battling all the commuters. Edmund had an aversion to public transportation so taking the train was out of the question. Edmund was making the throat-slashing motion again.

"Sorry, Gloria, I've got an appointment early on that I can't break. How about ten-thirty?"

"Okay, Russell," Gloria said with amusement. She could imagine how her request had been greeted by Edmund.

"See you tomorrow," Russell said, ending the call. Edmund sighed, grateful for the one small concession.

9.

406 PARK AVENUE
NEW YORK CITY
MARCH 2, 2011, 10:37 A.M.

Edmund and Russell entered the midsize high-rise along Park Avenue in midtown Manhattan. Predictably, Edmund had been in a sour mood on the Town Car ride down from Greenwich. Russell had insisted on sharing the ride—he wanted to see if he could soften his partner's mood before they met Gloria Croft. Edmund had been a bully all his life, and he felt uncomfortable in any situation where he wasn't in charge. Not only was he not controlling events here, it seemed like he was being played, and by a woman, and by a woman who used to work for him. Russell doubted whether his calming words had had any effect.

When they arrived, Gloria used a script she had learned from Edmund, and Edmund knew it. The two men were buzzed into the suite and shown into a glass-walled conference room, where they were left to stew for fifteen minutes. The receptionist was very polite, and they were offered coffee or water. Outside the room, the office seemed calm and peaceful, with only the hum of the air-conditioning system breaking the silence. The image exuded was of quiet authority.

Then Gloria emerged. She'd changed her look since Edmund had last seen her. There was now a slight wave to her mid-length, lustrous brown hair. She wore a well-tailored business suit with a lavender blouse and black heels. There was just the right hint of décolletage. She looked like ten million dollars.

"Gentlemen, I'm very sorry, something

going on in Singapore." Russell and Edmund had stood up when Gloria entered, and she walked over to each man and shook his hand. There was a slight, almost imperceptible smile on her face. She was clearly enjoying herself.

"Follow me!" She walked out of the conference room quickly, and Edmund and Russell gathered up their coats and briefcases and hustled after her.

"She's got us trotting along like a couple of poodles," Edmund muttered under his breath.

Gloria was already sitting at her desk when the men entered her office. Some giant, abstract, and presumably very expensive painting hung on the wall behind her. The desk itself was bare save for several large telephones; carrels behind Gloria were strewn with prospectuses and various files. One entire mahogany wall was inset with the mandatory array of televisions carrying the financial channels. Gloria pressed a button on the underside of her desk, and the office door soundlessly closed. When she spoke, she sounded coy even if Edmund knew that was something she was incapable of.

"I feel like I'm twenty-five again. Back then I was like a suckerfish hanging around the great predators, looking for the little scraps of food they missed when they fed. The ocean was full of blood. It was a lot more fun then than it is now, don't you agree?"

Edmund didn't like the way this had started out. Even he wouldn't have been this bold. Now she was the shark, and they were the suckerfish, and it was their blood she smelled in the water. He bit his tongue until Gloria started talking about the "opportunities" she had lucked into in the subprime field, opportunities she was grateful that the market (meaning Edmund and Russell) had made available to her.

"Well, Gloria," Edmund said, trying to control himself, "you're just not as smart as you think you are. That subprime stuff was never designed to succeed. We knew it was going to fail. We were shorting each other. We were shorting ourselves."

"Maybe you were, but not till the very end. I was buying swaps five years before you"—Edmund snorted—"and you guys were still leveraging your position selling the worthless bonds right up until Lehman went down. Tell me you weren't."

Gloria had at least one of her gloves off now. She felt she held a winning hand against LifeDeals. It might make for a longer game if she held her cards, but she had Edmund and Russell right where she wanted them, and she could enjoy witnessing their reaction if she played her hand now. She'd probably make just as much money in the long run if LifeDeals wasn't a public company. It depended on how far Edmund was going to push his luck. That morning before they arrived she'd looked at herself in the bathroom mirror and said, "Payback time."

Gloria cleared her throat and went on: "The traders who sold those CDOs should have gone to jail. The whole of Wall Street was tarred with that brush. Immoral, greedy, selfish . . . it was *stealing*."

"Nonsense," Edmund said. "You said it yourself: it was an *opportunity*. You destroyed those companies. Your fingerprints are on the bodies. The government mandated that mortgage lenders make subprime deals. Everybody should have a home. No one held a gun to anyone's head. . . . I don't understand why we're raking over all this again. We've moved on. You clearly haven't, but I'd urge you in the strongest possible terms to *get over it*."

Edmund was exerting as much self-control as he could, speaking slowly and evenly. Russell knew the plug on the volcano was shaking, the whole thing was threatening to blow. Robotically Edmund continued.

"We have the utmost confidence that LifeDeals is a winner and is going to prove to be so in the very near future."

"Oh really," Gloria said. "Well, I have half a million in credit default swaps on the line that says it won't. And I'm going to buy more. And you know what, I'll be glad when it fails, because I think you're stealing again, only this time you're stealing vulnerable people's life insurance, and you're paying them pennies. These are old people who are desperate for money because they need an operation and don't want to go bankrupt because our health system has written them off."

Edmund was massaging his temples. They were bankers, they made money, end of story.

"The Supreme Court has ruled that life insurance policies are equity that people can buy and sell," Edmund said.

"You're paying fifteen percent of face value. Ten if you can."

"We are offering a legitimate financial service to older Americans who need cash for whatever reason. We haven't created the need, we're merely filling it. It's of no concern to me whether an individual is paying for a new hip or a cruise to Alaska. Perhaps they just don't want their ungrateful children to get the money. There's nothing immoral or unethical about it. We're helping put money back into the economy. You should thank us."

"Oh, spare me, Edmund. Now that the mortgage market has dried up, some clever analyst zeroed in on life insurance. It's another gold mine and damn the consequences for the people involved."

Russell could see this was going nowhere fast. He moved forward in his seat. "Gloria, with all due respect, Edmund and I didn't drive down here to debate the ethics of life settlements, although I have to say they have been around for years with little protest. We'll have to agree to disagree.

We'd like to know why you're so sure we're wrong. I brought along some research as backup."

Russell placed financial statements in front of Gloria along with complicated graphs that showed bell curves for the life expectancy of people whose policies LifeDeals had purchased, separating them by the diseases the holders suffered. He gave Gloria the whole picture, letting her see her more information than was normally presented to prospective hedge fund managers. He then described the plan, how they would securitize the policies into bonds, resulting in vastly increased income that was then used to buy up more policies to make into more bonds. The bonds were weighted, the largest segment based on diabetes, the second largest on cardiovascular disease, and the third on kidney disease. While Russell talked, Gloria glanced at the financial statements and the bell curves. It didn't take her long. When she was finished, she tossed them aside as if she didn't believe any of it.

Finally Russell explained that since the bell curves could accurately predict when the policies would pay out, they could factor in all the other cogent data and determine their cash flow extremely accurately and buy as many policies as the revenue streams allowed. Their actuarial data was enormous, going back fifty years, and even longer if they needed it.

"We've left nothing to chance," Russell said. "It's foolproof, based on real numbers. Sure, a few people are going to have spontaneous remissions, but others will pay out faster than predicted. It's all based on accepted mathematics and the bedrock is the insurance companies. It might be the best investment opportunity ever, backed by the Supreme Court ruling, so there's no chance the insurance industry can lobby Congress to have laws and rules changed. The insurance companies are going to pay every penny the policies have accrued."

Russell suddenly stopped, out of breath. Russell and Edmund looked at Gloria, who stared back for a couple of beats. There was silence.

"Don't you see it?" Russell questioned.

"*I* see it," Gloria said. "You're the ones who don't see it."

"It's real. We've run the numbers up and down and confirmed it with all the actuarial companies. It's real. We're already holding fifty thousand policies—"

Gloria whistled. "How much are the premiums on fifty thousand policies, Russell? You must be paying out about four, five million a month. You're going to run out of capital by the end of next year if you don't start having significant income."

Russell and Edmund knew she was right. That Gloria was smart was not news to Edmund; he wouldn't have hired her otherwise way back when. But in this instance they'd be fine, they were going to be fully capitalized by the end of this year. He wondered if Gloria might be bluffing and was beginning to think she was. So far she'd given them nothing. He was getting tired of this.

"Gloria. All you've told us is that we are mean, heartless bastards taking money from old ladies," Edmund said. "But we knew that already. I think you're fishing. You told some guy you were shorting us knowing it would flush us out, and we'd come down here and explain our business plan. Which we have done. Congratulations. Now we should go and not take up any more of your time. We'll be more than happy to mail you a prospectus in due course."

Edmund's irritated expression had morphed into the insufferably smug look Gloria remembered from whenever he had dressed her down in days of yore. She pulled out the central drawer of her desk and found a red Sharpie on her desk. Looking at Edmund, she took one of Russell's graphs and copied the bell curve, only drawing it shifted to the right of the one printed on the paper. She held up the graph.

"What would it mean to you if this happened?"

Russell squinted at the paper—it was the diabetes chart.

"That's not going to happen."

"Humor me. Hypothetically."

"You're projecting chronically sick diabetes patients living about ten years longer than they're going to live. As I said, it's not going to happen."

"Let's say forty percent of your policies are diabetes patients. If we have a curve like mine instead of the curve like yours, I reckon that's twenty thousand policies you're stuck with for ten additional years.

That's, um, two hundred and forty million in premiums you weren't expecting to pay. Kind of cuts into your model, doesn't it? Perhaps they're half your policies. I think the curve needs to move a little more. Fifteen years and it's four hundred and fifty million. Your biggest source of revenue becomes a sinkhole of toxic assets."

"That's hypothetical, and it flies in the face of fifty years of actuarial data. Fifty years!"

Edmund was yelling but Gloria was looking at Russell. He looked worried.

"Yes, you have fifty years' worth of *old* data. But you're not looking at the future. Technology can make a monkey out of a table in a minute. If you have any more great ideas, please share them with me, I will be happy to take a position on them too."

"What the fuck are you talking about?" Edmund demanded.

"Do you know what an iPS cell is?"

"I've heard of them, yes," said Edmund. "Something to do with stem cells. But I don't see—"

"Induced pluripotent stem cells," said Gloria. "If you looked to the future and not to the past, you might know that iPS cells are going to have a huge impact on regenerative medicine."

"You mean stem cell therapy?" said Edmund. "That bubble burst ten years ago, all those biotechnology start-ups? Penny stocks today."

"Edmund, you're still talking about the past." Gloria had come this far. "You're ignoring the future."

"Okay, Gloria, what do you see in your crystal ball?"

"Have you heard of the Nobel laureate Tobias Rothman? Or Junichi Yamamoto? What they're doing at their research lab up at Columbia Medical Center?"

"No," Russell said, feeling that the ceiling was pressing in on him.

"Through a contact who follows biotech patents I've learned that Rothman has mouse organs, entire organs, that he has grown from iPS cells that he's transplanted back into the same mice that donated the cells. Any day now he's going to do it with human iPS cells if he hasn't already. He'll be able to grow pancreases. For humans. To make insulin. Pancreases that are custom made for a patient so no rejection. You know what that's going to do?" Gloria pointed to the graph she had drawn over and dragged her finger from Russell's bell curve to her red version.

"That."

Gloria sat back.

Russell had done the real math in his head. Thanks to some particularly aggressive salesmen in Texas and Florida, they were extremely long on diabetics' policies. Gloria had in fact undershot—they were almost two-thirds of their policies. Meaning they might be on the hook for almost $600 million in additional premiums. Who knew if the science was going to work and when, and not every patient was going to be helped, but still, if she was right, their paradigm would be in tatters. Was there any way they could dump those policies? Could they securitize them anyway? Would anyone invest in the company with this much doubt about the nature of the risk? These questions were occurring to Russell; Edmund just wanted to get the hell out of there.

"Think of LifeDeals as a swimming pool," said Gloria. "There's water pouring out already and there's going to be a lot less of it pouring in than you planned in the near term. You guys are going to be left high and dry with no life preserver."

Gloria was enjoying herself.

"You want some advice? I doubt it but I'm going to give it to you anyway. Hurry up and securitize and sell those tranches ASAP, before others start to see that the ground under LifeDeals is going to be more like quicksand than bedrock. Once that happens, your bonds are going to go begging. Some of the money that comes in from the bonds you might be able to squirrel away if you're clever, and I know you are, but you certainly aren't going to get back your seed money. Unless you want to break the law. Which brings us neatly full circle. Perhaps you'll end up going to jail this time."

"Russell, we gotta go," Edmund said, as Russell gathered up his papers. Edmund and Gloria held each other's glare. Gloria had played her hand, and she could see it had hit home.

"So sorry you guys have to run, but I have to go to lunch anyway," she said.

Gloria handed Russell some more of his papers. She'd already decided to strengthen her position against LifeDeals significantly later that day. Edmund was right in part— she had wanted them to tell her about their business plan, and she assumed Edmund would be arrogant enough to tell her too much. Now she'd seen their model, and it was even worse than she could have hoped. Or better. Maybe she'd cost herself some money, but she already had more than she could reasonably spend in three lifetimes.

That look on Edmund's face was price-less.

Edmund and Russell were silent as they waited for the elevator. Russell stole a look at Edmund's face, and it bore an expression he had never seen. It looked like grief. They got in the elevator.

"Hold these a second," Edmund said to Russell, handing him his case and his coat. Edmund stepped forward and slammed the elevator door hard with the fist he'd made of his left hand. He cried out and grabbed his hand. The pain, when it came, was a relief.

10.

COLUMBIA UNIVERSITY MEDICAL CENTER
NEW YORK CITY
MARCH 2, 2011, 1:00 P.M.

Pia had quickly learned to feel at home in what Dr. Yamamoto liked to call the "bathroom," the organ bath facility where the mouse kidneys, hearts, lungs, and pancreases were being nurtured. She had spent the morning in there, harvesting reams of data on the pH levels in the baths and using a handheld tablet to look at the histories of a few organs that had failed. They were later found to have very subtle variations in acidity or alkalinity from the rest of the samples. Pia's task was to monitor the baths, and she tried to figure out how she might rig up some kind of electronic alarm to her cell phone like Rothman and Yamamoto had that would alert her when a bath developed a slight variation in pH.

Dr. Rothman had come and gone a couple of times. Pia knew from speaking with Dr. Yamamoto that the team was running complex and time-consuming studies concurrently, both here with the baths and in the biosafety level-3 lab on the other side of Rothman's complex. Rothman's work on salmonella had made his reputation, and he wasn't about to abandon it, even if it meant working at superhuman levels of energy and concentration. He treasured his access to the highly virulent strains that NASA provided him with, and with the space shuttle program winding down, he didn't know when he might get more.

Lesley and Will had left the room to find Dr. Yamamoto. It had been decided that in addition to helping Pia, they would initiate their own study of the effects of slight variations in the temperature of the baths.

Unfortunately their study had reached a quick impasse, and they preferred to consult Dr. Rothman's associate rather than the man himself.

Dr. Rothman entered the room, moving to the last row of baths.

"We seem to have a problem with number nineteen," he said, apparently into thin air. Pia joined Rothman, who was fiddling with the monitoring unit under the bath.

"The blood flow is compromised. There's a blockage, so we may have to section the organ to see if the problem is developmental or some kind of embolus. There are few journeys longer from *in vitro* to *in vivo*."

"How long before you can start human trials?" Pia said.

Rothman flinched a little and looked around at Pia, apparently in surprise. Had he been talking to himself?

"We're a little closer with the kidney than with the pancreas. The kidney is basically a filter. Quite simple. But the pancreas is very complicated. It's fascinating to me that one gland would have so much to do, and such important tasks."

"Hormones and enzymes," Pia said.

"The islets of Langerhans. I always loved that name. They were discovered by a twenty-one-year-old German named Paul Langerhans in 1869. I remember when I was a teenager and first heard the term I thought they were named after some actual islands someplace."

Pia had rarely heard Dr. Rothman sound so jovial. He seemed to revel in his lair. Pia thought it fitted his temperament to enjoy the name of the hormone-producing cells of the pancreas that pumped insulin and glucagon into the bloodstream to regulate sugar levels. Or at least, they were intended to.

"Of course it was necessary to locate the pancreas adjacent to the duodenum so it could inject its enzymes into the digestive system. The ampulla of Vater, another of my favorites."

Rothman was referring to the junction of the bile duct and the pancreatic duct where food passing through the intestine was mixed with the agents necessary for its digestion and to control the level of acidity.

"But it's so deeply buried in there. It's very elusive. That's why pancreatic cancer is so hard to detect and so lethal. The organ has such a large blood supply cancers tend to spread very quickly."

Rothman's mind was wandering. He seemed so uncharacteristically relaxed.

"Its organogenesis is very elusive too. All the hormone- and enzyme-producing cells have to be genetically coded to create the gland, and we're just coming to grips with the process."

Rothman had moved to a different bath.

"The mouse pancreas is remarkably similar to ours. We're making strides here, but I want to speed things up."

Some scientists were working on implanting glucose sensors and insulin pumps into patients. Others were examining gene therapy solutions, with patients ingesting a medication containing a virus to cause the production of insulin in the presence of glucose. Rothman was tackling the issue the only way he knew: by swinging for the fences. Pia loved that confidence and ambition. She felt some of it had rubbed off on her in the time she had spent with Rothman over the last three years. She also knew how other people saw him. They saw that confidence as arrogance of the worst kind, but it could be arrogance only if the conceit was deliberate. It wasn't just that Rothman didn't care what other people thought, he didn't notice either.

"I wanted to thank you, Doctor," Pia said.

"For what?"

"For offering to lend me money to pay the Sisters."

"The Sisters helped you in the past, but the past is the past. You don't need them anymore. You need to move beyond all the problems foster care caused you, just like I did."

"I'm trying to," she said, referring to rising above the legacy of her childhood experiences. But about not needing the Sisters anymore, she wasn't so sure.

"My sons are not as healthy as I would like. I feel very guilty," Rothman said out of the blue, shocking Pia. He rarely said anything personal, especially something so very personal. The only other time was when he'd admitted having Asperger's.

"I'm so sorry," Pia said. "I had no idea."

"Nobody does," Rothman said, uncharacteristically wistfully. "I never talk about it. But it's a big part of my race with stem cells and stem cell science."

Pia didn't know what to say. What was suddenly clear was why Rothman had made such a deviation in his scientific pursuits after such success with his salmonella work.

Rothman continued to watch the tiny pancreas suspended in the bottom of the bath. Pia could only imagine what flight of hope his mind was taking him on now. She could see him almost physically shake it off. He took one more look at the figures on the monitor and wordlessly left Pia's side. It was amazing and distressing how he could turn on and off.

11.

After leaving Gloria Croft's office, Edmund Mathews, still steaming mad and nursing a sore left hand, turned east onto Lexington Avenue and found a Duane Reade pharmacy. He bought a bottle of Motrin and took four. His hand throbbed sharply, but he was certain he hadn't broken any bones when he slammed the elevator door. Had he used his stronger right hand, he surely would have. Russell Lefevre often found

Edmund's behavior during crises to be un-
predictable and alarming, but he knew Edmund had a laser-like focus that he could
bring to bear at times like this. Edmund had
the ability to break down complex problems and attack them piece by piece until
he had it licked.

Edmund had the car brought around
and the two men sat in it double-parked
on East Fifty-eighth Street. Russell swore
he could hear Edmund thinking.

"We have to get a head start on securitizing what we have," Russell said.

"Yes. For certain. And look at the diabetics whose policies we own," said Edmund.
"See if it mightn't be cheaper to cancel
some rather than carry them. And we
should lay off some of our sales force until
further notice."

Edmund had Russell call a contact at
Goldman Sachs, a man named McDonald
in the asset-backed securities division.
McDonald had been interested in Life-
Deals but was wary. Russell was still con-
fident they would get one of the major
players on board, and he hadn't spoken to
McDonald in a while. It happened that Mc-
Donald had a few minutes to spare an old

client, and Edmund and Russell headed down to West Street in Battery Park City and Goldman's global headquarters.

That guy's small-time, no vision," Edmund said, after the unsatisfying meeting. Russell had answered all the questions the traders asked about securitizing their portfolio of life settlements sooner rather than later. But the traders couldn't see what the hurry was. From their perspective the more policies they had to bundle, the better their product was going to be. And they hadn't done the grueling legal legwork to create the complex CDOs to be in a position to take them to market. What Russell and Edmund had been looking for was reassurance after their meeting with Gloria Croft. As they left Goldman they admitted to each other that the reaction they'd gotten wasn't exactly negative, it just wasn't wildly positive either.

In the car Russell and Edmund made another decision. As Gloria Croft had so devastatingly demonstrated, the main problem they were facing was with the mortality-rate bell curves that LifeDeals' viability was predicated on and the damage that medical advances might do in terms of moving the curve to the right.

"We need to go see Henry Green," Edmund said. Henry Green was CEO of Statistical Solutions LLC, the company that had produced all the actuarial data, including the bell curves. Edmund got out his BlackBerry. This was a call he wanted to make.

"Henry Green, please. . . . Okay, well, tell him Edmund Mathews is in the city and on his way over and needs to see him right away. . . . Well, I'm sure he'll understand when you tell him. Our key data has flaws. There's new information. We need to fix it." Edmund hung up.

"He'll see us," Edmund said.

LifeDeals had put Statistical Solutions on an expensive retainer. Russell wanted to be armed with the best available statistical analysis when they went on the road selling their product. One supposed lesson from the subprime debacle was that investors wanted to know exactly what they were investing in. It might appear to be self-evident, but it wasn't. Russell wanted to be able to show an investor the latest data, even individual policies, if they cared to see them.

For his part, Henry Green was less than pleased to be hearing from Edmund Mathews at all, let alone when he was demanding a face-to-face meeting without notice. While Russell Lefevre wanted the full breadth and depth of research that Statistical Solutions offered, he gave the firm time to accomplish what was asked for. In contrast, Edmund Mathews would call up and want immediate answers to complicated questions. Green had had to drive his people hard, squeezing every last cent's worth of work out of the company to comply. Edmund expected Henry to drop everything whenever he called.

Edmund and Russell arrived at the Statistical Solutions offices in Chelsea in short order and within a couple of minutes were sitting with Green in his office.

"Edmund, I gather you mentioned something on the phone about 'new information,'" Green said hesitantly.

"That's right," said Russell, who wanted very much to avoid having Edmund yell at Henry Green, which had happened in the past. "There's new material and we need your expert opinion to see if we need to be concerned about it."

Edmund sighed at the understatement.

"What my colleague is trying to say, Henry, is that you may have been wrong in some of your forecasts by amounts that could put us out of business. So I'd be very grateful, Henry, if you could get those geniuses you told us about who could have gotten jobs at Google to come in here and prove to us that they are in fact smart enough to tie their own shoelaces after all."

Edmund's voice was rising in volume but the dam held, just. Henry Green pressed a number on his phone pad and picked up the receiver.

"Yes, Laura, would you have Tom and Isabel meet us in the conference room right away?" Green hung up the phone.

"Gentlemen, shall we?"

Everyone Russell and Edmund could see around the office was young. Henry Green at least affected the look of a business-man with his dress slacks and dark shirt, but his messy hair was at least two inches too long in back. The numbers geeks, dressed in black, looked like they had just come in from an all-night party. Statistical Solutions was gaining a reputation for all kinds of data collection and algorithm solving, and a lot of their employees did indeed go on and work for Silicon Valley giants that paid for their dry cleaning and accommodated their dogs at work. To keep them, Henry Green had to be equally tolerant and generous. As long as they gave him six months of hard work, Henry Green didn't mind. Statistical Solutions was strongly in the black.

Anticipating that Russell wanted to speak, Edmund dove right in, addressing Isabel and Tom directly.

"What do you know about stem cell research in relation to the treatment of diabetes?"

"I know what stem cells are," Isabel Lee said.

"Did you build it into your projections?"

"Build what in?"

"The fact that a professor up at Columbia is making strides toward creating human pancreases outside the body to be used as transplants. If he succeeds, he'll be prolonging the life of diabetes patients."

"Which is a good thing, of course," Isabel said. Neither Isabel nor her colleague Tom Graham enjoyed working on mortality statistics for LifeDeals, even less when they found out what LifeDeals was doing with them. They'd mentioned their misgivings to Green, but he'd waved them off, saying they were not being paid to make ethical value judgments. Yeah, the concept of making money from people's deaths is creepy, but the pay is good.

"Yes, it's a wonderful day for medicine and fat people, less good for my investors," Edmund said.

"Listen, we gave you full license to draw up parameters for us, using actuarial data and cross-referencing it with our cash-flow projections, and nowhere did we see any information about this," Russell said, getting a nod of agreement from Edmund.

"Russell, we built in increases in life expectancy and added tolerances for unexpected developments, but they were capped at five percent," Henry said. "As we discussed, as you agreed. If there is about to be a major breakthrough like custom-made transplantable pancreases from stem cell research or fallout from the human genome project, we can't be held responsible. You can't anticipate once-in-a-century events."

"Then all this fucking statistical research is useless," Edmund snapped, throwing up his hands in frustration. "It's all nothing but mental masturbation."

"Na-ha," Isabel said, not at all intimidated. "It's good data for what we had. If there's a paradigm shift, then numbers change and graphs have to be adjusted to reflect it. Simple as that." She shrugged and sat back in her chair.

Tom Graham was looking at a fingernail and didn't respond.

"That's it! That's what we get! Whoops, sorry, wrong number. We didn't think of that! We were paying you to think of everything. It's not as if stem cells popped out of the blue. What sort of company are you running anyway?"

"Okay, let's not get worked up here," Russell interjected. "Henry, Edmund apologizes—"

"Don't apologize to me, apologize to them," Henry said, indicating Isabel and Tom. Isabel glowered at Edmund, who eventually raised a hand to speak. It was about as contrite as he was going to be.

"Henry, listen, we need some fresh models run based on some new assumptions that I can e-mail to you in an hour or so, soon as we get back. We need to see how our cash flow is affected in these new scenarios. You'll have to make assumptions as there is no real data available. We'd be very grateful if you could do it for us. And we need it right away. As you know, there's provision in our contract—"

"Yes, Russell, I know," said Henry. "In actual fact, I happened to take a look at our contract when you were on your way over. We'll do the work for you, have it for you tomorrow, as soon as we can. As *you* know, Russell, there's a mutual twenty-four-hour cancellation provision in the contract, under certain circumstances. I believe circumstances such as these cover the provision more than adequately. So consider this your notice."

More deflated than they had been on arrival, Edmund and Russell didn't have it in them to protest. They got up to leave.

12.

At her home outside Phoenix, Sally Mason sat on a bench next to the entrance making the most of the last of the morning air before the sun made sitting outside unbearable. Even though Sally had been born in the state and lived here all her life, the heat had always got to her. Sally was proud of the fact that she was a lifelong Arizonan. There'd been only about 450,000 people living in Arizona when she was born in 1933, and that was about the current population of Mesa, a place that was barely a dot on the map when she was growing up.

Today, Sally was scheduled to receive another visit from Howard Essen, the salesman she'd met a couple of times and spoken to on the phone frequently in the last few weeks. Sally appreciated the fact that Essen hadn't been too much of a hard-seller, not as relentless certainly as the man who sold her husband the life insurance policy in the first place. She'd actually enjoyed talking to Howard about his family, a wife and three children, to whom he was clearly devoted. He'd also shown interest in her story, about Arizona when she was a girl when they still tied up horses outside stores in downtown Phoenix, about her Preston, now twenty years gone, and about their only daughter, Jean, and her son. This was one of the good days, a day she didn't have to travel forty-five minutes for hours of tedious and uncomfortable dialysis.

Sally had decided that today she was going to tell Howard Essen she was accepting his proposal.

Howard agreed to Sally's request to come at noon, as she wanted to keep the afternoon free. She checked her watch—it was about ten of—and Sally closed her eyes and thought about Preston as she did most days. She'd been so young when they met, barely eighteen, and he looked so dashing in his Air Force uniform when he came into her pop's convenience store. The fifth day in a row he came in he ran out of things he needed to buy and he had no ready excuse: He was here to see Sally. Life with Preston hadn't always been easy, but he was always a caring man. Toward the end, he set up the life insurance policy for Sally and funded an annuity to make the payments with a little left over. Preston wanted to make sure their daughter, Jean, was taken care of, and he hoped that would be one less worry for Sally.

The money going to Jean under the policy always seemed like such a huge sum to Sally. That was until Jean's husband died suddenly, leaving her with a mountain of bills and debts she had no idea existed. The money that Sally had squirreled away after selling the house Preston bought in 1965, the best year he'd had in his plumbing business, had been diminished to help Jean pay her bills. Now Jean was having to give up most of her inheritance to help her mother. Sally protested a little, but Jean insisted, and Sally knew she was right. Preston Mason would never have hesitated—he'd have done whatever it took to help his wife live the best life she could.

Sally's kidney condition was at stage five, the end stage, and she needed a new organ. But there were thousands of people on the waiting list and the state had just decided to stop paying for lung transplants altogether, as well as some heart and bone marrow procedures. How long would it be before kidney transplants were added to the list? Sally didn't want to wait to find out. She didn't want to spend her last years chained to a machine; she wanted her freedom back but it came at a price. She needed at least $250,000 for the operation. Above and beyond the money she'd need to keep her place at Castle Towers, she had some savings and there was a little money Jean had promised she could have. But she was still tens of thousands of dollars short, which was the reason that when the idea of selling her life insurance policy was presented to her, she was receptive to it.

The call from Howard Essen came at a particularly apposite moment. It wasn't a coincidence, although Sally would have been upset if she'd known how it came about. Howard found potential clients through an informal network of contacts he'd established at more than two dozen retirement homes and nursing facilities. He paid a mix of orderlies and supers and front-desk staff to tip him off when a resident told them about certain medical or personal issues, like starting dialysis or visiting a heart specialist or not being able to afford to help with their grandchild's college tuition. Howard found it distasteful, but he felt he had little choice. These were tough times, and he had to find a way to keep his own family's heads above water. In this case, Sally had told a friendly orderly her predicament, and he mentioned it unthinkingly to the superintendent, who in turn called Howard.

For ten years, Howard had made a decent living selling starter mortgages to young Arizonans. When things were going well he'd been caught up in the all-pervasive hysteria of home ownership. Everyone was selling mortgages with no supporting documentation, so why shouldn't he? There was no one who said it was a bad thing. After more than six months out of work he'd found this job with LifeDeals. In fact, they'd come after him, looking for once-successful mortgage salesmen and offering a job paid almost wholly on commission. The cheaper Howard bought a policy for, the better his remuneration. It helped him sleep at night when he didn't squeeze that extra percentage point out of the policyholder. Not that he thought it would have been so easy to get Sally Mason to capitulate.

The first time he paid her a visit, Howard had introduced himself and Sally said, "Essen, like the city in Germany?"

"Yes, ma'am. Exactly." This was a sharp one, he could tell at once.

Howard presented his spiel, showing Sally the graphs and tables indicating how much money Sally would save if she didn't have to make the premiums and how much money she might make if she invested it wisely.

"So if I stop paying into the policy and use the annuity money, I can have this much cash when I'm, let's see, a hundred and two?" Sally pointed at a very large figure at the outer edge of one of the projections.

"That's right. Who's to say you're not going to live twenty years with your new kidney? And we base our projections on a historically average rate of return on a sensible mixture of investments. I can give you the name of a great investment specialist who could help you with that."

"I'm sure you can, Howard. And what rate of return might you expect?"

"As I said, using historical averages, about eight percent, give or take."

"Oh, Howard, I wish you'd called me thirty years ago. If you had, I wouldn't be in this position."

A couple of minutes before the hour, Sally saw Howard pull up in his Ford truck and park. She waved to him, and he walked over. "Hello, Mrs. Mason," he said.

"Good morning, Howard. Let's go do some business," and Howard smiled at her.

Sally's room was small so Howard and

Sally sat in the dining room of the home where she felt more comfortable. Howard had brought all the paperwork, and he laid it out in front of Sally for her to sign. Sally picked up her pen and put it down again.

"You know, Howard, when Preston bought this policy, he said it was going to set up our daughter for life. But instead of that I'm using it to give me another ten years because I can't trust the state I've lived in all my life to help me anymore. I'm almost out of money, my daughter's almost out of money. There's just my grandson, George, up there in New York at medical school who's always said he wants to make some money so he can help his mom out. He doesn't know anything about this because he's already further in debt than my kidney's going to cost me. No one's got any money, they've just got debt. How'd it get this way, Howard?"

Howard Essen looked down at his feet. They'd talked a little about Howard's previous career and the mortgage craziness and about how Sally's pop sometimes gave customers a little bit of credit at the store before the end of the week when they'd spent the previous paycheck. And how he almost always regretted doing it.

"I swear I don't know, Mrs. Mason."

"Oh, I think we have some idea, Howard."

Howard watched as Sally Mason signed the paper that turned over her half-million-dollar life insurance policy in exchange for just over $75,000, 15 percent of its value. Sally had gone quiet and didn't say much to Howard after the transaction was completed. Howard would come by in a few days with a cashier's check and Sally's copy of the agreement. When he finished up and said his goodbye and left, Howard felt like going back home and taking another shower. Sally decided she'd wait a couple of hours and call her grandson, George, and leave a message. She wanted to make sure things were still going well for him in New York.

13.

Edmund Mathews was sitting at his kitchen island with a cup of coffee when the house phone rang. Edmund picked it up in the middle of the first ring. It was Russell.

"Sorry if I woke you."

"God no, I've been up for hours. You hear anything?"

"Henry Green e-mailed me a couple of minutes ago. His team has put together some numbers, and they want to show us at nine this morning. What's the earliest I can pick you up?"

"You can pick me up now. What did he say about the numbers? Did you call him?"

"No, his message said not to call, just come by."

"So we have no idea what they came up with. Great. Well, just swing by whenever you can. I'm ready when you are." Edmund hung up the phone.

Nothing he'd thought about since the meeting at Statistical Solutions the previous afternoon had offered Edmund much solace. He wasn't a numbers-cruncher like Russell, but he understood how heavily they were exposed by the insurance policies they'd purchased from diabetics. These people had looked like such a solid foundation for their business: a widespread and chronic condition with severe complications and a lot of lower-income policyholders. He'd seen more than a few e-mails from salesmen saying they'd reached someone whose policy was in arrears just as they were about to lose it. These were the perfect candidates, people happy to settle for ten cents on the dollar for something that to them was worth nothing.

Edmund wasn't a man who spent a lot of time in regret or recrimination. If something was broken, you fixed it. The key was, you had to get ahead of the problem before it got serious. Edmund's favorite historical character, predictably enough, was General George S. Patton. Edmund appreciated such a man of action. If Patton had been allowed to reach Berlin first in 1945, and then been allowed to keep going to Moscow, how different would things have turned out in the world? Such great men of history were always thwarted by the weak and the small-minded.

Edmund hated nothing more than feeling powerless, which was where the events of the previous day had left him. Gloria Croft had fired the first shot, and then Henry Green provided the coup de grâce. Edmund felt completely blindsided. He hadn't seen it coming, and neither had Russell. Russell was supposed to be the details guy who knew people who knew what was going on, the one who had his ear to the ground. Edmund had said as much on the long car ride home from Statistical Solutions the previous evening. Gloria would have been gratified at how long they spent stuck in traffic.

By the time he got home, Edmund was done sniping at Russell, and a dark cloud had made its way across his face and stationed itself there. Alice spent another evening staying out of her husband's way and again, Edmund had few words for their son. With his scotch bottle as a companion, Edmund had taken up sorcery. He was trying to bore his way into Henry Green's simulation software, willing it to come up with some way of limiting the damage that was being threatened to LifeDeals' future. Short of relying on magic, he was certain there was something he could do. He had to get himself and his company to Berlin.

14.

The call early the previous evening from his grandmother Sally had jolted George back to a place nearer his usual moorings. One day before that, he had found Pia in the hospital cafeteria with Will McKinley. Lesley Wong had been there too, but George had fixated on the fact that Will McKinley had worked his way to Pia's side for a month's elective. Although George considered himself reasonably facile with women, in that he got along with most, Will was a more practiced seducer with fewer scruples. George wouldn't have imagined Pia would be interested in a guy like Will but what did he know? Jealousy was a cruel emotion and while the four of them had sat together he'd suffered through believing Will was reveling at the scale of George's discomfort. Will had never made any secret of just how attractive he found Pia. More than once, he'd asked George what he thought Pia saw in him. George secretly enjoyed Will's rude question because it implied that he as well as others saw him and Pia as some kind of couple.

George knew his grandmother well enough to know she would disapprove of Pia. Or, rather, she would find his continued interest in her to be unhealthy for him. With all that he had on the line, George wondered for the thousandth time what he was doing continuing his pursuit of Pia's affections. It wasn't so much the time that it took up, though it took up enough, it was the amount of emotional energy he expended on her, dissecting her words and actions, thinking of strategies to win her affections, worrying about her well-being. He needed to conserve that energy for his studies. More than anything, he wanted to be the best doctor he could be.

George knew how much his family was pulling for him to succeed. They had suffered so many reverses, and it seemed like they were sliding down a one-way slope like so many middle-class families. If he didn't make it, he knew his mother and grandmother might put a brave face on it but be devastated inside.

George also knew his mother, Jean, had money issues. She'd moved into a much smaller house in the same Baltimore neighborhood a few years before and still didn't seem to have any extra cash. Jean had had the misfortune or lack of foresight to work in decaying industries after George's father died. She had been a bookkeeper at the Bethlehem Steel works at Sparrows Point for a while, then she found and lost a job at the General Motors plant. She always said she was fine when he asked about her finances, and refused to let him look at her bank statements. Although George was on a full scholarship, she never failed to send him a twenty-dollar bill whenever she could.

"You're a student, George," she told him. "You concentrate on your education!"

When Sally had called it was five o'clock in the East, and she didn't expect George to pick up his cell phone. Her intention was to leave him an encouraging message without taking up any of his precious time. She had an exaggerated sense of how busy George was every minute.

"Busy day?"

"Not too bad. They're not killing us just yet. Actually it was a good time for you to call since I'm on a break. I'm taking a radiology elective, and they don't work themselves to death like some other specialties. How is your day going?"

"Oh, you know. It's pretty quiet around here these days. Have you spoken to your mother recently?"

"Not lately. What's up?"

"Something interesting did happen yesterday. I sold your grandfather's life insurance policy to a very nice gentleman. I'll be paid in a few days. How are you doing money-wise? Are you okay? I could send you some."

"I'm doing fine," George said, even though he was constantly short of cash. He couldn't wait for July 1, when he'd start his residency. Instead of money going out, he'd be getting a salary. It wasn't going to be great, but anything was better than it was at the moment. Even with his scholarship, he'd assumed a sizable debt.

"If you need any money, let me know."

"I will," George said, although he had no intention of asking his grandmother for money. "I've never heard of someone selling a life insurance policy. Is that common?"

"Mr. Howard Essen, the man who bought it, said it's very common."

"Oh," George said simply. He told himself he'd try to remember to investigate online such a scenario when he got back to his room. At that point he'd switched the conversation with his grandmother back to her health, which he knew was not good as she was being kept alive by kidney dialysis.

Later when George had looked up "Life Settlements" and read about the issue, he wasn't happy. It seemed to him that it was one more way that the elderly could be victimized, this time by the financial world.

He couldn't help but worry that his ailing grandmother had been taken advantage of, and such a thought had helped rearrange his priorities.

Grabbing his jacket from the closet, George headed down to the elevators. Once there he briefly thought about Pia, and wondered if he should go up to her room to make sure she was awake. But he hit the down button. Hell, if she was going to be spending the day with Will, she could get herself up. Instead he decided to grab a coffee, rewarding himself with a more leisurely entry into the day than usual.

15.

STATISTICAL SOLUTIONS LLC
CHELSEA, NEW YORK CITY
MARCH 3, 2011, 9:17 A.M.

As was his habit, Edmund made sure he and Russell were fashionably late for their meeting at Statistical Solutions headquarters. They were greeted coolly by Henry Green and hustled directly into the same conference room as the previous day. The mood was somber, if not funereal. The room was occupied by a half-dozen people, including the slacker Tom dressed in a plaid shirt, wrinkled, low-riding Bermuda shorts, and flip-flops. Isabel was not to be seen. Two of the other people in the room—a young man and a woman—were dressed in a similar casual vein as Tom; two additional men who were a couple of years older wore dress shirts without jackets, pleated pants, and striped ties. Their haircuts were neat, conservative. The final man was dressed in a full dark suit and had an ostrich briefcase at his side.

Henry Green spoke first. In front of him were several copies of what looked like a bound report.

"Thank you, gentlemen, for coming in today. As I mentioned yesterday, Statistical Solutions LLC has decided to exercise its option to terminate its consultancy agreement with LifeDeals, Incorporated, as of close of business today, March third, 2011. In doing so, we are acting without prejudice, and we adhere to the articles of our initial agreement—"

"Yes, yes, blah, blah, blah," Edmund said, interrupting Henry rudely. "We get it, Henry, you're reading us the legal fine print so we think twice about suing you for incompetence. 'If our information is useless, don't blame us.' Now, let's play a game. Hands up, who in this room's a lawyer? You?" Edmund asked, pointing quickly at Tom. Tom stared back at Edmund and didn't flinch. "Don't think so," Edmund commented with a snicker. "How about you two?" Edmund gestured toward the two men dressed in shirts and ties. "Wrong again. Looks to me like a couple of accountants."

"Mr. Mathews, I am trying to do this as painlessly and professionally as I can. Yes, I have asked our legal representation to join us, as you have so astutely observed—"

"He's calling me Mr. Mathews now," Edmund said, swinging around to address Russell. "He's definitely been talking to his lawyers."

"Okay, Edmund, that's enough," Russell mumbled. He was tired of making excuses for Edmund when he blew up in public like this. It was like traveling around town with a rebellious and obnoxious teenager.

In fact, Russell and Edmund had discussed whether they should bring their own lawyer to the meeting. Russell contended that if each side lawyered up, it was more than likely that the meeting would be aborted before it began. One lawyer would speak, the other would object, and Life-Deals and Statistical Solutions would be advised to leave the matter to their legal representation. What Russell had not anticipated was that Edmund saw red the moment he spotted Statistical Solutions' legal counsel, who stood out from the others like a sore thumb. On edge from everything that was going on, Edmund took the man's presence as a personal affront.

"If I may make a suggestion," Russell said. "We came here this morning for the report that you promised. Let's deal with the legal issues of our relationship after the fact."

"Okay, Russell, thank you," Henry said, glancing at Edmund, who appeared reasonably composed. *Well, you won't look so composed in five minutes*, Henry thought. "We'll proceed with our presentation. There's a copy of our termination letter in the packets we'll give you at the end of the meeting, as well as a completely nonprejudicial note from our legal department reiterating the reasonable scope of our services, which is what I was trying to do a few minutes ago. But I appreciate you're eager to hear the results. I want to assure you that we had our best people working on this. Isabel Lee, whom you met and who is unable to join us today, put in a solid shift on this. So did Tom Graham, who graduated two years ago from MIT. . . ."

Edmund rolled his fists one over the other, like an umpire indicating for play to proceed. He wanted the facts, not the support behind the facts, and the longer it took getting the information implied that it wasn't going to be to their liking.

". . . and Paul, who had more than five years' experience at the Department of Defense." Edmund drummed his fingers on the desk.

"Okay. The work we did last night—all night, in fact—was to estimate how a shift to the right of the bell curves we previously created on the timing of the redemption of the life insurance policies LifeDeals holds would affect cash flow. We'll have the formal report in a day or two but we can give you a preliminary one today. I have to say, we were surprised."

Henry paused and took a sip from a glass of water.

"We were surprised how quickly even

the slightest shift of the bell curves would affect the company's financial situation. It would create a period of time in which the payment of premiums would need to be continued to maintain policy values with limited income. This effect is predicted because of the steepness of the bell curves' slopes. As we know, once the policies start to be cashed out by LifeDeals, income can be expected to rise very rapidly, which is why we had strongly recommended that you maximize your purchase of life settlement policies in relation to capitalization. Everyone clear on this?"

Russell nodded vigorously. There was nothing new here.

"Okay, good. Next we looked at the lifespan statistics of individuals lucky enough under current procurement and distribution protocols to get a new organ, be it a lung, a heart, a liver, a kidney, or a pancreas, depending on which degenerative disease is involved. We found that getting an organ alters these people's life expectancies to a marked degree. Understand that we already factored in standard organ replacement rates in the preliminary data that we all approved, and it was at that time a small variable. But the new circumstances, the potential new circumstances, I should say, caused us to drill down into those statistics further and find different research that previously wasn't relevant."

Henry paused again to take a drink. Edmund was fit to burst.

"There are newer statistics which show how well new organs work for patients over a long period. The older figures implied that organ recipients still had the propensity, whatever it was, to affect the new organ and often adversely. But to a greater extent than we initially would have expected, new organs, or at least a large percentage of them, do very well over many years provided it's a good match. Of course newer antirejection drugs have helped as well. In many or most cases, ten to fifteen years of life expectancy can be added to patients' lives. In lay terms, it appears that you can put a new radiator in a beat-up car engine, and it doesn't matter so much how you drive. The radiator's going to hold up.

"We applied these newly developed statistics to the bell curves of LifeDeals' policy-holders and there's no way around it—the implications are pretty catastrophic for cash flow if a percentage of policyholders get new organs. The higher the percentage, of course, the more catastrophic the effect."

"What percentage?" Edmund barked.

"Well, the problem seems to be that the cash flow issue starts almost immediately with just a small shift to the right. Just a few percentage points."

"What do you mean by 'a few'? Five? Ten?"

"Er, five's not good, ten would be, as I said, catastrophic."

"So we'd need five to ten percent of diabetics to get a new pancreas," said Edmund. "What are the chances of that happening?"

There was silence.

"These are not rich people. They won't be able to afford it. It's fucking pie in the sky."

"Not necessarily," Tom Graham said, speaking up for the first time, his voice surprisingly deep. "What you said about people not being able to afford it. Look at the statistics. There might well be thirty-five million people with diabetes in this country. It costs something like a hundred and fifty billion dollars a year to treat them.

You think insurance companies won't want to jump on this opportunity? How about state programs that have to carry the cost of these people for decades? Not to mention Medicare, Medicaid. Even far-right politicians are going to find a way around their qualms about stem cells because who won't want to help get twenty, thirty million Americans healthy? It's a magic bullet. If it works, it cures people. And once the organ is accepted, it costs *nothing*. Pancreas doesn't work? We'll grow you a new one and you're welcome. People have been searching for decades for a way to reduce healthcare costs. Regenerative medicine is going to be the answer."

This was worse than Edmund had dared think. He was a salesman; he knew that even if not every diabetic got a new pancreas, the idea of buying diabetics' life insurance policies in a climate in which people could receive a new organ was suddenly looking very outdated, like investing in steam engines after the Model T Ford was produced.

"This is all laid out in the final report?" Russell asked.

"It will be," Henry said. "It's summarized in the report we'll be giving you today."

"Of course, this is all confidential."

"Of course."

"But it's all dependent upon the date induced stem cell organs will be available," Edmund said. "It's not happening next week. At least I assume it isn't. What is it—two years? Five years? Have you looked into that?"

"Perhaps Ginny here might speak a few words in that regard," Henry said. Sitting next to Tom Graham, a tall woman with long black hair nodded to Henry. She shared Tom's fashion sense and was wearing a T-shirt with a bright image of a robot on the front.

"I read the journals I could find online and tried to figure out some kind of timeline, but the articles in this arena aren't very speculative. It's a new technology so there are no statistics to predict such a big leap in something like regenerative medicine," Ginny said.

Ginny proceeded to talk about the rapid developments already accomplished for stem cell maturation into specific cell lines by researchers around the world. "The next step would be to turn these cells into organs or organ-like apparatuses by a process called organogenesis. This work is going on in Russia, in China, in Germany, but it's having the most success at Columbia University with Doctors Rothman and Yamamoto. Rumor has it that these two researchers have already formed whole organs, which have been transplanted back into the mice that donated the cells from which the organs were formed. Supposedly in the next month or so there's going to be an article in *Nature* about it with all the supporting data. Apparently they have had such success that they've already requested clearance from the FDA to do it on a human. They're waiting for FDA clearance for the next step," said Ginny.

"And when might that happen?" asked Edmund.

"I did talk to one scientist friend last night," Ginny said. "He told me no one knows, but the best guess is in the next couple of months."

"As far as the business angle on this, the numbers strongly suggest that partial remedy would be provided in circumstances like this if the party holding the policies were to raise capital immediately as a hedge against this newly raised eventuality." Henry was taking over in the hope of wrapping up the meeting. Edmund's fuse was getting shorter by the minute, he could tell. Henry was now practically reading verbatim from a script.

"We already ran revenue models for you based on the idea of securitizing tranches of life insurance policies, and while it's difficult to build into the models the prospect of degraded assets, in the final report there will be a recommendation that the securitization proceed immediately and that a significant portion of the funds obtained be set aside to satisfy premiums on those policies that will have to be carried longer than expected. As far as additional life settlements, it would make sense to buy only those life settlements involving individuals with clearly terminal illnesses like metastatic cancer . . . ALS . . . things like that."

The list was a lot longer but Henry's distaste had finally got the better of him.

Edmund thought that all this meeting had done was to confirm what Gloria Croft had told them less than twenty-four hours earlier. It figured: Gloria was one of the best analysts he ever had. And she knew about this before he did. Edmund was confounded by the fact that his great money-making scheme could be jeopardized by two geeks he'd never heard of.

"Let me ask you a question," he growled at Ginny. "You find this research and you find a scientist to call in the evening who says the FDA is going to green-light this project that could revolutionize medicine or whatever. So why am I not reading about this in *The New York Times*?"

"Because researchers and their universities have become much more sophisticated about patent issues. There used to be a rush to print because they yearned for the notoriety, but they're much smarter now. There are fortunes to be made in biotech, and this area of organogenesis might be the biggest yet. It will probably overshadow every other technological milestone in the history of medicine. Believe me, when the Rothman work hits *Nature*, it's going to be all over *The New York Times*, *The Wall Street Journal*, and every other media outlet."

. . .

Edmund and Russell rode the elevator in silence. It was the same car that Edmund had assaulted the day before. He'd taken a prescription painkiller from his cache, so he was feeling only a dull throb in his left hand. He looked closely and thought he could make out a slight indentation in the metal elevator door. The trouble was he felt like doing it again.

Only when they reached the street, away from any prying ears, did they speak.

"What do you think?" Russell said.

"I think we paid those idiots too much money. And we will sue them."

They met their car in front of the building and got in. Edmund thought for a moment. His mind was racing.

"Okay, here's what we're gonna do. Today. No more diabetics, obviously. Tell the sales force, even if they're hooked on the line, even if they're in the boat and you have the billy club in your hand, put 'em back in the water. Any contracts in the works—cancel. Checks being cut—cancel.

"Have someone go back and look at contracts of people who have diabetes and something else. We like the something else now. Get the lawyer to draft a letter in his best incomprehensible legalese to say we're no longer interested in diabetes and send it to these people. Scrub those people out of the stats. They never had diabetes. And we need new policies. Target smokers. I know they're the worst because none of them thinks they're going to get sick and when they do, they die too fast. Find out if we can target smokers or ex-smokers with policies who've missed a couple payments. They're all lying anyway. And offer them twenty-five percent—"

"But the model—" said Russell.

"Fuck the model!" roared Edmund. "Don't you understand? As of today, there is no model. We don't have a *business* if this shit goes down, never mind a *model*. Jesus. These are Band-Aids I'm talking about and we've got a head wound."

"Potentially," Russell said.

"Right, yes, there's a chance this research may not get anywhere. But still, we're up to our necks in this either way. Gloria Croft is already shorting us, and she won't be shy talking about it. We have to do something. It's not like we can sell our stock and walk away."

"Perhaps we should go and see Jerry

Trotter," Russell said, after an awkward pause.

"Yeah, I was thinking the same thing," said Edmund.

Dr. Jerred L. Trotter, an old friend of both Russell and Edmund, ran a very successful hedge fund. Trotter was a man who enjoyed outthinking people, which meant he wasn't above a certain amount of sharp practice if he was confident he could get away with it. There were so many areas where the regulatory authorities were lax, or there just weren't any regulations. It was by using Trotter's good offices, and through a number of disguises of Trotter's creation, that Edmund had purchased credit default swaps on his own company while continuing to sell subprime bonds to his corporate clients. It was just the kind of caper that Trotter relished. Especially when his cut was so generous.

Edmund had sounded Trotter out very early in the planning stage of LifeDeals. He sent Russell over on what looked like a fact-finding mission. Did Jerry think a model like this might work? Did Jerry think these were good assets to spin off bonds from? Did Jerry think enough investors would want to buy such a product? Russell never mentioned that they were seeking investors.

Three days later, Jerry had called, practically biting Edmund's arm off over the phone. He'd run the numbers, and he wanted in. Edmund, after pretending to think about it, pretended to reluctantly allow Jerry to invest $25 million of his own money and more of his fund's. Trotter would definitely want to hear about these new market conditions. He wouldn't be pleased, to put it mildly, but he was always a man of action and he'd think of something.

The driver had been awaiting instructions as the two men sat in the back of the car. Now Edmund gave the driver an address, and they set off.

16.

There was no way we could meet you guys today, no way. And then Russell said the magic word: 'Terrasini.'" Everyone laughed, even Edmund, who was making an effort to calm down.

Dr. Jerred L. Trotter, former plastic surgeon, current hedge fund maven and LifeDeals angel investor, was holding court alongside his longtime number two, Maxwell Higgins. There was always a table at Terrasini for Trotter, and the four men— Higgins, Trotter, Mathews, and Lefevre— were nestled at a table in a corner of the restaurant's front room.

"I thought it couldn't hurt," Russell said, attempting to sound breezy. Edmund and Russell were glad Trotter could see them at short notice, even if it had meant killing a couple of hours until lunchtime.

"You know it's my favorite place to eat. Unless I'm picking up the tab, right, Edmund?"

"There's no danger of that, Jerry," Edmund said. "Everyone knows it's against your religion to pay for lunch."

Trotter guffawed. "Damn straight," he said loudly, and waved expansively toward no one in particular and a waiter quickly came over.

"That glass of Barolo, make it a bottle. I trust that's okay, gentlemen? Second thought, bring the glasses and then the bottle in a few minutes. I need a real drink after the morning I had."

Edmund looked on, suppressed irritation sticking in his craw. That little sideshow just set him back at least a couple hundred bucks. But scenes like this were part of the cost of doing business with Jerry Trotter.

"No serious problems, I hope, Jerry," Edmund said.

"Everything's a fucking problem," Jerry said in his usual penetrating voice. A man in a Cucinelli sweater who'd brought his family to lunch turned around and shot Jerry a look.

"Whoops, apologies, forgot where I was," Jerry said to the man.

"I thought we should meet in the office," Edmund said. "You know, easier to speak freely." Jerry Trotter, like a lot of financiers, swore like a stevedore. Edmund didn't care about that but he wanted to discuss Life-Deals' predicament without having to hold back in front of the other diners.

"Got to eat, Edmund," Trotter said, picking up the menu.

"Of course, Jerry."

Edmund thought that Jerry Trotter probably knew the menu better than the restaurant's own waitstaff. Everyone insisted on playing these childish games, thought Edmund, aware that, once more, he was the one being toyed with. Edmund studied

Trotter's face. He knew the man was at least sixty, but he looked closer to forty-five with his sweep of gunmetal hair, a few trace laugh lines, and bright blue eyes still a shade of azure that caused more than a few people to take a breath when they saw them. If he'd had any cosmetic work done, it was very good.

"Max, what was that special again?"

The waiter was handing out the glasses of Barolo.

"The pasta?" Higgins questioned with his upper-crust London accent. "Orecchiette with sweet sausage, broccolini, touch of ricotta. Sounds marvelous."

"Ah, gives me a hard-on just to think about it. Of course. Times four, what do you say, guys? Cold day, calls for some soup, I think. The other special, squash soup, little bit of cream, am I right, Max? All around, sir, if you don't mind."

The waiter agreed it was a great selection. Edmund made a point of looking at his menu a couple of beats longer, then folded it and handed it over. He was too upset to protest. Now Trotter was swirling the red wine around in his glass. It was a lovely ruby color and on another occasion,

Edmund would have been rhapsodizing about it.

In the often flamboyant world of hedge fund management, Jerry Trotter was something of a celebrity. He'd already enjoyed one very successful career as a plastic surgeon, catering mostly to the moneyed ladies of New York's Upper East Side, for whom he performed face, eye, and buttock lifts. In truth, Trotter was a better showman than he was a surgeon. He knew, like everyone in the medical profession, that during medical training grades counted more than the need to display particularly good physical skills in obtaining training positions in such surgical specialties as the eye or brain, or in plastic surgery. Trotter had made sure he always got good grades to make up for his hand-eye coordination, which was poor enough for him to find surgery a taxing grind. But that was in the past, and he didn't need good hand-eye coordination to manage money.

Trotter had always enjoyed looking after his own money and taking the odd risk here and there. After years of working six days a week at his practice, he had a lot of it to manage. Trotter had known Max

Higgins for years and well enough to know he was keen to strike out on his own from his trading position at Goldman. Trotter made a proposition to Higgins: we'll set up a fund, you run it and teach me what you know, and I'll supply the money. It worked, and Trotter quickly found that his patients trusted him and were grateful and many were happy to let him invest for them. Trotter was a quick study and soon his fund, the immodestly and unimaginatively named Trotter Holdings, was heading toward the middle rank of name funds.

"So, Edmund, Russell, what was so urgent that we had to meet today?"

Russell looked over at Edmund before he started. The delay in Trotter being able to meet with them had at least allowed Edmund and Russell to decide how they were going to present their news to Trotter. They'd sat in a diner on Lexington Avenue for an hour and strategized.

"We have a potential public relations issue we want to give you a heads-up about. We thought you might be able to help us get out ahead of the possible publicity—nip it in the bud, so to speak."

"Edmund, has your checkered past finally caught up with you?" Jerry asked, not sounding as though he was joking at all.

"We've heard about some medical research that's taking place," Russell continued, to spare Edmund from having to respond. "It's at an experimental stage, with no guarantee it's going to work or anything, but in some quarters it's being taken more seriously than in others."

"How does that affect LifeDeals?" asked Jerry, who glanced between Edmund and Russell even though it was Russell who was speaking. All the joviality had left his voice. The two waiters brought over the soup and left it quietly, detecting the tension at the table.

"It may not mean anything," Russell added. "As I said, we want to get ahead of any potential bad publicity."

Jerry Trotter picked up his spoon and tasted a mouthful of soup. It was delicious, of course, but when he sensed he was about to hear something unpleasant, his appetite faltered. "Russell, you're going to have to tell me a little more clearly what's going on."

"Okay, Jerry, sure. There are a couple of researchers at Columbia who think they can grow artificial organs using human stem cells that they make from a patient's own cells. Obviously I don't know the details, but the process is called organogenesis. It's supposed to start what will be called regenerative medicine. If they can grow new pancreases, for example, they can help people with diabetes live longer. But at this point, it's a huge 'if.'"

"I read something about that idea in some research we did on our due diligence for LifeDeals, but it sounded like science fiction," Jerry said.

"Apparently not anymore. The future is now, as they say. Or it might be," Russell said.

"How many people know about this?" Max Higgins asked.

"Not many," Russell said. "Outside Columbia and the stem cell field, very few is my guess."

"How did you hear about it?"

There was a pause. This was where it was going to get a lot trickier.

"Gloria Croft told us," Edmund said.

Max Higgins quickly figured out the implications and, way ahead of Trotter, asked Russell the main question.

"Is she taking any action?"

"Yes."

"And knowing Gloria, she's shorting LifeDeals, am I right?"

"Yes."

"Hold on, hold on, wait a second," Jerry said. "LifeDeals is being shorted because of some work being done in a lab at Columbia?"

"I'm afraid so, Jerry."

Higgins went on, "Am I to assume that some numbers have been run looking at cash projections based on a potential breakthrough in diabetes treatment? And that the projections don't look so good?"

"Is he right?" Trotter asked. Higgins had got right to the heart of the matter in seconds.

"Broadly, but look—"

"So he is?" Trotter questioned.

"As I said, it's early in the—"

"Would you mind telling me how this . . . this fucking *disaster* is what you would describe as a public relations issue?" Jerry was hissing, using his soup spoon to point first at Edmund, then at Russell. The table was silent until Max Higgins spoke up again.

"The science may fail eventually, but with Gloria Croft taking a position, investors are going to be alarmed when they find out. Then it becomes as much about Gloria as about the science. She's a barometer. So from that perspective, they're right, Jerry, it's a PR problem first."

"And if the science succeeds?" Jerry said.

"Then we have a bigger problem," said Edmund.

Jerry put down his soup spoon and took a large drag on his $30-a-glass Barolo.

"You guys didn't see this coming?"

"Obviously not," Edmund said. "It's a once-in-a-century breakthrough if it happens. You can't do projections for being hit by an asteroid."

No one was eating now. The waiter, coming by for a second time, asked if anyone was still working on their soup and no one was. Yes, the soup was fine, but everyone was preoccupied. The uneaten soup disappeared.

At Jerry's insistence, Russell walked him through what they knew of the research. He made a point of saying that there was no guarantee it would succeed; the odds had to be that it wouldn't because in the vast majority of research projects there was always some major unanticipated obstacle that would arise to thwart the hoped-for result.

"So what are the chances it will succeed?" Trotter questioned.

Edmund said there was no way to know. He then had Russell talk about the effects such an eventuality would have on Life-Deals' cash flow. As Edmund and Russell had agreed before meeting with Trotter, Russell erred on the conservative side.

"What's our position vis-à-vis the public offering?" Jerry directed his question at Max, his partner. He didn't care that he might offend his lunch hosts.

"The lockup period expires May thirty-first," Max said.

When an investor takes part in an initial public offering, they can't sell their shares for a certain amount of time, in this case 180 days. Trotter Holdings was halfway through the mandated blackout period, meaning that Jerry Trotter and his fund were stuck with his shares for another three months.

"Shit. What are the chances of Gloria

Croft keeping her mouth shut for three months?"

"Listen, Jerry, life insurance is still a twenty-six-trillion-dollar business," Edmund said. "There's plenty of money to be made. These diabetes policies are basically a drop in the bucket. It's not a question of dumping LifeDeals shares, it's a problem that needs a solution. That's why we came to you, you're the man who deals with problems, everyone knows that." Edmund was being purposefully flattering and Trotter wasn't unhappy about it. It's true, he was a guy who could solve a problem, but this was a big problem and a new problem.

"Gloria Croft is so full of it you wouldn't believe," Edmund continued. "She was carrying on, telling us that our life settlement bonds were a bad product. Blah, blah, blah. She even told us that we should have been prosecuted over subprime."

"She is one sanctimonious bitch, I know that for sure," Jerry agreed.

"She was enjoying telling us about the research, twisting the knife."

The pasta was set at each man's place. There was slightly less tension around the table now—the problem had been identified, there was a common enemy, and the four of them were on the same side. Soup could be resisted, but the pasta was a different proposition, and each of the four men ate.

"Of course, there is a medical angle here, Jerry, that we think you can help us with. And Statistical Solutions is drawing up projections of the effect on revenue if we have to pull the diabetics' policies. We're going to need more capital. We can see if we can fill in these capital shortfalls with different initiatives. We've already directed our sales teams to go back and beat the bushes for metastatic cancer patients with big policies. It costs more money to buy those policies, but it's completely risk-free."

"More money, how so?" Higgins said.

"We've authorized the salesmen to offer more than the standard fifteen percent. Metastatic cancer patients are not going to cause us any problem about dying on time. It's just that we have to be more aggressive to find them."

"Okay, Edmund, I'm hearing you. Needless to say, Max and I will have to put our heads together and talk about this research issue. We want to see that Statistical Solutions data as soon as you have it, of course. And we have a bunch of meetings this afternoon, so I'm sorry but we have to eat and run."

Jerry downed another forkful of his lunch and chased it with the remnants of his third glass of wine. The leave-takings were quick and less effusive than the greetings had been when the four men met. Trotter and Higgins left Edmund and Russell behind, picked up their coats and got into their waiting town car on Fifty-fourth Street.

So?" Trotter asked when he was settled in his seat. They were heading south on Park Avenue.

"Gloria Croft," Higgins said. "She's a pit bull."

"I sense there's history there with Edmund—perhaps it's more about that than about the product."

"Maybe it's both. She's found a flaw in the model, and it just happens to be Edmund Mathews, so it's a bonus."

"Be that as it may, we have to do something," Jerry said. "And we can't leave it to those two. They're floundering, you can tell.

There's too much time till we can sell the stock."

"I agree. But Edmund has a point: it's still a good business even if there is a bump in the road with the current model. It will just take some juggling and deep breaths on our part. It's not a time to panic. Besides, since we can't sell the LifeDeals stock, we can't panic even if we wanted to. I also agree that in an ideal world, he should have seen this coming. But our due diligence didn't pick it up either. It's a function of the times. Technology's changing too fast just like markets are changing too fast. It's getting harder and harder to factor this kind of thing in."

"Well, I think we need to do some of our own research. A little more street-level. We can't rely on Edmund et al. for that, clearly. Let's get an investigator up to Columbia, sniff around a little. And someone can do some digging on Gloria Croft. A woman like that doesn't get where she is without pissing a lot of people off. And maybe cutting some corners. We need to get some angles to work with, get some leverage."

"Okay, I'll get right on it. This is a new

one on me—shorting stocks because of a medical breakthrough."

"It's new all-round. We may have to get creative," Trotter said, watching the Park Avenue traffic move slowly in a steady afternoon drizzle.

Jerry Trotter knew how to make an entrance into a room, and he also knew how to make an exit. Edmund didn't know what to make of what had just happened. Sure, Jerry was royally pissed when he first heard about the problem, but he seemed calmer when he left. The problem was that the departure had been so sudden.

"What do you think?" Edmund asked Russell. They had ordered cappuccinos.

"For me, Higgins is the brains of that operation, he sees the bigger picture," said Russell. "It didn't take him long to zero in on the heart of the problem. They definitely got the message."

"Do you think they'll come up with some suggestions?" Edmund asked.

"I do," Russell said. "I think it was right to tell them early in the game. It feels good to have Jerry Trotter and his team working on this with us. I just hope they get back to us soon."

"My guess is that he will," Edmund said. "Jerry isn't the kind of guy who's going to watch while his sixty million dollars turns into pocket change. But I do have one reservation."

"What's that?"

"I never can be a hundred percent confident Jerry's working *with* us."

17.

COLUMBIA UNIVERSITY MEDICAL CENTER
NEW YORK CITY
MARCH 3, 2011, 6:23 P.M.

Pia glanced up from her reading to see that it was almost six-thirty, and she wondered how long she was going to have to wait. She was sitting in the deserted lab outside her office, which continued to be off-limits. She was waiting for Rothman, who was still in the biosafety unit trying to finish up the data for the *Lancet* article. Yamamoto had told her to wait because

Rothman wanted to speak with her. What about, she had no idea. Whatever it was, it made her feel uneasy.

The day had been interesting in some regards although it had not been one of her best. She had spent the morning doing the lab equivalent of KP duty, washing and rewashing glassware. For the second day in a row Pia had been actually late, not just late by the secretary Marsha Langman's standards. For the second day in a row George had failed to appear at her door, and she wondered why. It irked her to a degree because she'd come to count on it, even though she was the first to agree that he wasn't obliged to come and wake her. She'd slept badly again, as she'd been doing for a week or more. As per usual it was nightmares involving childhood memories she'd battled to suppress and which surprised her in their lucidity. Even after years, they still possessed ample power to shock and disturb her.

The head technician, Arthur Spaulding, had seemed amused by Pia's punishment. He had made a point of detouring when in the lab to pass by Pia, saying nothing. He didn't have to, his smirk was enough.

Spaulding had been at the research center for years, and he liked things done just so. He'd started working for Rothman only in the last eighteen months, and Spaulding got on with him about as well as his predecessor had before he was fired. Spaulding seemed to take exception to any irregular request from Rothman, and Rothman being Rothman, most of his requests were irregular.

"Do you need something, Mr. Spaulding?" Pia said finally on about his fifth pass. "You seem to go out of your way to come over here."

Spaulding said nothing and left, as Yamamoto had suddenly appeared and come over.

"Miss Grazdani, we would like to see you in the organ bath lab."

Dr. Yamamoto hadn't directly said anything about Pia being late, and he didn't need to; Pia had gotten the message. She suited up quickly and went in the lab to join Lesley and Will, who had been in there all morning. They were standing in a side room with Rothman, who was holding a thick paperback book in one hand and pressing impatiently at the display of a newly installed machine that looked like a large inkjet printer.

"Dr. Yamamoto, it appears we have bought a lemon," Rothman said.

Will gestured down to the power strip in the wall, and Yamamoto bent down and flicked on the surge protector. The machine wheezed and babbled into life.

"Anyone know what this piece of machinery is?" Rothman said, not missing a beat and bending forward to stare into the innards of the device. As she moved closer, Pia could see how intricate the engineering on the device was, with tracking bars and a large array like the inkjet of a printer. Pia opened her mouth, but Lesley beat her to it. "An organ printer?" She had seen the cover of the book Rothman was holding.

"Yes, for three-D bioprinting. We have an older machine, but this one is new. Someone from the manufacturer is coming tomorrow to show us how to use it."

"Perhaps we should wait till then to turn it on, Doctor," Yamamoto said.

"No harm in warming it up. Mr. McKinley, what do you know about three-D bioprinting?"

"I think it works like a regular printer,

spraying living cells onto a sheet of . . . a sheet of something. It goes back and forth building up the layers into a three-dimensional structure. The cells can often organize themselves to function collectively. So far it has applications making skin and cartilage."

"Indeed. You can print a spinal disk. Which I may need to try by tomorrow," said Rothman, straightening up and rubbing the small of his back.

"We're all going to get up to speed on this machine together. As this engineering matures it might be quicker than growing organs. At this stage I'm thinking of using it to fix defects in the organs that we're growing. But who knows? The value of this technology is that an organ would be fashioned as the mirror image of the patient's by using data from MRI studies. As is often the case with organogenesis, the hardest part is not in replicating the function of the organ, or gland, but in connecting it to the rest of the body—veins, arteries, ducts, and so on have to be oriented appropriately to make the surgery feasible."

Rothman had found a switch and he toggled it on and off. He then reopened the instruction book and immediately became engrossed.

Yamamoto ushered the students away. Will looked back at Rothman.

"I hope that thing's still working when the guy comes tomorrow."

The students spent the rest of the day monitoring the organ baths. They'd found that some did experience small changes in temperature or pH spontaneously, and the three talked with Yamamoto about designing an alarm system even for those minor fluctuations. It seemed to them that even such small changes might impact the results. It was real science, demanding and exciting for each student. Will and Lesley worked closely, keeping a respectful distance from Pia, who was in her own world.

After Dr. Yamamoto dismissed the students for the day, he asked Pia to stay behind for a moment. "Dr. Rothman would like to speak with you later, after we're done in the level-three lab. I hope you don't mind."

"Of course not," Pia had said. What else was she going to say?

18.

ONE CENTRAL PARK WEST
NEW YORK CITY
MARCH 3, 2011, 8:30 P.M.

Jerry Trotter and Max Higgins left Edmund Mathews and Russell Lefevre with a souvenir of their lunch together at Terrasini. It was a healthy check, and as Edmund paid up, he hoped that Jerry and Max were going to do something to justify it. He was reasonably confident, as he knew them to be guys who did not sit on a problem. They were known to do whatever it took.

And Jerry and Max did not disappoint. Within an hour of leaving the restaurant, Trotter and Higgins had two of their best investigative guys working on the two separate cases, one on the Columbia regenerative organ situation, the other on the hoped-for dirty little secrets of Gloria Croft in hopes of having something to control her with. Jerry knew that everyone, especially Wall Street people, had their secrets. The PIs were also given Edmund's and Russell's full names so they could Google them for background information.

Jerry couldn't use his very best guy, who was in fact a woman named Jillian Jones, because she was already involved in looking at a company that Higgins thought might be tanking its results to pave the way for a takeover. But as PIs, Tim Brubaker and Harry Hooper were separated from Jones only by a sliver. They'd do a thorough job, and they were very quick.

This was the first time Jerry ever had three PIs on his payroll at once. Strictly speaking, Jones, Brubaker, and Hooper weren't on the Trotter Holdings payroll at all; each was employed off the books in a strictly cash-only arrangement. There was no paperwork—no pay stubs or invoices or receipts, the latter because Trotter trusted the three not to pad expenses. The PIs undertook enough on-the-books domestic surveillance cases to report to the IRS to show sufficient income to justify their lifestyles. They were usually able to piggyback a cash job for someone like Jerry Trotter on one that was recorded by the business accountant.

Jerry Trotter loved this semi-legal, clandestine work because it was so far removed from anything he'd done as a plastic surgeon or a money manager. He loved everything about it and even saying "Brubaker" and "Hooper" gave him a little thrill; to his mind, they were perfect PI names. For him it was like being in his own movie. Brubaker and Hooper were ex-cops and had seen everything; Jillian Jones had seen everything too but no one knew what work she had done prior to this and no one dared ask. In contrast to most PIs, she always acted anxious and quick to take offense. She also had a black belt in karate and was always armed.

As usual, Higgins took care of all the practical arrangements. He bought three use-and-lose cell phones and used one to place a prearranged marketing cold call to Hooper and Brubaker's offices. The call purported to be from a firm interested in talking to the business manager about the company's metered postage. This identified the source of the call. The first digit of the call-back number times one hundred was the rate being offered; the last four specified a time for a meet at the usual location. Brubaker and Hooper had a habit of checking their messages regularly and both picked up Higgins's call within a half-hour. The promise of a $300-an-hour rate drew them to the four o'clock meeting place in a back booth at Flanagan's bar on Second Avenue. It took Higgins five minutes to give them their marching orders, a cell phone for each to call in on, and a $1,200 down payment on their work.

Another aspect of the game that Trotter relished was asking his guys how they'd found whatever information they dug up. At first neither Brubaker nor Hooper wanted to talk about their MOs, but they'd come to indulge Trotter's whims. He did sign the checks, after all.

When the phone rang at eight-thirty,

Trotter was fixing his second Glenlivet in his apartment near the summit of the Trump International on the corner of Central Park West and Columbus Circle. Trotter lived so high up he didn't bother with drapes in the living room—he didn't want anything to interfere with his view of Central Park. Tonight, banks of low clouds and rain were all he could see. He was pleased to see it was Brubaker. The number on his LED was the cell phone Higgins had given him.

"It's B," Brubaker said. It was the code name Trotter insisted on his using.

"So soon?" Trotter could barely conceal the childish excitement in his voice.

"Yes, I got to speak directly with the laboratory's secretary by posing as a journalist. Couldn't shut her up. Thought she was doing her boss a favor talking him up. Thinks he's shy and needs the pub. She even said as much."

"So she was informative."

"Very. Don't understand half the stuff she was saying, but she was knowledgeable. I'm transcribing the tape myself word for word. I don't want any transcription service looking at this stuff."

"Of course, very prudent. So give me the headlines."

"Okay, the two names you mentioned to me are the guys for sure. . . ."

"Rothman and Yamamoto," Trotter said, talking over Brubaker.

"Shit, what's the point of the code words and all the cloak-and-dagger you insist on if you don't follow it yourself? Yes, those are the guys. The first one is the big cheese."

"Sorry," Trotter said, inwardly cursing himself.

"Okay, so she tells me all this stuff that they're doing, and I'm supposed to be a science reporter and able to follow it. So I asked her at the end for the Cliff Notes version that I can use for the readers."

"What paper does she think this is going in?"

"No paper. I told her I was doing the research to see if there was a story and if there was, I'd sell it and call her again."

"What if she calls you?"

"She doesn't have my number. I told her this was very hush-hush on my end, and I asked her not to tell anyone we'd spoken because this is such a big story that other reporters are going to be on it soon, and I want to get a jump on it. I'm actually thinking of writing it up for real—I wasn't lying to her, this is going to be way big."

Jerry's joy at playing Dick Tracy evaporated.

"What do you mean, 'big'?"

"Well, according to her, these guys are close commercially to growing organs outside the body, organs that will be perfect matches for the person who needs them. The trials have worked with animal subjects, and they want to move on to using human stem cells."

"When?"

"She did get a little cagey there. Not because she wouldn't tell me—I think she didn't know and didn't want to let on that she didn't know. But it's months that they will be moving to human cells, maybe even weeks and certainly not years."

"Weeks or months? The difference is important."

"Well, I guess I need to make a few more calls. But it's happening. And soon. He's working on something else too. Something about growing salmonella strains that cause typhoid fever on the space shuttle. Can you imagine? To think where our tax dollars go. It makes me sick."

"Tell me about it," Jerry said. "Okay, thanks, B. Keep me posted."

"Got it, boss."

After hearing from Brubaker, Trotter was impatient to know what kind of progress, if any, Hooper was making. Although it was technically against protocol, Trotter called Hooper's new cell.

"Yes," Hooper said after one ring. He was between calls on the Gloria Croft assignment and thought it might be one of the contacts he had made calling him back.

"Hi, it's the boss."

"Hi, boss."

"What's happening? Any dirt?"

"I'm only three hours in. Not even."

"What's the setup?"

"I'm a headhunter looking for someone for a major bank CEO job. The board wants a woman for appearances' sake. I'm asking around about people on my supposed list."

"Our friend doesn't need a job, she makes seven figures–plus a year," said Trotter with disappointment. He purposely avoided using Croft's name.

"I know that. They know that. But people like showing off how *much* they know. I think someone might tell me just how much she doesn't need a job in a bank. Or need the scrutiny of running a public company, more like it."

"So you want someone to brag about what they know."

"Sure, everyone does it. Most everyone. And the finance world is like a small, competitive club which feeds on gossip."

Okay, that was more like it. Jerry was struck again by how much Hooper and Brubaker sounded alike. They sounded like Brooklyn cops, which is what they both had once been.

"So you shake anything out of the tree yet?"

"Just spoke to a guy who knew her at Morgan, back in the day. I said someone mentioned him as a possible reference, and he laughed. Real asshole, thinks I'm a moron having gone to Brooklyn College nights. I don't like these Ivy League types. But he has something, I'm sure. Trying to fuck with me a little. Hope he doesn't push it 'cause he's messing with the wrong guy.

I can get his nice car towed tonight, and it ain't goin' to the pound."

"Yes, I'm sure you can. That's what keeps me honest in our relationship."

Hooper laughed, then added, "One other thing. He mentioned that I might ask one of the bankers Higgins mentioned when we talked this afternoon. He said if I wanted dirt on our friend to ask him, because he thought he had been literally and figuratively fucking her back in their Morgan days."

Trotter frowned. "Which one?"

"The thick guy with the short hair," Hooper said.

"Now, that *is* interesting," Trotter said. "Don't call and ask him directly. Make it part of your investigation. It could be interesting."

"Got it," Hooper said.

As Trotter hung up the phone, he smiled. "Edmund, you rogue."

19.

Pia waited more than two and a half hours for Rothman and Yamamoto to finish their work in the BSL-3 lab. She spent the time productively reading papers on tissue engineering and organ printing on the Internet, which is what she would have been doing anyway if she'd gone back to the dorm. As the time had passed and her empty stomach growled, she became progressively concerned it had something to do with her being late two days in a row. Eventually, Rothman and Yamamoto appeared. Yamamoto immediately left. Rothman wordlessly waved for her to join him in his office, where he got straight to the point.

"I want to talk to you about the future. Your future. I need to know that you are committed to this work."

"I am, truly," Pia said. She was panicked. "I know I was late this morning—"

"You were late two mornings in a row, at least according to Miss Langman."

"I'm sorry . . ." Pia stammered. Her fears were coming to pass.

"It doesn't help to be sorry," Rothman shot back. "I'm concerned about what it implies."

"I will make sure it never happens again," Pia offered.

Rothman waved her off. "Let me speak while I'm inclined to do so. As you know, I'm not accustomed to talking too much about this kind of nonsense. I don't have the time. Last year I confided in you some information about myself because I had been progressively confident that you were turning out to be the person I thought you could be. Remember, as I told you, I played a role in getting you admitted when others on that damn admissions committee where I was forced to serve were reluctant because of your foster care experience. Since I had the same experience, I thought you might have promise of being a researcher."

"I've come to the same conclusion," Pia blurted.

"Don't interrupt!" Rothman snapped. "Last year when I told you those secrets about me that are only known by my wife, bless her soul for putting up with me, concerning my foster care history and my Asperger's, I wasn't completely open. I said my sons were not as healthy as I would like. To be more specific, not only are they too on the Asperger's spectrum, but even worse, they have type 1 diabetes. Having passed on the Asperger's was reason enough for guilt and depression. The diabetes has put it over the top. The main reason I've turned to stem cell work is to see that my boys are cured in my lifetime. It's a quest that pulled me out of a serious bout of depression. Depression has been my bête noire."

"I'm so sorry to hear about your boys," Pia offered.

"I'm not telling you this to elicit any sympathy. I'm telling you this so that you understand me better. I have never ever agreed to mentor anyone, and it is not just because my Asperger's puts me at a social disadvantage. I feel I don't have the time for other people's nonsense, and this includes Ph.D. students as well as medical students. You were a first. I thought your foster care experience would make you thrive in the lonely pursuit of science and that you should have been given a chance."

"I think you're right," Pia said. "I know I struggle with social issues as well."

"Pia, commitment to research has to be total. Two days ago you came in here and told me that, yes, you were going to take me up on my offer to do your Ph.D. here in my lab. At the same time you told me you were going to do a simultaneous residency in internal medicine. And then you expected me to be pleased. Pia, that old myth of the doctor doing both clinical medicine and research at the same time is totally passé. It wasn't even true when it was current. Research is more than a full-time job."

For one of the first times in their three and a half years of knowing each other, Pia and Rothman held each other's eyes. It was a kind of Mexican standoff. Both were conflicted. Pia had struggled hard and surmounted considerable obstacles in her drive to become a doctor. And now she was so close. In months she would be getting her M.D. degree. The problem was she wouldn't yet be a doctor, one that can get a license from the state. A resident was on his or her way to becoming a real doctor. If she didn't take a residency, she'd always be a medical student with an M.D.

Both individuals looked away.

"I realize that I'm hard to read," Rothman said, breaking a short silence, "or at least my wife tells me so. She advised me to have a conversation with you."

"She knows about me?"

"She knows about everything in my life. It is the only way we could have survived as a couple. I'm not easy to live with."

Rothman had been rehearsing this speech for days so he was relatively comfortable once he had started talking.

"What I seek in a colleague is commitment. A med school graduate knows nothing. No offense. But if they're able to pass through medical school it means they have the basic intellectual wherewithal to do research. After the initial flash of inspiration that tells you what to look for, most of the success in research lies in doggedness. In covering every angle, tracking down every lead. I'm mixing metaphors but you know what I mean. Dr. Yamamoto was in fact a rather mediocre student, but he exhibited more application than ten other men who had better grades. I can already tell what kind of doctors your colleagues will be. Ms. Wong is desperate to help sick people, and she'll be very good at it. Mr. McKinley will probably end up doing something flashy but unchallenging, like surgery, and worse yet, plastic surgery."

Pia didn't know what to say.

"I'm pleased you made the right decision about the nuns. It shows me that you're orienting yourself in the direction of research, but I don't want you to make the same mistakes I made. For me, doing a residency in internal medicine was a big waste of time."

Rothman paused.

"I think we're similar in a number of ways."

Pia's eyes opened wide, and she flushed and looked down at her feet. She didn't share Rothman's newfound comfort in discussing such personal matters.

"I need more help here. Dr. Yamamoto can't do everything, and I can't rely on med students rotating in and out of the lab. No offense. The two of us are spread thin, working on salmonella and organogenesis at the same time. But the university is committed to helping us, and I hope we'll be able to add laboratory staff and take over more lab space to ramp up our organogenesis work. We need at least another researcher. Which is why I'm talking to you about commitment. Although I usually have no time for excuses, tell me why you were late the last couple of days."

"There's no excuse, really," Pia admitted. "But I've been having trouble sleeping." Silently she cursed George for her getting accustomed to him waking her up even though she knew it was totally unfair.

"Why have you been having trouble sleeping? Anxiety?"

"Nightmares."

"About what, if I may ask?"

"Childhood memories. Ancient history."

"Pia, I think I need to know more about you. You've told me little about yourself even though I've tried to be open with you about me."

"What do you want to know?"

"Everything!"

Pia took a deep breath. Occasionally in life there is a key crossroads moment that can be identified as such even as it's taking place. Pia understood she couldn't hide or keep quiet. The time to talk was now. Except with her caseworker, Sheila Brown, she'd never talked about her childhood. She took another breath. She felt as if the room were closing in on her. The only light in the room was a small library light on the desk, which put Rothman's face in shadowy relief.

"I do remember my mother—not much, just little things. She was also a Pia. My first name is actually Afrodita, but we were both called Pia. Sometimes out of the blue, a scent on someone or a gesture will make me think of her. But she died when I was little. I don't know how, and I don't even know how I know she died, but I do. I lived somewhere in the city with my father, Burim, and his older brother, Drilon, who stayed with us. They were Albanians, real Albanians, just off the boat, very rough around the edges. My father was away a lot, and I had to spend time with my uncle, who was a real creep. Have you got any water or anything?" Pia's throat was dry.

Rothman got out a bottle from a small fridge under the Nespresso machine. He pushed it and a cup across the desk's leather surface.

"He hit me a couple of times, my uncle. He used to touch me, never when my father was around, he was very careful. He made me touch him inappropriately, to say the least. He took pictures of me, you know, and developed them himself, and I think he used to sell them to other creeps like him. It developed into a side business for him. One night I had enough, and I went for him."

"What did you do?"

"I tried to stab him in the penis with a pair of scissors. Unfortunately I missed the target. It bled a lot. I remember later during first-year anatomy when the professor was talking about the femoral artery and joked about how you should avoid puncture wounds there. I suppose that's where I must have stabbed my uncle.

"When he got out of the hospital, he beat me up pretty well, and I guess someone called nine-one-one about a little girl with a bruised face because the police came and grabbed me. My uncle and my dad both got arrested. So I became the property of New York City Child Protective Services."

Pia took another drink of water.

"And your father?"

"He vanished. Years later I made Sheila Brown, my final and best caseworker, tell me what happened. She managed to find out that the two of them made bail and disappeared into the city. I've no idea where he is, if he's even alive. I guess I convinced myself that my father wasn't to blame for what his brother did to me. When I was in foster care, I used to fantasize that he would suddenly appear and rescue me from those places I was in, but he never did. I gave up hoping after a few of years."

"How old were you when you were taken into care?"

"Six. I was a problem for the foster care people from the get-go. My father hadn't officially given up his parental rights, so I couldn't be adopted. He had to register with Child Services before—I wasn't in school, I guess—and genius that he was, he said I was a Muslim, which, as an Albanian, he may have been. Sheila said he must have thought I'd get better treatment if I was a minority, but it just meant none of the religious agencies wanted me. Back then the system was dominated by Catholic, Protestant, and Jewish organizations. So instead of having a chance at some reasonably appropriate placement, I was put in a kind of temporary group home, and a janitor there tried to abuse me like my uncle did, but I fought him off. I complained about it, and I guess that marked me down as a troublemaker.

"I ended up in juvenile court a couple of times. I was lucky not to get locked up, I suppose, but I was designated a 'person in need of supervision'—I love that phrase. So the first dump I got sent to was called the Wilhelmina Shelter for Troubled Children. I got in trouble a lot. They'd write me up for not looking the staff in the eye, which they interpreted as being insufficiently remorseful, that kind of thing."

Pia looked at Rothman. His face was impassive. He nodded almost imperceptibly.

"When I was twelve or so, I got shipped to the Hudson Valley Academy for Girls, in a town called Eden Falls. It sounds nice, right? Eden Falls. The supposed school was a nineteenth-century institution. They used to send teenage prostitutes there, you know, to reform them, but when I was there it was all the hard cases who'd been thrown out of everywhere else—the girls no one wanted to adopt or deal with appropriately. The girls lived in these cottages. The paint was peeling, the plumbing didn't work. Roasting in summer, freezing in winter. That was bearable. It was the other girls that were the problem.

"The place was run by these girl gangs that were like crime families. Well organized—'daddies' at the top, then 'housewives,' 'cousins,' 'uncles,' and so on. They'd take your money, make you do their chores, beat you up for no reason. They came out at night. There was a lot of abuse—you know, physical stuff, sexual stuff sometimes. The staff knew, but they didn't care—the girls kept much better order than the staff ever could. I tried to stay out of the way, but they got everyone in the end. They found me hiding one night and attacked me in a bathroom. . . ." She paused.

"Anyway, I found an old book on boxing in the library and a couple of the younger girls knew some karate so we did a make-shift self-defense class. I was determined. Every time they came looking for something from me, I fought back. So I never joined their 'shadow society,' as one social worker called it. I got into a lot of fights, spent quite a lot of days and nights in the little punishment room, which was the moniker for solitary confinement. I spent a week there once. What I did was get the girl who was the leader of the group that attacked me in the bathroom off by herself and gave her one hell of a beating."

Pia worried that she was saying too much, but Rothman simply nodded again when she looked at him.

"I worked really hard at the lessons that were available at Hudson Valley Academy. It was my escape. There were some teachers who cared. I was determined not to end up pregnant on welfare or in jail like most of the girls did when they left. For the most part the staff didn't care what happened or what anybody did as long as we didn't actually kill each other. Excuse my English, but it was like a goddamn garbage dump. Leave the trash there till it's eighteen and had developed a taste for drugs and then release them into the world with no supervision. Good luck.

"The superintendent there, he knew it was the system that created as many problems as it fixed. Papitano was his name. He tried to get better therapists and teachers. He even tried to have the place shut down, but he was threatened so he stopped trying.

"I knew about that because the superintendent lived in a big mansion on the school grounds and a few of us used to clean his house and make his meals. He helped me out by putting me on that detail and getting me the good teachers. But he was a real sad sack and abusive—I guess his wife had left him, and he never saw his kids. I was sixteen, and I was around his house a lot and he got it into his head that I was interested in him even though I had resisted all his advances. One night he got really drunk, and I was in the library reading—it was the only library in the whole school—and he came down and said he loved me. He was really pathetic, but he got me in a corner, and I don't like being cornered. I think he said he got the black eye falling in the shower.

"I think Papitano was more embarrassed than mad at me because nothing happened to me. Except he wanted to get me out of there, which was a good thing. In retrospect I don't think it was for me, but rather so he wasn't tempted again or whatever his problem was. But his intercession worked by finding me a good and competent case-worker."

"Sheila Brown," Rothman said.

"Sheila Brown. She was very persistent, and she went to court, and Child Protective Services agreed to move me to a group home so I could possibly get my high school diploma before I was 'emancipated' out of the system. Emancipation, which is a very well chosen word. So I left Eden Falls, thank God. I was happy to leave, but that Papitano guy, the superintendent . . ."

Pia's voice trailed off and she paused to collect herself. When she resumed she talked very quietly, leaning forward, practically addressing Rothman's desk.

"You know, I really had grown to trust

him. I thought we had a connection. But before I got shipped out, he got drunk again, and he was a big man. He caught me alone in the library again. I'd let my guard down, and he betrayed me."

Pia stopped talking. They were sitting so still that the motion-detector-operated switch in Rothman's office doused the lights. The sudden pitch darkness caused both Pia and Rothman to jump. The lights came right back on.

"Jesus, I thought they fixed that," Rothman said. "Used to happen to me all the time."

"You must think I have an antisocial personality disorder," Pia said, regretting saying so much about her violent past. It had been like a dam bursting. "I've never really talked about it straight out like this. Not to anyone except maybe Sheila. But with her it wasn't all at once. It was over time."

"I don't think you have a personality disorder in the slightest," Rothman said. "You did what you had to do. I admire you. My foster care experience was nowhere near as bad. With Jewish parents, I got a decent placement right off. It wasn't a picnic, and I had to do without much nurturing, but I was older to boot. I was eleven at the time. Also I got to spend vacations with an aunt who wasn't the warmest of souls but at least was family. Even though my label then was only ADHD, my parents couldn't deal with me, so they had given up. In their defense, I was a handful. They had four older children, and I just figured that my mom and dad had run out of love by the time it got to me.

"Listen, Pia, I'm not trying to make you feel grateful to me, or feel any different about me because of what I've told you. I'm just saying that I understand some of what you went through—more after what you've been willing to share tonight. It's no wonder you have nightmares, and to tell you the truth, your being late doesn't bother me as much as it bothers Marsha and Junichi, especially with what I know. Ironically, it bothers them because they believe it bothers me. The major point I want to leave you with is that research is the calling where I found myself despite my past and despite my Asperger's. I think it could be for you as well, but you're going to have to make a decision. It can't be halfway. It's got to be either research or clinical medicine. It can't be both."

"Reactive attachment disorder," Pia said. "One of the social workers at Hudson Valley Academy told me I had reactive attachment disorder. It's supposed to mean I can't establish a relationship with anyone."

"Well, I guess we make quite the pair then," Rothman said, and smiled. Pia had never seen Rothman smile before and his whole face lit up for a second. "You think about your future. You don't have to say anything now. But I have to know soon so I can prepare. Once our article for *Nature* comes out, things are going to accelerate."

Rothman stood up. "Now I have to go back in the biosafety unit for another hour or so." Typical of his Asperger's syndrome behavior, he didn't comment further, just left.

Pia remained sitting after Rothman had departed. Except for the sounds emanating from some of the automatic equipment out in the lab, there was silence. Even the desk lamp went out again until she waved her hand in the air. She'd been taken aback by the evening's events. She felt exposed, emotionally naked, and found herself worried that Rothman might decide on further thought that she was much too big a risk. She sat in her chair for at least ten minutes before she got up and left. As she descended in the elevator, she started to feel better, relieved to a degree that she'd been as open as she had. Having been in foster care himself, Rothman understood her. All at once Pia felt confident all was going to work out. It was her opinion that you can trust only a man whose actions match his words, or better still, who acts without asking for anything in return. The only person she knew who fit that bill was Dr. Rothman. She knew that even George, as generous as he was, had his own agenda.

Exiting into the cold night, Pia didn't know exactly what she was going to do, but she had to admit that Rothman had made a lot of sense. And as unbelievable as it was, she felt he'd morphed into the father figure she'd never had.

20.

When his home office phone rang just after eight in the morning, a very anxious Jerry Trotter snapped it up. He'd been hoping it would ring, and he was hoping it would be Harry Hooper.

"I just had breakfast with that Morgan guy I was telling you about last night," Hooper said, launching right in after Trotter picked up.

"You met with the guy? Sat down in front of him and ate breakfast?" Trotter was surprised. Brubaker and Hooper were usually more indirect, avoiding face-to-face meetings.

"He wouldn't say anything more over the phone. He wanted a meeting, insisted on it. At six-thirty in the morning. He thinks I'm a headhunter for real, and he wants a new job, like yesterday. I couldn't see the harm in it. It's not like I'm going to see the guy again."

"But what do you know about being a headhunter?"

"What's to know? I just asked the guy to tell me about himself, about his strengths, where he sees himself in five years, all that BS. I said I didn't know of anyone who needed someone exactly like him, but I'd keep an ear to the ground, keep him in mind."

"Didn't he ask you for your business card?"

"Said I was all out," Hooper said. "Said I'd been meeting with a lot of bankers the last couple of weeks and underestimated demand. Almost convinced myself I was that busy. Anyway, we finally got around to talking about your woman friend. She and the thick guy who she was working for at the time definitely slept together. More than once. Not just some drunken hookup at a convention but an actual affair—hotel rooms in the afternoon, that kind of thing."

"And he knows this how?"

"He was going out with this woman who was good friends with your girl. Real good friends, like girlfriends who told each other everything. So your friend tells this woman she's seeing this guy who's married. Then she says it's her boss. She swore the friend to secrecy, made her swear she'd never tell anyone, all that. But the woman told my guy. Information's valuable, as you know, and it all depends on the circumstances. This woman thought it would help in her relationship with my guy, bring them closer, having a shared secret. It didn't work. They broke up after a while."

"So why'd he tell you?"

"Like I said, information can be valuable. I was asking about your girl, he knew something. Maybe he wanted the supposed job I was checking out your friend for. I don't really know. I guess I may have led him to believe I'm better connected on Wall Street than I am."

"He's going to be pissed when you disappear all of a sudden."

"What's he gonna do, tell his boss? Anyway, I plan to call him next week, start letting him down slow. It looks like I'm going to be downsized myself. Sure is a cruel world."

"Okay," Jerry said. "Give me a second to think."

Jerry held the phone in both hands. This was good—Gloria Croft and Edmund Mathews had slept together ten, twelve years ago. And clearly it hadn't ended well because Gloria was apparently enjoying trying to ruin Edmund. But for what Jerry had in mind, there had to be more. This was good, but it wasn't enough.

"Okay, I like this, but I need more. Keep digging. Try and figure out why it ended between them, and why it ended so badly."

"All right, got it."

Jerry sat back in his chair. He was a man with a lot of secrets, which is why he assumed everyone else had them. Some of Jerry's secrets concerned the fact that he was unfaithful to Charlotte, his wife of twenty-two years. He had had affairs with some of his patients, one of which continued after Trotter ended his medical practice and went into finance. It was still going on, with trysts at an apartment Trotter maintained in the Village for that express purpose. Trotter didn't feel any guilt about Charlotte. He thought of it as a kind of deal even though Charlotte had never been approached about it. He played around, and she lived the high life. Shopping was her sport.

From Jerry's perspective risk was a big part of life. Everybody handled risk differently. He thought he handled risk well, which was what made him a good hedge fund guy. Others handled risk poorly. The real question that dogged Jerry's mind at that moment was how much would have to be on the line for someone to do something truly desperate. He was just beginning to think there might be a way to solve the problem that Edmund had tossed into his lap.

Jerry Trotter had another secret, one that weighed on his mind more heavily than any other. It had nothing to do with women. Not only had Jerry taken a very sizable personal stake in LifeDeals, in addition to the position his fund had acquired publicly, but he had made a third and completely clandestine investment that was larger than the other two stakes combined. Jerry had studied what Edmund and Russell had set up with LifeDeals, read the business plans, and pored over the sales reports. He had commissioned his own secret research and paid lawyers hefty fees to set up financial instruments ready to be sold at a few days' notice. And then, masked by a series of offshore shell companies, he had set up the bare bones of a parallel company that would mimic LifeDeals, right down to the type of policies it went after. As Edmund never tired of saying, life insurance was a $26 trillion business in the USA alone. There was plenty of money to go around.

Edmund and Russell's bad news about regenerative medicine had hit Jerry Trotter like a hammer blow, much more than Edmund could have guessed. His due diligence had completely missed it, as had Edmund's. To his partner and his firm, LifeDeals' predicament was unfortunate but it hardly threatened the hedge fund's success, even in the short term. But Jerry stood to lose much more. His personal stake was very large but also survivable. But if the shadow company that he was rolling out went down, he was probably ruined. The various subsidiaries were already buying policies. Individually, each was tiny compared with LifeDeals'. Together, Jerry had once been proud to think, they were larger.

Over the course of approximately eighteen-plus hours, from the moment he'd left the Terrasini restaurant, Jerry Trotter had become an extremely desperate man. He hadn't slept all night, instead using his old calculator and various files and portfolios to try to figure out ways in which he could emerge from this intact. He knew he was clutching at straws with Harry Hooper, but he was hoping against hope that Edmund Mathews had something more than just money at stake, something that would mean Jerry didn't have to try to fix this mess all on his own. Jerry had few qualms, but he much preferred to delegate the truly dirty stuff, the stuff that could get you thrown in jail or worse.

21.

ONE CENTRAL PARK WEST
NEW YORK CITY
MARCH 4, 2011, 11:55 A.M.

By noon Jerry was near to being a basket case. After finishing the call with Harry Hooper, he went back to doing what he'd done at the end of the night: surfing the Internet just to have something to do. Jerry was buzzing on the amphetamines he'd taken to keep him awake and he knew he had thirty-six to forty hours until he crashed. Every couple of hours he drank a

Red Bull, and he chugged Diet Cokes constantly. His wife, Charlotte, had no idea what was going on but was familiar enough with the routine to keep well out of her husband's way. For Jerry the Internet was a wonderful resource and babysitter, so to speak. You could find out anything you wanted to know on it, as well as plenty of things you didn't know you wanted to know. It couldn't help much with finding the Fountain of Youth or proving the existence of God, but otherwise, it was golden.

The Internet was particularly useful when it came to providing practical solutions to all manner of problems. Jerry had recently discovered how to tune his universal remote so that it operated the controls on his TV, and he was grateful for that. This was a different kind of problem. As he sat alone in his darkened study with the shades drawn, he stared at the screen on his Mac, following threads in obscure discussion groups, piling up memberships in esoteric organizations, clicking on links that took him to some tortured recesses of our collective consciousness as represented on the World Wide Web.

Some of Jerry's on-screen reading

reminded him of being at medical school. What he wouldn't have given to have had this resource back then! The dry phrasing of the medical material hadn't changed in thirty years. Jerry thought he'd perhaps spent a couple of hours reading about salmonella when he was a student. He'd always been slightly germophobic, especially when it came to the more powerful microbes, and reading about this one made him uncomfortable. But Dr. Rothman's first specialty, the one that brought him his first Nobel, was fascinating.

It was such a versatile and dangerous bacteria.

The longer he sat at his desk, the more convinced Jerry became that only one course of action was open to him. He was initially horrified by the thought, but it looked like there were no other options, and he hated to be backed into a corner. Whenever he got squeamish, Jerry pondered the prospect of being broke and disgraced. If it all came crashing down, he'd be a laughingstock. Some ambitious hack would write a book about him, and he'd come across like a buffoon, an idiot. He would avoid that fate at any cost.

Once Jerry had the idea percolating in his mind, really all he needed was the resolve and the money. Spending hours researching certain specialized activities on the Internet had convinced him of something else: Money really could buy you anything. He had the money. He just had to convince himself he could follow it through.

Now, toward midday, the throwaway cell phone rang again. Trotter was hoping for Hooper, but he got Brubaker.

"What do you have?" Trotter said.

"Confirmation that those two guys are definitely the leaders in this organ-making field. Way out in front. Independently confirmed beyond that source I mentioned. And no one can be precise on the timeline because it depends on the results of tests that no one can predict. They might do a test and it doesn't work, which sets them back a week, a month. Or it does work and it's on to the next one."

"But eventually it's going to work?"

"That's what I'm hearing."

"Too much to hope that it blows up in their face."

"If you're looking for them to fail, doesn't

look like it's gonna happen. From every source, they're very confident."

"How do you know?"

"So I'm told. Plus they've formed a private company to control the patents that have been applied for. And it's not one patent. It is a whole series of patents to be sure they'll control the whole field."

"Thanks, I figured. That means they're close."

"Not necessarily—just means they're confident they're going to get there."

"How'd you find out about the company?"

"You really wanna know?"

"Indulge me."

"Okay, boss. I have a friend in the New York State Division of Corporations. Can find out when people register corporations or LLCs. Comes in handy when guys set up limited liability companies to hide money from their wives."

"I'll bear that in mind."

"Rothman Medical they call it. So it wasn't hard to find. Registered two weeks ago. They probably registered it overseas too, in better tax locations. As I said, they're being thorough."

"And who are the partners?"

"The members of the company? Just the same two guys."

Jerry ended the call. Rothman and Yamamoto. It seemed like the two of them were piloting the whole ship on their own. Jerry checked his watch. It was nearly twelve-thirty, almost four and a half hours since he'd spoken with Hooper. Suddenly Jerry felt crushingly tired. It was vital to him that Hooper find something he could use as leverage on Edmund Mathews. His brain was close to fried; he had to have someone help him with this. He knew Hooper would call him the second he had anything, but like the previous evening, he couldn't resist calling.

"It's me," he said redundantly when Hooper picked up.

"Is there a problem?"

"Just checking in," Jerry said, trying to control his voice.

With his antennae constantly up, Hooper sensed there was a problem, and the problem was Jerry. Jerry had said only five words, but it sounded to Hooper like Trotter was tweaking on crystal meth. Having been a policeman, he'd had to deal with all manner of drugs. "You don't sound so good."

"I'm tired is all."

"Well, I got some lines in the pond," said Hooper. "Just waiting for a bite. Just try and relax."

Sure, thought Jerry, as he broke the connection. *That's easy for you to say.*

22.

The night before, Pia had taken the time to set the alarm that George had given her as well as her own cell phone and had awakened refreshed and ready to go at 6:30. She'd slept like a rock. First time in more than a week. After showering, Pia had taken a trip to the cafeteria and knocked on George's door bearing a toasted bagel with cream cheese and a cup of coffee.

"Wow, this is a first," George had said when he answered the door. "And you brought breakfast. Come in!"

"I'm just returning the favor. Or favors. But where were you yesterday and the day before? I was late both days, and yesterday I ended up scrubbing beakers for two hours as punishment."

"Oh, I . . ."

"Doesn't matter. I have some news."

"Good news?"

"I think so."

George had continued getting ready while Pia sat on his bed.

"Rothman wants me to work in his lab full-time when I graduate."

George had come out of the bathroom holding his toothbrush. His mouth was agape and foaming.

"Can he do that?"

"I think around here, he can do pretty much whatever he wants. All he has to do is threaten to go to Harvard or Stanford."

"So what did you say?"

"I didn't say anything. For one thing, I was too stunned, and for another, he told me to think about it. But it's a no-brainer. I'm going to say yes. I'll talk to the dean about postponing my residency. I imagine I can still qualify as a Ph.D. student. But the important thing is to work in his lab. You can't believe what's happening in there. He's going to become even more famous. I wouldn't be surprised if he wins another Nobel."

George had returned to the bathroom and stood in front of his mirror. He looked himself in the eye and bit his tongue.

"That's great, Pia. Congratulations." He had tried to sound convincing, but didn't think he managed it.

"I thought you were going to give me one of your rants about Rothman."

"Hey, if this is what you want to do, I think you should do it." He bit his tongue again.

"My thoughts exactly. Come on, George! Hurry up, we're going to be late."

The early morning had been dark and a cold drizzle was in the air. March was not one of the best months in New York City. George and Pia had hurried to their assignments, talking about how their first days had gone.

"So what's it like working with Will McKinley?"

"He's a bit of an ass and into himself. Rothman thinks he'll go into plastic surgery. Anyway, he's holding his own since he's smart enough. I do like Lesley."

"I'm sure that Rothman's comment was not meant as a compliment. I've heard he's never said anything positive about anybody."

Pia had merely raised her eyebrows without commenting.

"McKinley reckons he's God's gift to women. I'm sure you figured that out."

Pia had shrugged, as if to say, "And?"

"Is he leaving you alone?"

"I can handle Will McKinley, believe me. He is quite cute though."

George had caught up the stride after momentarily lagging behind Pia. He looked across at her. She was smiling, having a laugh at George's expense. He couldn't help but laugh along with her. Silently he chided himself for being such a wimp.

The morning passed uneventfully for the students. They spent their time on their respective projects in the organ bath unit. Pia also spent several more hours reading about pH buffers designed to be used for tissue culture. The maintenance man had still not finished in her office or in Rothman's office either and wires still hung out of both ceilings. The electrical blueprints that had been in Pia's cubbyhole were now in Rothman's office. Pia had gone in to see if the worker was there as he wasn't in her space. She wanted to give him an earful about the job not being done. But he wasn't in there either, and after starting her reading, she forgot about him altogether.

As if taking a cue from jealous George, Will showed up and tried to engage Pia in small talk. Pia wasn't sure if he was hitting on her or not but couldn't have cared if he was. She answered his first few questions but then told him directly she wanted to concentrate on her reading. He took the hint and vanished.

At twelve thirty-five Rothman and Yamamoto appeared from the depths of the BSL-3. Pia couldn't help but notice that they were acting out of character. They were actually talking excitedly to each other. Pia didn't stare directly but watched out of the corner of her eye. The lab was quiet, which was why she had heard them emerge. It seemed that everybody was at lunch.

All at once Yamamoto came toward her as Rothman disappeared into his office but without shutting his door. Even that was out of the ordinary. Pia sensed that something was going on.

"Where are the other students?" Yamamoto asked when he reached Pia's side. His voice had what Pia would have described as an anticipatory ring.

Pia looked up. "I believe in the organ bath unit," she said.

"Good," Yamamoto said. "I want you in there too. Rothman and I want to show you students something."

Five minutes later all five people were in the organ bath room attired as per usual in caps, gowns, masks, and booties.

"Okay," Rothman said, clasping his gloved hands together in excitement. After Pia's surprising talk with him the previous evening and now his excited behavior, she felt she was seeing a side of Rothman that she never imagined existed. "Dr. Yamamoto and I want to show you something but in the strictest confidence. You will be here a month, Pia longer, but we would be very grateful if you could keep what you're about to see to yourselves in that period and thereafter. Agreed?"

The three nodded their assent.

"Good. We don't want anyone to get excited prematurely. The stakes here are very high."

As he talked, Rothman edged toward the back of the room. Set in the wall was a door with another security pad like the one on the main door outside. Rothman shielded the code pad with his body, punched in a code, which Pia assumed was the same as for the other security doors, and pulled open the door. Dr. Yamamoto held it as Rothman stepped over the threshold, followed by the students. Yamamoto stepped in and closed the door behind him.

They were standing in a room that was maybe ten feet square, an identical but smaller version of the one they had just left. The five people made the room feel crowded. The same bluish light filled the room, which had its own HVAC system that hummed a little louder than its larger neighbor. The recessed ceiling light illuminated two carts like the ones they had been working with next door. They stood side by side, but only one was operating.

Rothman gestured toward the bath atop the one cart. It was similar to the ones out in the main room. In it was a kidney much larger than the mouse organs. Soon they learned that it was a human kidney, and like the human kidneys in the outer room, it had been made from Yamamoto's fibroblasts. It was a pale color and appropriately kidney-shaped. The difference was that this organ had ports through the Plexiglas wall that were connected with Y connectors to the organ's artery, vein, and ureter.

"What you're looking at is what is going to be the world's first human organ exo-plant made from induced pluripotent cells. This morning we received official sanction from the FDA to go ahead and attach this organ to Dr. Yamamoto's cannulated in-guinal artery and vein. We will be allowing the organ to function as it would if it were transplanted into Dr. Yamamoto's abdo-men."

"You've volunteered for this?" Will asked Yamamoto.

"Yes, of course," Yamamoto said with enthusiasm. "It is a great honor for me."

"When will you do it?" Pia asked. It seemed as if she was being overwhelmed on a daily basis in Rothman's laboratory.

"As soon as we can schedule it with the surgery department. It will be done in one of the main operating rooms for safety's sake. We'll allow the organ to function for several hours while we monitor it carefully. It's going to be a big day. A milestone really."

But what Pia could see before her seemed like a destination in itself. The dreams inherent in what was growing next door were being made into a reality in this tiny secret chamber. Pia felt a sense of awe, that she was present at the creation of something immense and extraordinary. No one in the room was saying a word. Pia stared at the artificial kidney sitting in its nutrient solution, the blue light reflecting in the bath and flickering over her face. She had been working in Rothman's cathedral but now she had seen the shrine. She knew that Rothman would have preferred the organ to be a pancreas, but she knew he knew that would not be far behind.

She could hardly wait to see that happen.

23.

Jerry Trotter was slumped in his study, his head twisted awkwardly as it rested on his desk next to his slender Mac keyboard. As he snored fitfully, Jerry was having a particularly lurid dream. He is sitting as far back in a chair as he can while a man is yelling right in his face. In the dream, Jerry is late for a vital appointment, but he doesn't know what it's for, and he can't find out until the man stops yelling at him and gets out of the way. Jerry twitched himself half awake but didn't move. He'd drooled on the desk and his head was pounding. A phone was ringing somewhere nearby.

After an hour that morning, Jerry had turned off the ringers on all the phones in the house and on his regular cell phone. It appeared that there were plenty of people who wanted to talk to him. He hadn't shown up at work so they figured he was at home or at least somewhere where he could pick up his cell phone. But the only calls Jerry cared about would come in on the device that Max Higgins had given him. So that must be the phone that was ringing.

Jerry sat bolt upright and pulled something in his neck. A quick spasm of pain ran up into his head as he scrambled for the phone. It stopped ringing.

"Shit, shit."

Although he was one-part asleep and couldn't orient himself properly, Jerry found the phone and pushed at the unfamiliar buttons. A 917 number came up and he pressed the green button. The phone redialed. It wasn't Higgins, and he couldn't remember Hooper's number or Brubaker's.

"Let it be Hooper," he said quietly, with purpose. "Let it be Hooper."

Someone picked up the call.

"Where've you been? I called twice."

It was Hooper.

"You got something?"

"Bingo."

"What is it? You gotta tell me. . . ."

"We need to meet. The Starbucks on the corner of Sixtieth. Opposite the Mandarin Oriental."

"That's right across the street."

"See you in ten minutes."

Jerry Trotter looked at his Rolex again and then around the Starbucks. Harry Hooper had said ten minutes and that was almost a half-hour ago. Jerry had come straight down to the street from his skyscraper aerie and hurried across Columbus Circle, and he'd reached the place in four minutes flat. Max Higgins would be at the apartment at any moment too. Jerry had quickly called him and asked him to come up from the office with the car. Things seemed to be moving.

As usual, the Starbucks was jammed. There was a line of people snaking around the store, all waiting to order, and customers to their left waiting for their beverages to be delivered. Most of the two-tops were occupied by individuals with laptops and a lot of notebooks. Who were these people? Jerry wondered. Didn't they have homes? Or offices? A homeless guy had wedged his shopping bags and himself into a corner. He had a cup of water and as long as he stayed awake, he could sit there for the rest of the year.

What sort of venue was this for a meeting? Jerry wondered. There was little chance of finding somewhere to sit and less chance of talking discreetly. Jerry took out the phone and was ready to call Hooper again when he felt a hand squeeze his elbow, and not lightly. He twisted around. Hooper.

"Let's take a walk," he said.

Hooper guided Jerry out of the store and across the street so they skirted the front of the Time Warner building. Hordes of people were coming in and out of the doors.

Hooper turned right on Fifty-eighth Street and walked toward Columbus, steering Jerry through traffic to the south side of the street. They entered a pair of light green glass doors and took an escalator up to the lobby of the boutique hotel on the corner. Hooper led Jerry to a quiet section of the expansive lobby and sat at a table where a drinks menu was resting.

"A little quieter in here," Hooper said.

"What was all that about? We could have just met here."

"You sounded very tense on the phone," Hooper said. "I'd say nervous was more like it. And nervous people make me nervous. Just basic precautions."

Jerry looked at Hooper. How old was the guy, fifty-five? He was smaller than Jerry remembered, no more than five-eight, with dark hair that might be dyed but which was all his. He had a pinched, smoker's face and friendly eyes. Trotter trusted him not at all.

"Shall we have a drink?"

"Sure," said Jerry, who was running on fumes. Hooper waved a hand and a waiter came over from a bar.

"Scotch, rocks, a little water," Hooper said.

"Vodka martini with a twist," Jerry said. "Thank you."

"You look a bit rough there, boss."

"Didn't sleep well," Jerry said. "Nothing some good news won't cure. I'm presuming it's good news because you couldn't tell me over the phone."

"I wanted to have a little word with you, face-to-face."

"Oh, yes."

"I'm kinda wondering why you're so interested in this guy."

"Well, what's it to you, Harry? I asked you to find out some information and you seem to have found something. Obviously I want to have some leverage over this person, but it's nothing you need worry about."

"I'm curious how valuable the information might be."

Jerry paused while the waiter served their drinks. Was this little asshole trying to shake him down? The waiter left, and Jerry picked up his glass slowly.

"Cheers, Harry." Jerry knocked back half of his drink and put it down. "I'd say the information is worth the three hundred an hour I'm paying you. That was our agreement, I believe. A very generous one."

"Agreements are made to be renegotiated," Hooper said.

"What do you have in mind?"

"Another ten grand."

"Ten grand? Are you kidding?"

"Not in the slightest."

Jerry laughed, he couldn't help himself. Ten thousand was chicken feed. Anticipating that Hooper would try something like this, although not quite so unsubtly, he had brought fifty thousand dollars with him and was willing to spend it.

"Let me think about it," Jerry said, pretending to look pensive. "You must think I'm an idiot," he added, taking another gulp of vodka. "You and Brubaker both. Do you call each other and say, 'What an idiot that Jerry Trotter is, thinking he's some kind of spy'?"

Hooper looked at Jerry coldly. He didn't say no.

"I'm an idiot, but I'm not a total idiot."

Jerry reached into the pocket on the front of his leather jacket and took out a small digital recorder of the type Hooper was familiar with.

"What's that?" Now Hooper was smiling.

"I taped our calls, Harry. Not on this machine but another one just like it. What did you say—'basic precautions'? I prefer to think of it as insurance. Ha, me and insurance." Jerry finished his drink and held up his glass for the hovering waiter. Hooper hadn't touched his drink.

"There's nothing on there. I never say anything on the phone."

"Oh, really? Then you've got nothing to worry about."

Hooper's eyes darted around the room briefly, and he took a sip of his drink.

Jerry had got him thinking, he could see that.

"We're in this together, my friend. I have no intention of doing anything with the recordings. As you say, there's probably nothing there. But we've definitely entered a new phase in our relationship. You were very honest with me—you want more money. Okay."

Jerry reached into his jacket again and took out a thick manila envelope. He threw it down on the table next to Hooper's drink. Hooper picked up the envelope, held it below the level of the tabletop, and opened it with a finger. He flicked through the bills and looked up at Jerry. Jerry thought that if Hooper had ever seen that much money before, it was evidence he'd seized in an investigation, and it was going under lock and key.

"I don't get it," Hooper said. "That's a lot more than ten."

"Yes, it is. That's fifty."

"Fifty grand! Holy shit."

"Ah, Mr. Hooper, your grim exterior is slipping." Jerry finished off his drink. He was feeling a lot more like his old self.

"What do I gotta do?"

"You tell me two things, and I give you another one of those envelopes in a couple of weeks. That's all. First, I'm going to tell you what I think. I think you're a greedy little man. I know you pad your bills for me—that's fine, everyone does it. But this is real money. And I have more real money that I intend to keep giving you as long as we can help each other out. Because we really are in this together. I also think you don't know exactly what I have on tape. Hmm?"

Hooper had regained his composure and was looking Jerry right in the eye.

"I notice you already took the money. I also think you're thinking, Screw it, I want the money. It's easy money too, Harry, because I know you already know the first thing—that's why we're here. And I really think you'll find out the second one very quickly, a man of your experience."

"You're playing a dangerous game. You're an amateur."

"I know." Jerry closed his eyes and smiled. "But I'm a quick learner. So tell me what you found out about Edmund Mathews and Ms. Croft."

In a few sentences Harry Hooper told Jerry Trotter what he'd been told and about the source of the information. There was no doubt in Hooper's mind that it was true.

"Thank you, Harry. That might just be enough for me."

"So what's the other thing you want to know?"

Jerry leaned in toward Hooper.

"I want you to tell me how I get my hands on some polonium-210."

24.

It was thirty miles, give or take, from Columbus Circle in Manhattan to Edmund Mathews's house in Greenwich and by some miracle, Jerry's driver, a former New York State highway patrolman, made the trip in just over fifty minutes. After leaving Harry Hooper in the hotel bar, Jerry had found Max Higgins waiting in the limo in front of his building. He got in and called Edmund Mathews immediately, pretty much ordering him and Russell to leave their Greenwich office and meet at Edmund's house within the hour. Jerry had told Max nothing. Max thought Jerry looked terrible—red-rimmed eyes, unshaven cheeks, hair in disarray, and wearing a strange and rumpled shirt-and-khakis combination under an old leather jacket such as a biker might wear. And he could smell the alcohol on his breath. Max would have to wait for an explanation because as soon as he'd spoken with Edmund, Jerry stretched out in the limo's generous backseat and fell into a noisy and fitful sleep.

In the hours since their lunch with Jerry and Max the day before, Edmund and Russell had done nothing significant in terms of solving their problems. Russell had busied himself overseeing the implementation of some of Edmund's ideas about buying different types of life insurance policies and legal staffers had started combing through existing diabetics' policies looking for what Russell had called "anomalies." Anyone who'd used a middle initial on one document and not on another, they were to see if that was grounds for termination of the policy. Any agreements in progress were halted pending investigation. But these were stopgaps. If there was to be a macro solution, Edmund and Russell hoped it would come from Jerry.

When Edmund received Jerry's summons, he was optimistic that salvation was at hand. Jerry had sounded hoarse, and he was even more abrupt than usual. But no matter. Russell had been positively giddy as the two men waited for Jerry, Edmund more reserved. From experience Edmund knew that if Jerry had thought of something, it wouldn't be pain-free. There'd be a price to pay somewhere down the line.

Jerry's limo pulled up to Edmund's front door. As Edmund watched from a second-floor window, the driver hopped out and held the door open for Jerry, who slowly stepped into the chilly winter air. Even from this range, Jerry didn't look so hot. As Edmund made his way downstairs, his wife, Alice, ever the good hostess, opened the front door.

"Alice!" Jerry said jovially. "I was hoping I'd see you. You look as lovely as ever." And she did, her blond bob tucked back behind her ears, her light green eyes set off by a mint-green sweater, her gym-toned legs setting off a sharp, knee-length skirt.

"Hello, Jerry, how are you?" Alice grabbed Jerry's elbow and leaned in to kiss his cheek. Jerry had tried to tame his hair and had quickly polished off half a roll of breath mints, but he hadn't completely overcome his dishevelment. Nor had he done anything about a subtle ripeness that hovered around him like an invisible cloud. Alice recoiled a little.

"I was just saying to Max," Jerry continued as Edmund joined them, "what a wonderful couple Alice and Edmund are. And little Darius makes three. Beautiful wife, a healthy heir, this stunning house. Edmund, you are a lucky SOB. The man who has everything. Wasn't I just saying that, Max?"

"Absolutely, Jerry, and who could disagree?" Max had no idea what Jerry was talking about, but he played along. Two minutes earlier Jerry had been all but dead to the world.

Jerry had his arm around Alice's shoulder as the group filed into the house. Edmund wondered what on earth was going on. Jerry had never shown the slightest interest in Alice, nor Edmund in Charlotte Trotter. They didn't have that kind of relationship—it was all business.

"Russell here? Ah yes, there you are," Jerry said, spying Russell emerging from the library.

"Can I get you gentlemen anything?" Alice asked, extricating herself from Jerry's grip. Jerry moved to lean against a wall. From Edmund's perspective it appeared as if Jerry was having trouble standing up.

"I'd love a coffee, thanks, Alice. You have one of those fancy machines, right? As strong as it comes, and in a large mug if you wouldn't mind. Didn't sleep so well last night."

Alice moved toward the kitchen and the four men stood in Edmund's expansive entryway.

"We don't have all the paperwork from Statistical Solutions corroborating the concerns we have about the bell curves," Edmund said, eager to get the ball rolling.

"I don't care about that," Jerry said. "It's as bad as you thought. Actually, it's probably worse than you feared. We have to preserve the capital we've invested, and the only way to do so is to act quickly and decisively. Like now."

"Well, shall we go into the library and sit down and talk about it?" Edmund asked. "Or the living room?"

"No, Edmund," Jerry said, suddenly sounding more focused. "You and I are going for a little walk outside."

"A walk? It's freezing out there! It's going to snow later."

"Don't worry, Edmund, you're not going to freeze to death. Go grab a coat."

As Russell and Max moved into Edmund's library, Edmund and Jerry stepped outside, Edmund fortified by a woolen overcoat, Jerry by the coffee Alice had made. It was five shots of espresso staining the inside of a Syracuse University mug.

"They've set up a company to control the patents for the organogenesis techniques," Jerry said. "Rothman and Yamamoto. These are the guys, no doubt about it. They're the problem."

"I'm glad you're taking the issue to heart," Edmund said. They walked along an ornamental path in the front of the house, past rosebushes that had been severely pruned back for the winter. Patches of snow lay on the lawn in the shadow of the hedges.

This was as barren as Edmund's garden ever looked.

"We have to act at once. Those bell curves move at all to the right, it's a disaster."

"I'm pleased you see the same problem we do."

Jerry stopped walking just short of the lawn.

"Unfortunately, we don't see a simple financial solution, like selling ourselves short through an intermediary or securitizing our policy holdings immediately. With Gloria Croft shorting big-time, we probably couldn't find any institutional buyer."

"I agree," Edmund said. "But the life settlement concept is still sound. It's maybe the best business opportunity I've ever come across. It would be a shame to have to give up at this early stage."

"I agree," Jerry said. *And more than you know*, he thought, more than even Max knew. "Which is why I've come up with another plan."

There was a silence, then Jerry went on.

"It's a little unorthodox, but it's the best plan that serves all of our interests. Believe me, I've thought about nothing else over the last twenty-four hours. But it's not for us to do—it's for you to do. It *was* your idea, this whole thing. Your mess to get out of. Just you and I will speak of it, nothing will be in writing."

Edmund nodded. He didn't expect anything different. Not from Jerry.

"There's only one solution, and it's the way it has to be because this guy Rothman has got himself out there so far ahead of the pack."

Another silence ensued.

"I think Rothman's momentum has to be stopped. If it is, I think we'll have a good five years before the rest of the research community catches up to where Rothman is today."

Neither man said anything. Jerry's words hung heavily between them as if they were written in the air. Finally Edmund broke the excruciating silence.

"How do we stop Rothman's momentum, Jerry?"

"Easy," said Jerry. "You kill him."

Edmund turned and walked away from Jerry, back toward the house. He took a path on the side of the building and Jerry set his empty coffee cup down and followed him to the rear garden, where Edmund sat on a bench with a view of Long Island Sound. Jerry sat down next to him.

"Murder, Jerry? Like having him shot?" Edmund was appalled. At the same time he didn't think he had the luxury of dismissing any idea out of hand no matter how preposterous it sounded.

"No, not at all. The two of them should die in a way that doesn't invite suspicion of homicide. It must look like an accident. There shouldn't even be an investigation, although I suppose that would be inevitable. But there can be nothing that makes this look deliberate. Because it wouldn't be beyond the realm of possibility that any semi-competent murder investigation would lead right to LifeDeals. You sat there yourself at Statistical Solutions and talked about what this could do to the company's bottom line."

"Do you have any specific suggestions, Jerry?" Although the proposal was outlandish and terrifying, Edmund wanted to find out what Jerry was proposing. It wasn't as if Edmund had any plan B waiting in the wings.

"As a matter of fact, I do."

Edmund continued to stare out at the water.

"I'll tell you," said Jerry, "most of the medical people will know that Rothman's first interest in research, before he became involved in regenerative medicine, was salmonella, which is the number-one cause of food-borne illness in general and typhoid fever in particular. He's investigating the virulence of the bacteria—what causes it to be a tremendously deadly bacteria on the one hand, and a bothersome but nondeadly cause of gastrointestinal distress on the other. Why does one type give you the runs but another kills you? We did a little research. He's found that growing salmonella in outer space produces a very lethal strain. He should be fed some of this particular strain.

"A lot of people don't care for the man—they're jealous of his Nobel Prize, and they think he's got an attitude. If he dies from the bacteria he's studying, a lot of people are going to say, 'Oh, that's terrible,' and then smile at the irony of it later."

Jerry made it sound so easy.

"I suppose that would be clever," Edmund said. He felt he had to say something.

"That's not the half of it. The typhoid fever he'd immediately develop might or might not kill him. There has to be something else that will kill him quickly and definitively, but it's got to be something you can't easily detect. There's a substance called polonium-210—very radioactive and deadly if you ingest it but not harmful otherwise. We'd use it because it produces many of the same symptoms as typhoid and would be masked by it. It's what killed Alexander Litvinenko in London a few years ago."

"I remember that. That was just a theory, surely, the polonium."

"I think it was more than that," Jerry said.

"Why do we need it?"

"To make sure the guy dies. It's very potent. The challenge is that Rothman and his sidekick work in one of the premier medical centers in the world. The salmonella, no matter how virulent it might be, cannot be counted on by itself. One or both of them could be saved. That's a chance that cannot be taken. We need to be sure. One-hundred-percent sure, ergo the polonium, and a massive dose of it to boot."

"So where the hell do you get this stuff? Who's going to buy it? Russell?"

"You hire the right people. Professionals."

"You've been watching too many movies," Edmund said. "So tell me, Jerry, who is going to procure this deadly radioactive poison for us?"

"Albanians."

"Albanians?" Edmund's voice betrayed his skepticism.

"There's an Albanian Mafia that's grown big in New York in the last twenty years. Very violent, very ruthless. But also very reliable, if you do business with them. Their word is their bond and all that. The FBI put a crimp in their operations in the nineties, but they've grown back and they're looking to make names for themselves again. You're going to ask, how do I know? I got this from a man who spent years of his life trying to put these guys in jail. He gave me a name."

Jerry held out a piece of paper, folded in half, for Edmund. Edmund thrust his hands in his coat pockets and looked at Jerry.

"You're out of your fucking mind."

. . .

Jerry let Edmund stew for a couple of minutes. Edmund had moved down to the edge of his property and was standing, looking out at the gray water of the Sound. Jerry could imagine Edmund's state of mind—part of him horrified to even consider such a thing, another part telling him he had no option but to consider doing it. Which side was winning? Jerry decided to play his trump card. He didn't want to have to do this either, but again, there was no choice. He walked down to join Edmund and stood about four feet to his right, looking ahead.

"I know about you and Gloria Croft."

"What about me and Gloria Croft? You mean personally?" Edmund waited a beat, then turned to look at Jerry, who was stony-faced and staring straight ahead.

"What's that got to do with anything?"

"So you know what I'm talking about?"

"Yes, yes. Gloria and I had a . . . a thing when we were working together."

"When you were her boss."

"Yes, Jerry, *Jesus*, what does that have to do with *anything*?"

"You got married young, I believe."

"I was married at the time. I admit it, I was a bad boy. I got carried away, and I wasn't the only one who's ever done that. You tell me you never did. But I learned my lesson. I steer very clear of bitches like her."

"So no harm, no foul is what you're saying, right, Edmund?"

"Jerry, I swear I have no idea what the relevance of this is. You just asked me to *kill* two people, for Christ's sake." Edmund turned his head as he said it, checking that no one had joined them. "Are you trying to put pressure on me with *this*?"

"There's something I don't think you're aware of. I was hoping I wouldn't have to bring this up, but it seems like you leave me no option." Jerry looked at Edmund. He had crossed one bridge with Edmund a few minutes ago. Now he was going to burn it down.

"When you were sleeping with Gloria Croft, she got pregnant—"

"Oh, bull*shit*, Jerry—"

"She got pregnant, Edmund, and she had a termination, and it didn't go well. She used a good clinic, I can give you the name, but the procedure had some serious complications. I can give you details, if you need them. She survived, but it left her sterile, so she can't have children. And I would imagine it also left her with a lot of resentment for the man involved."

"Why should I believe this?" Edmund's face was dark with fury, his hands bunched into fists still thrust deep into his coat pockets, his left hand throbbing from punching the elevator door. He leaned toward Jerry, almost goading him.

"You're trying to blackmail me? I can't believe you."

"The information came up quite by chance," Jerry said. He was surprised how remarkably calm he felt. "We were looking for dirt on Gloria when we heard about this. I know someone who has contacts in the records department at certain hospitals, and he found the relevant file. The timing's right, we checked, and there's even a note in there saying that she only had one sexual partner. They were ruling out some STDs, so they asked. My guess is that partner was you."

"Bullshit."

"You use a condom every time, Edmund? She miss a bit of work around the time you stopped seeing each other? You might not remember, but I doubt you liked your analysts taking a lot of time off. And perhaps she left the company soon after that, am I right?"

Edmund sighed. He felt deflated, almost literally, as if the air had been sucked out of his lungs. He stared back out at the water again.

"So what will you do with this information? And I'm not saying it's true."

"I said just now what a lovely wife you have, what a beautiful home. It's true, of course. I'm just pointing out to you what's at stake here, Edmund. You might not see things as clearly as I do. We've all worked so hard to get what we have, and there are so many people who are jealous of us, who say we don't deserve all this, but we both know the truth. We earned everything we have. Without us, this country would be starved of innovation. Nothing new would be created. Okay, so someone's going to grow organs outside of the body, but not now, not when they'll destroy this wonderful product of yours. It's a fantastic idea that you had. And you have to protect it."

Jerry paused.

"Now you say what I just told you is

bullshit. It's not all bullshit, is it? It can't be. And what's Alice going to say if she gets a note that says her husband slept with his analyst, and she got pregnant? I doubt she's going to be placated that easily, just by telling her it's all bullshit."

Edmund said nothing.

"I'm telling you, these Albanian guys can make all of this go away. I assure you they have done more difficult things than this. It turns out that it's true what they say: money really can buy you anything. Just look around you, Edmund, you just have too much to lose."

"What about Gloria Croft?"

"Don't worry about her," Jerry said. "She'll get hers when LifeDeals share price skyrockets."

Jerry held out the piece of paper again. This time, Edmund wearily put out his hand and took the scrap, unfolded it and read it. Jerry touched him once on the shoulder with his left hand and turned and walked back toward the house. Edmund stood where he was, staring at the name written on the paper, a name that meant nothing to him, and everything.

PART II

25.

Tobias Rothman was happiest when he could work uninterrupted in the safe confines of the lab, with Dr. Yamamoto at his side. Yamamoto was like Rothman's right arm. He could hold out a hand, and Yamamoto would know what he wanted without him having to ask for it. The two men communicated by looks and pointed fingers and sometimes, Rothman swore, by intuition. If Rothman could intuit anything as they worked together under the hood in the biosafety level-3 lab today, it was that his colleague didn't feel so good because a couple of times he'd uncharacteristically missed Rothman's cues. In truth, Rothman hadn't been feeling particularly well himself for the last hour or so. He had some mild gastric distress but worse was a kind of light-headedness, as if he were walking on eggshells. It had started about an hour after their coffee break at nine. They'd been in the unit since six.

Rothman looked over at Yamamoto. He was facing the wall, resting his hands on the lab bench, breathing hard. Yamamoto turned to look at Rothman, and Rothman could see that he was shivering. With a hood and mask, all Rothman could see of Yamamoto's face were his eyes, which reflected fear. Suddenly Rothman felt it too, and began to shiver himself. It was as if he'd just jumped into a bath of ice water, yet he was sweating, and he felt nauseous. It was impossible that what flashed through his mind could be happening—they'd taken all their usual precautions, and their safety record was perfect.

The next moment Yamamoto's eyes rolled up in his head, and he collapsed limply onto the floor. Rothman tried to steady himself before going to Yamamoto's aid, but he felt suddenly much worse. The room swam before him. He knew he was going to black out and just before he did, his hand reached for the red button on the wall.

Pia was sitting in her office comparing notes with Will and Lesley. It was crowded but quiet. They'd taken refuge in there despite its diminutive size as there was yet another workman in the lab proper, again working up in the ceiling with all the electrical wires. He'd briefly been in her office as well as Rothman's but thankfully had left both. Luckily it wasn't the same guy, Vance, who'd been such a pain weeks earlier.

The three students had formed an effective unit in their three weeks together and were making good progress with the temperature and pH issues with the organ baths. They'd spent almost all of their waking hours including weekends in the lab, but none of them begrudged a minute of it.

Then, in an instant, it was as if a riot had broken out at the door to the lab.

"What the hell?" Will said, as the three students piled out of Pia's office.

From her vantage point, all Pia could see were people barging in through the door. The place was being invaded—she must have seen twenty people dressed in gowns, hats, masks, and booties rush toward the biosafety unit. Bringing up the rear was a pair of gurneys sprouting IV poles with plastic bags of IV fluid slapping against the metal poles, pushed by more gowned-up figures. The gurneys disappeared into the biosafety unit, whose door had been propped open with a doorstop. Pia felt a terrible sensation growing in the pit of her stomach.

One man stopped by Marsha's desk and stood next to the terrified secretary, who had a hand clasped over her mouth; another blocked off the entrance door, which was again closed, denying access to the corridor and the rest of the medical center. The laboratory staff crowded into the center of the room and there was a ripple of loud conversation and shouted questions.

"Is this a drill?" Lesley said. "What's going on?"

The figure by Marsha's desk pulled down his mask. He was a fifty-something African-American man with skin as black as ebony; his voice was calm yet commanding.

"Okay, folks, this is not a drill. We have a situation, and I need you all to stay right here, right where you are. Is everyone in the lab accounted for?"

People looked around, checking for coworkers among the fifteen or so technicians and support staff standing around. Pia could see the maintenance man in his coveralls standing at the back of the room, gaping like everyone else.

"Everybody here? Okay. My name's David Winston. I'm from hospital security. These other people are a mixed group from the hospital ER and the Department of Infectious Disease. I'll give you more information when we have it. I am asking you to please remain in this area. Thank you for your cooperation."

The staff stood in small groups and talked among themselves. Pia, unable to stay still, walked around in a small, tight circle. Whatever was happening, she knew it wasn't good. A wave of anxiety washed over her.

The lab door opened abruptly and a tall, distinguished-looking man walked in quickly and made his way through the cordon toward the biosafety unit, conspicuously avoiding eye contact with anyone. He was dressed in protective clothing like the others except his mask hung down on his chest. Under the gown was a suit, not scrubs like the others. Pia knew this was the chief of Infectious Disease, Dr. Helmut Springer, as she had attended several lectures he'd given during second-year pathology.

The background buzz of conversation grew louder. Most recognized Dr. Springer. Everyone in the lab was well aware that they worked with highly virulent and contagious microorganisms. Was it possible there'd been some contamination of the lab? Where were Dr. Rothman and Dr. Yamamoto? Springer's appearance only heightened the tension. The man by the door was on a cell, apparently quarterbacking whatever was happening. "We're on our way, ETA five minutes," he was heard to bark into his phone.

Quickly tying his mask in place, Springer pulled the biosafety unit door fully open. As if on cue, the gurneys reappeared, the one in front carrying Dr. Rothman, Dr. Yamamoto in the rear. Both men had IVs and were wearing oxygen masks. Rothman passed right in front of Pia, who pushed forward to take a look. She could see he was deathly pale and shivering violently. His eyes were fixed straight ahead, staring at the ceiling. He looked like death.

As fast as they had come, the cavalcade of medics was gone. Only Dr. Springer and Winston remained. Springer addressed the shell-shocked staff, a few of whom were clutching each other for comfort, others holding their hands over their mouths in disbelief at what they had just witnessed.

"As you can see, Doctors Rothman and Yamamoto have been taken ill. At first guess, we have to consider it to be severe typhoid fever. Both men are presenting the classic symptoms—fever, sudden prostration, abdominal distress, delirium, right lower quadrant borborygmi." Springer counted off the symptoms on the fingers of his left hand as if he were on formal grand rounds. Once a professor always a professor, thought Pia. "Obviously, they were working in the biosafety unit. But can anyone tell me what they were working on exactly?"

Lab technician Panjit Singh stepped forward. "They were working on salmonella strains grown in the space station lab. I know that for a fact because I set everything up for them this morning. They've been working on it for weeks."

"Okay, thanks, that's very useful. Do you know if there are any antibiotic-sensitivity studies available for these special strains?"

"Yes, lots of them. I can get them for you."

"That's good, I'm going to need them, thank you. Mr. Winston here will talk to you about procedure a bit later, but here's a thumbnail: no one is to go into the level-three lab until it's cleared. The Rothman lab itself will be off-limits until further notice. I've already put in a call to the CDC to get their help on the epidemiology side so we can find out how this contamination occurred. Right now, everyone needs to follow me to the Infectious Disease Clinic, where you'll be screened for typhoid fever. Everyone will also need to take a prophylactic course of antibiotics. This is very important. For the next week you'll have to monitor your own temperature twice a day. Anything unusual, come in right away. A degree either side of normal, I want to see you. Any questions?"

"Who raised the alarm?" Singh asked.

"There's a panic button in the biosafety lab," Springer said. "One of the doctors must have hit it. We'll check the tape."

"Does everyone need to come to the clinic?" Pia asked. "Even people who haven't been in the biosafety unit today?"

"Absolutely. And Mr. Winston will also be gathering names of everyone who's been here delivering supplies or takeout or whatever. We want to see everyone who has set foot inside this lab. That's it. Thank you for your cooperation."

The din of conversation erupted again.

"Oh my God!" Lesley said. "Did you see how they looked? It must have come on fast."

"Dr. Yamamoto told me he didn't feel so

hot this morning," Will said. "But yeah, I saw how they looked. I guess we better go do what the man said."

Pia looked around. The maintenance man was hanging back, and though Pia didn't want to talk to him, she knew he needed to follow the protocol.

"There's a medical issue," she said to the man. His temporary name tag read "O'Meary." "You have to come to the clinic with everyone else."

O'Meary looked nervous and didn't say anything. Winston called out to Pia.

"Time to go," he said. "We're locking down." There was clearly no room for argument. Pia waited for O'Meary to leave and exited in front of Winston. As the last person out, Winston pulled the door shut and talked to two figures in full hazmat suits standing outside.

"No one gets in," Winston said. "Put up the caution tape." The men in the hazmat suits nodded and set to work.

As they made their way to the elevator, Pia could see that the whole floor was being cleared, with other personnel being led down the stairs. There were more people in hazmat suits that looked like robots. On the elevator ride down, Pia could feel her heart beating too fast, and she had to concentrate on breathing deeply. She felt some dizziness from her shallow breathing. As she walked along the sidewalk she was gripped by what felt like panic—everything around her felt very close and incredibly far away at the same time. She had stopped walking and was holding on to someone. Voices were loud in her ear.

"Come with me," a woman is saying. It's a hot sunny day but Pia's freezing cold. The woman has a nice smile and she's holding Pia's hand. This is a new place, Pia knows that. She hasn't been here long. This is the first smile she's seen, though it's odd now—grown-ups don't keep smiles on their faces the whole time. Pia and the woman have come inside and they're walking up to a large door. It feels like they're walking uphill. "This is the headmaster's office," the woman says. She opens the door and pushes her in. Pia can hear the lock being turned. "Hello, Pia," says the man. He's smiling too but it's a twisted smile, not a smile of welcome. . . .

Pia looked up. She was sitting on the ground on 168th Street with traffic passing by. Winston was supporting her with his hand, looking down at her.

"You okay?"

"Yes, I think so."

"You fainted. Or almost fainted. You're not perspiring, so I don't think you have a fever. I think you're okay. Ready to get up?"

Pia waited a second and allowed Winston to pull her to her feet. Then she remembered where she was and what had just happened. With disturbing clarity she saw Rothman lying on the gurney, his face looking like death, and the image terrified her. Over the course of three and a half years she'd come to rely more and more on the man's strange friendship, particularly after their heartfelt conversation a few weeks ago. Up until then, their relationship had been akin to two people comfortably wandering around in a darkened room, occasionally sensing each other's presence but not much else. But after the conversation and the personal revelations, she felt they'd moved to another level. Rothman had become the ersatz father she'd always pined for. Most important, she'd allowed herself to begin to trust Rothman despite having learned not to trust anyone, not to allow anyone into a position where they could betray her, like so many had done.

Now, as she stumbled along the street, Pia was overwhelmed by the thought that just when she'd allowed Rothman into her world, he was going to abandon her. Why was he doing this? And why now? It was irrational to think so, but did he do this to spite her? Did he purposely set her up? After all, he'd admitted to being depressed. She was almost paralyzed with anxiety.

At the Infectious Disease Clinic, Pia was shaking when she was handed the Z-Pak prophylactic antibiotic. She sat down in the waiting area and her head started to clear. She was aware that several people had tried to talk to her, but she didn't hear them.

"Miss Grazdani!" a nurse called out sharply, standing directly in front of Pia. She was on the brink of calling the ER if the young woman continued in her fugue-like state, thinking Pia might have to be admitted.

Not quite awakening, Pia sat up straighter and focused on the nurse's face.

"I'm here," Pia voiced. "I'm sorry. What did you say?"

"I said that you can't go back to the lab. It's going to be closed until the CDC epidemiologists get here from Atlanta and declare it clean. What you should do, as we have advised the others, is go home, start your antibiotics, and watch your temperature. Is there someone we can call who can meet you there? Miss Grazdani? Are you okay, Miss Grazdani?"

"I'm just fine," Pia assured her.

26.

COLUMBIA UNIVERSITY MEDICAL CENTER
NEW YORK CITY
MARCH 23, 2011, 2:37 P.M.

It wasn't a warm day, but Pia had wanted to sit outside. She had found a bench set in a small rectangle of public cement, what in New York City is called a park, and sat down, hands in her coat pockets, her chin down, hood pulled over her eyes. Her mind played over the scene she had just witnessed several times. There was a surreal quality to it, like it was one of her nightmares. Unfortunately it was real.

After she had gotten herself reasonably calmed down, Pia got up from the bench and started to walk toward the dorm. She got halfway, changed her mind, and turned and headed back to the hospital. There she took the first two of her antibiotic tablets at a water fountain before heading to the internal medicine floor.

At the main nurses' station, she asked for Dr. Rothman and was directed to the infectious disease wing a floor above, where Rothman and Yamamoto had been admitted. She wanted to check on Rothman's status, hoping that he'd revived with treatment, and if so, she wanted to ask him if he knew how he and Yamamoto had become contaminated. Pia knew the epidemiologists would certainly be asking the same questions, but she had a personal reason for finding out—the crazy thought that he'd done it on purpose, an idea she knew to be irrational but which demanded, in her mind, to be investigated.

Pia had another concern. Experience had taught her to absolutely distrust authority in any institution and to assume that nothing would happen the way it should. She knew Rothman was disliked by almost one hundred percent of his colleagues in the medical center. He was rude, seemingly arrogant, and antisocial. While medical protocol and simple human decency demanded that each patient receive the undivided attention of medical staff and the best care available, she couldn't help but think Rothman's reputation might degrade the standards.

Pia used her medical student credentials to get on the floor and found that the two researchers were in adjoining, negative-pressure rooms where air flowed in but not out. They were in strict isolation but there was no one guarding the rooms. Pia started to put on the isolation gear in the anteroom—the gown, hat, mask, gloves, and booties—but just as she was about to put on her mask, Dr. Springer emerged from Rothman's room. He undid his mask and stared at Pia.

"What on earth are you doing here? You're Rothman's student, aren't you? You're supposed to be home."

"I took my antibiotics and my temperature's fine. I know I'm clean—I wasn't in the biosafety unit today, or even in contact with Dr. Rothman or Dr. Yamamoto. It's very important I speak with Dr. Rothman."

"Good God! Of course you can't speak with him. The only people allowed in are medical staff assigned to his case. No family, no friends, and certainly no medical students."

"There's no one in there looking at him now. Are you sure of the diagnosis? Is this the best place to treat his condition?"

"What do you mean, 'is this the best place?'" Springer shook his head in disbelief.

"I know what people around here think of Dr. Rothman—"

"Young lady, I don't know what you're implying but everyone at Columbia Medical Center gets the same superb care as everyone else, friend or foe, rich or poor. It makes no difference whatsoever. And I happen to like Dr. Rothman."

"Okay, okay. Sorry, I'm just upset." Pia didn't want to get thrown off the floor. "I've been working with both men for more than three years on the salmonella strains that are probably involved, and I thought I might be able to help."

"Okay," said Springer. He relaxed a degree. He sensed Pia's intentions were good even if totally unrealistic.

"I have to tell you that both men are delirious. Even if I let you in there, you wouldn't get anything out of Dr. Rothman. Follow me." Springer took off the protective gear and tossed it into the covered hamper. Pia did the same.

Springer took Pia back to the nurses' station and, sitting down, itemized the laundry list of tests that had been ordered, including a complete blood count, electrolytes, blood cultures, urine cultures, stool cultures, stat DNA microbiology tests, and the appropriate X-rays. At that point the tests that had come back confirmed that the infectious agent was one of the salmonella strains Rothman and Yamamoto were working on, which Rothman had named the alpha strain, the most virulent of the three grown in space. He also mentioned that the white cell count showed a mild leukopenia, meaning the white cell count was mildly depressed, something often seen with typhoid fever. He declared the electrolytes, meaning primarily sodium, chloride, calcium, and potassium, were normal. Springer concluded by telling Pia that Rothman's and Yamamoto's temperature, heart rate, blood pressure, degree of oxygenation of blood, urine output, and central venous pressure were being monitored, and that at the moment the only thing abnormal was the temperature.

"They're both in bad shape, especially considering how quickly the illness came on," Springer added.

"What antibiotic are they on?" As Pia knew from her studies with Rothman, there was debate about which was the best to use in serious salmonella cases.

"That's a good question," Dr. Springer said. "Actually Dr. Rothman briefed me recently on findings he had made in his studies of antibiotic sensitivity on these zero-gravity strains. All three strains he was working on are very sensitive to chloramphenicol. That's an antibiotic that at one time was considered the best choice for typhoid, but it went out of favor in the seventies because newer strains of salmonella were becoming resistant. Dr. Rothman said that because these strains were grown in space, they were more virulent but somehow they'd also lost their chloramphenicol resistance. He was interested because drug resistance is a big problem with salmonella."

"Have you thought of trying ceftriaxone?" Pia asked, referring to a newer antibiotic.

Springer hesitated, giving Pia a once-over look. He'd been trying to be nice to her, as she was obviously concerned about her mentor. When he resumed speaking his voice and syntax had changed. There was an edge. "I actually wasn't requesting a consult by speaking with you. It's purely as a courtesy that I'm filling you in on Dr. Rothman's condition and course of treatment. But to answer your question, if it was a question, there is some sensitivity to ceftriaxone but significantly less than there is to chloramphenicol."

"Chloramphenicol can cause aplastic anemia," Pia said, missing Springer's signal that she was pushing it.

"Yes, we've taken into account the side effects, of course. Excuse me." Springer suddenly got to his feet. Abruptly he left Pia, talked briefly with one of the residents helping with Rothman's and Yamamoto's care, then left the floor.

Pia waited for a few minutes before wandering over to the same resident, who was reading a chart.

"What do you think of Dr. Springer? Do you think he's qualified?"

"What do I think? He's the best in the country. I wouldn't be here otherwise."

Puzzled by the question, the resident walked away, leaving Pia standing by the nurses' station, alone.

27.

News of the Rothman/Yamamoto event spread rapidly through the Columbia medical community. George Wilson, like everyone else, had heard about it, and he could only imagine the effect it was having on Pia. Concerned, he had looked for her. It took some searching but George finally managed to track her down. She didn't answer her cell phone and neither Will nor Lesley had seen her, so he had had to physically find her. George struck gold in the library stacks, a place he knew she found comforting. After some cajoling, Pia agreed to go with him back to the dorm cafeteria.

Pia was as distraught as she could ever remember being. She was especially upset because her emotions were so conflicted. Usually in her tumultuous life, distress had a definitive cause, but now she didn't know whether to be upset about Rothman's dire condition or angry at his carelessness in getting infected with the bacteria he'd been working on. And there was an undercurrent: Pia was terrified about her own future, which she thought she'd been so careful about but now seemed to be in the balance. She was also furious with herself for allowing Rothman to penetrate her well-constructed protective shell. And now she had the added distraction of George, who was trying to be solicitous but making things worse with all his questions.

"I can't sit here anymore," Pia said suddenly, interrupting George, but she didn't care.

"You haven't eaten anything," George said, looking down at her tray. "You've got to eat."

"I can't eat," Pia complained. "Feeling I'm in control is important to me. I don't feel in control. My life is coming apart. I've got to see Rothman. I have to."

Security was essential to Pia, as was control. At the moment she felt neither.

"Is he allowed to have visitors?"

"I don't even know if he's conscious. But I'm not a visitor, I'm concerned about the course of treatment he's on."

"I'll come with you," George said.

Pia didn't know whether she wanted him to come or not.

"Don't you have things to do?"

"Nothing important. I want to help you."

"Whatever!"

Pia jumped up from the table, leaving her tray of food untouched. George stuck her turkey sandwich, still in its wrapper, in his jacket pocket and hustled after Pia. As she marched to the hospital, George trailed along in her wake. He tried to talk to her but gave up when she wouldn't answer. She was on a mission.

The floor housing Rothman and

Yamamoto was bustling with staff and orderlies. There were few patients in evidence. Most were too sick to be up and about. Pia found the resident on duty, Dr. Sathi De Silva. As the sole infectious disease resident, she had her hands full, not just with her two celebrity patients but a ward full of others, and several more people in the emergency room awaiting her attention. Pia and George were in their medical school white coats so Dr. De Silva accepted them as students most likely on their internal medicine rotation. Dr. De Silva took her teaching responsibilities very seriously, so when Pia started asking questions about Dr. Rothman, she stopped what she was doing. "To answer your question, both Dr. Rothman and Dr. Yamamoto are dangerously ill. They're both delirious and uncommunicative."

"I understand they're on chloramphenicol. What's your feeling about such a choice?"

Dr. De Silva shrugged. "I think it's a good choice. Yes. It's a unique situation because there are newer antibiotics, but in this case we have sensitivity studies that show the involved strains of salmonella to be uniquely sensitive. Dr. Springer believes it's our best hope. We're monitoring for side effects, but we haven't seen anything. If there are any problems, we can always switch to one of the newer, third-generation cephalosporins."

"Strange case," Pia commented.

"One of the strangest," Dr. De Silva agreed. "And not a little ironic."

"Do we know how they got infected?"

"If we do, I haven't heard anything. I know the CDC epidemiologists went through the lab and particularly the level-three containment area where the salmonella strain was kept. I think their initial concerns were about a malfunction of the hood, but apparently it was working fine. There was some bacteria in the hood itself, but you'd expect that. They took cultures, I know, and we'll get results in twenty-four hours. I'm hearing all this secondhand. My job is to look after them."

"Of course," said Pia. "Has the CDC finished with the lab?"

"Dr. Springer said an hour ago that most of them were already headed back to Atlanta."

Dr. De Silva's cell phone beeped, and

she glanced at a text message. "Oops, gotta go! Nice talking with you."

"Can we see Dr. Rothman?"

"I don't see any harm, but you're not going to be seeing much," Dr. De Silva said, already walking away. "As I said, he's delirious. If you do go in, just make sure you put on all the gear and don't bring anything out!"

Eagerly Pia set off toward Rothman's room. George stumbled after her.

"What are you doing?" George complained. "You can't go in there. He's sick, he can't tell you anything. Why take a chance?"

Pia didn't answer. She suited up as per the Universal Precautions established by the CDC, which were posted on the outer door. George continued to try to talk Pia out of the visit, but she ignored him. He found a set of protective gear for himself and followed Pia into the room. As they passed through the door they could feel air entering with them.

Pia walked directly over to the bed. Several IVs were running, each laced with antibiotic.

"Dr. Rothman? . . . Dr. Rothman?"

Rothman stirred and half opened his eyes.

"Dr. Rothman, can you hear me?"

"What are you *doing*?" George's nerve was failing him on many counts. Neither of them was on an internal medicine rotation, so they had no business or excuse to be there, and why was Pia trying to talk to Dr. Rothman? The man was delirious. Apart from the trouble they could get into, George was nervous about the salmonella that was making Dr. Rothman sick. The man looked gravely ill, with an ashen coloring and loose strands of hair matted to his pale forehead.

"He doesn't look good at all," Pia commented.

"Tell me about it," George said nervously.

"My gosh, look! He's losing some hair." Pia pointed to tufts of hair on Rothman's pillow, but George wasn't interested. Rothman had become agitated now, twisting against his restraints while mouthing some words. Pia grabbed his chart and was flipping through the pages.

"His temperature's up—not a lot, but up nonetheless."

"Pia . . . let's *go!*" George stage-whispered.

"You go, George, I'm not leaving. Not yet." From working with Rothman, Pia had learned a great deal about typhoid fever and its cause, salmonella typhi. She knew the danger signs of the illness and the fact that the disease attacked the small bowel, concentrating in lymphoid tissue in the small intestine called Peyer's patches. Rothman's gown was pulled over to one side, and Pia exposed Rothman's abdomen a little more. She slowly pushed in on his upper abdomen, and Rothman squirmed and moved his head from side to side.

"He's definitely showing signs of discomfort, maybe pain in his abdomen," Pia said. "This is not a good sign."

George was beside himself. He could see a few people passing by in the outer hall through the wire-embedded windows in the two doors of the isolation room. He walked over and closed the blinds, hoping to buy Pia some time. When Pia suddenly let up on the pressure she was exerting, Rothman reacted slightly, to Pia's surprise, as if that caused more discomfort.

"Did you see that? He recoiled. Would you say he recoiled?"

Pia repeated the maneuver and got the same result.

"He definitely recoiled."

"Whatever it is you're doing, it's going to get both of us kicked out of school if we don't leave right now. We're pushing the limits on a couple of celebrity patients."

"It's rebound tenderness," she said. "It's a sign of peritonitis, inflammation of the lining of the abdominal cavity. It means the bacteria have penetrated the lining of the small intestine."

Pia reached over and punched the intercom button. The nurse at the station picked up.

"Is Dr. De Silva available? If she is, get her in here stat. The patient has developed rebound tenderness."

George was hopping from one foot to the other. *Now she's really done it*, he thought.

At once, Dr. De Silva came in the room, palpated Dr. Rothman's abdomen and confirmed Pia's finding.

"And look, he's losing some hair," Pia said.

"That could be the chloramphenicol. But regardless, the rebound tenderness suggests the chloramphenicol is not controlling the infection. We'll have to change the antibiotic. I'll call Springer and get his suggestion. Thanks for your help."

Dr. De Silva ducked out of the room.

"He's getting worse," Pia said, looking at Rothman forlornly.

"Rebound tenderness isn't a good sign, I know that," George said. "But you've done all you can do. Let's go. You heard her, she's calling Springer."

By the time George and Pia took off their gear and got back to the nurses' station, Dr. De Silva was on the phone with Springer. Pia stood where she could hear Dr. De Silva's half of the conversation. It sounded like Springer was doing most of the talking.

"Okay, ceftriaxone . . ." she said. ". . . And the hair loss . . . Right, of course we'll stop the chloramphenicol. . . . Okay. I'll see you soon, and I'll call Dr. Miller."

Dr. De Silva turned and saw Pia. She hung up the phone and redialed immediately. She covered the receiver with her left hand and talked to Pia as the phone rang.

"Dr. Springer's on his way in. He wants to check the rebound tenderness for himself— Oh, hello. I need Dr. Miller. . . . Dr. Miller, this is Dr. De Silva in Infectious Diseases. I'm treating Dr. Rothman and Dr. Yamamoto. Dr. Springer would like a consult. We're seeing rebound tenderness in Dr. Rothman and may have to remove the infected bowel. . . . No, just Dr. Rothman at the moment . . . His temperature is up slightly. Other levels—blood pressure, pulse, oxygenation—are the same. Okay, thanks."

Dr. De Silva hung up the phone and exhaled. She was a small woman of Sri Lankan descent who prided herself on running a tight ship. She was embarrassed that a medical student had picked up an important sign that she'd missed. "I just checked him a few minutes before you two showed up. Temperature was holding steady," she said, half to Pia, half to herself. She turned to Pia.

"It can come on very quickly. Dr. Miller, the chief surgical resident, is coming in. And Dr. Springer's on his way over. So, who's your preceptor? I should at least give you credit for what you found. And how did you know what to look for? I'm impressed."

"Actually I'm not on internal medicine at the moment."

"Are you on an infectious disease elective? If you are, I haven't heard your name."

"I'm not on an infectious disease elective either."

George was desperately trying to get Pia to shut up. Out of Dr. De Silva's line of sight he was frantically making a time-out gesture like a football official.

"Well, what brought you here?" Dr. De Silva asked.

"I just happen to know a lot about salmonella."

"Really? From whom?"

"Dr. Rothman," Pia said, as George grabbed her arm and literally pulled her away, angling her toward the elevators.

George felt a sense of relief as they left the hospital. With as busy as Dr. De Silva was, he hoped she wouldn't say too much about the two mysterious med students, one of whom had been very helpful. Actually he doubted she would. He knew that there hadn't been any negligence on Dr. De Silva's part, but he knew that in the competitive atmosphere of the academic center, she was probably chagrined that she'd been, in a fashion, upstaged by a medical student. Pia had detected the change in Dr. Rothman's condition before she did. But George's relief was short-lived.

"I want to go back to the lab," Pia said, stopping suddenly. They had just reached the corner where 168th Street turns into Haven Avenue. "I want to see if there are any clues as to why or how he got infected. He's so careful, I don't understand it. He's so detailed and compulsive about his work, his organization, his technique, it's all flawless. It doesn't make sense."

Still lurking in the back of Pia's mind was the thought that Rothman had infected himself intentionally. But why would he involve Dr. Yamamoto? It couldn't be the case, or could it? What she wanted to do was completely eliminate the idea as even a remote possibility. If Rothman died, it was going to be a betrayal of sorts, but she didn't want it to be his betrayal. Betrayal by fate she thought she could ultimately handle. Personal betrayal by Rothman would be something entirely different.

George groaned inwardly. Visiting Rothman had been bad enough. Visiting a lab that was off-limits by order of the CDC was something else entirely. "The lab is closed," George said in a fashion that wouldn't brook discussion. "Order of the CDC. Let's head up to your room. I saved the sandwich you didn't eat." To prove his point, George pulled the food from his pocket.

"I'm going," Pia said.

"What on earth do you think you're going to turn up that the CDC hasn't?'"

"I don't know, but I can't do *nothing*. You can come with me or not, I'm going anyway. Of course two sets of eyes may be better than one."

George realized Pia was asking for his help, however indirectly, which was a first. Still, it wasn't an easy decision. He was okay with bending the rules, but not breaking them like this. He couldn't afford to get kicked out of medical school. It had been his goal as long as he could remember, and he had his family to consider. But George had no time to ponder his decision. Pia had already turned around and was heading toward the research building.

"You're not worried about getting typhoid fever?" he asked, catching up to her.

"I was in there this morning. And there's protective gear we can put on just like we used in Rothman's room."

Pia entered the building. George followed. It was like making a decision without making a decision. They showed their IDs to the security man and headed for the elevators.

As George had expected, the door to the lab was crisscrossed with yellow caution tape. "See, just as I expected. We can't go in."

Pia didn't respond. She merely peeled back the necessary tape and tried the door, which was locked. It didn't deter her. Many times over the last three and a half years, Pia had been asked to take a reading in the lab at night, or monitor an automated experiment. She took the key she'd been given for those eventualities, opened the door, and stepped over the threshold.

"Pia, this is crazy," George said. Reluctantly he came in after her. It was dark, and very quiet.

"Relax. The security cameras are out, they've been working on them again for days. Who's going to come in now? I just want to check the refrigerated storage facility in the biosafety lab and take a peek at the logbook. And before you say it, I know the CDC has probably investigated all that. They might have even taken the logbook. Be that as it may, I need to make sure they didn't miss anything."

Pia turned on the minimal light necessary. It was a small lamp by the communal coffee machine. She then quickly checked her own office, and Rothman's. George trailed after her like a shadow. As far as she could tell, nothing had been disturbed in either office. Pia pointed out Rothman's desk to George. The in-tray, the few files, the pictures—everything was just so.

"See how orderly he is?" said Pia.

All George could think about was getting out of there. An air circulator kicked on and George jumped half out of his skin. He followed Pia to the biosafety level-3 room and they donned the protective gear once more. Pia used the coded punch pad to reach the lab itself. Since there were no windows, Pia turned on the overhead lights. The ventilation system was still running and there was an eerie calm in the place. Pia checked the logbook, which the CDC had not taken. There were the usual entries; the next to last one was Panjit Singh, when he went in that morning to set up. Then there was Rothman and Yamamoto's entry. There was nothing abnormal. She then went to the refrigerated storage unit. Using a separate keypad, she was about to open it when she heard a noise that caught her attention.

"Did you hear that?" she whispered intently to George.

"Hear what?" George said nervously.

Pia held up a hand and went to the door and cracked it open. There were quiet sounds but unmistakable—voices in the lab outside. Voices getting louder.

"In here . . . c'mon," she said urgently.

"Shit," George said under his breath. He'd heard the voices. "Shit on a brick," he mumbled to himself.

Silently but urgently Pia waved for him to follow her. George saw where they were heading and beat it out through an emergency exit in the far corner of the lab. The door complained when he pushed it open as it hadn't been opened since it was installed back when the lab was last renovated. It had also been made airtight.

Pia followed close behind George. She

might have stayed and faced the music had she been there by herself, but she was well aware of George's utter fear of authority. Where that had come from, she had no idea.

The unit's emergency door led to the lab storeroom where Pia and George pulled off their protective gear and stumbled out into the main part of the microbiology department that housed Rothman's lab. Staff on the evening shift at the microbiology clinical lab were curious to see two young people running by, then stunned to see them followed a minute later by three figures in full hazmat gear.

Microbiology led into the anatomy department and George and Pia crashed through the connecting doors and into the familiar surroundings. As first-year students they had spent a good deal of time in the department. George was leading, but he didn't know exactly where he was going. All he knew was that he wanted to avoid getting caught. He ducked into the darkened anatomy room, dimly illuminated by night-lights. For the benefit of the current first-year students who were taking anatomy at the time, the room was well stocked with cadavers, most covered with oilcloth shrouds. Several torsos sat upright on the head teaching table. They'd been cut across the upper chest and then halved in a sagittal section so that half the gullet and half the brain were visible. George was eye-level with the torsos, the exposed whites of their eyes seeming to glow in the half-light.

George and Pia ducked behind the long teaching table, but there was nowhere to hide. A moment after their arrival, the banks of ceiling lights flickered and came on. Three security guards in hazmat suits stormed into the room. Pia stood up and George, very reluctantly, followed suit.

The security men were angry, demanding Pia's and George's identification cards. They then made several calls on their radios before turning back to the students. George was cowering, Pia taking it all in stride. "You're coming with us," said the nearest figure to George, grasping his arm and marching him out of the room. Pia was escorted out behind him.

The group wended their way past the few onlookers in the clinical microbiology lab and down to the street via a service elevator. George's mind was racing but he couldn't think of any way Pia could talk her way out of this. As they walked across the campus, the group attracted a lot of stares and comments from passersby. Some of them wondered if they were watching some med-student prank.

George and Pia were taken through a featureless corridor in the hospital bowels to the security department. They walked past a bank of TV screens being monitored by two bored-looking men, down another corridor and into a small office with a hand-written sign on the door: DUTY OFFICER. Standing up, watching a couple of monitors mounted on the wall, was David Winston, the man who'd taken charge in the lab earlier that day. He recognized Pia, having helped her when she fainted in the street.

"Ah, you again. I see you're feeling better than when I last saw you."

"Mr. Winston," Pia said. "My friend and I were just retrieving some of my belongings from my office."

Winston referred to a list on a clipboard resting on his desk.

"Miss Grazdani, and . . ." He looked at George.

"George Wilson."

"George Wilson. Not on my list. You a fourth-year student as well?"

George nodded.

"Well, you'll be taking antibiotics too," Winston said. "Folks, there's a protocol we use in these situations. You broke into a secure, potentially contaminated area. I actually saw you do it myself, sitting right here. The cameras might not be operating inside the lab, but outside they work just fine. So I see two people go into the lab, and I have to send three of my guys in full body gear to go in and find you. And it turns out to be you two. So the protocol is, I make a call to the dean of students, who loves to hear from me, as you might imagine. It's just a heads-up because my next call is to my friends at the Thirty-third Precinct, and I'll have a full and frank conversation about criminal trespass."

George was aghast. If the police got involved, he was screwed.

"I don't know why you guys went in there, and I'm not going to ask. The CDC might have cleared it, but the caution tape was still over the door. Especially you, Miss Grazdani, as you were specifically told the lab would be off-limits. Frankly, I'm dumbfounded. But I've never understood medical students since I took over this job heading the center's security."

Pia started to speak, but Winston held out his hand to silence her and called the dean of students. He explained the situation. He then listened for a good two minutes and hung up the phone.

"She's coming down. I don't know who I'd rather deal with if I were you, the dean or the Thirty-third."

Winston showed George and Pia into a small side room and closed the door. George was too agitated to speak; Pia started pacing around the room. She couldn't sit still. After what seemed like an age but was in fact thirty minutes, the door opened and a tall, dark-haired woman in sweats and a ski jacket came in and shut the door behind her. Her name was Helen Bourse. She had been dean of students for almost a decade and was well liked but hardly a pushover.

"What the hell did you think you were doing? You two have made me cash in more favors than I actually own, stopping Mr. Winston from having you arrested. I want you to convince me I did the right thing."

"I'm so sorry, Mrs. Bourse," George said. He took one look at Pia's defiant face and decided he should speak for the both of them.

"*We're* very sorry."

"So what in God's name were you doing there? In a lab that was sealed and potentially contaminated."

"The only part that might have been contaminated was the biosafety unit," Pia said, interrupting George, who'd started to respond. "We took the necessary precautions. I wanted to look for myself. I just can't understand how Dr. Rothman managed to get infected, knowing him as I do."

"So you weren't picking up your stuff as you told Mr. Winston. And what, you're suddenly epidemiologists? We had a team of actual epidemiologists check out the lab today both from here and from the CDC. They combed the place, including the biosafety unit."

"What did they find?"

"Nothing, but that's not the point."

"I've been working in there on and off for over three years. I wanted to check it out. If something was different, I might have been able to see it, probably better than strangers from Atlanta."

Some of Bourse's vinegar lost its acid. She realized that Pia had a point. Still, it didn't justify what these two otherwise gifted students had done, something totally foolish and out of character. After a pause she asked, "Well, what did you find?"

"Nothing, but we were interrupted. Do you have a report from the epidemiologists?"

"Certainly not from the CDC. Not yet. But I spoke to the head of our own team. Apparently nothing was found amiss."

Dr. Bourse knew that Dr. Rothman was closer to this student than to anyone in the whole medical community. She knew quite a bit about Pia, more than she guessed Pia surmised. Bourse had had access to all the deliberations of the admissions committee, which she had pored over in great detail. Up until the call from Winston, she'd had high hopes for her, hopes she wanted to maintain. For Pia, Bourse's intent was to try to keep the damage from the evening's escapade and poor judgment to a minimum. Such was the burden of being dean of students. Earlier that evening Bourse had had to deal with an even more difficult issue: A third-year student had been caught stealing prescription drugs from the medical floors. Bourse turned her attention to the second delinquent. At least he met her eye, which she couldn't get from Pia. "So what's your excuse?" she asked George, with a certain resignation in her voice.

"No excuses. I was helping my friend," he said as evenly as he could.

Dr. Bourse studied George. He too was a top student, more liked in general than Pia, who could be considered standoffish. Bourse was well aware of George's apparent infatuation with Pia, so she took his excuse at face value. Once again she marveled at how such an apparently accomplished young man like George could be reduced to such a lovelorn teenager that he'd risk his future like this. If Bourse had allowed Winston to have him arrested, it could have affected his becoming a doctor.

"All right," Bourse said. She took a deep breath and regarded the ceiling for a moment to clear her head. "Here's what we're going to do. You're going to go back to your rooms and stay there. You won't fraternize with anyone or talk about this episode with anyone. You'll monitor your temperatures and take your antibiotics as directed. George, I'll make sure you get some. And I'll see both of you in my office at seven tomorrow morning. We'll discuss your elective then, Ms. Grazdani. Mr. Wilson, tomorrow you will return to Radiology. Both of you will also say a prayer for me and thank the Lord that I'm in a benevolent mood. I'll now go and square this away with Mr. Winston. If I can."

With the dean out of the room, George let out a deep sigh and sat back in his chair. "Oh my God, I thought we were dead. If the police aren't involved, it's just an internal thing. It won't be on our records. It'll be like this never happened." George looked at Pia, who didn't respond. Her face was a blank, her mind clearly still back at the lab.

"You can't let this drop?" George questioned.

"Of course I can't let it drop," Pia shot back. "Something had to have happened. Something out of the ordinary."

"What about one of the technicians messing up, either by accident or design? I mean, Rothman was like a bull in the proverbial china shop. I imagine there are a lot of people who aren't crying tonight about what happened to him."

Pia shook her head. "There were people in the lab who found him unpleasant. But the same people admired him greatly. I can't imagine anyone in the lab being involved in any underhanded way."

"So what are you thinking?"

"I don't know what to think," Pia said. Her mind was swirling. Her first concern was whether or not Rothman would pull through. At the same time she was reconsidering the two possibilities for what had happened: Rothman contaminated himself by accident, or he did it deliberately. But then, another idea started to take shape in her mind. She realized there was a third possibility she hadn't yet considered.

28.

COLUMBIA UNIVERSITY MEDICAL CENTER
NEW YORK CITY
MARCH 24, 2011, 5:05 A.M.

Although it was only a little after five in the morning, Pia finally quit trying to go back to sleep and got out of bed. The previous night she'd returned to her dorm room from the security office exhausted mentally and physically. Before she and George went to their respective rooms, he gave her the turkey sandwich that he'd saved. It was flattened to a degree but still recognizably a sandwich. Once back in her room, she'd eaten a corner of it, then threw the rest in the trash and went to bed, hoping to get some rest. She'd not slept well, but at least she couldn't remember her dreams.

Pia showered quickly and dressed. She understood how essential it was to her future that Rothman pull through. Despite the hour, she knew she had to go over to the hospital to check and make sure he was okay. Her hope was that the new antibiotic had worked wonders and was controlling his infection. In that case, she further hoped that his delirium had cleared up and she could have a word with him. She wanted to ask him if he had any idea what had happened in the biosafety lab the previous morning.

Emerging from the dorm onto Haven Avenue, Pia felt conspicuously lonely. It was morning although not yet light. She felt like the only person in the world as she made her way over to the hospital. Once inside, it was different as the hospital never slept. Quickly she made her way up to the infectious disease wing.

When she got to the ward she was perplexed. She felt she must have gotten turned around because the room she thought was Rothman's was being disinfected in preparation for its next inhabitant. But no, this was his room. So Rothman had been moved, perhaps because he was showing signs of improvement following the new course of treatment. Pia didn't allow herself to think that anything else could be the case. She checked Yamamoto's room. His room was also being cleaned. He'd been moved as well.

Pia turned around and went back to the nurses' station to find out where Dr. Rothman and Dr. Yamamoto had been sent. The station was humming, even at that time of the morning, in preparation for the shift change at seven.

"Excuse me," Pia said to one of the night nurses standing at the counter filling out one of the millions of forms they were required to do. "I'm looking for Dr. Rothman and Dr. Yamamoto." Suddenly Pia felt nauseous and an overwhelming sense of panic rose within her. *They weren't moved because they got better.*

"Please, tell me where they are," Pia pleaded, hoping against hope.

"And who are you? Are you related to Dr. Rothman?"

"I'm Dr. Rothman's medical student. Please, where is he?"

The nurse took Pia by the arm and walked her away from the busy nurses' station into the waiting room, which was empty at that hour. She didn't turn the light on and the two women stood in the semi-darkness. Pia was worried her legs were going to give out and she would collapse on the floor like a rag doll.

"Listen, we only just told the families," the nurse said. "I'm sorry, they both passed. Dr. Rothman first, then Dr. Yamamoto about an hour ago."

"What do you mean they 'passed'?" Pia asked, but intellectually she knew what the nurse meant. But just maybe . . .

"They died, sweetheart, I'm sorry. Dr. Rothman died being prepped for surgery. That's all I know. That's all I can tell you. Look, I have to go." The nurse put her hand on Pia's arm and left the room.

Pia went down on her haunches, her mouth open in a silent scream. She clasped her arms around her knees and pulled herself tight into a ball, as if she were trying to hide somewhere within her own body. Pia felt like she'd been punched in the gut. She was disoriented and angry—angry at the hospital, angry at the world, angry at Rothman himself. If she was going to judge a man by his actions, what had he done? She'd been abandoned. Betrayed. Pia stumbled out of the room and off the ward, descended in the elevator, walked outside in a daze. The sky was now light in the east, but the sun had yet to make it up over the horizon.

29.

Pia staggered down Fort Washington Avenue like a drunk, clutching her stomach. Thinking she was about to throw up, she stopped by a garbage can, but she was only able to bend over the rim and dry-heave a couple of times. Pia stood up and breathed deeply in and out. She had to get a grip on herself, but what was she going to do? There was an immediate issue to contend with, and she was almost grateful for the distraction: She remembered that she and George had to see the dean of students at seven, so she went to the dorm to find George.

George had set his alarm for 6:15. He was accustomed to sleeping soundly, even if the rigors of medical school meant it might be for only three or four hours at a time. But last night he'd been unable to sleep save for brief snippets, constantly turning over the events of the evening in his mind. At one point he'd given up and sat for almost an hour in the semi-comfortable armchair by the window and nursed a glass of Jack Daniel's from a bottle that had lasted through his whole medical school career. Through the window he could see a portion of the George Washington Bridge and a bit of the New Jersey Hudson River waterfront. He was totally confused and humiliated about his motivations.

Last night, Pia had come desperately close to wrecking all of George's plans. George stopped himself; it really wasn't Pia's doing that he had tagged along with her. He had to take some responsibility.

The problem was that he cared about her too much to let her blindly charge into these predicaments by herself, and whether she acknowledged it or not, she needed his help. Still, he knew there was a point where he'd have to stop and put his own interests first. He just didn't know where that point would be.

He'd been asleep for only a little more than an hour when the alarm went off, and George unknowingly swept his hand over the snooze button. Nine minutes later he did it again, and he would have done it a third time if Pia's knocking hadn't woken him up. He was pleased to see her until he saw the look on her face and realized there was something wrong.

"What happened . . . ? Wait, what time is it? We've got the dean . . ."

Pia walked into the room like a reanimated zombie and fell full-length on George's bed. She mumbled something into George's pillow.

"What's wrong?" George saw what time it was and started to get dressed. After a few seconds, he went over to the bed and sat on the edge and moved a few strands of hair from Pia's cheek. She was a basket case.

"Tell me," he said quietly.

"He's dead. They're both dead."

"Who? Rothman? Yamamoto?"

"Yes."

"Oh, Pia, I'm sorry. I'm so sorry." George laid his hand on Pia's shoulder. "Pia, I don't know what to say. God, this is really a tragedy. From what you've told me, they were on the verge of something huge. What a setback for regenerative medicine, probably years, maybe even a decade. There's no one to fill their shoes."

Pia was silent. George removed his hand. She turned to look up at him. Her face no longer looked blank, just angry.

"Right now, I don't give a flying fuck about the future of regenerative medicine. Jesus!"

Pia sprang up from the bed and stormed out of the room. George followed her, tucking in his shirt. At first he couldn't see her but heard footfalls receding down the stairs.

"Pia, wait up!"

George ran down the street after Pia, who was speed-walking toward the dean's office. He caught up with her and jogged alongside.

"Pia!"

Pia waved her hand, dismissing George. "Look, I'm sorry."

She stopped dead in her tracks, clenched her fists with her arms by her sides, and let out a low scream in exasperation. She turned and looked George right in the eye.

"George, don't tell me you're sorry. Please just *shut up!*"

With that she walked off and left George standing in the street like a just-dumped lover. George's shoulders fell. Condolences clearly weren't his strong suit although he hardly thought he deserved such a brush-off. He thought back to his long night of self-examination. If this woman needed him, especially now, she sure had a funny way of showing it.

30.

COLUMBIA UNIVERSITY MEDICAL CENTER
NEW YORK CITY
MARCH 24, 2011, 7:00 A.M.

Pia and George arrived separately at the suite of offices of the dean of students. They were each buzzed in by the dean herself as the secretary, due in at eight, had yet to arrive. They sat at either end of the leather couch outside the office proper, avoiding eye contact, not saying anything. For Pia, such silences came naturally, while for George, who'd happily talk to anyone, it was a strain not to communicate. At the same time he had no wish to be told to shut up again by Pia, which was what he was certain would happen since all he wanted to do was apologize, again, for inadvertently upsetting her. It was part of his nature to feel responsible.

A few minutes after the hour, Helen Bourse emerged from her office.

"Thank you for being on time this morning," Bourse said, beckoning Pia and George to follow her. She gestured to a couple of straight-backed chairs for them to sit in. She had seen a note in Pia's file, which she'd read overnight, written by a particularly zealous clinical preceptor during her second-year introduction to surgery. It said that Pia had difficulty arriving on time for early-morning appointments, even after being admonished that such behavior was not tolerated in surgery. Although it was usually only about five to ten minutes, it was consistent, and the preceptor indicated that she thought it was a serious lapse.

Dr. Bourse sat down and regarded her two students. "To begin, I'm afraid I have some very bad news." Her voice had the gravity appropriate to the situation. "There's no way to say this other than just to say it. Doctors Rothman and Yamamoto both died this morning. They were being prepped for surgery for rapidly developing peritonitis, but they didn't make it."

"I know," Pia said.

"How do you know?" Dr. Bourse was confused. She had just learned it herself.

"I went to the infectious disease unit this morning. I woke up early. I thought maybe the new antibiotic would have had an effect, but I was told they had died."

Dr. Bourse stared at Pia, whose voice sounded as if all the fight had gone out of her. She could see that the young woman's eyes were rimmed with emotion and fatigue. Dr. Bourse sighed. Here was yet another example of Pia's marked willfulness, as she herself had told both Pia and George in no uncertain terms to go back to their rooms, check their temperatures regularly, and stay there until this meeting. Yet Pia had willfully ignored the order.

Dr. Bourse sighed again, still looking directly at Pia, whose eyes were, as usual, diverted. "Okay, I'll try to overlook the fact that I told you to stay in your dorm room. I gather you went to the hospital because of your closeness with Dr. Rothman?"

Pia nodded. She had an urge to admit that for her, Rothman had morphed into the father she never had, but she held her tongue. It wasn't in her to be forthright with her secrets.

"At least you made no attempt to go back to the lab, or did you?"

George looked quickly at Pia, worried. The thought that Pia might try to go back to the lab without him had not occurred to George.

"No, I didn't," Pia said quietly, and George exhaled.

"Did you both check your temperatures as I asked?"

Both students nodded, although George had had to abandon his thermometer when Pia flew out of his room that morning.

"And I assume everything was fine. Okay. Rothman's and Yamamoto's deaths are a blow to everyone here at the medical center, particularly the school. I knew Dr. Yamamoto a little, and he was a fine colleague. Dr. Rothman I knew better, of course, and I understand you got along well with him, Miss Grazdani. He certainly took a keen interest in your progress and afforded you more privileges than he did other students." And any fellows, thought Dr. Bourse. "I viewed that interest as a compliment to your abilities as a researcher and to the potential that Dr. Rothman recognized in you."

Pia was staring at the ground.

"Of course it's terribly ironic that Dr. Rothman, who spent so much time uncovering the pathogenicity of salmonella, should die from the same organism he'd come to understand so well. . . ." Bourse let the thought drift.

"So, Miss Grazdani, I have arranged for you to do research, starting today, with Dr. Roselyn Gorin, who is one of the most talented people on campus. She has a Lasker Prize, as you may know, and she's doing absolutely groundbreaking work on the differentiation of stem cells into specific adult cells. Roselyn is a friend of mine. She's a wonderfully warm and understanding person. I just talked with her ten minutes ago, and she's very happy to take you on. *Happy*'s not the right word in these circumstances, but she's very willing to help."

Dr. Bourse smiled hopefully.

"Today? I can't possibly start today," Pia said.

George winced as it was apparent to him that Dr. Bourse's first reaction was of intense irritation.

Dr. Bourse paused in order to gain control of her emotions, as she was as irritated as George had sensed. Roselyn was a friend, but in fact she hadn't been overjoyed about taking on a new student, especially Rothman's student, who had built up a reputation of her own, fairly or not. Dr. Bourse wanted to tell Pia to get her act together, but she held her tongue.

"I'm very grateful for what you've done," Pia said quickly, trying to sound sincere. "Really," she added, as if she sensed she was pushing it. "But I just got this news an hour ago, and I really can't think straight. I need a couple of days. To get my head together."

Dr. Bourse sighed again. Pia was not the easiest individual to get along with. At the same time what she was saying was undoubtedly true. Everyone at the center was going to be shaken by the deaths. Dr. Yamamoto was a very popular presence and even if few could tolerate Rothman on a one-on-one basis, his death was still a blow, especially under these circumstances. He was, after all, the center's scientific celebrity.

"Okay, Miss Grazdani. Today is Thursday. Monday morning, first thing, I shall expect you to resume your responsibilities as a fourth-year medical student. I am also reminding you to stay away from Dr. Rothman's laboratory. This is compassionate leave, not an opportunity for you to play epidemiologist again. We have real epidemiologists who are qualified to do the work. Do you understand?"

Pia nodded.

"Please say, 'I understand,'" Dr. Bourse said. She wanted to be absolutely clear.

"I understand," Pia said, almost inaudibly.

"Mr. Wilson. You'll return to Radiology today—"

"Absolutely, Dean," George said, cutting her off.

"And you will also cease enabling Miss Grazdani. Perhaps you might want to ask yourself why you, with a hitherto spotless record, are drawn into the kind of behavior we saw last night. *Gnothi seauton*—do you know what that means? It means 'Know thyself,' and it's something that we as physicians need to remember always.

"I doubt that it was your idea, Mr. Wilson, to break into Dr. Rothman's lab, and I hope that in the future you will let your actions be guided more by your intellect than by your id—by your cerebrum more than your hypothalamus."

George eagerly nodded agreement.

"Everyone clear?" Dr. Bourse said. Pia and George nodded in unison.

"Well, thank you. You can go."

Dr. Bourse watched George hold the door open for Pia, who left without acknowledging George. She acted as if George holding the door for her was a matter of right.

Dr. Bourse sat at her desk for a few minutes of contemplation. Since a large part of her job was to get to know her population of medical students at the Columbia University College of Physicians and Surgeons, she thought about the strange relationship between Pia and George. Of course, fraternization between students was not necessarily encouraged, nor was it discouraged, provided it did not interfere with performance. In this romance, it was pretty obvious what he saw in her as she was the source of considerable gossip around the center as a particularly beautiful, intelligent, but enigmatic young woman. What wasn't so clear was whether there was any reverse attraction.

Relations between staff and students, on the other hand, were officially frowned upon, but it was difficult to enforce a ban when the parties were all consenting adults and the students mostly in their late twenties. There had been persistent rumors concerning Pia Grazdani and Dr. Rothman. Again, Pia's exotic beauty and obvious intelligence were lost on few people, but what she might possibly have seen in him was beyond most people's comprehension. But nothing was ever substantiated and while there was every reason to believe that Dr. Rothman had given his student significant responsibilities and privileges, there was never any evidence that he had done so inappropriately. And now, Dr. Bourse thought, the conundrum of their relationship would just have to remain one of life's little mysteries.

31.

After leaving the dean's office, Pia spent the rest of the morning stewing in her room. Her feelings were in absolute turmoil, emotions and thoughts swirling in and out of her consciousness so that one minute she felt utterly depressed, the next she was sharp and motivated. She was still angry at Rothman for getting sick, and also at Springer, the chief of Infectious

Diseases, for letting Rothman die, which she believed he did by selecting an outdated antibiotic despite the supposed sensitivity testing that Rothman himself had done. And why did it have to be her, a lowly fourth-year medical student, who made the diagnosis of the incipient peritonitis, the onset of which had heralded the man's death?

But most acutely, Pia knew she was devastated by the simple fact that Rothman was dead. She was depressed at the thought of what it meant to her future. Pia had a lot of practice at dispassionately breaking down a situation and identifying how it affected her. It was the emotional aspects of her state of mind that she struggled with the most.

Pia had been completely convinced by Rothman's argument that she wasn't suited to clinical medicine, since she actually didn't like most people, especially when they were sick and complaining about it. She had little sympathy for illness and none at all for any kind of complaining. At one point during her residency, after thirty-six hours without sleep, she had had to take blood from a patient, a tough-looking young policeman who was deathly afraid of needles. As the man wriggled and squirmed and Pia couldn't for the life of her find a vein, she told him to "quit whining like a baby." Fortunately, no one overheard her, and the man didn't complain, although the staff did wonder why he made such an effort to avoid Pia for the rest of his stay.

With Rothman gone, she didn't know if she had it in her to follow through with getting a Ph.D., which was a requirement if she was serious about pursuing a future in research. Most of all, the nagging issue of what had happened to Rothman wouldn't leave her alone, and she mulled it over continuously. It could have been an accident, she knew, but it seemed very unlikely knowing Rothman as well as she did. He was too careful, too compulsive. And the two of them getting sick simultaneously? It didn't make sense. But the alternatives seemed equally unlikely, especially the idea that he did it deliberately. The only other possibility, namely the idea that someone else did it deliberately, like Panjit, who might have had the opportunity, seemed even more unlikely.

The longer Pia sat in her room, the more

agitated she became and the more motivated to take some action. But what? She
paced around the room as best she could,
given the close confines of the living area.
She lay on her bed, but that was intoler-
able. She thought about calling Will or
Lesley, but she didn't know what she would
say to them. She walked down the corridor to the soda machine, but she didn't
want anything to drink. Her mind was
buzzing, racing, overheating.

Suddenly Pia knew what she could do
to get herself centered, to regain some focus. George had been hanging around,
offering to help. She thought there was
something he could do for her, as he'd done
a few times in the past. George wasn't so
different from any other man she'd ever
encountered. But each time it had happened, when Pia thought George would
have been put off by her needs, there he
was, back again the next day.

Pia imagined that George would be on
his lunch break, one of the benefits of a
rotation in something predictable like radiology or pathology. There was a predictable schedule. She wanted to call him, but
she couldn't find her cell phone. And when

she did find it, in the pocket of her coat, she saw that the battery was dead. She plugged the phone into the charger and called George, catching him as she had hoped on his way over to the cafeteria.

"I was going to swing by later to make sure you were okay," George said. They hadn't parted on the best of terms after meeting with the dean, and George's perennial insecurity about Pia had surfaced again.

"You offered to help. Is that still the case or are you still mad at me for getting you in trouble?"

"I'm not mad at you, I'm just worried about you."

Pia rolled her eyes.

"So you'll help me?" This was awkward. Pia wanted George to say yes, I'll be right over. Instead, he said, "Not if it means going back up to the lab."

"No, George. What I'd like you to do is come over here for a few minutes."

"Right now?"

"Right now, George! I assume you're on lunch break?"

"Okay," George said. "I'll be right there."

Pia prepared. Almost to the minute of

his expected arrival there was a knock on Pia's door. She pulled it fully open.

George's eyes sprang open to their fullest extent. He was clearly taken aback. Nervously he glanced up and down the dorm hallway to make sure no one could see what he could. Pia was standing in the open doorway buck naked.

"This isn't quite what I expected," he managed, as Pia pulled him into the room. She was shockingly deliberate, as she had been on previous occasions, and again, as on those previous occasions, he didn't resist. Under the circumstances she was a force greater than him, and he was powerless. Pia grabbed at the belt in George's pants, and he obliged. She then pulled his sweater and T-shirt over his head. Pia pushed him onto the bed and handed him a condom just as she had on the other occasions. He was ready—achingly so—and Pia got up on him immediately. She closed her eyes and looked up, rocking herself rhythmically and hard against him. He knew it was simply sex, that she was looking for the endorphin rush, and she found it fast, shuddering slightly as she did so.

As soon as she was finished, Pia put

her hands on George's chest and slipped off him. She looked right at him, but it was like she didn't see him. "Thanks. I needed that," she said. She walked over to her bathroom, turned on the shower, and, after a couple of seconds, jumped in.

George put his hands behind his head and looked down at himself for a few beats. He then slipped off the condom, walked into the bathroom, and flushed it away. From a birth control perspective, it had been a waste. Pia had finished showering and was toweling off. George couldn't help but admire her athletic body, exquisitely shaped breasts, and deep, flawless, honey-colored skin.

"Would it kill you to kiss me?" George was bemused; he didn't know what to think. He was being used, he knew, and didn't understand why.

"I don't like kissing. Doesn't do anything for me."

George could tell Pia's mind was already elsewhere. There was no point in him saying, "Well, what about me?" He could hear her reply: "What about you?" George didn't know what else to say. Each time they had sex, George hoped it meant

they'd made a breakthrough, that their relationship had climbed out of its curiously
stalled state into a level of true intimacy.
But it had never been the case. Nor was it
now. She was a train running on a totally
separate track. In many respects his role
was irrelevant, as if it could have been
anyone lying there.

"Thanks," Pia repeated airily as she
passed him coming out of the bathroom.
There was no modesty, whether pretend
or real. In her upbringing there had never
been an opportunity for even pretense.

"What for? I didn't do anything."

"No, you did! Really. You've given me a
reboot like what needs to be done with a
modem once in a while. You've made it
possible for me to see what I have to do,
rather than sit here paralyzed."

"Is that what it was? I want . . . I want
us . . ." George felt like that hopeless teenager again. Pia was dressing quickly.
George was standing naked and felt very
self-conscious. He slipped on his boxers.
"So tell me. What are you going to do?"

"Get in more trouble, I expect."

"What does that mean?"

"You should just leave, George. My problem is I don't think Rothman was treated correctly, whether people believe it or not. There was something wrong about how he got sick and there was something wrong about how he was treated. Chloramphenicol? It's almost never prescribed these days. Third-generation cephalosporins are where it's at now, so why give him something old that potentially causes truly catastrophic side effects?"

"You told me yourself. They used it because of Rothman's own sensitivity studies."

"That's what they said. He shouldn't have died, period, yet he was dead within what, fifteen, sixteen hours? He got sicker in the hospital—there was no delay in treatment, he was taken straight to the ward right after he showed the first symptoms. I think the treatment made him worse."

"Okay, I understand you're frustrated," said George, "but the dean told you directly not to interfere. Not to play epidemiologist. Do you want to get kicked out of here in your fourth year?"

"I've got time off, I'm not sitting here, I'll

lose my mind. I'm going to talk to Springer about the treatment and why it didn't work. No one said I couldn't talk to him."

"Springer! Everyone knows he hates med students. By reputation he was second only to Rothman. You pull him as a preceptor for your rotation in internal medicine and half the students try to switch within a week. And the other half are lining up on the roof to jump off the building. Not to mention the fact that you've already pissed him off."

"Don't worry, George, I'll be my normal diplomatic self."

"That's exactly what I'm worried about."

32.

COLUMBIA UNIVERSITY MEDICAL CENTER
NEW YORK CITY
MARCH 24, 2011, 2:05 P.M.

As Pia sat and sat in the narrow waiting room of Dr. Helmut Springer, her determination to see him didn't waver. Her tryst with George had succeeded in establishing in her mind what she needed to do. She had a burning need to know two things. The reason why Dr. Rothman became sick was one issue; another was why the vaunted and lauded Columbia medical staff had, in her mind, apparently screwed up his treatment. She knew she was only a fourth-year medical student, but from her perspective she couldn't come up with a compelling reason why Dr. Rothman and Dr. Yamamoto should have died at all, let alone died less than a day after the men were admitted to the infectious disease ward at the hospital. It wasn't as if they were in some backwoods operation—this was one of the absolute premier medical institutions in the world.

Though Springer probably wouldn't be happy to see her, she was hopeful that if she talked with him he could aid her quest to find out what had happened. He was, after all, a world-renowned infectious disease specialist. She knew his reputation of not treating medical students with anything close to respect and she knew their meeting the day before had not ended well; still she was optimistic. If he didn't know that she was the one who first recognized Rothman's incipient peritonitis, she was going to tell him herself, thinking it should count for something.

After forty-five minutes of waiting, Springer's receptionist finally announced to Pia that the doctor could see her now. Pia quickly entered his office. Springer was at his desk facing into the small room. There were no other chairs; it was Springer's way of keeping meetings short.

"Dr. Springer, I'm sorry to bother you again, and I know I annoyed you the last time we met. I apologize for all that. But I'm a medical student, and if I can't learn from my experiences, then I'm a pretty poor excuse for one. And I apologize for questioning—"

"Yes, yes," Springer said, cutting Pia off midstream. Her apologies sounded rehearsed and there was nothing resembling contrition in her eyes. Worst of all, his schedule was completely full with residents, at that moment, awaiting his arrival in the emergency room. He cleared his throat. "From our last chat I suspect you believe you know better than some of the foremost authorities in the land what has taken place here. Well, I want to disabuse you of that notion. Also I'd like to say that I wouldn't have even taken the time to see you this morning were it not for the fact that you discovered the early signs of peritonitis in Dr. Rothman. Dr. De Silva told me about a medical student who she assumed was on rotation catching rebound tenderness in Dr. Rothman's abdomen, which had not presented itself previously. We'll overlook the fact that this medical student was not, in fact, on rotation and had essentially broken into the ward and was wholly unauthorized to approach the patients. Of course, I later learned that this medical student was yourself."

It took Pia a couple of seconds to realize that Springer was paying her a slight compliment, even if it was cloaked in a sardonic reprimand. Pia took it as an opening. "I fully admit it was, and perhaps I shouldn't have been there," she said. "But it was an important discovery with important consequences. The man was clearly getting worse, which makes one wonder why the original antibiotic was chosen."

"Please," Springer said, his face empurpling. "This is where we left off last time. I just indicated that we were grateful for your help, and now you're back with this nonsense. I can't win. Again, there is nothing to indicate that chloramphenicol wasn't doing the best job under the circumstances. And, as we have said about fifty times, we were informed by the sensitivity studies carried out by Dr. Rothman himself that it was the correct choice of antibiotic. We are working under the assumption that Dr. Rothman's work in the study was as thorough and accurate as was customary."

Pia couldn't believe what she was hearing. Was Springer attempting to shift some of the responsibility onto Rothman? In this case it seemed especially crass to even suggest blaming the victim. "So how come, considering those sensitivity studies, neither Dr. Rothman nor Dr. Yamamoto showed any sign of response to the chosen antibiotic?"

Springer closed his eyes for a moment. "The answer to your question is simple. The virulence of the involved strain of salmonella overwhelmed both the antibiotic and the patients' defenses. Remember, antibiotics, contrary to myth, do not cure. It is the patient's immune system that cures. Obviously with Rothman and Yamamoto, their immune systems were completely overwhelmed. Simple as that."

Pia started to respond, but Springer cut her off. "Listen, we've been over this issue. And let me add that a department head at this hospital does not have this kind of conversation with a medical student. A department head does not have this kind of conversation at all—there are protocols to be observed, there are panels that are convened if there are questions about the diagnosis or treatment. It's not clear in this case that there are any questions. Jesus, why am I justifying myself to you? This is not how we conduct business around here."

Pia wasn't picking up on Springer's rising sense of outrage. She had him in the room and she wanted answers. "Why weren't Rothman and Yamamoto being monitored more closely?"

"They were being monitored extremely closely. Each had his own nurse."

"Closely? How did it happen that a medical student had to pick up on the signs of developing peritonitis?"

"That was a fluke. It would have been picked up very quickly. Trust me. Now, is there anything else I can help you with, any other hospital policy you might want to critique for me?"

Springer's sarcasm was lost on Pia.

"This case confuses me," Pia continued.

"In fact, it's one of the worst cases of salmonella or typhoid that I've ever come across."

"In your vastly broad experience," Springer said.

"In my experience, yes."

"Well, what are you alluding to? I'm sure you're alluding to something. So enlighten me, please."

"One of the first things they told us when we got here was about diagnosis. 'When you hear galloping hoofbeats, you should think of horses, not zebras.'"

"Yes, of course, it's the oldest saw in medicine. What about it?"

"Should we be looking for zebras here, Dr. Springer?"

"*We* are not looking for anything here, Ms. Grazdani. But I am dying to know what it is that you are looking for. So enlighten me again."

"Okay. Is it possible that this case represents some exotic form of an antibody/antigen reaction the body can have, like a Shwartzman reaction? In which case would it not have made sense to use Decadron or some similar anti-inflammatory agent, something potent, to try to head it off at the pass?"

"If that is your great revelation, well, I'm sorry to say it's not much of one. Because we used Decadron in the evening when it became clear that the two researchers were approaching extremis. Perhaps you should review the patients' charts before making accusations like that."

"Of course. If I had been given access to the charts I wouldn't have made the mistake. But I'm not making accusations, I just want to get to the truth, Dr. Springer."

"We all do, Ms. Grazdani."

Springer was suddenly overcome with fatigue. Talking with Pia Grazdani was frustrating, and he had more people he was going to have to deal with that afternoon who were going to be even more of a burden. There would be the inevitable press and the patients' families. It was not going to be a good day, since ultimately, it was the patients he cared about.

"Do you think perhaps there could have been yet another bacteria involved besides salmonella, a bacteria or a virus that was being covered or camouflaged by the salmonella? And maybe it was this bacteria that was totally resistant to chloramphenicol and was the real killer?"

There was silence while Springer tried to control his anger. This was simply too much. His eyes drilled into Pia's while she maintained her composure, waiting for an answer while looking down at her feet. Finally Springer exploded with bottled-up emotion.

"I cannot, for the life of me, imagine a more ridiculous scenario. We made the diagnosis by fulfilling Koch's hypothesis. The illness was caused by salmonella, whose presence we ascertained in multiple ways, but most convincingly from blood culture. We classified the strain in multiple ways as well, particularly by DNA analysis. The offending organism was, without an ounce of doubt, the alpha strain of salmonella typhi that Rothman himself had had grown in space with the cooperation of NASA. There was no other pathogen, for Christ's sake. The blood cultures only grew out the salmonella. Nothing else! Nothing at all!"

Undaunted, Pia changed the subject on a dime. "What about the hair loss? Does serious salmonella infection cause hair loss?"

Springer was having difficulty controlling

himself, yet the woman seemed completely calm. "The stress of almost any severe illness, particularly one presenting with high fever, can cause hair loss. Anyway, what hair loss are you talking about?"

"I saw hair loss with Rothman before I discovered the rebound tenderness. The resident suggested it could be attributed to the chloramphenicol."

"That's not something I am aware of," he said. And then, suddenly and angrily, "Oh, for God's sake. You wait here!"

Springer bounded out of his desk chair, pushed past Pia, and disappeared. Pia stood in the room and waited. Within a few minutes, Springer reappeared and sat down, giving Pia a nasty look. Thinking she had probably maximized what she was going to get out of the conversation, Pia eyed the door.

"I told you to wait," Springer said. "Stay there!" Confused, Pia did as she was told. There was silence except for Springer's labored breathing. *The man's boiling*, she thought. *I'm not getting anywhere.* Pia eyed the door again.

"Dr. Springer, I sincerely thank you for your time."

"Stay where you are!" Springer said brusquely.

Pia rolled her eyes, confused. *First he can't wait to get rid of me, now he wants me to stay. . . .* Then, bursting through the door came Dr. Helen Bourse, dean of students.

"Ah, Dean Bourse, it's simply not possible for me to do my job if I am to be hounded by a medical student who thinks she should be running my department. She goes onto the floor and sees patients with no authorization, which I am sure could open us up to all manner of liability issues. She repeatedly questions my medical ability and second-guesses decisions that were made, and now she's come up with an outlandish suggestion that we might have completely missed another organism which was responsible for Rothman's and Yamamoto's untimely deaths. First it was the choice of antibiotic, now it's a second pathogen. This is outrageous and it has to stop."

Pia looked at Springer, and she was unable to conceal the contempt she was feeling. He had run off like a coward and got the dean to come tell her off. She glanced at Bourse, who was standing arms akimbo, a hard expression on her face. She was angry and dumbfounded.

"I would like Dr. Springer to understand that I'm not trying to do his job," Pia said in her defense. "I'm just trying to answer some questions that I would have thought were important ones. My sense here is that something is wrong."

Neither Springer nor Bourse could believe the gall of the young woman. The question in both of their minds: Who the hell does she think she is? Springer found his voice first.

"Do you see what I'm talking about? This woman is off the wall. I'm going to talk with Groekest about the advisability of rescinding the position she was offered here as a resident/Ph.D. candidate. This is absurd."

At the mention of the chief of the internal medicine department, Helen Bourse signaled with a snap of her head that Pia should leave Springer's office. Pia was happy to oblige. Bourse then nodded to Springer to indicate that she had the situation under control. "I'll get back to you. Sorry about this." Bourse then followed Pia out of the office and into the hallway. Pia might be temporarily unbalanced, but Springer was a bully, and he'd made his point. Before Pia had a chance to say anything, Bourse lit into her.

"What the hell do you think you're doing? When we spoke this morning, and I gave you time to get your head together, I don't believe I said you should go see Dr. Springer and belabor the head of Infectious Diseases about his patients or his diagnosis. Where is your social sense? Good grief, woman! It's common knowledge that Springer is not a fan of medical students in general, but this episode has pushed him over the edge. I have never heard him as exasperated as he was when he called."

Pia started to speak, but Bourse wasn't done with her.

"You're fast developing a reputation as a troublemaker, Ms. Grazdani, and that will not look good on your résumé if it gets recorded. You are here, essentially, as a guest of the institution, and guests do not behave like this. If they do, they're usually asked to leave. I gave you a couple of days to get over the tragic death of your mentor and that wasn't supposed to be time for you to come in here and stir things up again."

"But don't you think these questions need to be answered?"

"No, I don't, not if he doesn't," Bourse said, gesturing at the door.

Pia started to speak again, but the dean had had enough. "Have you shown any signs of a fever?"

"No."

"Then get yourself back to your room. If I hear you're causing any more trouble over this unfortunate affair, I will think seriously about rescinding your welcome here as a medical student. Which would be something of a tragedy for you, considering you only have a couple of months left before you graduate. And it would be a tragedy for us because we'd be admitting we made a mistake in taking you in the first place. I don't think Dr. Springer will go to Dr. Groekest on his own, but he might. So be careful, young lady. You are now officially on very thin ice. I must not have made myself clear last time we spoke. Am I making myself clear now?"

"Yes," said Pia. "Perfectly."

33.

For Pia, being in trouble was as natural as breathing in and out. She'd spent most of her life under some kind of probationary supervision undertaken by people who didn't know her, care to know her, or understand her situation. Long ago, Pia had wondered how it was that she was the one who ended up in front of some panel or other. She never instigated the trouble, she was always reacting to someone older and more powerful trying to take advantage. Somehow that fact got lost in the paperwork. More often than not, it was only she who suffered the inquisition and the punishment that followed. For her, injustice belonged with pain on the same one-way street.

By the time she reached age twelve, Pia had simply stopped questioning the way of the world as it concerned her. This was just how it was and how it was going to be. Over the years she'd come to know how the individuals of influence in her life operated. Dr. Springer was a familiar type. He was fiercely protective of his own reputation and would adopt any position that protected him, even at the expense of reason and fact. Quick to take offense, Springer had no backbone. When Pia pushed back and kept pushing, Springer literally ran away. He went and found someone who did have some fortitude—Dr. Bourse— and he hid behind her. Bourse was a different proposition. She wasn't afraid, Pia could see that, and she wasn't willing to take the easy way out and simply dispense with the problem—Pia—which she could have done.

Pia had spent the afternoon anxiously mulling over Springer's behavior. She'd learned nothing. There was also the fact that no one seemed concerned about the medical issues she was raising, which couldn't help but fan Pia's semi-paranoid belief that the medical center, and the Infectious Diseases Department in particular, hadn't looked after Rothman and Yamamoto properly. And how could anyone prove that some medical center personnel had nothing to do with their getting sick in the first place? Pia was starting to consider the idea that some kind of cover-up might be under way, orchestrated by Dr. Springer.

And Rothman was still emotionally in her head. If she hadn't let him take such an influential role in her life, she wouldn't have found herself in her current predicament. If you let people into your life, she thought, you were bound to hurt sooner or later.

A knock on her door jolted Pia out of

her agitated state. It was George. Who else?

"What happened with Springer? I was so worried I couldn't concentrate all day."

"It was a disaster."

"I'm sorry. I'm also sorry I didn't offer to go with you, really I am. You shouldn't have to do this all by yourself."

"George, stop saying you're sorry, please! Besides, I never expected you to come with me. In fact, I never gave it a thought. And after what happened, I'm glad you didn't come. Springer was a lot angrier at me than he was the first time. He went and fetched the dean to tell me to stop interfering. And he threatened to go to Groekest if I didn't."

"So, are you going to?"

"Going to what?"

"Stop interfering."

"How can I? They're the ones interfering, covering things up, not me. They're sitting on something, I'm sure of it."

"If you don't mind me saying so, that sounds rather paranoid."

"So be it. And remember, even paranoid people have real enemies."

"So you got confronted by the dean again?"

"Afraid so."

"What did she do?"

"Bawled me out big-time. Gave me a lecture about being a troublemaker. Threatened to have me kicked out of school."

"Shit!" George commented.

Pia checked her watch. "Actually I was just about to go back to Rothman's lab. I'm just waiting until it's late enough. I don't want to run into anyone, especially not the dean."

"Pia, the last time I looked, the dean isn't working security. They have a whole staff for that, and they caught us in about five minutes the last time we went to the lab. Bourse made it pretty clear you're not supposed to go back to the lab. Now she's spoken to you a second time. Maybe they're right. You *are* crazy."

"I think I have an aptitude for science, George. There are facts here, evidence that doesn't add up. No scientist is going to just walk away from that."

"Then tell me this: What are you going to do when you get kicked out of this place?

That would make you an ex-scientist. Or not even. More like an ex-almost-qualified scientist. I don't think there's a great deal of demand for them in the job market today. You're going to graduate in a couple of months, if you're lucky. Yes, Rothman's death is a bad experience, a terrible one, but you might be compounding it and throwing away a career before it's even started."

"Career? Right now I don't see that I have a career. And I couldn't live with myself if I gave up now. Do you know if Rothman's lab is still officially closed?"

"How would I know? Well, I do know it's closed to you."

"The epidemiologists must be done by now," Pia said, ignoring George's point. "If they're not still checking the place out, there's no reason I can't go. I do have stuff I left in there. The dean was upset that we went in when it was still officially closed. If it's still officially closed, I won't go in, I promise, but if it's not off-limits, I will. At the very least I need to check the contents of that storage freezer in the level-three biosafety unit, which we didn't get a chance to do last night, remember? I'm one of the few people who knows the code that Spaulding uses in the logbook for the storage freezer. I want to be sure that all the samples that should be in the freezer are in the right place."

"Who's Spaulding?"

"The head lab technician. Rothman and Spaulding used to argue about the state of the storage freezer. Rothman thought the freezer was a mess, Spaulding disagreed. Rothman was thinking of sacking him. But that wasn't unusual—everyone thought they were about to get fired. Spaulding was the only one who pushed back."

"This is all very interesting and maybe you might find something is amiss in the storage facility. But even if you did, then what? Remember, it's not Rothman's lab anymore. All that is history. Unfortunately. And *you're* going to be history if you keep doing what you're doing. And are you really suggesting that the senior lab tech might have had something to do with Rothman's death? That's crazy."

"Actually, I don't know what I'm thinking. I do have some wild ideas, like these two scientists plotted together to carry off a dual suicide."

George looked at Pia with consternation.

"I'm kidding. I'm kidding. But there are so many things bouncing around inside my head right now, so many theories, and I can't rule anything out. Maybe it's something someone didn't do rather than what they did do—what do they call that? A sin of omission, not commission. The only thing I *know* is that something about this whole situation is not right."

"Of course the whole situation isn't right, Pia—two people died. That can never be right. But it doesn't mean there can't be a simple and logical explanation for why it happened."

Pia thought for a moment. She considered opening up to George and talking about herself and her state of mind, but that was something she had always been loath to do. That was what she had done with Rothman and look where it had gotten her. She glanced at George's face. He'd been looking at her the whole time; she had been mostly looking at the floor. He looked less eager than usual and more serious. Pia took a deep breath. She decided she'd at least try.

"I don't want to think Rothman had anything to do with his own illness. But I'd like to be sure. If he did, it will mean that he let me down. In a real way, he betrayed me. Rothman was very important to me, and it's hard for me to admit that anyone has such an influence on my life. Now he's gone, I feel like I'm starting at square one. And I don't want it to be his fault."

George nodded, but he was having a very hard time understanding Pia's reasoning. Even if Rothman accidentally infected himself, why would that mean she should think less of him, that he "betrayed" her?

"It was Rothman's idea to start the research track of my training, and it was going to be under his direction. Who's going to do that for me now? I was going to be working in his lab for my Ph.D. Where am I going to go now? Once again I've been abandoned."

George was a little taken aback at what sounded like self-centeredness in the face of Rothman's and Yamamoto's deaths. "I'm sure the university will find you another lab," he said. "They found you another rotation. Will and Lesley are already doing theirs."

"Maybe they'll find me one, maybe they won't."

George hesitated for a moment. He knew there was a risk Pia would take what he was about to say the wrong way. But he decided to say it anyway. "Pia, I'm sorry, but I don't understand how Rothman could have 'betrayed' you, as you put it. He got sick and died. It's tough for me to understand you sometimes. I don't think you should insert yourself into this where you don't have to. If you're now thinking Rothman's death wasn't an accident and that there's a cover-up going on, I don't see any other way for this to end but badly."

"Unless it's true."

"You're talking about murder. Who would want to murder one of the best research teams in the country?"

Turning it over in his mind, George could think of only one reason why someone would be so willing to risk their career without blinking an eye. He knew for sure this line of reasoning was going to get him into trouble. "Look, it's none of my business, and I've never said anything to you that would make you think I was jealous of any other guy, er, getting close to you, but your relationship with Rothman, well . . ."

George was cut off by Pia's loud laugh.

"Oh, God! Is that why you think I'm caught up in all this? You think I was sleeping with Rothman?"

"No. Well. Yes. Maybe. I don't know. It might explain why you're so worked up about it. It's what some people are saying on campus."

"So I have to be sleeping with a guy to care about how he died? Thanks a lot, George. I did let him get close to me but not like that. Typical male. I'll say it if it helps: No, there was nothing physical between me and Dr. Rothman. Zip. Believe me, I can tell when a man is interested in me like that, and he wasn't. He was actually happily married and devoted to his family, despite how asocial he seemed."

Pia was steamed and George didn't know what to say. The thought he'd expressed had taken on a life of its own in his mind. But as soon as he had voiced it, he knew it was very unlikely. Now he was just embarrassed he'd even mentioned it.

"All right, that does it, I'm going to the

lab," Pia said. "I really do have stuff there that I need to get. I worked there for more than three and a half years. And don't worry, if it's off-limits, I'll come right back like a good girl."

"And if it isn't?"

"Then I'll check out the storage freezer and get my stuff."

"I'll walk over to the med center and wait for you in the library."

"You don't have to do that."

"After Springer, it's the least I can do. Really."

"I guess I can't stop you."

George knew that was as close to an invite as he was going to get.

34.

Pia and George walked over to the Black research building and passed through security with their medical student IDs. They were bucking the tide, as it was past five o'clock and most of the staff was streaming out, having finished work for the day. Pia and George parted at the elevators, with Pia telling George she would come find him in the library when she'd finished her visit.

In the elevator, Pia was glad George wasn't with her. She'd be able to do what she wanted more quickly without him. She was pleased but not surprised that the caution tape was gone from the lab entrance. More good news: The door was unlocked, meaning the lab was officially back to normal. But the positive feelings were short-lived when she saw that a few of the familiar denizens of the lab had taken the same opportunity to show up and get on with whatever business was pressing. Marsha Langman was tidying up her desk, its previous pristine neatness a victim of CDC investigators who had gone through most of the lab's records. Unfortunately the head technician, Arthur Spaulding, was also there, for similar reasons, trying to get everything back to normal.

Seeing Spaulding was a disappointment. His presence precluded her plan to visit the biosafety lab. If he saw her, particularly if he saw her in the refrigerator storage facility, he would undoubtedly make a scene. Pia cursed under her breath that she hadn't gotten into the lab before any of the others. Neither Marsha nor Spaulding, nor any of the other technicians who were there, greeted her, or obviously snubbed her—it was like she wasn't there at all. It surprised her, because they were all going through the same trauma involving their bosses' deaths. It was like they were a group of automatons.

Pia headed toward the open door leading into her small office, thinking she might have to get her stuff, leave, and then return later that night to check out the biosafety microbiological storage freezer. In the process she practically collided with the maintenance man from the day before, O'Meary.

Obviously he knew Pia's name. "Miss Grazdani! Nice to see you again. We just heard ten minutes ago that we can get back in here tomorrow morning to finish up. I'm just checking the site, making sure all the tools are here." He then leaned toward Pia and whispered, "I'm not a hundred percent happy about being in here after what happened yesterday. But the job's gotta get done. You think it's safe in here now? Our boss says so."

"I think it's safe," Pia said. "I don't think it was ever unsafe."

"Good to hear." O'Meary straightened

up to his full height. He jerked his thumb toward Pia's ceiling. "I think we've isolated the problems with the short. It's up there, so we should be outa your hair by lunch tomorrow."

Pia didn't respond. She doubted the problem would ever get solved. Besides, she wouldn't be there at noon tomorrow or any other day.

"I hope we won't be bothering you too much tomorrow," O'Meary said, trying to be considerate. He tried to go around her. Pia stopped him.

"I know you've only been here a couple of days, but did you see anything unusual yesterday morning? Before all the excitement started. Anything that struck you as odd?"

"That Springer guy asked me already, and the Disease Control people. They took a long time about it."

"I'm sure they were very thorough, but I'm wondering, because you were in here all morning and in different parts of the lab with your wires, if you saw anyone early on who you didn't see in the lab later. Anyone who looked like he didn't belong."

O'Meary narrowed his eyes, but playfully.

"What are you, a cop now?"

"No, I'm not a cop."

"I wasn't working in that bio unit where they got sick, so I wouldn't know about anyone in there. Are you sure this place is safe? The disease people were asking about contamination, like 'Before the contamination . . .' and so on. Is it really safe in here?"

"I'm sure it's safe. I came back and I'm not about to take a risk with that bacteria."

"So why the questions? You're making me nervous."

"I'm just making some of my own inquiries. Supposedly nothing abnormal was found here in the lab or in the biosafety unit. Did you see Dr. Rothman or Dr. Yamamoto at all?"

"I didn't even know which one was which. There was a lot of people in and out of this lab, dropping stuff off."

"Do you know Arthur Spaulding, the head technician?"

"Yeah, he was introduced to us when we first came on the job."

"Did you see him when you were in Rothman's office?"

"Sure, a few times. Quick ins and outs."

"Anyone else more than once?"

"The secretary, Martha."

"Marsha."

"Whatever, yeah. You know, you sound an awful lot like a cop."

"I'm not a cop, just a student who has a few questions. Sorry to keep you. But if you think of anything unusual, just find me."

"Are you gonna be here?"

"Actually, no. Let me give you my cell phone number. If you remember anything, please call. I rarely use it, but I'll pick up a message." *A message that I can ignore if it's not germane,* thought Pia. She usually made it a point not to give out her cell number. O'Meary wrote it down.

"Okay, I got it."

Over O'Meary's shoulder Pia saw Spaulding say good night to Marsha and leave. She silently applauded. She was now free to go and check out the storage freezer.

To be on the safe side, Pia did a circuit of the lab to see who else was around. A couple of the other support personnel were tidying up in the main lab area, and

Marsha was busy around the front desk, but there was no one there who might go into the biosafety unit. Stepping into Spaulding's office, she took the microbiological storage freezer log from where she knew Spaulding kept it in his desk. In the anteroom of the unit she quickly suited up, and once inside the unit itself, she used her own key to enter the large walk-in storage freezer. The door closed automatically behind her. She was surprised the interior light was on, which was odd, because Spaulding was scrupulous about turning it off when he left. As Pia started to contemplate what that might mean, the door was yanked open. Pia's heart leaped in her chest. She found herself face-to-face with an equally surprised Arthur Spaulding.

"What are you doing here?" Pia asked quickly, feigning indignation.

"I came to turn off the light. More to the point, what are *you* doing here? This is off-limits to anyone but Nina Brockhurst, Panjit Singh, Mariana Herrera, and me. You know that. And how did you get in, damn it?"

"I have a key," Pia said, producing it and dangling it in front of her masked face. "Dr.

Rothman gave it to me, and he gave me authorization to come in here."

Spaulding snatched the key roughly out of Pia's hand, causing her to start again.

"Maybe you didn't hear, but Dr. Rothman isn't around anymore to give you his authorization."

"I bet you're happy about that," Pia blurted. As soon as the comment left her mouth she regretted it.

"For now I'm in charge of this lab, and from this point on, you no longer have authorization. And I'll take that too." Spaulding snatched the logbook that Pia was holding.

Pia stood there for a couple of beats, deciding what to do. She'd recovered from the shock of Spaulding's unexpected appearance and now was just angry. She'd never liked the man. She brushed past Spaulding heading toward the freezer door.

"You're not the princess anymore, Pia darling. Your access to this entire lab is revoked, as I'm sure the dean would be happy to confirm if I asked."

Pia said nothing. In the anteroom she took off her protective garb and passive aggressively left them where they fell.

Seething, she walked back into her tiny office and packed up the few belongings and files she'd accumulated in three-plus years. She found an empty box and put them in it. Without looking back, she closed the office door and walked toward the entrance to the lab. Marsha Langman didn't look up as she passed by. What a bunch of jerks, Pia thought.

In a huff, Pia headed back to the dorm, but then she remembered George in the library. Reversing her direction, she quickly found him and got his attention. She then left. He quickly closed the journal he was reading and followed her out into the hall. He had to jog to catch up with her. It was no secret she was angry.

"Can I ask what happened? You weren't gone long. Was the lab still off-limits?"

"Maybe it would have been better if it had been," Pia said. "I hope you're hungry because I'm starved."

"I'm hungry enough. Let's go to the cafeteria."

"Fine," Pia said.

They exited the hospital. It was cold and dark. They walked quickly.

"You still haven't told me what happened," George reminded Pia.

"What happened was that prick Spaulding surprised me at the storage freezer and ended up kicking me out of the lab for good. The dummy left the light on and came back to turn it off. My bad luck he's so anal. Figures, he's a huge asshole."

"You can't be surprised he got mad. And why do you care if he kicked you out of the lab? You're going to another lab come Monday. You can strike another staff member off your Christmas card list."

"I don't send Christmas cards."

"It's a figure of speech, you know what I mean. So now the lab's really off-limits, right?"

Pia nodded. "I guess so."

"So there's not much more you can do, unless you want to break into Springer's office."

Pia looked over at George with confusion.

"I'm joking. Seriously, there's nothing more you can do. You've talked to the doctor in charge of Rothman and Yamamoto's care and now you can't go back into the lab. You have to let it go and let the authorities do their work. You can be sure there's an investigation going on. So you should drop it. Yes?"

Pia wasn't hearing George's plea at all.

"Pia, are you listening to me?"

Far from dropping it, Pia was now wondering whether Spaulding was hiding something. Yet what could she do? And what was she going to do with the rest of her life? Without her mentor and his program, was research still a possibility? Becoming a physician had seemed to offer safety in her life, something she coveted. But Rothman had made her realize that her discomfort with patients, with other people in general, might not bode well for such a career. She was at a crossroads in her life and had no answers. Thinking about it made her anxious.

Pia let out a sigh and George asked her what was up. Pia ignored the question. She suddenly knew that her preoccupation with finding out what had happened to Rothman was allowing her to avoid thinking about her career and the decisions she was facing. It was her first line of defense.

The future could wait. Pia stopped walking and pulled George to a stop just outside the dorm.

"I'm not giving this up. I've got to find out why this tragedy happened. There are too many questions. Every time I stop and think, there are more questions; more people acting strangely. The infectious disease people insisted on using a fifty-year-old antibiotic and the patients died within hours despite being diagnosed and treated. And no one, I mean no one, liked Rothman. All his colleagues were jealous of him having a Lasker and a Nobel and possibly being in line for another. Okay, Spaulding was mad that I was in the storage facility, which he has always been weirdly proprietary about, and he knew I'd been in his desk since I was holding the logbook. But he was acting bizarre, like the lab was now his. The moron is only a fucking technician. He's not a researcher. And what about the fact that I, a mere medical student, was the one to pick up the peritonitis? Maybe if they had gotten him to surgery sooner, he would still be alive."

"What do you want me to say?" George

asked. He tried to look Pia in the eye but she avoided it.

"Does it really sound like I'm paranoid? Don't answer. Whatever, I'm not finished looking into all this as there doesn't seem to be anyone else doing it."

"How many times do I have to remind you that this is one of the premier medical centers in the world? Do you really believe you have anything to add? You're going to flame out, Pia. Is that what you want? Do you have a career death wish?"

Pia thought for a moment. "Maybe."

"Even if you persist in this self-destructive investigation or whatever you call it, I don't see what your options are. Springer, Bourse, Spaulding—you're on a last warning from all of them."

"I'm not afraid of Spaulding. He took my key, but I still know where Rothman kept his. He was acting like he had something to hide."

"As I said before, I think this is crazy. Look, if you insist on pursuing it, why don't you check out the autopsies? There's probably a simple pathological explanation for Rothman and Yamamoto's clinical course. Or even a complex explanation, I don't know. But that's where you're going to find the answers, not pissing off everybody in the hospital. The autopsies were probably done today so they could dispose of the bodies because they're still hot."

"Hot?" Pia said.

"Yeah, hot, as in contaminated with salmonella," George said sharply. Sometimes Pia could be a little slow on the uptake. She still looked bemused, as if her mind wasn't making a connection. "You understand what I'm saying?"

"Like you'd say someone full of virus is 'hot.'"

"Exactly. No Pathology Department wants to keep hot bodies around. I tell you what you should do: Find one of the pathology residents tonight and ask what they know, or what they can find out. You haven't worn out your welcome in that department yet. Have you?"

"Actually, that's a good idea. I didn't think of that."

"If you want to look into that, I'll come with you, so you stay within the lines." George smiled as he said it. He wasn't reprimanding her, he was joking because he knew he wouldn't be able to keep her out of trouble if she was determined to get into it. She'd more than proved it.

"But I'm not going back to the lab," he added. "If you want to do that, you're on your own. Spaulding is bound to have alerted security. And what does it mean if there's a sample missing in the freezer? What does it prove? Other than the fact that Spaulding's not as good at his job as he'd like to think. Which is another thing you knew already."

"I don't think Spaulding would alert anyone. He doesn't have that kind of authority, despite his big talk. But at the moment I'm not thinking about going back to the lab. I think I'll follow your suggestion and check with Pathology. As I said, I hadn't thought of that. It's a good suggestion."

"Then I'll tag along. I know, I'd feel guilty if I don't go and you get carried away again and get yourself kicked out of school."

"I don't care one way or the other," said Pia. She was intrigued. She wondered why she hadn't thought of it.

35.

The wind blew fiercely down Haven Avenue and into the canyon of 168th Street. Pushed from behind, Pia and George made rapid but chilly progress from the dorm toward the medical center. It was raining, and George struggled with a cheap umbrella until it finally turned inside out for the third time. He stuffed it headfirst into a trash can. Pia strode on, head down, the hood of her sweatshirt pulled tightly over her head.

Once inside the hospital, they descended into the labyrinthine bowels of the nearly century-old building to the morgue. It was malodorous and poorly lit and filled with outdated equipment. The morgue served as a way station for the dead: In simple cases, bodies would be picked up by a funeral home. A van from the OCME, the Office of the Chief Medical Examiner, would come if there were complicating factors.

Both Pia and George found it difficult to reconcile this run-down, dirty place with the hospital and medical center as they knew it. Some campus buildings were slightly shabby on the outside but pristine and modern within. The morgue was unkempt inside and out, and at this time of the evening seemed to have been deserted by anyone from the realm of the living. Old-fashioned wooden meat-locker-style doors with metal signs proclaiming that only authorized personnel were to be admitted were the order of the day. The only noise in the godforsaken place was a low-grade electrical hum and the drip of water onto cement floor.

Following their noses, they walked into the tiered amphitheater of the abandoned autopsy room, which looked like the set of a horror movie depicting Victorian times. Some of the seats were broken. The pit area, with its two ancient autopsy tables, was being used as storage for a random collection of pipes, old sinks, and discarded toilets. With the constant fight for space in the medical center, George wondered out loud why the area hadn't been retrofitted.

Finally Pia and George walked into the morgue itself. Arranged along the walls was a series of walk-in coolers. The fifteen or so corpses in the room were on separate gurneys, some covered by sheets, others fully exposed. Still in place on a few of the bodies were the various tubes and wires used to treat and monitor them while they were still alive. A couple of the bodies were clothed, others naked. Most still wore the hospital johnnies they expired in. Mixed in were a couple of long black body bags.

Pia and George were wondering why they couldn't find anyone working there when the night diener, or mortuary attendant, startled them.

"What do you want?" the man asked. It was obvious he was unhappy at being disturbed. He was perhaps fifty or sixty, small of stature, wearing a stained lab coat. He had a bulbous head too large for his body with a badly maintained comb-over wedged on top. He wore small oval glasses and squinted through them at his uninvited guests. The casting department for the Victorian horror movie had done a good job.

"And how did you get in?" he added before Pia or George could answer his first question.

"We came in that way," Pia said, indicating their entrance route.

"That's the back entrance. Visitors are supposed to come in the front. No one ever comes in the back way."

"We're here to ask about a couple of autopsies," George said. "Autopsies that might have been performed down here today. The patients would have been two staff members who died early this morning, Dr. Rothman and Dr. Yamamoto?"

The attendant laughed cynically, as if this was the funniest thing he had heard in ages.

"There hasn't been an autopsy done down here in fifty years. I never heard of either of those patients. They're not here, if that's what you want to know. And if there was an autopsy, it would be done in the anatomy department of the medical school, where they still do them. On account of the teaching. You need to get in touch with the pathology resident on call. And you can go out the front way." The man pointed in the direction of the usual exit. He then stood there implacably.

George looked at Pia, who didn't seem in the mood to argue.

"Okay," George said. "Thanks."

As Pia and George waited for the elevator to rumble its way down to them, George snuck a look back toward the chamber of horrors.

"Can you believe that guy?"

"I've been in some creepy places, but that's the creepiest."

"Do you think he ever leaves?" George said.

"You get the impression that he lives down here."

"I'll be happy if I don't see that face again."

"I should think so," said Pia. "If we come back down here, it means we're dead."

Back in the land of the living, George called the on-call pathology resident. Dr. Simonov agreed to meet with them and asked that they come up to the clinical path lab. When Pia and George found him, Simonov was taking a break in a small windowless office with a giant mug of strong coffee on the desk in front of him.

"So what can I do for you guys? It's not often I get called by medical students. What's up?"

Simonov was Russian but had lived in the West long enough to almost completely lose his accent. Only the occasional dropped article gave him away. He'd gone to both college and medical school in the States.

"We're wondering if there was an autopsy performed today on either Dr. Rothman or Dr. Yamamoto or both," George said. He had suggested to Pia that he do the talking this time. She didn't care. "They died early this morning when—"

"Yes, I know who they were," Simonov

said. "Everybody in the medical center knows about them. Why are you asking?"

"There are questions about how quickly they died," Pia said before George could speak. "It was a relentless downhill course despite maximum treatment so that we—"

"No autopsies were done on them here," Simonov said, cutting Pia off. "Not a lot of autopsies are done anymore in general. It's a pity, but it is reality. There's no money. But Rothman and Yamamoto, they would not have been done here under any circumstances. Having died like they did of an infectious disease while working meant that they are definitely medical examiner cases, pure and simple. All we did here was put the bodies in body bags, seal them up, and decontaminate the exterior. They were then picked up by the OCME." He spelled out the acronym, explaining it stood for Office of the Chief Medical Examiner.

"I know what the OCME is. So do you know the results?"

"Results!" Simonov laughed at Pia's question. "Maybe in three weeks or more," he said. "They get a lot of bodies down there, and they generally take their time."

"Down where?" Pia said. "Where exactly is the OCME?"

"You gonna go down there now? I wouldn't advise it. But, okay, whatever. It's on East Side, First Avenue and Thirtieth Street, near NYU Medical Center."

"Thanks. If we call them up, do you think they'll answer our questions?"

"Now?"

"Tomorrow."

"How would I know? Maybe they never had medical students asking questions. But then again it is affiliated with NYU Medical Center, which is a teaching hospital. For all I know they may have a medical student elective."

"Who should we call? Should we ask for someone in particular?"

"I knew one of the MEs, but he's no longer there. But they have a PR department. I'd call them. Maybe call the medical legal investigator on the case."

"Do you think they'd tell us the results if we called?" George asked.

"You mean call the ME's office?" Simonov smiled and let out a quick, knowing laugh. "You think in this great big city bureaucracy you can just call and they jump and tell you results? Not in a million years. This case is important, they were important guys. It's going to be a media event. There's probably going to be lawsuits about safety, that kind of thing. Since it's an infectious case, the autopsies have probably already been done, but they're not going to release any results for three, four weeks after the toxicology screens are completed. But there's not going to be general access to the information, and they definitely won't give the results to a couple of green medical students."

"You're probably right," Pia said. She knew more than most people about city institutions.

"If I were you, find something else to do. But it's your life. If you insist on looking into the case, I'd go down there. I wouldn't try calling on the phone. If you're there in person and meet with someone who more or less takes pity on you or likes you, you might learn something." Simonov winked at Pia. She got his inference but ignored it.

"So if you're really committed," Simonov continued, "go to the OCME. Just don't count on getting any answers. As for calling, you might as well call three-one-one."

Simonov was referring to the citizens' help line—people called to report a cat stuck up a tree or a loud movie set on the street. Simonov checked his watch and picked up his coffee.

"If you decide to call three-one-one, tell them there's still a big pothole on my street. Been there since Thanksgiving."

Back out in the rainy night, Pia and George slogged along 168th Street, keeping as far away from the curb as they could. Every time a yellow cab zipped by, it splashed water up onto the sidewalk.

"Well, that was almost useless," Pia managed against the wind.

"I'm not sure I'd write it off as useless. He reminded us about the politics involved. He also emphasized that there's undoubtedly going to be a thorough investigation as a prelude to any legal action. I think that's information you should take to heart. It's time to drop all this, Pia."

"Dreamer," Pia said. "I'm in this until I get some answers."

"You are impossible," George commented, as a sudden gust of wind came down from Haven Avenue, halting their forward progress for a moment. They had reached Fort Washington Avenue. Looking to the side, Pia realized they had come abreast of the Black research building.

"What time is it?" Pia asked.

George managed to glance at his watch. "It's after ten. Time for us to be in bed." For George the idea of bed had immediate appeal. It brought up the fact that they had had sex that day, or at least Pia had had sex. Ever the optimist, he wondered if just maybe, after his accompanying her back over to the hospital to check on the autopsy, she might consider a continuation. George closed his eyes and screwed up the courage to speak.

"Do you want to come to my room? Stay the night? Or we could go to your room, whichever you prefer."

"What for?" Pia asked, blankly.

"Well, for one thing, we ended things a little quickly this afternoon. Maybe if we had more time . . ."

"That's a thought," Pia said in a preoccupied fashion. "Have you noticed where we're standing?"

George looked up. In truth he hadn't

been particularly aware of the immediate surroundings.

"We're just outside the Black building," Pia added. "It's after ten, as you said. I want to go up to the lab for another quick visit to check out that damn micro storage locker. I'm not going to be satisfied until I do it, and this is the best time. I've been in there fifty times at night like this."

"No, Pia!" George said firmly. "It's too big a risk."

"I don't think there's any risk whatsoever. You head back to the dorm. It'll only take me twenty minutes at most."

George looked ahead at the dorm looming in the misty night. It beckoned as a haven of warmth and security. He looked back at Pia. She was smiling up at him, confident as usual. Most important, she hadn't said no to his suggestion that they sleep together. "You really think it'll be safe, that no one will suddenly pop in?"

"Absolutely. Twenty minutes it'll take me. I'll call you as soon as I get back to the dorm."

"And you remember that whatever you find out, it won't prove anything?"

"I'm aware of that."

George's mind went into overdrive. Maybe it was a good idea. Maybe if she got the damn micro storage locker out of her mind, she'd give up on her self-destructive investigation.

"All right," George said with sudden resolve. "I'm coming with you. Maybe I can help speed things up." He grabbed her hand and started to pull her toward the Black building entrance.

Pia resisted. "Are you sure?"

"I'm sure," George said. In his mind's eye what he could see mostly was them climbing into bed, holding each other tightly.

Pia shrugged. "It might be quicker with two people. All right, let's do it."

Without another word, Pia and George ducked into the Black building. The security man knew Pia well and didn't bat an eye. Pia used her key to open the main door, a key Spaulding had not asked for. The logbook was back where she expected it would be, in Spaulding's desk. Inside the biosafety unit she used Rothman's spare key from his office to open the storage locker. They worked quickly and efficiently.

George wouldn't have wanted a physician to check his blood pressure at any point during the visit, but Pia seemed icy cool and focused.

Pia had George read out to her how many of each sample were recorded in the logbook while she counted the actual samples. As Pia suspected, there were three samples missing from the storage freezer, at least according to the book. There were supposed to be thirty samples of the zero-gravity salmonella typhi, divided evenly between what was called alpha S. typhi and beta S. typhi. One of the missing samples was from the beta salmonella strain and the other two were the alpha strain, which was the strain that had infected Rothman and Yamamoto. Out in the main part of the unit near the hoods, Pia found a small collection of six labeled petri dishes in the incubator. Each was labeled with either an alpha or a beta.

After Pia and George had left the biosafety unit and removed their protective clothing, Pia found two of the same type of stoppered containers used in the storage facility without labels sitting next to Spaulding's sink.

After replacing the logbook and the

spare key, Pia said to George, "Okay, we're done."

George's heart rate calmed down once they had exited the lab without incident.

"What does all this mean, Pia?" George asked as they rode down in the elevator.

"I don't know," Pia admitted. "It might not mean anything, but information is information. What I'd like to do is go over the discrepancies with Spaulding if I can figure out how."

"Good luck with that," George said.

Pia and George fought their way through the weather back to the dorm. Though he was exhausted, George felt strangely exhilarated. He and Pia had actually worked together. George knew he'd been useful and was acutely sensitive to Pia's gestures, like the way she had put her hand on the small of his back to encourage him to precede her through the outer dorm door. She was obviously pleased with what they had accomplished. They stopped in the lobby and pushed the elevator button. Both cars were on upper floors.

Pia stared at the elevator's slow-moving floor indicator. George cleared his throat to speak, but Pia didn't want to hear what he had to say. She just wanted to get to her bed and try to sleep.

"Pia, you must know how I feel about you. I've tried to tell you a hundred times. More than that. Pia, would you look at me?"

Pia reluctantly turned to George. He had that earnest look.

"You know I worry about you because of my feelings for you. I love you, you must know that. I think about you constantly."

On hearing the words, something in Pia's brain fizzed into life. A laboratory animal learns to stop engaging in a certain behavior, like touching a red button, if it gets a painful shock every time, even if previously it got a reward, like a piece of food. In Pia's mind, there was a connection between protestations of affection and pain. She had learned that the people who said those words would cause her pain, and should be avoided, like an electric shock.

Pia pressed the elevator button again, as it appeared that the car was stuck on the eighth floor. She said nothing.

"Our relationship can't be totally one-sided."

"What do you mean, 'relationship' . . . ?

Look, George, this isn't the time or the place for this."

"When is the time, Pia? I've wanted to tell you I love you for years."

The elevator finally arrived, the doors opened, and a cluster of students noisily piled out. A party had started in someone's room and now was moving to a bar up on Broadway.

George pulled Pia aside as the door closed. She rolled her eyes.

"George, come on. Not now."

"I'm sorry, but I have to say it. I know you don't want to hear this, but I don't understand you."

"That makes two of us."

"But we need each other, don't you think? I know I need you."

"I don't know what that means—to 'need' someone. Someone needing me, I don't want that responsibility."

The second elevator arrived with a straggling student who hurried to catch up with his friends. Pia got in the car and held the door for George.

"Get in, George, Jesus."

Pia punched the eleventh floor for her room and seven for his. Message delivered. George reluctantly got in. Pia's mind was already full of competing problems— Rothman, the Sisters, Africa, the rest of her life—and now here was another one. She wondered what it was like to think about someone constantly as George said he did of her. It was an alien concept. She glanced at George, who was looking at the floor. She had no idea what he was thinking or feeling. The elevator stopped on seven and Pia reached out and pressed the hold button. George hesitated for a moment, than stepped out.

"Good night, George," Pia said.

George just nodded as the doors closed. To Pia he looked pathetic.

36.

George knew something about loss. His own father, Morgan Wilson, died when George was three, and no matter how hard he tried, George couldn't really remember anything specific about him other than a vague sense of contentment. He did have a few vague memories, but they'd been pieced together from photographs shown to him by his mother, Jean. There was one silent home movie of a time Jean and Morgan took George to see his grandparents, Sally and Preston, in Arizona. George had watched the film over and over and his father always looked impossibly young and endearing. In the short film Morgan is holding George on his lap and alternately kisses him on the cheek and hugs him. Morgan's absence had caused George a degree of melancholy similar to the melancholy he was feeling at that moment.

George got up from his bed where he'd flopped after Pia's rebuff. He needed to get out of his room if only for a short interval. There was always the vending machine room on the first floor. He needed to see people, normal people, and there were usually students getting sodas or bags of chips.

As George headed toward the elevators, he tried to concentrate on how much he was loved by his family. He'd always had that to fall back on whenever he felt lonely. He knew that Pia did not have an equivalent situation, which made her behavior even more confusing. Why did she so consistently reject the love that he wanted to share with her and finally had the courage to voice? It just didn't make sense.

George slapped the down button. Almost as if the car had been sitting there waiting for him, the elevator doors opened. Inside was Will McKinley, perhaps the only person in the world who could have made George feel even lonelier.

"George!" Will said. "What a coincidence. You heading down for a snack? Hop in!" Will took George's arm and pulled him in. The ground-floor button had already been pressed. George lacked the strength to resist.

"What's the matter, George? You look terrible."

"I'm just tired. It's been that kind of day."

"How's Pia? Have you seen her? She must have taken what happened to Rothman real hard."

"She did."

"Lesley and I tried to call her but she's not picking up."

"She's not great at staying in touch with people," George said.

The elevator reached the ground floor and Will guided George off.

"Listen, George, if there's anything I can

do to help Pia, just let me know. Really. We want her to get through this in one piece, she's a great girl."

George simply nodded. Will walked away toward the vending room. When he realized George wasn't accompanying him, he turned and waved to George to follow.

"Come on! My treat."

George sighed, wearily turned, and pressed the button once more to call the elevator. He wanted company but not Will's company.

37.

COLUMBIA UNIVERSITY MEDICAL CENTER
NEW YORK CITY
MARCH 24, 2011, 11:30 P.M.

The moment the elevator doors had closed on George, Pia had already relegated him to his proper place in her mind, well down the list of her immediate concerns. She didn't like being abrupt with him, but she didn't want to get into a long-drawn-out conversation either. She was exhausted from not sleeping well the previous night. Unfortunately, when she reached her floor, she had a bit of bad luck. She had run into Lesley and had had to have a conversation about Rothman and Yamamoto. Curious if Lesley had any interesting thoughts, Pia had tolerated the chat, but after ten minutes or so, when it was evident Lesley was not about to add anything significant, Pia broke it off.

Pia put the key in the lock and opened her door, walked in, and hooked the door with her right heel to slam it shut. In complete darkness, she felt the wall with her left hand to find the light switch and flicked it on. With her right hand she tossed her keys in the general direction of the desk. All Pia wanted to do was take a quick shower before going to bed. She'd been on the go all day and tomorrow wasn't going to be any quieter with a planned visit to the OCME.

Pia walked over to the window and closed the blinds. She took off her lab coat and tossed it over the arm of her reading chair. Next she removed her sweater and laid it on top of the jacket. She opened her closet door and kicked her shoes directly inside, first the left, then the right. Next she shucked off her black skirt and then her bra and let them fall to the floor. Pia couldn't wait to get into a hot shower. She put her hand on the bathroom door and thought it was odd that it was closed—she never closed the bathroom door, even when she was using the toilet.

Before Pia could process another thought, the door was yanked open away from her and the handle wrenched out of her hand. A tall figure materialized in the doorway and put the heel of his hand on Pia's breastbone and pushed her hard to the ground. Pia's head snapped back and smacked against the floor. A reflex cry rose in her throat, but it was choked off by the man, who was straddling her now with his knees on her arms, his left hand over her mouth. Pia tried to clear her head, but her ears were ringing. The man kneeling on her was wearing a balaclava, and she could see a second figure, obscured by the first. He was also hooded. Both wore hospital security uniforms.

The first man struggled to keep Pia still. He reached behind him with his right hand and the second man handed him a roll of duct tape. The first man looked back again and waved the tape.

"Cut me a piece," he said in heavily accented English, and his colleague obliged. He freed Pia's mouth, took the strip of tape in both hands, and clamped it down over Pia's mouth before she could let out more than a stifled screech.

"Stop moving. We're not going to hurt you," the first man said. Pia wriggled once more but stopped. She was struggling to get enough oxygen through her nose and her head was throbbing where she had hit it on the floor. Her arms were getting numb where the man was kneeling on them. She looked into his eyes and nodded.

"Okay. I'm going to let you up. Don't do anything stupid."

The man got to his feet, digging his knees into the fleshy part of Pia's arms as he did so. He stood back and she got up. She felt small. She was wearing only a pair of panties, and even though they were wearing balaclavas, she knew the eyes of the two men were moving up and down her body. She was going to be raped, she was certain. Pia raised her arms to rub her sore triceps and cover her breasts.

Pia thought, *It's only ten feet to the door.*

Pia thought, *They're not expecting me to do anything.*

Pia thought, *I don't want to be raped. Not again.*

Pia looked from one man to the other and then down at the floor. She wanted them to relax, even slightly. Then she got up on her tiptoes, tapped her right foot on the floor behind her, and in one move, using her arms first for balance and then for forward thrust, she drove her right foot heel-first into the front man's groin. He doubled over and staggered back and into his colleague, and Pia stood square at once, moved forward and reached over and hit the second man in the face twice, boxing jabs that fit the narrow space she was in. Both men were hurt but not enough. Pia got in a couple more kicks that would leave bruises, but the two men quickly regained momentum and charged her. The first man, his groin aflame, feinted a couple of times, then smashed Pia in the jaw with a right hook, knocking her unconscious.

When Pia woke up her head hurt like hell, and she couldn't move her limbs. She understood why: She was duct-taped to her chair, her arms bound behind her and her ankles fixed together. Pia's eyes were barely open, but she could make out one of the men coming toward her, his arm moving back and then quickly forward. She flinched, then took a face-full of cold water that the man had thrown over her using the Tupperware container she some-times fixed oatmeal in.

"That's what you do when I say do noth-ing stupid, huh?" The man's concealed face was very close to hers. His blue eyes bored into Pia's. She tried to speak, or at least snort.

"You are a good fighter, but we are more experienced, and there are two of us. We have respect for you because we are fam-ily men. But we know some young men who are less, what is the word? Civilized. They are, in fact, animals. If they were here now and not us, then God help you."

The man was speaking in a whisper. The fight and the overturned furniture that resulted had prompted the upstairs neigh-bor to bang on her floor to ask for quiet. The men didn't want to try the neighbor's patience.

"I say this only once. We are here to give you a message. Stop what you are doing. Stop asking questions. Your doctor was careless and got himself and the other doctor infected, and he put the whole medical center in a compromised position. It will be dealt with quickly and quietly and everyone will move on."

Pia was rocking back and forth in her chair, her eyes wide with fury. It was her rebelliousness surfacing.

"Stop rocking!"

Pia didn't stop. The man slapped her in the face, not hard but well placed enough to make her jaw throb even more severely than it had been. Pia sat still.

"You will be watched. Not by us, by our friends. If you keep meddling, if you call the police, our other friends, the animals, will come and take you away and you will ask them to kill you after a couple of days. You will beg them. You understand?"

Pia stared at the man. He moved even closer than before and the rough material of the balaclava touched her skin. She could feel his hot breath through the damp wool. He spoke in barely a whisper.

"You understand?"

Pia waited a beat, then nodded.

"You will tell no one we were here. If you talk with anyone here, like that boy you are with, they will be killed too. If you go to the police or the medical authorities, you will be killed. It's easy. Just stop, go about your life, and all this goes away."

The man stood up. His colleague stepped forward and jabbed the needle of a syringe hard into Pia's thigh. She gasped at the pain, then fell unconscious almost at once. The men tore off the duct tape binding her, leaving her skin red and swollen where it had been in contact with the tape. When they pulled the tape from her mouth it tugged at the wound on her jaw and further opened a tear in her lip. Blood trickled down her chin. The first man wiped it off with a tissue he got from a box on Pia's dresser. He pocketed it after using it. He picked her up and laid her on the bed with her head over the side. He knew that the drug he'd given her had the tendency to cause vomiting.

The men removed their balaclavas and prepared to leave. If Pia had been conscious she would have seen at once that the face of one of the men, the leader, was marked with a cleft lip. The other man had a peculiarly and memorably pointed nose. The first man cracked the door open and, seeing an empty hall, quickly exited the room, followed by the second man. They put on their official hats and, adjusting their uniforms, made their way quickly to the stairs.

38.

COLUMBIA UNIVERSITY MEDICAL CENTER
NEW YORK CITY
MARCH 25, 2011, 8:07 A.M.

Pia woke up in stages. First, when it was still night, she skimmed the surface of consciousness but quickly fell back into the darkness. Then, later, it had become light outside, and she was aware of her own breathing and a sharp pain in the back of her head and a throbbing along her jaw. Finally, she awoke and was hysterical—there were men in her room, chasing after her, she had to get away. She tried to get up, but her body wasn't obeying her commands. She slumped back on the bed and closed her eyes.

Then she remembered. Men had been hiding in her bathroom and had attacked her. The last thing she remembered was getting jabbed with a needle. She felt her leg at that spot, and it was sore. She looked down at the puncture wound. So she had been drugged, and hit. No wonder she felt so bad. She reached down and felt between her legs: nothing; she experienced a modicum of relief.

Dazed with the fog of her drug hangover, Pia was unsure of what to do. Her mind clicked over to George. Pia remembered the conversation they'd had in front of the elevator, the confessions George made to her and the look on his face when Pia said she wasn't thinking about those kinds of things right now. Last night she wanted George to leave her alone; now she wished he were here with her.

As the drug gradually started to wear off, the pain in Pia's jaw intensified. She stood up. She was dizzy. She managed to get herself into the bathroom. She looked at her face in the mirror, and it was a mess. A livid red welt with a small laceration covered much of the left-hand side along the jawline. Pia's lip was swollen and bloody, and there were red marks where the duct tape used to gag her had ripped at her skin. She remembered the fight, how she'd kicked one of the men in the groin and been smashed in the face in return. Pia leaned in and looked at her eyes. She saw that they were puffy and ringed with dark circles. She hadn't had a normal good night's sleep in an age. Being unconscious for hours didn't count. Pia looked at herself again and hoped to get an answer to the question: What was she going to do now?

She washed her face with cold water and took a long, hot shower. She put on her most comfortable sweatshirt and pajama pants. She located a bottle of Advil in her travel bag and took four tablets, washing them down with two glasses of water. Then she called George on his cell phone. When he didn't answer, she didn't leave a message, fearing she wouldn't be able to say anything coherent. She sent a text message instead: "Something's happened. Please come over. Urgent. P."

Pia lay down on the bed and waited.

George's phone vibrated in his pocket. He hung back a little from the group doing radiology rounds and read the message. He had a coffee break coming up, and he figured he could wait until then to reply. Pia had probably found a way of indicting someone else in her conspiracy theory, and he had been enjoying being a regular medical student for the last couple of hours. George put the phone back in his pocket and caught up with his group.

George called Pia after finishing a cup of coffee in the X-ray technician lounge. It was 9:45. At first, George thought he had a bad connection because he couldn't understand what Pia was saying. He moved out of the room with its background chatter, into a corridor, and stood by a window.

"Pia, can you hear me? You're very faint. What is it?"

What Pia was trying to say was "Please can you come to my room?" But it didn't sound like that at first.

"Say that again, Pia, I can't understand you."

Pia repeated herself.

"You want me to come?"

"Yes."

George was confused by the sound of her voice and wondered if Pia's state of mind had anything to do with the way their conversation had ended the previous night. It crossed George's mind that Pia was drunk, but it sounded more like she had a mouth full of cotton.

"Okay, I'll be right there."

George asked one of the other students to tell the resident he'd been called away on hospital business and headed to Pia's room. He found he was less eager to see her than usual. The previous night he'd made a decision, recognizing that he was probably barking up the wrong tree with Pia. George wasn't confident he could follow through with his decision, but he was going to try. It was for his own peace of mind.

Fifteen minutes later George knocked on Pia's door. When she opened it and he saw her face, all of his plans, doubts, and recriminations were washed away. He was instantly morphed back into the slavish dog he'd been for three years.

"Oh my God, what happened to you?"

Pia shook her head and pointed to her jaw. George fetched Pia's desk chair and sat her down.

"Take your time, tell me what happened."

"There were two men in my room. Last night," Pia said. She spoke slowly and deliberately.

"Last night? This was last night? Why didn't you call?"

"They drugged me. I just woke up."

"Jesus. Who were these men? What did they do? Did they . . . ?" George hesitated, not sure he wanted to hear.

"No, they didn't rape me, if that's what you're asking. They warned me to stay away from the Rothman case."

"Jesus, Pia. Do you want to lie down?"

"No, I'm okay."

"I'm going to call security. And then the police."

"No! Don't!" Pia said. She shook her head vigorously, an act that hurt a great deal. She was still dazed from the sedative, but the clouds were clearing.

"No security and no police. I have to take what they said seriously. They were waiting for me in my room. They said they'll be watching me. I mean, they already had been watching me. You see what this means, George? It means I was right. There's a conspiracy behind Rothman's and Yamamoto's deaths."

"Wait a minute, Pia, slow down," George said. "These two men, who were in your room, who obviously beat you up, they said specifically, 'Stay away from the Rothman case'?"

"Not like that, but they said it."

George was horrified, but his first instinct was one of skepticism.

"Did you recognize the men at all?"

"They had ski masks on. But they were dressed as hospital security. Shit, George, maybe they *were* hospital security, you know? That would mean the hospital is covering it up. Spaulding, the dean, Springer, all those guys . . ." Pia stood up as if she wanted to flee.

"Oh, come on, Pia. This is New York City. In America. Maybe in a movie or some Third World dictatorship they kill off their own doctors and beat up medical students, but not here. I can't believe you could think that. Get a grip."

"Well, someone did this!" Pia said, pointing at her face, shaking, partly with rage, partly with fear. "I know what institutions can do, George, what people can do to someone they're supposed to be looking after. If you grew up in the system I grew up in, maybe you'd be a little more cynical. I know one thing: Everyone has their own agenda. If you're in the way, things like this happen to you." Pia sobbed once and her shoulders heaved.

"Okay, Pia." George stood and reached out to Pia, and she went into his arms. He held her tightly.

"I think we should call the police. You need an ambulance as well—"

"No!" Pia pushed George away. "I need to think about what this means. If we call the police, they'll call the administration and security here, and for all I know, they were the ones who attacked me. I need to think." Pia grabbed both sides of her head and shook herself. "The drug, I can't think straight."

"Maybe we should go to my room," George said.

"They know all about you, George. It won't be any safer there. They won't do anything now, I'm just sitting in my room."

George looked around. "You think they're watching you that closely?"

"Well, think about it. Every time we moved, we got caught. It happened twice in the lab."

"One time it didn't."

"But we didn't find anything important then, remember? And we were allowed to go through the morgue just fine because there wasn't anything there to find."

"I'm having a hard time believing all these people are in on a conspiracy. Bourse, Springer . . . Dr. De Silva, who was treating Rothman. Why, Pia? What are they conspiring about? And there's no proof the deaths were anything other than accidents."

"Let me remind you again. You have no idea how much people hated Rothman. I saw it every day I was in his lab. No one liked him—he was rude, disrespectful, mean. And they were all jealous of him, how he got special treatment from the hospital, how he got a Nobel and might well get another. He had a lot of enemies, all sorts of reasons, including people in his own lab."

"Okay, but you don't kill someone because you don't like them. It's too much, it's so theatrical!"

"Well, how do you explain this?" Pia gestured to herself. "I was attacked," she yelled. "I was ordered to stay away. Now I'm sure Rothman was killed. His death wasn't accidental, it was deliberate. The only thing I'm not sure of is why they didn't kill me too last night rather than just warn me. They must be more afraid of how people would react to my disappearing than afraid that I wouldn't respond to the warning. As they said, if I keep quiet, all this goes away. If I disappear, they talk to you and find out what I was thinking."

George felt a sudden chill. If Pia was right, he might be next in line for a visit. But how could she be right? It was so farfetched. George needed some time to think too.

"Can I get you some ice for your face? I'll just be down the hall."

"Sure, thanks."

George went to the ice machine at the end of Pia's corridor, but it was out of order. He could go down to the cafeteria where he knew ice was always available, but that meant leaving Pia on her own in her room for a few minutes. George walked back to her door and opened it, startling Pia.

"Shit, George, can't you knock?" she said.

"Sorry. The ice machine's out. I'm going downstairs to get some. I'll be right back."

39.

George returned with the ice. Pia was sitting at her desk, writing furiously on yellow legal paper, trying to make sense of what had happened in the past forty-eight hours. George took some ice and wrapped it in a towel for Pia to hold to her face. The rest he put in her sink. He then sat on the bed and watched her write on page after page.

Pia tested her prodigious memory, trying

to isolate fact from speculation. She worked backward from the undeniable fact that she'd been attacked and threatened in her own dorm room. That was obviously a criminal act—but what else of all the events of the past two days had constituted unlawful activity? While she worked on the what, she also worked on the who. She tried to piece together a cast of characters using the information she was certain about. There had been two men in her room—but who else was involved and how broad was the conspiracy she now knew existed?

After an hour, Pia stopped.

"This is getting me nowhere. It could be anyone. And there's so much that's happened, and I bet we don't know the half of it."

"What about trying to establish a timeline? Isn't that what they do in those cop shows on TV? They use a whiteboard: 'six forty-two P.M., suspect seen in O'Leary's bar . . .'"

"But we don't know who the suspects are unless we just include everyone. And we can't really investigate anything. Say we think Springer was involved somehow. The only times we know what he was doing are when I was with him. I can't pick up the phone and demand he answer any questions about his whereabouts at any other time."

"This is why we should call the police," George said. "They can investigate to their heart's content and ask him anything they please."

"Given that there's a conspiracy, one of the things we don't know is why."

"Only, as you keep saying, Rothman was hated by half the human race. Of course that raises the question, why kill Yamamoto as well? He wasn't unpopular, was he?"

"Not at all, people loved him. He was devoted to Rothman. They were like two peas in a pod, working together. If they weren't working together in either the biosafety unit or the organ bath unit, Yamamoto was in Rothman's office. They even ate together if they took time out for lunch, which wasn't always the case. Yamamoto was the only one Rothman allowed to use his private coffee machine or drink the bottled mineral water from his private office fridge. They were like Siamese twins."

"So there's much more we don't know

than we do know, as far as what other people were thinking and what they were doing," George said. "So what *do* we know, other than the fact that you were attacked last night and told to stop involving yourself in this?"

Pia turned back to her desk and picked up her pen and underscored a couple of lines on the page.

George looked at his watch. He was concerned about getting back over to the hospital but decided he was more worried about Pia. The resident to whom he'd been assigned for the day was rather laid-back, to say the least, and probably didn't even realize George wasn't around. Besides, George wanted to stay and humor Pia for a while. He was worried that she might have a concussion from the attack, and he wanted to make sure her mental status didn't change. In addition, he reasoned, she couldn't get into any more trouble while they were there in her room.

Suddenly Pia turned back around. "You know what we know the most about?"

George shrugged.

"We know the most about Rothman and Yamamoto's illness even without the autopsy results and even without seeing their charts. I was in the lab when it presented, I saw them in the hospital, I talked to the doctor who was treating them, I examined Rothman myself, I diagnosed new symptoms, I spoke with the department head involved."

"Good, yes," George said. They had gone over all this before but under the circumstances, George was happy to do it again. Pia tore the sheets she had written on off her legal pad, crumpled them into a ball, and threw the ball in the general direction of the trash basket. She missed. Pia began writing again, more slowly this time.

"Okay," she said while she worked. "We do have a timeline of the infection. The onset was extremely rapid. Rothman or Yamamoto pressed the panic button and there was a medical team in the lab almost at once. I saw them arrive. Rothman and Yamamoto knew what to look out for, so from the first symptom to the medical team arriving may have been only ten minutes, at the outside. Springer showed up, and he went into the lab. Then he stayed and talked to the staff while Rothman and

Yamamoto were taken directly up to the infectious disease floor and put in isolation, and treatment was started. I'd say they were there in five or six minutes. And Springer told us it was classic typhoid fever—high temperature, delirium, and so on, so it was diagnosed immediately. No delays. They got antibiotics within an hour of the initial symptoms."

Pia had the pad on her knee.

"So Rothman and Yamamoto got all the symptoms straight off. It apparently wasn't the usual sequence where a patient gets one symptom initially and then another a few hours later. It happened like a bolt of lightning. As far as I know, that's not the way typhoid fever develops. Then the patients got the more ominous rebound tenderness by that evening. It's all so speeded up."

"You said this was a particularly virulent strain," George said.

"True. One of the zero-gravity strains. The alpha strain. But still."

"And you also said that Rothman's own sensitivity studies suggested that the strain should have been knocked out by the antibiotic he was given."

"That's right, the chloramphenicol and later the ceftriaxone."

"So what are you saying? Are you suggesting that it can't have been that strain of salmonella?"

"No, I'm not. The strain had to be involved since Koch's postulates were satisfied."

"Meaning that they managed to grow the culture from samples taken from the patient."

"Or by using more modern DNA techniques, yes."

"Pia," George complained, "you're confusing me. What's the bottom line here? What are you trying to say?"

"I suggested to Springer that there might be a second bacteria involved, a bacteria or a virus that was actually more virulent than the salmonella typhi and that was resistant to the antibiotics. It could explain the shockingly fast clinical course Rothman and Yamamoto experienced."

"What was Springer's reaction to your suggestion?"

"He went bonkers on me," Pia said with disgust. "That was the end of the interview because he went out and called in reinforcements, meaning the dean."

Pia put down her pad and pen back on the desk.

"So you think there might have been two bacteria involved," George said.

"Right at this moment that's the only thing I can think of. The clinical course was just too fast, especially in the face of two antibiotics given within hours of initial symptoms and known to handle salmonella. I know it's contrary to recognized diagnostic rules, the major one being that one should look for a single causative agent even with seemingly multiple symptoms. But it's the only way I can explain what we've seen with Rothman and Yamamoto."

She turned back to her desk and read from her notes.

"We have all the symptoms right here: fever, delirium, prostration, temperature elevation, sweating, low white cell count known to be associated with salmonella, all leading up to abdominal rebound tenderness. From intestinal perforation and finally death."

George got up from the bed and headed into the bathroom. Pia was overwhelming him. He was amazed she remembered Koch's postulates from second-year microbiology. He certainly didn't. He put some of the ice that was melting in her sink into a fresh towel, rolled it up and brought it to her desk. He exchanged it for the first one he'd made. Pia was staring at the paper, her back to him.

"Here's some more ice," he said.

Pia swiveled around in her chair, and George winced when he saw her jaw at such close quarters.

"How's it feel?"

"It's not too bad. A bit better with the ice."

Pia took the fresh towel and held it to her face. An image flashed into her mind: Rothman lying on his deathbed, sweating into his pillow, delirious . . . Suddenly she stared directly up into George's eyes with a fierce intensity that made George look away.

"The hair loss!" Pia said slowly, with emphasis. "What about the hair loss?"

40.

Pia got up from her chair, put the ice-filled towel down on the desk, and started pacing her room, circling George. First he'd been unnerved by the intensity of Pia's stare when she had her epiphany, whatever it was; now she was stalking around the room like a cat closing in on a mouse.

"What hair loss?" George questioned.

"Rothman's! Remember I saw there was

some hair on his pillow before we found the rebound tenderness."

"Yes, I remember. You pointed it out to the resident, and, as I remember, she suggested it might have been due to the chloramphenicol."

"Exactly," Pia said.

She stood still. "Can I use your computer?" Pia's laptop was old and slow; the year before George had invested in a new Dell with a much faster processor.

"Sure. Let's go!" George picked up the wet towel from Pia's desk and gestured toward her with it. Pia shook her head. George took the towel into the bathroom while Pia changed from her pajama pants into sweats. She also quickly downed more Advil.

Gathering up her notes and heading for the door, Pia paused and looked back. She'd experienced a flash of anxiety. Although her room was where she'd been attacked, she still felt safer there than outside. Her attackers were lurking out there somewhere. Perhaps they really were watching her, as they'd threatened. George sensed her trepidation and put an encouraging hand on Pia's shoulder and

squeezed lightly. They exchanged a reas-
suring glance. Pia breathed deeply and
walked out of the room, shutting off the
light as she went.

"Let's take the stairs," Pia said, and she
and George descended the four flights,
walked along the corridor, but then stopped
in front of George's door. Both had the
same thought: If they knew about George,
they probably knew his room number.

"What do you think?" he asked. It
wasn't crazy to imagine that the two men
might have it in their mind to pay George
a visit too.

"Now I think we're being paranoid," Pia
said.

"But as you correctly said, even paranoid people have real enemies. Wait there!"
George unlocked the door and pulled it
fully open. He and Pia were prepared to
flee if anything looked amiss. Nothing did.
George entered his room, making sure
nothing had been disturbed before throwing open the bathroom door. "All clear," he
said with a sigh of relief.

"Let's get to work," Pia said.

George booted up his laptop and
checked the wireless signal before giving

up his desk chair to Pia. He went and sat on the bed. His room was a mirror image of hers.

Pia quickly went online, typed "hair loss" and "chloramphenicol" into the search engine and scrolled through the results for a few minutes. "There's nothing that lists hair loss among chloramphenicol's side effects. Actually, there are some alternative healers who sell chloramphenicol to reverse hair loss. Wow, De Silva was so wrong when she said chloramphenicol might be the cause of the hair loss."

Pia continued surfing. "Springer attributed it to fever and stress," she said as she read. "It seems that stress can cause hair loss. But I don't think it could be involved in this case. I mean Rothman and Yamamoto were certainly being stressed with their fevers and all, but for stress to cause hair loss I think it has to be over a period of months, not hours."

Pia continued her search. George couldn't see the screen from his vantage point, but he could see the light flickering on Pia's face as page after page flashed by. Suddenly there was a steady light, and Pia leaned forward in her chair. "Yeah, here we are. Hair loss and stress. Yup, I was right." Pia read out loud: "'Unless the stressed patient is pulling his own hair out, severe stress merely changes the hair follicle from an active state to a resting state. The hair doesn't fall out immediately but rather over a period of months.'"

Pia looked over at George. "Clearly Springer's suggestion wasn't much better than De Silva's."

"So what are you thinking?"

"Since I've never heard of salmonella causing hair loss, we have to think of something else to explain it, bringing us back to the second-agent idea, like another bacteria or a virus. But if there was another microbe involved, it would have to be one whose clinical symptoms mimic typhoid fever because all the other symptoms were consistent with typhoid fever. Are you following me?"

"I think so."

"I'm saying that we have to come up with an agent that mimics typhoid fever symptomatically but which also causes hair loss and can kill in hours in the presence of chloramphenicol and possibly ceftriaxone. Of course, without access to the charts, I can't be sure they ever got the ceftriaxone, but for the sake of argument, let's assume they did."

"You know what I wish?" Pia said after a few minutes of silence. "I wish that we examined Yamamoto as well as Rothman. Just to be sure he was suffering from the same signs and symptoms."

"Maybe we can ask Dr. De Silva's opinion."

"I don't think she's going to want to hear from me. Let's keep going."

Pia looked up at the corkboard on the wall behind George's desk. A business card for a taxi service was tacked next to a picture of George's mother and grandmother. There was a postcard from Hungary alongside it. Suddenly Pia snapped around again.

"What are the usual causes of hair loss besides what I've mentioned?"

"This sounds like internal medicine rounds, which I'd like to forget. That was one venue where I did not shine in the slightest."

"Come on," Pia said. "What causes hair loss?"

"Er, hormonal changes, alopecia areata,

stress like you said." Pia motioned for George to come up with more. He thought harder.

"Dermatological diseases of the scalp, particularly cicatricial diseases. Wow, that's a good one. That's the kind of response that would have gotten me kudos on rounds. Trouble is I always choked up."

"What else?" Pia commanded. She waved her hand, indicating she wanted more.

"Okay, certain drugs."

Pia nodded and looked expectantly at George, as if she knew the answer and was waiting for him to get it. It was like a game of charades.

George became impatient, ready to give up before he remembered something else.

"What about chemotherapy and radiation?" George sounded uncertain. Sure, they caused hair loss, but what could be the relevance?

"Right on!" Pia exclaimed. "Radiation! You saw people undergoing radiation when you were on oncology during internal medicine."

George nodded.

"Chemotherapy and/or radiation destroys

the hair follicles and the hair falls out immediately."

"What are you getting at?" George noticed that Pia's face had brightened considerably.

"I said I was wondering if Rothman could have been infected with another bug besides the salmonella, another bug that was not sensitive to chloramphenicol or the third-generation cephalosporin he was given."

"Right, the ceftriaxone."

"I suddenly don't think there was another microbe," Pia said. "Damn it, George, you said it yourself, remember? You said they had to autopsy the bodies the same day the men died because they were 'hot.' I thought at the time it was a strange word to use, but I think you were more right than you knew. I don't think they were hot because they were full of bacteria. I think they might have been hot because of radiation."

41.

Laurie Montgomery had been sitting in her office at the Office of the Chief Medical Examiner catching up with an old friend, Detective Captain Lou Soldano, when the phone rang. She saw it was her boss, apologized, and took the call. She was soon rolling her eyes, and Lou smiled.

Laurie Montgomery had been back at the OCME for eleven months, since the harrowing events of the infamous Satoshi Machita case, involving both the New York mob and the Japanese Yakuza, which led to the kidnapping of her infant son, John Junior. The story had been plastered all over the media for several days as the details of the case unfolded. After JJ's rescue, Laurie had come back to work but only after she had found a live-in nanny, Paula, who immediately proved to be a godsend. With Paula looking after JJ, Laurie felt secure. Right now, her husband and fellow ME, Jack Stapleton, was working in the same building, and JJ was safe with Paula at the couple's home on 106th Street. It didn't hurt that she and her husband had friends like Detective Captain Lou Soldano either. Right after the kidnapping, he'd insisted on a twenty-four-hour security detail for the Stapleton home.

From Laurie's side of the conversation and from knowing Laurie's boss, Dr. Harold Bingham, Lou sensed he'd be in for a wait. He took his copy of the *New York Post* from his briefcase and flipped through it until he saw the story: IVY SPACE GERM DOCS DIE. He quickly reread the first few paragraphs. He had wanted to show the article to Laurie, which was one of the reasons he'd stopped by.

"Sorry, Lou," Laurie said, hanging up the phone. "That was Bingham."

"I assumed as much. No problem. Did you see this article?" He held up the paper.

"Yes, but not that one specifically. There was the same story in the *Times*."

"Crazy and scary at the same time. It says that two researchers at Columbia contaminated themselves in a lab with some virus grown in the space station or something. The bodies were supposedly brought here to OCME. Is this all true?"

"Most of it. But the contamination agent wasn't a virus. It was a bacteria called salmonella typhi that causes typhoid fever. Jack did both autopsies yesterday. Very sad. I understand they were stem cell researchers who were making huge strides growing human organs."

"That's what I understand," Lou said. "Anything unique about the autopsies? There were some wild theories about the deaths in the article. Apparently one of the guys was a big-deal researcher who was not particularly liked by his colleagues."

"Jack didn't mention anything other than that he was impressed with the pathology. He'd never seen an entire gut in both patients in such bad shape. Typhoid fever isn't usually so generalized. Anyway that was the case I was just talking to Bingham about. He expects there will be some political fallout. If there's a press conference scheduled, he wanted to give me a heads-up that he might want me to host it. He knows Jack hates doing it and isn't the most diplomatic."

Lou laughed because Jack was one of the most undiplomatic men he knew. "You guys make a good pair because you complement each other." Changing the subject, he said, "What about a bite of lunch today? Do you have time for a quick one?"

"I'm sorry, Lou, they're dropping like flies out there."

Lou laughed again. He was glad the public couldn't hear the black humor that was often engaged in within the OCME walls.

"I hear you."

Lou levered his stocky frame out of Laurie's chair, put his trench coat back on, and made his farewells.

42.

The first time George heard Pia's theory, he thought she had lost it for sure. She said she believed that Rothman and Yamamoto were murdered using a radioactive agent, polonium-210, that was masked by the salmonella bacteria they had also been given. George had sarcastically asked which James Bond movie she'd gotten that from, but Pia was, as ever, deadly serious.

"George, it's actually happened before so it's a copycat crime. Someone was actually murdered in this fashion. Truly. The man's name was Alexander Litvinenko, a Russian. He was killed in London in 2006. Don't you remember? It was all over the news."

"I don't remember," George admitted.

Pia waved George over to the desk so he could see several of the newspaper stories she had found online, then she filled him in on the basics of the case.

"Litvinenko was in the KGB, then the FSB, which is what replaced it. He fled Russia and was given political asylum in England. He wrote a couple of books that were critical of the Russian president, Putin. You'd think he would have been super-careful, knowing what he did. He meets these guys, ex-KGB like him, in a London hotel bar for tea. Within hours he's sick and hospitalized. After several days he's diagnosed with radiation poisoning, which is later figured out to be polonium-210. He gets progressively worse, since there was not a lot the doctors could do, and dies about three weeks later."

"Three weeks. That's a lot longer than Rothman and Yamamoto."

"Yeah, I know. But polonium's effects are dose-related. We don't know how much polonium was used and when Rothman and Yamamoto were poisoned."

We don't know if *they were poisoned,* thought George, but he kept it to himself. Pia was on a roll.

"So the Brits investigate and find out about the bar and the tea, and there was radiation all over the place, especially in the teapot. Ultimately it was proven that he died from deliberate poisoning. They did an autopsy and the pathologists had to wear hazmat suits. Litvinenko's GI tract was very hot, to use your word. The guy had to be buried in a lead-lined coffin."

"Okay, I can see why one spy might use something like this to kill another spy, but why use it on doctors? If you want to kill them, why go to all that trouble? Why not just shoot them?"

"That's the clever part. Whoever did this did not want anyone to know it was an assassination. They wanted it to appear like an accident. The symptoms of radiation poisoning are camouflaged by the salmonella: fever, prostration, delirium, GI symptoms, low white count. Everything's the same except the hair loss. They were counting on the fact that no one would think to look for this kind of agent because of the typhoid fever diagnosis. Polonium is unique in that it decays by only emitting alpha particles, which would only be detected if someone thought to look specifically for it, but nobody would because the diagnosis of typhoid was so obvious."

Pia was picking up steam again. It all seemed to fit.

"Nor would the alpha particles make anyone else sick, which obviously has been the case. Alpha particles can only travel about a centimeter, and they can be blocked by as little as a sheet of paper. It's only if the polonium-210 is breathed in or ingested that it's dangerous, and then it's *really* dangerous, especially in a large dose, which can be rapidly fatal. Even as little as a millionth of a gram can kill you."

Pia sat back in her seat with a look of triumph on her face. "What do you think, George?"

George was overwhelmed both by the amount of information Pia had thrown at him and by her enthusiasm. Things fit, but he couldn't help but wonder if Pia was getting ahead of herself. "You have to assume the hair loss had no other cause," George said. He thought a little more. "But I guess this would explain why the antibiotics didn't work. Or maybe they were working, but the radiation overpowered them."

"Exactly," Pia said. "It is diabolically fiendish. Whoever is involved is smart—probably a doctor or a scientist who knows a lot of medicine."

George thought about it some more. He started pacing the room.

"I guess it's possible," George said. He could see no insurmountable problems with the theory. "So let's tell the authorities, let them figure it out."

"No, we can't. We don't know who did it."

"I guess you have to assume that the guys who attacked you had something to do with it."

"No doubt, but this has to be a major conspiracy. You know what this stuff is used for? They use it to make firing mechanisms for nuclear weapons. No one admits to making it, although the major source is supposed to be Russia. I just read about it two minutes ago. So the FSB can just call someone and get it. But how do you get it in New York City? There has to be a lot of people involved. Serious people with access to this material. And I believe those guys when they warned me not to go to the police. I'm not going to the authorities till I have enough proof to go to the media at the same time."

"The media?"

"I told you, I don't trust 'the authorities.'" Pia made quote marks in the air with her fingers. "If I give this story to the newspapers, whoever is involved won't be able to bury it."

"So what proof do you need?"

Pia turned back to the computer and made another search.

"Okay! Polonium-210 has a half-life of a hundred and thirty-eight days, meaning that it takes a hundred and thirty-eight days for it to lose half of its radioactivity. So if that's what they used, there has to be some trace around someplace, either in the lab or in the rooms Rothman and Yamamoto occupied in the hospital. Even if someone was very careful giving it to them, there's bound to be some residue just like there was in London in 2006."

George joined Pia at the computer, looking over her shoulder. "How is polonium detected?"

"Here it is," Pia said, pointing at the screen. "Alpha particles can be detected with a Geiger counter. Pretty simple."

"Where are we going to get a Geiger counter?" George said. "Oh, let's use mine. It should be in the bottom drawer on your right."

"Very funny," Pia said. "Geiger counters are not all that uncommon, especially around a medical center like this. They must have them in Nuclear Medicine. We'll go over there and see if we can't borrow one."

"I couldn't help notice that you said 'we,'" George said. "So is this a formal invitation?"

"Of course it is," Pia replied.

"Well, thank you," George said. Actually there was no way he would have allowed Pia to go over to the hospital without him. He reached out and felt along Pia's jaw. "Maybe we should get you X-rayed while we're there. I know a technician who would do it as a favor."

Pia pushed his hand away. "I don't want to take the risk."

"All right, here's the plan," George said. "I'll help you look for a Geiger counter, but first I have to talk to my resident and come up with an excuse for not being around."

"Fine," Pia said. "I wouldn't mind a few minutes of rest. Whatever drug I was given has me feeling sleepy again. I could use a bit of rest while you take care of business. Do you mind if I just lie down here on your bed? Call me when you're ready." Pia moved from the desk chair over to the bed and lay down. She closed her eyes and let out a sigh. She was tired and wired at the same time.

George went over to her and, taking out his pocket light, made her open her eyes. He quickly checked pupillary light reaction. It was normal.

"Jesus, that's bright," she complained, turning her head to the side. "What the hell are you doing?"

"I'm just worried about a concussion," George said.

"That's a happy thought," Pia said.

"It's something to think about, especially if you're sleepy."

"Good point, but I think I'm fine, just tired."

"I'll go back to Radiology and make my excuses. I'll be right back. Wedge the chair under the door handle. Do you have your phone?"

Pia nodded.

"Make sure it's charged. My charger's on the desk. And call me if you need me."

George would have been far happier calling the police or renting a car and driving Pia as far out of the city as he could. But he'd come this far with her. He just had to cover himself, and he'd be clear to stay with her for as long as it took to resolve this thing. They'd get a Geiger counter and find the proof if it existed. Or they wouldn't find the proof, and Pia would have to drop this theory as she had all the others. Perhaps then she would quit sleuthing.

43.

Pia's brief sleep was interrupted by George knocking gently on his own door. She woke up with a start and recognized that she was in a room that was not her own. She sat up feeling like she had a hangover. All at once she realized where she was, and the whole previous night's experience came flooding back. Pia got up from the bed, swayed for a moment, and went to the door.

"Who is it?"

"It's George." Pia took the chair away from under the door handle. She then hurried into George's compulsively clean bathroom and checked out her face, wincing when she touched her bruised left jawbone and wincing again when she noticed for the first time that she also had the makings of a good black eye. Reflexively, she closed her uninjured eye to make sure she could see normally. She also examined her cut lip, and then wiped away a bit of blood encrusted in her nostrils. Then she began to fill the sink to wash her face.

"What time is it?" she called through the open door. Her mind was clearing, and the dizziness she'd experienced when first getting off George's bed had totally disappeared.

"It's about two, a little after," said George. "You want something to eat?"

"No! There's no time. We have to get moving. The longer we wait, the less chance we have of finding anything. As we learned, polonium has a relatively short half-life and you can just wash it off normally, like dirt."

"So you're sticking to the polonium

idea?" George had half hoped Pia would have cooled to her rather outlandish scenario by the time he got back.

"Absolutely. It fits so well. You agreed it fit, didn't you?"

"It seems to," George said. "Provided we can't think of another reason for the hair loss. But the practicalities seem so daunting. And you're sure there was hair loss, right?"

"Oh God, yes, George, I'm sure. You saw it yourself."

George looked at Pia as she emerged from the bathroom. She had an intent expression on her face. It seemed that Pia was pleased with the power of her deductive reasoning, or else with the elegance of the plot to murder her mentor.

"Do you have any idea how hard this must have been to pull off?" she said. "It makes the Kennedy assassination look easy."

"I think Oswald acted alone."

"Okay, bad example. This has to be a sizable conspiracy, with a number of people involved. Once we confirm the polonium, I can't let the authorities spin the story, which they will. I need to make sure my version of the story, which is the truth, gets out."

"But if there's proof, the police will protect you."

"Bullshit. It's the police I'm most afraid of. Listen, the more I think about it, the more I think it has to have been other researchers or doctors. The science behind it is impressive. I mean, it had to be someone with a medical background who thought all this through. Otherwise, as you said, why not just shoot them?" Pia stopped herself.

"I'm jumping the gun. We've got to look for radiation left in the lab. If it's going to be anyplace, that's where it will be, I'm sure. We need that Geiger counter. But let's make a quick detour back to my room. I need to dig out some concealer. The fact that I look like I got run over is going to raise some eyebrows."

"Let's make it quick," George said. "I've only managed to wrangle a couple more hours. I have to be back in the Radiology Department for an important lecture at four o'clock."

Pia and George were able to borrow a Geiger counter from a resident in the department of nuclear medicine with ease. It was an out-of-commission machine awaiting recycling that was actually better at detecting alpha particles than the newer models. With the detector in hand, they hustled over to Rothman's lab to check for any leftover radiation.

Once at the lab's outer door they hesitated. "The only person I'd rather not run into is Spaulding," Pia said. "He's the only one who might cause us trouble. I never got the impression that any of the other technicians liked me much, but I can't imagine they would physically stop us."

"Want me to duck in and ask if he's around?" George questioned.

"Good idea," Pia responded.

It took George less than a minute. When he reappeared he said that the secretary told him Arthur Spaulding was taking a late lunch.

"Lucky us," Pia said. "Let's do it."

The pair entered the lab with Pia in the lead. Marsha Langman looked up. Pia said she was just coming by to get some personal items. Marsha shrugged and went back to her work, whatever that was.

Pia made a beeline for the biosafety

unit. They quickly donned protective clothing. They were in a hurry and didn't want to be interrupted. Pia wanted to start in the unit because it was there that Rothman and Yamamoto had spent the entire morning on the fateful day, as well as the day before.

The Geiger counter was a small yellow box about the size of a large flashlight, with a handle on top. Pia held the main instrument in her left hand and ran the sensor, much like a microphone, over the bench surfaces. The machine made a slight crackling sound from background radiation every few seconds. To Pia's chagrin, they found nothing, even under the hood itself.

As they removed their protective clothing they didn't talk. Emerging back into the lab, they detoured to Pia's small office for Marsha's benefit. Pia had said she was there for some personal items so it was a command performance. As per usual, O'Meary was still there, half up in Pia's ceiling space. He poked his head down when he heard the students enter.

"Miss Grazdani, you back? My God. What happened to your face?"

Pia said nothing.

"Good news. I found the short after all this time. It was between here and the doctor's office. We'll be out of here today. Sorry about the inconvenience."

Pia ignored him.

"Is that one of those Geiger counters?"

"We did some radioisotope labeling in here," Pia said. "We're just checking the place is clean. Which it is."

"How does that thing work, then?"

"Look it up online. Like I did."

It made George uncomfortable that Pia was being so short with this guy. As his family was blue-collar, George felt a kinship with people like maintenance workers.

Disappointed at not finding any contamination in the biosafety unit, Pia was beginning to feel a big letdown. Yet there was one other place she wanted to check: Rothman's office. Besides the biosafety unit and the organ bath unit, that was the only other place where both Rothman and Yamamoto spent any time. The problem was Marsha and her guard-dog mentality. Even with Rothman gone, she suspected Marsha would be Marsha.

As Pia and George returned to the lab proper, Pia was running through her mind possible ways to handle Marsha. Luckily the problem solved itself. Marsha was no longer sitting at her desk. Pia guessed and hoped she'd taken a late lunch like Spaulding.

With Marsha no longer standing guard, Pia and George hustled into Rothman's inner office. Inside, there had obviously been some packing going on because scattered around were open cardboard boxes half full of books and papers. Pia ran the probe around the desk, the shelving behind the desk, the couch, and the coffee table where Rothman's guests, usually journalists, would sit and hope that they would be the one to breach Rothman's famous guard. They were inevitably disappointed. Next they tried Rothman's private bathroom, which his celebrity status had afforded him; no other lab had a bathroom like this. But the Geiger counter stayed mostly silent except for the background crackle, just like in the biosafety unit.

Pia almost forgot about it but there was one more room—not so much a room as a storage area, where Rothman used to keep supplies scientific and secretarial. The place was stacked with toilet paper and paper towels, cases of beakers and test tubes, reams of paper, and old files. And here also was Rothman's beloved Nespresso machine. Well, maybe, thought Pia. Just maybe.

There were a few wayward clicks from the Geiger counter next to the coffee and cappuccino maker that made Pia's pulse pick up speed. Next to the coffeemaker was a dish towel, folded in half and carefully spread out in a small space between the coffeemaker and the coffee fixings themselves. The towel was supporting four white porcelain coffee cups: two espresso size and two regular size. They were sitting upside down. There were a few more clicks as Pia ran the probe over the bottom of the two regular coffee cups. Then she held the counter in her left hand and turned the cups over. She put the probe into one cup, then another. There was definite activity. It wasn't off the chart but there was more activity in the cups than in the rest of the lab.

"They got Litvinenko with his tea," Pia

said excitedly. "Maybe they used the coffee here. It would explain how they both got hit at the same time and no one else was affected."

"Doesn't sound like much radiation. You think it's significant?"

"It's not much, but it is registering alpha particles. The cups were probably washed but there's still something left. Anyway it's definitely significant. Let's get out of here."

Pia took one of the coffee cups and held it gingerly by the handle. She took a padded envelope, slipped the cup inside, and put it in the reusable shopping bag in which she'd brought the Geiger counter.

George and Pia reversed their steps and emerged into the main part of the lab. Unfortunately they were in for a surprise. Marsha had apparently not gone for a late lunch, and Spaulding had returned from his. Both of them, with indignant expressions, blocked their way. Spaulding in particular had his hands on his hips and glared at Pia. "How dare you!" he said haughtily. "I told you not to come back here. And what are you doing with that?" He pointed at the Geiger counter.

Pia motioned for George to follow her.

Her intention was not to engage them in conversation. She started to skirt Spaulding, but he grabbed her arm. Protectively, George moved to get in between them.

"It's all right, George," Pia said in a calm voice. "Arthur, let go of my arm or I'll file a complaint with the medical center authorities for sexual harassment."

Spaulding let go of Pia's arm. "Whose Geiger counter is that? Does it belong to this lab?" He was sputtering.

"Don't worry, Arthur, we signed it out from the appropriate department."

"But what are you using it for in my lab? I demand you tell me."

"It's a bullshit detector, Arthur. Oh, look." Pia held the sensor up to Arthur's face and it crackled with its background noise. "It appears to be working just fine after all."

Pia pushed past Spaulding and shot Marsha an indifferent look before leaving the office.

44.

George was relieved to get away from Spaulding and the lab unscathed and hoped their trespass wouldn't be communicated to Bourse. He hustled to catch up with Pia and found her waiting for an elevator.

"Third strike you're out with that guy, and you're at oh-and-two. Now you really should stay away from him."

"That's okay," said Pia, "I have no reason to go back to the lab. We picked up some clicks from the coffee cups, but it was hardly what I was hoping for. I don't know if that's going to be conclusive enough. We need more evidence."

"I was worried you were going to challenge Spaulding about the freezer log."

"I thought of it. He's such an ass. He has no authority to bar me from anywhere. I have no idea if what we found in the storage facility has any relevance whatsoever. If someone used a sample of salmonella from the freezer to infect Rothman and Yamamoto, there's no way we're really going to know."

"So do you really think Spaulding had something to do with Rothman's death?"

"If he did, he was a very small part of something larger. He's not smart enough to think that up all by himself."

Pia thought about what that might imply, about who might possibly be involved if there was a broad conspiracy. If Spaulding had been recruited, anyone could be a threat to her, a thought that made her shudder. She felt extraordinarily vulnerable, as much as or more than anytime during her childhood. As difficult as it was, she just had to keep her nerve and find some more evidence.

"George, can I stay in your room tonight? I don't want to be alone."

"Of course you can," George said. He was pleased she was asking. He only wished the circumstances were different.

When they reached the street, George expected Pia to head back to the dorm. Instead she accompanied him toward the hospital. It was raining and the wind was blowing sideways. People were moving along with their heads down, collars turned up against the cold.

"So you're not satisfied with the readings from the coffee cups?" George said. "You don't think it's enough to go to the media with?"

"I really don't think so. The few clicks we heard might not be that uncommon. I really don't know. The cups obviously were rinsed out, I think, but not scrubbed clean. I want to check the infectious disease ward. The killer may have been able to clean up after himself at the lab, but they wouldn't have been able to get onto the ward. Unless they have people on a cleaning crew."

Which was entirely possible, thought Pia.

"So that's where we're going?" George asked. He checked his watch. He still had time before the lecture he had to attend.

"Yes."

They reached the ward and quickly saw the futility of the mission. There were new patients in the rooms that had been occupied by Rothman and Yamamoto. An infectious disease ward had to be kept spotless because of the nature of the illnesses and infections treated there. The hospital was always aggressive with its general precautions, here even more so.

After a couple of minutes of scouting around, Pia looked at her watch.

"We're wasting our time here. Let's go back to the morgue."

They took the elevator down to the basement this time, taking the approved route. In daytime, there was slightly more activity than they had found on their visit the night before, when the place was presided over by the mortuary diener from central casting. The place itself had gained no luster. Without windows it could be day or night, still bleak and decrepit. There were several quite normal-looking men in their fifties whose job it was to handle the comings and goings of the corpses. They were helpful, seemingly appreciating a visit from live people. Pia and George asked them if they remembered handling Rothman's and Yamamoto's bodies. They did, because there had been quite a bit of fuss, including a warning about the possibility of typhoid and instructions about general precautions.

"We disinfected the body bags on the outside after the bodies were put inside," the first man explained. "Of course we used full precautions the whole time."

Pia and George could see no ID tags on the men and thought it prudent not to offer their own names.

"So which gurneys did you use? And were they treated afterward?"

"Sure they were treated," the man said. "And they're still where they were treated."

"Do you mind if I take a look?"

The attendant took the two students to another old autopsy room. This one had a special ventilation system because it was used for "dirty," or decomposing, cases. Pia proceeded to run the radiation detector around the gurneys, but she found nothing.

"What are you looking for, exactly?" the diener asked.

"One of the patients had had radioactive isotope therapy," Pia said, thinking quickly. "We want to make sure there wasn't any leakage. Which there hasn't been, so thank you."

As Pia and George made their way back to the elevator, George complimented Pia on her quick thinking in reference to the radioactive isotope idea.

"I had to come up with something. Maybe I'll use the same story when I go to the ME's office." Then she added, "Nix that! I couldn't get away with it with a medical examiner. From the autopsy they would already know neither of the men had cancer."

Pia pondered again. "I know. I'll say that Rothman and Yamamoto were using a radioactive alpha emitter in their research, and we want to be sure they didn't contaminate themselves with it as well as contracting the salmonella. I'll tell them that it's a safety issue."

"Sounds good," said George.

By now they were inside the hospital lobby.

"I have to have something to eat before I go downtown. The ME's office closes at five, I think, but I'm going to faint if I don't eat something. I don't even know if I ate anything yesterday. I know I haven't today. How are you with time?"

"I've got a few more minutes before my lecture."

They went to the hospital cafeteria. It was busy, even at off-hours like this, as illness and its treatment didn't operate on a convenient nine-to-five schedule. Staff, patients, and visitors alike had to grab something to eat when they could. Pia got something substantial while George grabbed a coffee and a cookie.

"So," George said, "what about revisiting the idea of going to the police and telling them about the clicks we got with the Geiger counter? I just can't believe it's a large conspiracy. Even if it was murder with polonium, I'm sure the explanation is going to be something much more banal. Something we haven't thought of. I don't know, perhaps he had gambling debts?"

"I couldn't disagree more. If it was polonium, it would have to be a high-level operation of some kind. Polonium is impossible to get. It would mean there would have to have been intense planning for weeks—months, even. There has to be powerful people involved, there has to be. I essentially *lived* inside a conspiracy for years. I told you, George, if you saw what I've seen, you'd know people are capable of anything."

George was aware that a couple of other diners, people he didn't recognize, were looking over at them from other tables. Pia's makeup couldn't conceal all her bruises, especially in the harsh fluorescent light of the cafeteria. George leaned in toward her and lowered his voice.

"So what do you intend to do exactly before you give up on this thing?"

"There's only one more place to check for significant radiation—the bodies at the OCME. If there is none or I can't get in to check, then I'll give up my investigation. Is that good enough?"

"How are you going to get in the door at the ME office?" George asked, remembering their conversation the previous evening with the pathology resident.

"I don't know that yet," she said, with a

touch of irritation. "If I just tell them what I believe, they'll think I'm crazy. 'Remember those research guys from Columbia that were brought in here? Well, I think someone put polonium in their coffee. . . .' I may go with the alpha particle emitter idea I mentioned. I don't know. I'll see how the land lies. I'm just going to have to wing it."

"Maybe you should just go and hang out in your room. Hold off on going to the medical examiner's for today. You've been running around like crazy and you got beat up last night, for Christ's sake. I can't go with you this afternoon, but perhaps we can go together in the morning?"

"Tomorrow's Saturday. I have no idea if the ME's office is even open. I don't know how long they keep the bodies there, either. I would imagine the office encourages families to arrange to take their relatives to the funeral homes as quickly as possible. Plus, if we go tomorrow, they're likely to be short-staffed. They'll probably say, 'Come back Monday.' And I just can't sit around. I have to know."

"You're probably right about Saturdays," George said. "But—"

"No, George, I'm going today. You go to

class. There's no way I can get in trouble at the OCME."

"You're very resourceful," George said with a wry smile.

Pia ignored the comment. "I'll leave now. Would you mind hanging on to this coffee cup? I'll keep the Geiger counter and hope I need it."

George took the bag. "Not at all. We'll meet up as soon as you get back." He watched a focused Pia leap up and lift her cafeteria tray. "And be careful! Try to stay out of trouble!"

Pia merely glowered at him before leaving.

George watched her wend her way among the tables, deposit her tray at the window, and then leave. The idea occurred to him to call the police now that Pia was safely out of sight. But he knew if he did that, whatever the outcome, Pia would never talk to him again. He was certain that she would consider it an act of betrayal.

Tossing back the remains of his coffee, George got to his feet. At least he was going to be on time for the lecture.

PART III

45.

BELMONT SECTION OF THE BRONX
NEW YORK CITY
MARCH 25, 2011, 3:28 P.M.

Aleksander Buda ended the call on his cell phone and held the device in his hand, then used his spatula-like index finger to tap the end-call button. There was now a problem in an operation that had gone so smoothly up to now, and he hated problems. Problems gave him terrible heartburn. He found the container of different-colored antacid tablets he always carried, took a handful, and chewed them quickly, one after another. Buda was fifty-something—fifty-what he didn't know for sure, because his family had left Albania with a few pots and pans and a little money but no documentation indicating when he was born. Over time, first in Italy and then in the United States, he had acquired the paper trappings of the immigrant, including a date of birth in 1958, but he had no idea if it was true.

Buda wasn't a big man, perhaps five-nine, but he had close-cropped hair with a scar that ran into his hairline on the right side of his broad face and enough prison tattoos on his arms, should he care to show them, to make anyone think twice about approaching him. Buda dressed unobtrusively, today in a tan long-sleeved shirt and jeans and sneakers. One might imagine he actually was a handyman for a group of East Side co-ops, work he showed up for every now and again, rather than what he really was: the head of a crew in the Albanian mob.

Buda's crew, or clan, was less hierarchically organized than a Cosa Nostra family, and leadership was often fluid and based strictly on results. Through a combination of caution and brutality, Buda's power had remained unchallenged for years. The members of the crew shared their compatriot's reputation for ruthlessness and violence, gained over more than twenty-five years of aggressive criminal activity. The Albanians had come late on the New York scene and they had been keen to make up for lost time. They took low-level positions in Italian organizations only to rise up and challenge the longer-established Mafia stalwarts.

In Europe, Albanian groups established a strong presence in hard and soft drug trafficking, dominating the heroin trade in many countries, running the raw materials from Afghanistan through Turkey to Albania. Processed heroin and other drugs could then be distributed anywhere in the world, through hubs like the terminals at Port Newark, New Jersey. Heroin was just one business the crews were involved in. They also had interests in such prosaic activities as extortion, loan-sharking, and illegal gambling. Aleksander Buda had lieutenants working such operations so he could keep a low profile and take on more lucrative projects, such as the one he was working now, the one with a problem.

Buda was very aware that Albanian crews had developed a profile. One based in Queens had been taken down by the FBI a few years before; another in Staten Island was broken up in 2010. There were now more than two hundred thousand Albanians in the New York metro area, maybe three hundred thousand. The vast majority, all save a couple of hundred, were hardworking and law-abiding. Buda and his men drifted in and out of this Albanian diaspora, hiding among them in plain sight. The mob groups were clannish and secretive, hypersensitive to any kind of insult, and quick to use violence for the sake of vengeance. Under the Albanian code of *besa*, a man's word was his bond and a handshake was a cast-iron seal. Buda had an agreement to complete this task, and he realized he was going to have to expose some of his men to take care of this particular problem. And doing work in public was another thing that made him nervous.

After Jerry Trotter made his proposal to Edmund three weeks previously, it had taken Edmund two days to call the number Trotter gave him. Ten, fifteen times he had told himself that he wouldn't call, that he'd throw the piece of paper in the fireplace and forget all about it. Other times, he convinced himself that this was a test of his resolve set by Jerry, that if he called the number, Jerry himself would answer the phone. But at times, usually in the dead of night, when he sat by himself in his study drinking whiskey, Edmund ran through what such a call would be like to make. Say this guy actually was a killer for hire; how do you introduce yourself to someone like that? What do you say? He figured that if you called on business like this, you didn't use your own phone.

Edmund finally called the number from a pay phone in a Laundromat on Second Avenue in the Sixties in Manhattan, a busy spot without any obvious security cameras trained on it. Edmund steeled himself, inserted his money, and dialed the number. Someone picked up but didn't speak, and Edmund ran through his rehearsed lines.

"Hello. I got your number from a friend. I have a proposition for you. This isn't a joke."

Edmund didn't say any more; the phone line quickly went dead.

An hour later, Edmund called again, from the same pay phone.

"Can we meet somewhere? I think you'll want to hear what I have to say—"

Click.

The next day, on the fourth attempt, at ten in the morning, a thickly accented voice said, "Call in an hour. Pay phone bank at Grand Central. Main-level concourse."

Edmund did as he was told.

"Take six train to Morrison Avenue, exit platform north side and wait."

Edmund was at a point of no return. All he'd done was make a few phone calls, but now he was going to meet someone he knew was a killer. He looked at the commuters walking through Grand Central, ordinary people like him. If he went ahead with this, he would no longer be ordinary. In the recent endless days and sleepless nights, Edmund had weighed the possible costs of doing what Jerry demanded and doing nothing. If he failed to act, he'd be ruined financially and personally. But Jerry's terrible scheme gave him a chance.

Another thought had occurred to Edmund

and was proving impossible to ignore. These doctors were destroying his business. It was their fault he was in this position, and he was damned if he was going to let them get away with it.

Edmund rode the subway north to a section of the Bronx he'd never visited before. He got off the train on a windswept elevated platform. There was hardly anyone else around at eleven in the morning, just two men who had alighted at the station—one who had sat in Edmund's car, another from the car behind his. Edmund left the station, walked down to the street, and stood by the exit. He checked his phone, and crossed and recrossed the street, looking for some sign of life.

Suddenly, a dark blue panel van drew up, and the back doors opened. A voice from within told Edmund to get in, and he did. The van drove away, and immediately Edmund's arms were seized, tape was secured over his mouth, and a cloth bag was roughly forced over his head. His body was patted down, hands thrust into his armpits and groin. Then his clothes were removed, all of them, and he was left naked, bound, and gagged on the floor of the van, first as it rattled along the street and then, for what seemed like an age, parked someplace.

"Okay, Mr. Edmund Mathews, rich banker man from Greenwich, how did you get that phone number?" The voice came from the front of the van somewhere.

Edmund tried to talk but his mouth was taped shut. He mumbled and the voice said, "How rude of me. Let the man speak."

The tape was ripped away crudely, and Edmund reeled from the shock.

"A friend of mine gave it to me. He wouldn't say where he got it."

"We'll see. So what you want?"

Edmund laid out what he wanted. It didn't take long, but he had to explain a couple of times the need for using polonium to effect the killings.

"Okay, this is what we do. You come to Middletown Road subway station, eleven tomorrow. Bring a deposit for me. As a gesture of goodwill. Say, fifty thousand dollars in Ben Franklin notes. Nonrefundable. Give the man back his clothes."

Edmund's arms and legs were freed, and he dressed quickly. The van moved again and stopped after a few minutes, and the doors opened. Edmund got out in a bleak parking lot behind an abandoned building. He figured out where he was, less than a half-mile from where he had been picked up, and he took the subway back to Manhattan.

More than at any point throughout the whole ordeal, Edmund's flight reflex was strongest that night. If he called the FBI, surely he could give them Jerry and this guy, whoever he was, and at least he would be free from this crazy plot. But he wouldn't be free of LifeDeals and Gloria Croft and his own imminent destruction. The Statistical Solutions data had finally come in, and merely underscored what Russell and Edmund already knew. Their model was shot to pieces the moment regenerative medicine became a reality. His need to stand and fight kicked in.

Edmund traveled again to the Bronx, and was again driven away in a van, this time of a different color. Again, he was bound and stripped, but his clothes were returned more quickly this time and his mouth wasn't taped, a small mercy for which Edmund was grateful. He could feel that the envelope with the $50,000 was no longer in his jacket pocket.

"Thank you for the money," the same voice said. "A more cautious man would throw you out of the van now and be happy with good takings for one day's work. But I read about you, Mr. Mathews, and I am intrigued. Then I read about the people you say you want to die and I think, *What are they doing? I don't understand, I am a stupid peasant.* Then I think, *This guy must be for real.* I don't know why but I do. I also think this is a very expensive idea. Someone has to go to Russia, buy this radioactive material from some very bad men and not get caught. They have to give this material to the marks, plus the bacteria, and not get caught. We can do it, but not for one million dollars."

"How much, then?"

"Two. And a half."

"Jesus."

"Mr. money guy, I see where you live, how much money you make. You are not doing a trade, here, on Wall Street. I don't negotiate—that is the price. And tomorrow, the price is more."

"Okay."

"Sorry, speak up, please."

"Okay," said Edmund.

The two men met once more, three days later. Edmund told Russell he needed a huge amount of cash but not what it was for. Russell asked once, and Edmund bit his head off so Russell just did what he was told. It took Russell two and a half days to assemble one and a half million dollars from various business and personal accounts. Edmund packed it into a large baseball equipment bag and drove to the address he had been given on the phone. It was the same parking lot where he had been let out the first day. Once more, Edmund got in the van and went through the same degrading procedure.

"I guess you trust me," the voice said. "I now have one-point-five-five million dollars from you and I haven't done shit. But I am a businessman, and I will fulfill my end of the deal."

The man gave instructions for paying the rest of the money once the job was finished. The job would be done sometime in the next month. Edmund said nothing.

"But one more thing first. Something I

need to know, otherwise I am afraid I won't be able to go ahead."

Edmund said nothing.

"Who gave you my phone number? Was it your partner, Mr. Russell Lefevre?"

"No."

"So, who was it?"

Edmund was silent.

"I really want to know."

So Edmund told him.

"Okay, thank you. Now release Mr. Mathews."

From the front seat of the van, a man turned back toward Edmund. He was wearing dark glasses and a baseball cap but Edmund could see a livid scar on the man's forehead running up toward his scalp. The man was holding out his right hand.

"Shake my hand, then we have a deal."

The men shook hands, and Edmund heard nothing more, until March 25.

Aleksander Buda thought some more about the information he'd just received, and with his phone still in his hand, he called Edmund Mathews.

"Yesterday we followed to the letter the course of action you recommended, and it didn't work. I didn't think it would. Someone I have on-site tells me he saw her going around today with a Geiger counter, her and that guy she hangs out with. You know what that means? It means someone's seen through your brilliant plan."

"Shit."

"Yes, shit. As in what we are standing in up to our knees. Unless we do something right now, it's going over our heads."

The conversation was much too specific for Buda's liking. But he felt he had to get the okay from the banker and make sure Edmund realized the price had gone up. The job itself shouldn't be difficult, the girl was hardly being discreet, but he had a troublesome task to take care of. When he heard the girl's name was Grazdani, he paused. It sounded Albanian to him, and he wanted to be very sure that killing an Albanian girl wasn't going to step on anyone's toes. He didn't want to be the cause of a blood feud like there'd been in the 1990s. He'd have to snatch her, hold her, and put feelers out to see if there were any Grazdanis in the crews in the neighboring areas. But what were the odds?

"Okay," Edmund said finally, feeling the

same numbness he had felt when he agreed to the deal in the first place.

"There are two of them, actually," Buda was saying. "It will be another ten percent."

"Ten percent of the total or the balance?"

"Ah, ever the money guy," said Buda. "The total."

Buda ended the call and summoned Prek Vllasi and Genti Hajdini to his office in a trailer parked inside a low-ceilinged warehouse. Buda dressed his senior lieutenants down severely in Albanian.

"You were useless last night. She wasn't put off at all. Didn't you do anything to her?"

"You see," Genti said to Prek, "we should have done her when we had the chance. Like I said last night, knocking her around wasn't going to be enough." He turned to Buda. "She's a tough bitch."

"I can see that," Buda said. Genti had been nursing a black eye all day. "Now this whole thing is about to go down the drain because of her. She knows what happened, God knows how. You gotta get back over there right now and take out her boyfriend and grab her off the street."

"Boyfriend?" Prek said. "What boyfriend? You mean the kid she was hanging around with last night? Unless he's with her when we grab her, I don't know if we'd recognize him."

"He's the guy with his tongue in her ear!" Buda snapped. He was steaming, but he quickly realized Prek was right to be cautious. Killing the wrong man would be counterproductive.

"I'll get a picture of him from the medical school database and send it to your phones. His name is . . . George Wilson," he said, referring to a note.

"And remember, pick up the Grazdani woman," Buda said. "And don't touch her, you animal, unless she's not related to anyone important, in which case she's all yours. Understand, Genti? Word is she was in Rothman's lab just a few minutes ago, poking around. Take her to the summer house and call me when you get there. And take Neri Krasnigi with you. It seems like the two of you can't handle her."

Krasnigi was relatively new to the crew, younger, inexperienced, and more vicious than either Genti or Prek. The two men were affronted by the order but didn't show it.

As the men exited the trailer, Buda shouted after them, "Use the white van for the pickup and then dump it. Take the blue one to the house."

Prek gave a thumbs-up sign and walked away.

Prek and Genti found Neri Krasnigi sitting in a battered old armchair at the back of the warehouse reading a German *Playboy*. Prek told him to follow, and the three men got into the white van. The plates were obscured with what appeared to be dried mud but which was actually cleverly painted plaster.

As they pulled out into Lorillard Place, heading quickly toward East Fordham Road, Prek filled Neri in on the afternoon's operation. What they had in mind to pull off was a pair of Albanian specialties: a blindingly fast hit and snatch, in broad daylight if necessary. In the Albanian mind-set, it didn't matter. Neri was excited; this would be his first official hit. They checked that their automatic pistols were loaded. Duct tape, blankets, balaclavas, two Columbia University Medical Center police uniforms, and a can of Ultane, a volatile, rapid-induction anesthetic, were piled into the back of the van.

The white van pulled into a garage and Genti got out and climbed into a blue van. Starting it up, he followed Prek in the white van. They parked the blue van near the George Washington Bridge and set out again in the white van toward Columbia University Medical Center.

46.

COLUMBIA UNIVERSITY MEDICAL CENTER
NEW YORK CITY
MARCH 25, 2011, 3:54 P.M.

Unbeknownst to George Wilson, at the same time he was thinking about contacting the police, Pia was too. Not seriously, but it had crossed her mind. It was certainly true that if an investigation needed to be done, they were far more capable and could turn over rocks she couldn't even approach. But then there was the issue of what she would tell them. Would she say that she'd picked up a few lonely alpha particles in a coffee cup and thought it was evidence of a grand conspiracy? Of course not. There was no doubt in her mind that she would not be taken seriously, which ultimately would increase her vulnerability rather than decrease it. The police would think she was crazy and probably call the dean, believing they were acting in her best interest. Of course, going to the police had another downside. They might be tempted to look her up in their computer, and even though bad stuff about her teenage years was not supposed to be there, it might be. No, she would not go to the police. Instead, as planned, she'd go to the OCME in a final attempt to figure out the affair. If that didn't yield overwhelming evidence of wrongdoing, she'd give up, just as she'd told George.

When Pia had reached the street coming from the hospital cafeteria, her intention had been to head down to Broadway to take the subway downtown. But feeling the temperature and noticing that the rain had increased, she decided to take a quick detour back to the dorm for a better coat and an umbrella. She knew the subway would get her only so close to the OCME and that she'd end up walking. How far, she had no idea.

In the dorm she hesitated outside her door, just as she and George had done outside his earlier. Being attacked in her room the previous night made her paranoid. She didn't know how the men had gotten into her room.

Repeating what she and George had done, after silently unlocking her door, she opened it suddenly, prepared to flee if needed. She also carefully checked her bathroom to make certain it was empty. It was.

With a warmer, rain-resistant coat and an umbrella, Pia set off on her way to the subway. She had put the Geiger counter in another shopping bag to make it easier to carry. She checked the time. It was almost four, so if she was going to make it to the OCME before it closed, she had to get moving.

Walking quickly in the darkening day, Pia passed the Black building. She went another fifty feet along West 168th Street when she saw two hospital security police up the street, walking toward her. She stopped. She couldn't see them well in the fading light with mist rising off the pavement, but she could see their uniforms well enough. They were the same uniforms her attackers had worn the previous night. To make matters worse, they seemed approximately the same height and build.

Fighting the urge to flee, Pia stopped dead in her tracks. Ahead to her right was a porte cochere for the hospital. Pia considered racing to it and into the hospital where she could vanish into the crowds, but she'd hesitated too long. She'd have to pass the security guards before she got to the entrance.

She looked behind her and saw there were surprisingly few people on the street. She thought about dashing back to the Black building but thought that if the men wanted to catch her, they probably could before she got inside. Turning back around, she eyed the approaching guards. They seemed to be staring intently at her. She froze, suddenly remembering a similar scene imbued with the same fear and dread.

She was thirteen at the time and had been at the Hudson Valley Academy for Girls for maybe a year. The stress of constantly being on guard, the fear of being attacked at any time, wore on Pia. A couple of times she'd cracked and tried to run away from the school, and she did so again. This time she got lost and had to spend a harrowing moonless night in the woods surrounding the school grounds. The night wore on and on and hummed with threat. Pia tried and failed to make her way back to the academy in the hope of breaking back in before anyone realized she was gone.

Pia had spent the hours before dawn slumped against the trunk of a tree, dozing fitfully. She arose at first light and walked east toward the sun until she found herself on an unfamiliar street winding downhill. It was then that she saw two policemen in the middle distance. They were implacably and threateningly walking toward her, staring at her unblinkingly, silent like automatons. Pia froze, as if by standing as still as possible they might not see her. When they were within ten feet of her, they parted, one walking to her left, one to her right. Perhaps they hadn't seen her! Perhaps they weren't looking for her at all! But when the men came alongside her, they suddenly lunged at her, roughly grabbing an arm each. Once again she was a prisoner of the state, totally vulnerable.

Now the same feelings flooded Pia's brain. The security guards were coming at her with the same silent intensity, drilling her with their beady eyes. Pia stood stock-still and closed her eyes. Just like the Eden Falls policemen, the men parted right in front of her and went on either side . . . and moved on. The man to her left brushed past her upper body, then turned and said something—was he apologizing or saying "Get out of the way," or making a lewd remark? Pia didn't know. She breathed out with relief, unaware that she'd been holding her breath.

Pia was embarrassed by the depth of her paranoia. She shivered and a chill ran down her spine. The unnerving episode had taken only seconds. She wiped perspiration from her forehead and then hurried on toward Broadway. By the time she passed the hospital entrance, her breathing and pulse were almost back to normal. On Broadway she relaxed further as there were significantly more people. She felt safer there—she was safer there. In the near distance loomed the subway entrance swallowing pedestrians like an insatiable monster. A gust of wind blew the umbrella she was holding almost out of her hand, and she fought with it for a moment to get it under control. Once she did, she closed it and hurried forward to the stairs.

47.

Holy shit, there she is!" Genti shouted, pointing, as Prek made the right-hand turn from Broadway onto 168th Street running between the Columbia University Medical Center on the left and the Armory on the right. Genti's glance had alighted on the woman carrying a shopping bag when the wind blew her umbrella, threatening to lift her into the air. He saw her face clearly, and it was the Grazdani girl, no doubt about it. She was walking quickly toward the subway entrance. "Stop!" Genti shouted as Prek slowed.

"Who's with her?"

"No one, I didn't see no one," shouted Genti. "Let me out. Wait for me here."

Genti, who was riding shotgun, leaped from the van the moment Prek was able to stop. He ran after Pia, who he guessed was maybe twenty yards ahead of him, making her way toward the subway entrance. As he ran, Genti checked that the gun was secure in his jacket pocket. He wasn't certain what he'd do if he caught up with her—should he shoot her in the street? Grab her and bring her back to the van?

He just knew the one thing he couldn't do was lose her.

Genti watched Pia disappear from his view as she descended quickly into the station while he weaved in and out of the cars, gypsy cabs, buses, and vans on the busy corner of Broadway and 168th Street. He reached the subway entrance and rushed down the stairs but couldn't see her. Was she catching the A train or the 1? Probably the express train, the A, he thought. He was desperately looking ahead for her, half pushing people out of the way.

"Excuse me, excuse me." He didn't want to get too aggressive: New Yorkers were liable to get aggressive right back at you. Genti rarely rode the subway and didn't have a Metro card that he could swipe to get through the turnstiles, and he certainly didn't have time to stop and buy one from a machine. Hoping there were no cops looking out for fare dodgers, he followed a schoolkid and pushed through the turnstile behind him.

Genti had to choose, the A or the 1. Changing his mind, he opted for the 1, and as he neared the giant, aging elevator that took riders to the platform deep underground, he caught a glimpse of Pia at the head of a group of passengers who'd just got on. The doors began to close. He saw she was standing to the side, ready to be first off. He raced forward.

"Hold the elevator!" he shouted. "Hold it."

Genti reached the doors as they were almost closed and frantically tried to stop them. For a moment his hand was trapped and he was forced to pull it out quickly. He looked around. Stairs. Genti wasn't careful anymore; he pushed past an old woman and leaped down the refuse-strewn stairs three or four at a time. He didn't know that the platform was the equivalent of eight stories below and pressed on, dodging the few passengers walking up or down, yelling at everyone to get the fuck out of the way. He was breathless but reached the bottom only to find that the elevator had already discharged its load of descending passengers, and new ones were already boarding.

Genti took in lungfuls of air, his hands on his knees. He was the first to admit not being in the best shape. Then he heard nearby the high-pitched squeal of a subway train's brakes. Uptown or downtown? He guessed she was going downtown, as the majority of people were doing. He pushed forward and heard the mechanical sound of train doors opening. He entered a barrel-ceilinged passageway leading from the elevators to the station itself. Suddenly there was a crowd of people coming toward him, filling the tunnel from one side to the other. They'd just disembarked from the train, and he had to fight his way through them. When he reached the platform, he looked up and down its length, spotting Pia farther down the platform.

Genti saw her clear as day. She was right there, maybe thirty feet in front of him. She stepped into a car.

Then Genti made a mistake. While he waited for the "Please stand clear of the closing doors" announcement that always preceded the train's departure, Genti marched down the platform intending to board the train through the same door she did. Then, as he drew level, the doors closed without warning. Genti banged on the door and looked back toward the conductor about twenty feet away. "Hey, man, the door!"

The conductor ignored him, and the train's brakes released with a hiss of air. Genti looked into the car. Pia's and Genti's eyes locked for a brief second before the train began to pull away from the station. All Pia saw was another guy trying to push his way onto the train.

Genti turned to stare down the conductor, who drew his head into his cab with a slight smile on his face as the train picked up speed. Genti watched it disappear into the tunnel, keeping his eyes on its taillights until they disappeared into the gloom.

He'd failed.

Genti walked back to the elevator. In some ways he was embarrassed that he'd missed the girl, but he rationalized that it probably was for the best. Maybe he would have had trouble getting her out of the station without interference. Besides, he reasoned, if they were supposed to get the boy too, it would be easier to get them together and deal with them at the same time. If they'd taken the girl, the boyfriend might have gone to ground and been hard to find.

By the time Genti had ridden up in the elevator he was feeling much better about having missed Pia. And he had been reminded of what a beauty she was. He looked forward to snatching her off the street and taking her to Buda's isolated summer house where no one could hear anything going on inside.

Genti stepped onto the street and looked for the white van but couldn't spot it. He called Prek, who told him he was down beyond the Neurological Institute where he'd been able to snag a great parking place between the medical school and the dorm just beyond where 168th Street turns into Haven Avenue.

Genti walked west and soon saw the van. He got in and related how he'd just missed her in the elevator and then missed her a second time, as she was getting on the subway car. He said he was so close it was frustrating.

"It's not the worst thing," Prek said, echoing Genti's earlier thoughts. "This is the perfect spot right here. Hopefully, if we're lucky, when she shows up it will be with the boyfriend, and we'll be waiting. I'm thinking we need to get them together."

"How will we know which one he is?" Genti said. "I bet she has a lot of boyfriends."

As if Aleksander Buda were reading their minds, Prek's cell phone buzzed. It was an e-mail from Buda with an attachment. When Prek opened the JPEG he found himself staring at George's medical school admission photo listing his height and weight.

"He's six-one, one-ninety, with blond hair," said Prek. "Taller than most. We shouldn't have too much trouble picking him out."

"Perhaps he'll come by on his own," Genti said.

"No, my sense is they'll be together since they seem to be spending a lot of time together recently. I know I would if I was him. I imagine they'll meet up when she comes back from wherever she's going."

48.

CORNER OF FIRST AVENUE AND THIRTIETH
STREET
NEW YORK CITY
MARCH 25, 2011, 4:40 P.M.

As the last of the daylight threatened to
fade away completely thanks to the low
clouds and rain, Pia paused outside the
Office of the Chief Medical Examiner, gaz-
ing at the front of the half-century-old
building. It wasn't inviting in the least, with
its weird façade of blue glazed tiles that
reminded her of the Ishtar Gate of ancient

Babylon. She'd seen pictures of the latter in an almost equally ancient *Encyclopæ-dia Britannica* at the academy. She glanced at the tile and then at the outdated 1960s-style aluminum-framed windows. World-class ugly.

Pia had been worried about making it in time, but she'd been lucky with the trains. Now that she was there, she wasn't as confident as she had been about going in cold like this. She had no contacts there, no one she knew she could trust, no one she knew on any level, and this wasn't a feeling she liked. She was very aware that this was the *New York City* OCME and she'd had a lot of bad experiences with various city agencies as a child. The state may have provided her with food and shelter, but it had also fed and sheltered her enemies and abused her. There was not a lot of reason not to worry that this city agency wouldn't be equally as nasty.

Pia had another thought. What would happen if she went in there and actually succeeded in her mission? What if she asked to see Rothman's body and somehow got permission and then found that he had in fact been irradiated, proving that he and Yamamoto were murdered? Her mind raced. There'd be a huge police action, and she'd be at the center. It would be a media circus. She and George would be questioned, she'd have to voice her myriad suspicions and assist with inquiries and make statements and possibly appear in court. But then she touched her tender jaw and remembered the beating and the warning she'd gotten the night before. She had no choice. The answers to her questions lay in this building, or they were nowhere at all.

Taking a deep, fortifying breath, Pia tucked her umbrella under her arm and went in the front door.

The reception area showed every bit of its fifty years. It was dark and somewhat dingy with a worn dark brown leather couch and a few other worn, mismatched chairs. The linoleum floor was cracked and scarred. On a low coffee table were some dog-eared magazines with the address labels torn off the covers. There was a crowd of people sprinkled on the furniture and some leaning against the wall. Soon it became apparent they were all together, members of a grieving African-American family with at least three generations represented. Two teenaged girls were hugging in a corner, crying softly.

"Excuse me," Pia said, approaching the receptionist. A security guard sat at another table off to the side next to a set of glass doors. The receptionist, carefully dressed and pleasantly plump, was wearing a name tag that read "Marlene." She looked up. She had a friendly smile.

"Yes, honey."

"Hi. I'm a medical student and I'd very much like to talk to one of the medical examiners."

"Are you here to find out about teaching opportunities at the OCME, like the elective for medical students?"

"Maybe," Pia said, wanting to keep her options open.

"Maybe?" Marlene questioned, with a smile. "What is it exactly you want to talk to the medical examiner about?"

Pia hesitated.

"Actually, I'd like to discuss a specific case. Two cases, to be more precise."

"Are they relatives of yours?"

"No."

"Perhaps it's best if you talk to the

department of public relations if it's information about a specific case you want, seeing as you're not a relative."

Pia saw she was losing ground. The last thing she wanted was to be shunted off to the public relations department, where she surely wouldn't get access to Rothman's corpse. Fearing she might be turned away, Pia studied the receptionist's face, trying to think of an approach. Marlene seemed to be a congenial person and for a brief moment Pia toyed with the idea of telling at least a partial truth. Quickly she decided against it. Any way she explained the reason she was there that approached the truth would sound too bizarre.

"Actually, I also want to talk about the teaching opportunities here. The two cases I mentioned are teaching cases that I've heard about. I've come all the way down from Columbia." Pia smiled to try to cover up any potential inconsistencies. "I've become interested in forensics. Very interested."

Marlene was confused—what did this girl really want? She was also impressed that she had come all the way from

Columbia Medical Center way up in Washington Heights. That took some effort, especially late on a Friday afternoon. Marlene didn't have the heart to send her away without talking to someone. Besides, she was a pretty thing, and Marlene knew exactly who would be more than happy to speak with her.

"Okay then. I'll call Dr. McGovern."

"Is he a medical examiner?"

"He's a medical examiner and he also happens to be the coordinator for teaching at OCME."

"Thank you." Pia was delighted.

Marlene put in a call to Chet McGovern and motioned for Pia to take a seat. Pia stepped away from the receptionist's desk. She didn't sit down as there were no chairs available. It was close to five o'clock, so she had to make a quick impression on this McGovern guy. A moment later the glass doors opened and a heavyset woman in a lab coat appeared, holding a clipboard. She introduced herself to the grieving family as Rebecca Marshall, an ID coordinator, and asked them to follow her. Dutifully the entire clan disappeared through a door marked ID Room.

Pia took one of the newly vacated seats and tried to be patient. While she waited she tried to decide what approach to take with the medical examiner. Should she be aggressive or coy? Eventually she decided she'd have to wait and see what kind of man Dr. McGovern turned out to be. She was hoping for someone on the youngish side, someone she could flirt with to a degree. Over the years she'd learned she had an effect on most men, and she thought that this was one of those situations where it could work to her advantage. Usually it was the opposite.

A few minutes later her prayers were answered when a youngish man came through the inner doors in a long white lab coat with the confident air of a doctor. When he took one look at Pia, who was the only person in the waiting room, his face lit up. Pia recognized the reaction. She'd seen it too many times not to. He appeared to be in his forties, early fifties at most. He was blond and good-looking in a masculine, all-American way, somewhat like George, and Pia could tell he was in good shape.

He came right over to Pia like a bee to

honey and introduced himself. Pia did the same, avoiding his stare. She recognized the type immediately: an irrepressible Lothario who undoubtedly saw every attractive single woman younger than him as a challenge. She was encouraged.

After the introductions, which included him repeating proudly that he was indeed the current coordinator for teaching at the OCME, he said, "Let's go up to my office and see if we can't help you out. Thanks, Marlene."

McGovern winked at Marlene behind Pia's back, and Marlene rolled her eyes.

As McGovern escorted Pia to his third-floor office he peppered her with questions about where she was at medical school, what year, and what she thought she might like to specialize in. He mentioned how interesting medical forensics was and offered up his credentials.

Pia played along, answering McGovern's questions, acting as if she were interested in his life story and achievements. They entered McGovern's small office and sat on either side of McGovern's untidy desk.

"Sorry about the mess. So what can I

do for you, Miss, er . . ." McGovern's eyes shone with the struggle he was having remembering her name.

"Grazdani. Thank you for seeing me with so little warning."

"My pleasure, I'm sure."

"I want to know about autopsies that were performed here on Dr. Tobias Rothman and Dr. Junichi Yamamoto from Columbia University Medical Center. They died the morning of March twenty-fourth—yesterday—of typhoid fever." Pia was all business, taking McGovern aback. "I'm assuming autopsies have already been done," she said.

"Er, well, er, I wasn't involved in either one, and I haven't heard much scuttlebutt around the office other than one of them was the famous Nobel-winning researcher. All I heard was that he died of an extremely aggressive infection. But let me check what we have."

McGovern keenly wanted to be helpful. He looked at Pia, and she half smiled back at him. Using the computer on his desk, McGovern looked up the names to get the OCME accession numbers and then brought up the individual cases.

"Here we are. Yes, it says the autopsies were performed the afternoon of the twenty-fourth, so that was, er, yesterday. The day they died." McGovern scrolled through one file, then the other.

"They certainly were both serious infectious cases with severe erosion of the gut, both small intestine and large. Wow! Anyway they're considered OSHA cases, which was the main reason they were autopsied."

"OSHA cases?" Pia questioned. She'd heard the acronym but couldn't remember what it was for.

McGovern looked up. "The Occupational Safety and Health Administration. It's a government agency that gets involved when there are deaths in the workplace involving public safety issues. The autopsy results will be reported to OSHA as the OCME is required to do by law."

McGovern looked back at his screen.

"Okay. Both cases were done by Dr. Jack Stapleton. He's our super-doc who does more cases than anyone else. He's never satisfied, always pushing for more, works hard like he doesn't have a life.

"Let's see. The cause of death for both

cases is listed as infectious disease—typhoid fever—and the manner of death is accidental. Let me ask you, do you know why the manner of death is considered accidental?"

Pia said that she didn't, not adding that she might be challenging that official verdict.

"If the two researchers had come down with typhoid after eating at a restaurant, like the hospital cafeteria, then their deaths would have been labeled natural, since typhoid is a food-borne pathogen. But since they contracted the disease in a laboratory, or in a workplace setting, then it's accidental because it certainly couldn't be considered a natural process."

McGovern was trying his best to sound authoritative.

"And if for some reason the researchers infected themselves on purpose, then the manner of death would be suicide. And last but not least, if someone purposely infected them, then it would be homicide."

McGovern laughed and held his hands out wide as if to say, "See what a good teacher I am."

Pia didn't laugh with him or even smile.

For her he was acting stereotypically transparent. *He's talking to me like I'm a college coed*, she thought.

After a slightly awkward beat because of Pia's lack of response, McGovern said, "Do you have any specific questions about the autopsies? If you do, I can call Jack and ask him directly. I know he's still here."

Chet McGovern would have liked nothing better than to have Pia indebted to him for his help. An hour earlier he'd learned his Friday-night plans had fallen through, and he hated spending the best night of the week on his own. He was about to ask her if she was free and if she might like to have a bite of dinner when he noticed she was lifting her bag up onto the desk. She then reached into it and pulled out a yellow instrument, a lead, and mike-like device attached. It took McGovern a minute but he recognized it as a Geiger counter.

"Well," Pia said, "to be honest, what I'd really like to do is check if Rothman and Yamamoto might be emitting a small amount of radioactivity. I mean, if that would be all right."

"I suppose," McGovern said, not wanting to say "no" but confused by the strange request. There was obviously something she wasn't telling him, but he decided to play along. "Why do you think they might be emitting radioactivity?"

Here was the thousand-dollar question. She still hadn't decided how she was going to respond, even though she had been reasonably certain it would come up. She could go for broke and voice her suspicions or be more prudent and try to be obtuse about it. On the spot she decided on the latter.

"I'm involved in a project for a thesis involving radioisotopes used for research," she said. Pia decided this wasn't the time to raise suspicion about why she was really there at the OCME. She didn't want to show her hand just yet. She didn't want the OCME calling up the medical center and talking about her visit because it would reveal to whoever was involved in the conspiracy that she hadn't stopped her meddling.

"I worked in Dr. Rothman's lab for more than three years, and I know that certain isotopes were used in that period for various experiments. I just want to be sure there hasn't been any contamination to the personnel. I checked Rothman's lab and there was a very small amount of what we want to believe was rogue radiation in the office by his coffeemaker. I hope you can help. It's for everyone's peace of mind."

Pia stopped. She knew what she had just said didn't make total sense, but it sounded good. She smiled as pleasantly as she could. She hoped her smile didn't look as fake as it felt. She could tell that McGovern was suspicious and hesitant, but that he hadn't ruled out granting her request.

"Is that what you told Marlene down-stairs?" he asked.

"I told her I was interested in a couple of particular cases."

"Oh, okay. She said you wanted to know about the OCME electives. Never mind. Listen, we have radiation detectors down in the mortuary area just in case, and noth-ing has sounded recently, especially not yesterday. I know that for a fact."

"Well, that's not surprising because the isotopes we've been using in the lab were all alpha emitters for targeted alpha ther-apy such as bismuth-213 and lead-212, which wouldn't be picked up by general radiation detectors made for beta and gamma radiation."

Pia smiled again and McGovern nodded knowingly, even though he had no idea what she was talking about. The last time he read much about radioisotopes was over a decade earlier when he was studying for his boards. McGovern looked pensive. Pia thought he was thinking about alpha particles. In fact McGovern was running a mental checklist. At first he'd questioned himself, but no, he was certain. He'd never seen a better-looking medical student, which was saying something as they were, in his opinion, getting better-looking every year, at least at NYU, which was where most of the medical students he met in his position as OCME teaching coordinator were from. He should spend more time at Columbia, he thought.

"So you just want to make sure Rothman's and Yamamoto's bodies are not emitting alpha radiation?" McGovern asked, just to be certain he understood.

"That's right. That's why I brought this Geiger counter. It's specially programmed for detecting alpha particles."

McGovern went back to his monitor.

"Let's see. There might just be a problem. The bodies of infectious cases like these don't stay around here very long, for obvious reasons. . . . Yup!" he said suddenly, tapping the screen with a forefinger. "Just as I thought. There's a problem. As I said, in serious infectious cases like typhoid fever and a few other communicable diseases, the bodies aren't held here in the OCME. After the autopsies are completed and the cause and manner of death corroborated, the bodies are released to the families and the respective funeral homes and cleared for cremation. In other words," McGovern said, "the researchers' bodies are no longer here. You're about twenty hours too late."

Pia mouthed a repressed "shit," which McGovern caught and appreciated. He associated colorful language with feistiness, and he loved feistiness in a woman. It was his hope that now that he'd ascertained the bodies were no longer at the OCME, perhaps they could move on to more interesting topics, like Friday-night plans. Meanwhile, Pia stared into the middle distance, thinking. She could hardly reproach herself;

twenty-four hours ago, when the bodies left, she'd never even heard of polonium-210.

Watching Pia's expression, Chet suddenly was afraid that after hearing the news she might get up and leave. She was clearly disappointed. In his mind, her leaving at that point would be a major tragedy because so far he'd not gotten either cell phone number or an e-mail address from her.

"The guy who did both autopsies is just down the hall," Chet reminded Pia. "And he's a friend. So if you have a specific question about what he found, I'm happy to go ask him."

Pia was disappointed. It had never occurred to her that Rothman's and Yamamoto's bodies would have already been sent to funeral homes. She thought briefly about trying to find out the names of the funeral homes, but she didn't know how she would do that without raising a lot of suspicion. As for talking to the ME down the hall, what would possibly be the point?

49.

COLUMBIA UNIVERSITY MEDICAL CENTER
NEW YORK CITY
MARCH 25, 2011, 5:25 P.M.

Earlier, while Prek and Genti had sat in the van, Neri Krasnigi, the recruit foisted on them by Buda for God knows what reason, had been continually walking along 168th Street and the small portion of Haven Avenue from the medical school entrance back to the van. He'd been ordered to have his cell phone in the radio mode to act like a walkie-talkie to stay in contact.

Neri was dressed in one of the security guard uniforms, which now looked pretty wet from the rain. Prek knew he was taking a chance that Neri might bump into one of the real security guards, but he had been willing to risk it. Prek wanted as much notice as possible when either Pia or George appeared, heading in their direction on their way to the dorm. Nevertheless Neri had been ordered back inside the vehicle.

Prek was as content as he could be given the situation. He was certainly keyed up as he always was before a hit, especially with a couple of Red Bulls under his belt. He had another beside him just in case he needed it. The radio in the van was playing heavy metal with the volume turned low. As he sat and waited, Prek methodically rubbed the scar on his upper lip. It was a habit that he wasn't even aware of. It was now almost five-thirty.

Aleksander Buda had called to check in at five o'clock, and Prek had to explain that they had spotted the girl but lost her in the subway. When Buda exploded with a string of choice expletives in Albanian questioning the virtue of Prek's mother and parentage, Prek had held the phone away from his ear and even blushed slightly. Neri, who could hear Buda clearly even though he was sitting on a milk crate in the back of the van, let out a chuckle before he could stop himself, earning a scowl from Prek. As soon as Buda's volcano subsided, Prek held the phone to his ear again.

"Was she carrying anything, like an overnight bag?"

"No. Just a shopping bag and an umbrella. I'm sure she's coming back."

"She better be. . . . What about the guy?"

"No sign of him yet. He may be in class or whatever it is medical students do. They're just getting out now, streaming by the van. Of course he could be in his dorm room having passed by before we got here. But from watching her like we did, I'm sure they'll meet up. And we'll be here."

"Don't fuck this up," Buda said, and ended the call.

Prek looked around the floor of the van by his feet and picked up one of the empty Red Bull cans he'd dropped there and hurled it into the back of the van in the direction of Neri.

"You ass, you think this is funny? Get the dry hospital security uniform on. You're going back out for a walk."

The command-performance radiology lecture George Wilson had made a point of attending had finally finished. Unfortunately it hadn't been great. The speaker had a soporific voice, and George and the rest of the attendees had had a difficult time staying awake. Late lectures were a problem in that regard for most people, especially when the lights dimmed for the de rigueur slides. Halfway through the talk, George's mind had wandered to what Pia was finding downtown and whether or not she was safe and keeping out of trouble. George knew that if she caused trouble and the OCME called Bourse to complain, it would probably be the end of Pia's medical school days, at least at Columbia. As the lecturer had droned on, George found himself wishing he'd gone with her.

George got his stuff together and exited the lecture hall. He certainly hadn't learned anything. Reaching the street, he donned his coat and turned up the collar. It wasn't raining so much as drizzling. He had a knot in his stomach from worrying about Pia. He was worried that he'd allowed her to go on her own and wondered when he'd hear from her.

Along with a large clot of first- and second-year students, George walked through the early-evening air toward the dorm and past a young security guard who seemed to be patrolling the front of the building. George looked at him quickly, as he had no umbrella and his black fake-leather coat with its fake-fur collar appeared soaked. He looked about seventeen, and George paid him no mind. He walked into the dorm building and waited with the throng of students for an elevator. For the fiftieth time, George checked his phone. There was no text message from Pia, no call or e-mail.

When he reached his room, George flopped down on the bed, exhausted and hungry. He suddenly felt alone and afraid. He knew he wasn't nearly as tough as Pia. Armed with what little he knew of her up-bringing, he was aware of how much she'd been through in her life. It was so much more than he had ever experienced. Sure, his dad died when he was young, and there hadn't been a lot of money around when he was growing up, but his mother had always made sure he was loved and looked after. She paid attention to his education—made sure he studied and guided him through high school and college and on to medical school. She was always there, making sure he worked hard enough to justify the scholarships he needed to attend Arizona State University and then Columbia Medical School. All in all George had had support and security all his life, exactly the opposite of Pia. Vaguely he wondered where he would be today had he shared Pia's experiences. Probably in something like a hamburger joint slinging hash.

Suddenly George missed hearing a friendly voice. He called his mom but got the ancient answering machine she still insisted on using. He didn't leave a message. Then he looked at his watch and called his grandmother Sally Mason in Phoenix. He thought the middle of the afternoon would be a good time to catch her, but it was not meant to be. This time he left a message.

After George had passed by and entered the dorm, Neri went to the driver's-side window of the van. Prek lowered the window and looked at the rookie and felt sorry for him. He looked bedraggled with his dark hair plastered against his forehead. "Okay," Prek said. "Get back in the van but stay in the uniform."

"Thanks," Neri said, and meant it. He quickly entered through the van's sliding door.

Prek watched him in the rearview mirror as he pulled off the wet jacket. Genti was tapping a pencil against the dash in time to the music.

"Did the George fellow look at you?" Prek asked, still watching the underling in the mirror. It was easier than turning around.

"He did. He looked me right in the eye. Why do you ask?"

"Just curious."

"It doesn't matter, does it?"

"Can't imagine," Prek said. "I was hoping they'd be together, but what can you do. When you finish getting settled, bring that milk carton up to the front and sit between us. I want you to look out the windshield for the Grazdani girl along with us. Six eyes are better than four." The trickle of medical students had swelled to a horde. Like livestock returning from the pasture on their way back to the barn.

The van was parked on the west side of Haven Avenue facing southeast. Prek et al. were facing the medical students coming from the medical center complex, passing the van on the passenger's side.

"We have one bird in the nest. Now, where the hell is the other one? Where the devil did she go?"

50.

Chet McGovern waited with anticipation for the beautiful med student sitting in front of him to tell him if there was anything she wanted him to ask Jack Stapleton, who had performed the autopsies on the dead researchers she was interested in. McGovern tried to read her face. She'd looked crestfallen a few minutes earlier when he told her the bodies were gone, but now she seemed to have brightened. After a few moments' contemplation, something seemed to have occurred to her.

"Well, maybe there is something you could ask," Pia said.

"What? What would you like me to ask him?" McGovern said. He tried to mask his eagerness, worried it might scare her off.

Pia remembered Rothman's rebound tenderness, which she had been the first to find. It heralded the peritonitis, which bore witness to what was going on in Rothman's gut. Typhoid's target organ was the small intestine. From her recent research she knew that the gut was also sensitive to radiation, particularly the cells that lined the gut. But it was the whole gut, not just the small intestine. If polonium was involved, then the whole gut would have been damaged.

"I'd like to know if the autopsy findings were typical for typhoid fever."

"Let me go and find him," McGovern said with alacrity. "Not a problem. Don't move!"

He jumped up before Pia could change her mind and dashed out of the room, heading down the hall to Jack Stapleton's office. He knocked on the door and barged in without waiting for an answer. To his dismay, the office was empty.

"Damn!" He then ran down to the office of Jack's wife, Laurie, whose door was ajar as usual. To his delight both Laurie and Jack were there.

Laurie and Jack liked to hang out in one of their offices after the rush of the day and go over their cases and maybe make plans for the evening. The rush-hour traffic, particularly bad on Fridays, would subside a little if they waited to leave until six, and with the live-in nanny at home tending to JJ's needs, there was no rush. This was their quiet time, and they relished it because it was in short supply considering how busy they both were.

"Jack. Thank God. Oh, hi, Laurie, how are you? Jack, listen." Chet was talking excitedly and loudly at first but got mock-conspiratorial. He looked behind him and pushed Laurie's office door almost closed so no one else could hear.

"Jack, I have got the best-looking fourth-year medical student in my office that I've ever seen. I mean ever. I need you to keep her interested until I can get her info. I had nothing to do tonight, but then she showed up. It's like a sign. You gotta help me, man."

As usual, Jack was amused by Chet, his former office mate and longtime friend. Jack had heard innumerable episodes of McGovern's social antics. Laurie, on the other hand, had wearied of Chet's incessant womanizing. She couldn't resist baiting him a little.

"Chet, how old are you?" she said.

"I know," he said, pretending to be sheepish.

"No, seriously, how old *are* you?"

Jack thought he should step in at this point, between his wife and his friend.

"How can I help you, Chet?"

McGovern stuck his head around the door and looked down the corridor to make sure Pia hadn't left.

"Listen! This Columbia med student just came in asking about those two typhoid cases you worked on yesterday. Actually, she came in supposedly interested in an elective, but I guess that was a cover story. For some reason she wants to check the corpses for evidence of alpha radiation because they'd been using some alpha emitter radioisotopes in the lab where your two patients worked. She even brought in her own Geiger counter. When I told her the bodies had already gone she was disappointed. Thanks for being so over-the-top efficient with the death certificates and signing out the cases, Jack!"

"You're welcome, buddy."

Jack and Laurie smiled knowingly at each other. This was typical McGovern behavior. Each week there was a new hot prospect. It used to be Laurie felt badly for the man because she thought he was lonely. But that had changed. She was now convinced Chet did not want to find a mate. It was the chase he wanted, and he never tired.

"When I told her the bodies were gone, she wanted to ask you whether your findings were typical for typhoid."

"Tell her the findings were indeed typical for typhoid, but a very serious case of typhoid from a remarkably virulent strain."

"How about coming and telling her yourself? She'll be more impressed."

Jack looked at Laurie, who shrugged as if to say, "It's okay by me." Jack heaved himself to his feet, told Laurie he'd be right back, and followed Chet back to his office.

Chet made the introductions, and Jack could understand Chet's enthusiasm. Grazdani was fetching. He noticed the Geiger counter. He quizzed Pia about her interest in his cases. She gave him the same story she'd told Chet, and Jack purposely didn't challenge her although he was tempted. Instead he said, "My understanding is that you're interested to know if the autopsy findings were typical for typhoid fever. Yes, they were: a very virulent form of typhoid fever. The gut, the target organ of the disease, was in bad shape, which is why they died so quickly. There were multiple perforations into the peritoneal cavity."

Pia sat up straighter in her chair. "Have you seen anything like that before?" she asked.

"Well, no, not to that extent. But you have to remember that typhoid fever, and especially such a bad case, is rarely seen these days. It's no longer the scourge it used to be before we had antibiotics."

Laurie suddenly appeared. She'd decided

not to be left out. Chet introduced her to Pia. Pia shook her hand and then turned her attention back to Jack and said, "The strain they were working with and which caused their infections was particularly virulent because it was grown in space, under a NASA program."

"Really?" Jack said. He made a mental note to ask why no one had mentioned that fact.

"Was the involvement just in the small intestine or was it the whole intestine?" Pia asked.

"It was the whole intestine," Jack said. "From the duodenum all the way down and including the rectum. In that sense it was unique. Usually it's just in the small bowel. It was unique enough that I saved some rather large specimens in formalin. I thought they could be used in the future for teaching purposes. We take our teaching responsibilities very seriously around here, right, Dr. McGovern?"

The dig got Chet McGovern to mumble something, and Jack laughed. Pia looked confused, but in actuality she was giddy. She hadn't even heard Jack's sarcastic comment. All she had heard was that he'd saved sections of the gut! The bodies were gone, but pieces of the involved intestine were still available.

"I mean, I can't show you any slides because the specimens haven't been processed yet because the autopsy was only yesterday. But if you want to view the gross specimens, I'd be happy to show them to you. As for slides, if you provide your contact information, I'll either tell you when they're ready and you can come back, or, if you'd prefer, I could send some slides up to you at Columbia Medical School."

"Oh, absolutely, I want to see the gross specimens," Pia said. "And I want to see the slides too, when they're ready."

Jack looked at McGovern with a smile. "Dr. McGovern, make sure you get Miss Grazdani's contact information."

"I'll be happy to do so," McGovern said, beaming.

"Well, let's go up," Jack said, and all four trooped out of Chet's office and headed for the stairs. Pia carried both her umbrella and the shopping bag holding the Geiger counter.

On the fourth floor they all filed into the histology lab. The supervisor, Maureen

O'Conner, was still on duty. Jack could swear that since redheads had become very cool recently, Maureen's red curls had gotten redder.

"So what do we have here on a Friday night?" Maureen quipped. "Is this a party or is it work?" She looked from Jack to Laurie to Chet to Pia. Chet made the introductions and Maureen shook hands with Pia.

"I want to look at some samples, if it's okay, Maureen," Jack said. "I know it's late."

"Ah, it's never too late for you, Jack," Maureen said, and Laurie rolled her eyes. Maureen had taken an early liking to Jack and babied him with special attention. Jack's slides were always available a little quicker than everyone else's.

Under Jack's instruction, Maureen took out a number of formalin-filled sample bottles from the sample storage area and put them on an available and reasonably empty bench.

After donning gloves, Jack took out the pale intestine samples and put them on the countertop. He showed Pia the perforations and the marked erosion of the internal, mucosal epithelium that lined the organ. When she saw that Jack was ready to put them back into the sample bottles, Pia asked a question as casually as she could.

"Would you mind if I checked the sample with my Geiger counter?"

Jack shrugged. "It's okay with me."

Pia pulled the Geiger counter out of the shopping bag. After opening up the mica port specifically designed for alpha particles, Pia turned on the machine and positioned the Geiger counter as close to the intestinal sample as possible without touching it. Immediately the counter started giving off the clicks that announced the presence of radiation. As Pia moved the instrument even closer the clicks intensified until they were a continuous noise. Then the needle on the counter's gauge went off the scale.

"Whoa," said Jack. "What's that about?"

Pia said nothing and moved the counter away from the sample and then back. It was unmistakable, the sample was emitting radiation, a lot of radiation. She did it again just to be certain, then turned off the Geiger counter and slipped it back into the shopping bag.

The three shocked MEs looked at one another and then at the young med student. Something wasn't adding up at all. The sample of intestine had come from a man who had been signed out as having died of salmonella poisoning, yet the sample was emitting extremely high levels of alpha-particle radiation. This student had said that they had used radioisotopes in the laboratory as part of the experimental regimen, but could that have caused this radiation?

"What's going on here?" Laurie asked, addressing Pia. Her voice was even, unchallenging. "This is all rather surprising. Do you have any explanation?"

Pia's heart was racing, and she felt as though she might actually be in shock. She was not prepared to face the reality that Rothman's and Yamamoto's deaths might be a copycat of Alexander Litvinenko's in London. Pia was terrified of not being able to get to the truth. Now, when it appeared that she'd found it, all she could feel was a rush of anxiety and paranoia. All she wanted to do at that moment was to get the hell out of the OCME, go back to the dorm, and give herself an opportunity to think about the implications of the discovery and what her next step should be.

"Miss, we need you to tell us what you think is going on," Laurie said, her voice hardening to a degree. "This is an unexpected and very significant finding."

Pia said nothing. She could feel the eyes of the MEs boring into her. She'd never had any reason to trust anyone in a position of authority. These three weren't the police or hospital security, but they did work for the city. Who are the bad guys and who are the good guys? She didn't know. The bigger question was, are there ever any good guys? She had to get away.

Jack was as flabbergasted as anyone else. "You mentioned isotopes, radioisotopes being used in Dr. Rothman's lab?"

"Um, I'll have to find out for sure," Pia said. "I can get back to you in the morning. Do you come in on Saturdays?" She picked up her umbrella and hooked the shopping bag over her shoulder. She eyed the door to the hall.

Chet McGovern was trying hard to think of what Pia had told him about alpha emitters. "Earlier you mentioned something about lead and bismuth, something like lead-213 and bismuth-212, was that it?"

"It was the other way around: lead-212 and bismuth-213, actually. But yes, I did mention those isotopes, and now I have to go back and check to make sure they were the ones being used. I really need to leave." Pia checked her watch. "Oh my goodness, it's almost six o'clock. I promised to be back by six and it's a forty-five-minute subway ride up to Washington Heights."

The MEs could sense Pia's acute anxiety. No one was convinced by her display of surprise at the time.

"I think you need to stay here until we get to the bottom of this," Laurie said. "You might have been exposed yourself. Alpha emitters are dangerous if either ingested or breathed in. There might be other people who need to be checked out."

"Thank you so much for your help," Pia said nervously, looking at Laurie and Jack but not quite looking them in the eye. She was itching to get away. "I can be in touch about the isotopes tomorrow."

Pia didn't want to be trapped there when the MEs called the authorities, which she knew they would do shortly. She had to finish this on her terms.

"Young lady, what's going on?" Jack said. "You show up with a Geiger counter in a shopping bag and bruises on your face. Are you a medical student at all? Who sent you here?"

"No one sent me," said Pia. "I can see how this must look, but I am a medical student. You have to trust me—no one else was contaminated, I'm sure of it. But I can't stay here, I have to get back, I'm sorry."

Pia started backing toward the door, and Jack stepped toward her.

"You can't hold me here if I want to leave," Pia said. "And I want to leave. Right now!"

Laurie touched Jack on the shoulder, and he paused. Pia turned and walked away quickly. Chet followed and looked back at Jack, puzzlement written on his face. He had no idea what to do. He didn't even have her cell number. Pia and Chet disappeared. Maureen was confused too, wondering if she should call security.

"She's right, Jack, we can't keep her here. She said she's at Columbia, so she won't be hard to find."

"If she wasn't lying about that too."

Part of what Jack and Laurie liked about their work as MEs was the unexpected. This was something very new.

"What do you make of it?" Laurie asked.

"I dunno," said Jack. "There's a lot she isn't saying. She suspected there'd be radiation in the bodies. Of course she did, she brought her own Geiger counter! But when she found what she was looking for, she was completely spooked. More like terrified."

"Definitely," Laurie said. "We need to get someone to track her down."

"I agree."

Jack thought for a second.

"Let's check the other guy quickly."

Maureen was glad to have something to do. She fetched Yamamoto's specimens. They looked for all intents and purposes the same as Rothman's, mirror images in fact. But whether they were radioactive they had no idea. Pia had taken her Geiger counter with her.

"Should we call DeVries to find out how we can determine what the radioisotope we're dealing with is?" Jack asked, referring to the OCME head toxicologist.

Suddenly Laurie remembered a disaster kit that the OCME had put together after the agency had recovered from 9/11, the events of which had caught them, and most of the city agencies, completely unprepared. The concern was that if 9/11 had been a nuclear terrorist event, OCME would have been completely unable to cope. So as not to be caught unawares, the disaster kit had been put together. "I think there's an instrument in the disaster kit that detects radiation," Laurie said. "And it should be able to identify the radioisotopes involved. You remember? Bingham insisted on getting it."

Jack didn't recall, but he trusted Laurie's memory. When she left to see if she could find the device, Jack called John DeVries, the toxicologist, and asked him how they could identify the radioactive material.

"I honestly have no idea, Jack. My whole career I've never had to, thank goodness. The only radioactive cases to come through the OCME in my experience were patients being treated by nuclear medicine so we already knew the identity of the radioisotope. I guess you'll use atomic absorption somehow but I'll have to get back to you. It's Friday night, you know, Jack."

"I know it is, John. Many thanks."

That was a dead end for now. Then Laurie returned. She'd found the disaster kit and in it a Berkeley Nucleonics Corp. handheld Model 935 Surveillance and Measurement System, capable of identifying individual isotopes. Together Jack and Laurie read the directions and then used the machine to measure Rothman's intestine's emissions. After about five minutes, the result was available. Although mostly alpha particles were being emitted, there was also a low level of gamma radiation. It was the gamma radiation that yielded the result. It was polonium-210!

"The death certificates are wrong, both of them," Jack said. "Damn it, I missed this completely. This was no accident."

"Obviously. Do you know much about polonium?"

"I happen to know a little bit about it. First of all, there are no medical uses for it. In fact, you know what it's mainly used for? It's mixed with beryllium such that the alpha particles from the polonium cause the beryllium to release neutrons to act as a trigger for nuclear weapons."

"Good God!" Laurie exclaimed. "How do you know *that*?"

"I don't know how I know it, but I know it," said Jack. He remembered something else. "It was used to kill that Russian guy in London, you remember that?"

"Oh, yes, the defected former KGB officer?"

"Right."

Laurie and Jack had taken a professional interest in the case a few years back as did most forensic pathologists.

"We have to report this to Homeland Security," Laurie said.

"Yes," Jack said. "It doesn't mean Rothman and Yamamoto were making nuclear weapons, but it does mean that they didn't die from typhoid fever alone. They had typhoid fever from the salmonella, but they obviously had radiation sickness on top of it. My guess at this point is that the typhoid was a mask for the polonium, which, in retrospect, was probably the lethal agent. I should have questioned the fact that the entire gut was involved."

"Don't be hard on yourself," Laurie said. "I can assure you that no one could have made this diagnosis."

"I suppose you're right," Jack agreed, although he wondered for a moment if he wasn't just making an excuse for himself. "I have to say, it's a rather devilishly ingenious way of murdering someone. And whoever did it nearly got away with it. It fooled me. It would have got past everyone if not for that girl. What happened to Chet—maybe he talked her into staying?"

Jack got out his cell phone and called Chet.

"Chet, that girl, is she still here?"

Jack listened for a second.

"All right. You better get back up here." Jack disconnected. He looked at Laurie. "She's gone. According to Chet, no matter what he said, she literally ran out of the building. And he didn't get her contact information."

"She's got to be found. She could be in danger," said Laurie.

"You've got that right. If whoever is involved in this knows what she knows . . ." Jack didn't finish his sentence. Laurie instinctively knew what he meant. Instead Jack said, "I'll call the chief. This is going to be a bombshell and a media circus."

"And I'll call Lou. And then Paula. It looks like we're spending more of our Friday night here."

Jack nodded. He looked over at Maureen. "Sorry about all this," he said. "A bit of an emergency. Would you mind getting the rest of the specimens? They're going to have to be put in a shielded container of some kind."

"Will do," Maureen said. She'd picked up on Jack and Laurie's anxiety.

Jack and Laurie then ran out of the histology lab, down the stairs, and back to Laurie's office. As he punched in the numbers for Dr. Harold Bingham, the OCME chief, Jack could already see the problems that lay ahead: It was a high-profile case involving prominent medical researchers and the cause of death and the manner of death had been missed. At least they'd found it now, but that was unlikely to appease Bingham. It was Bingham who would have to report the findings to the various government agencies and deal with them, a job that Jack was thankful he did not have to do.

While Jack was calling Bingham, Laurie called Lou Soldano on his cell.

"Lou, it's Laurie. Can you talk?" She dispensed with any pleasantries.

"Hey, Laurie, nice to hear your voice,"

Lou said, his tone becoming wary. "What's happening?"

"We have a situation here at the office. It seems we have a case of polonium poisoning. Remember that case in London four or five years ago?"

"Of course I do!" Lou said gravely.

Laurie took Lou through what she knew— about the mysterious medical student arriving with her Geiger counter, about how she was upset not to find the researchers' bodies but able to test the tissue Jack had saved, and about her extreme reaction at the findings.

"If you're right and it's a copycat of that Russian guy and you mention the words 'KGB' and 'radiation,' this is going to be a shit storm, pardon my French. All the alphabet agencies, the media . . . And if the Russians are involved, it's serious trouble. You gotta keep a lid on it."

"Jack's on the phone to Bingham right now. I'll call the PR people and get them in lockdown mode."

"Appreciate it, Laurie. Now we gotta find this girl. Any reason to think she's not going back up to Columbia?"

"Hold on a second, Lou, Chet just walked in." Laurie turned to McGovern.

"Chet, the woman, she say where she was going?"

"No, she half jogged down Thirtieth Street, heading west. I assumed she was heading back up to Columbia. Why are you asking? What's going on, Laurie?"

Laurie ignored Chet.

"I'd guess she's heading back to the subway, Lou. Ten, fifteen minutes ago now."

"Lou? Are you talking to Lou Soldano?" Laurie waved him off. Jack was standing in the corner, on the phone with a finger in his other ear and saying a lot of "yessirs" and "nosirs."

"I'll put out an APB if you can give me a description. You said she seemed scared?"

"Very. She couldn't wait to get out of here," Laurie said.

"Sounds like she knows more than she should. So how would you describe her?"

"Maybe five-six, slim, about what, one-ten? Black hair, just down to the shoulder. Lovely skin."

"'Lovely skin' ain't a description, Laurie."

Jack had finished talking with Bingham,

and he piped up. "She's incredibly attractive. Maybe French/Moroccan/Slavic. Chet McGovern here was panting like a dog."

McGovern took the phone from Laurie.

"I'd say she's more likely Italian. Dark skin, like olive color. Soft features, dark brown eyes. Gorgeous, like a supermodel. She told me her name is Grazdani, that's all. You think she's in danger?"

Laurie snatched back the phone.

"Lou, it's Laurie again. Remember I said she's a fourth-year medical student at Columbia."

"Good point," Lou said. "If we're lucky, we might be able to get a picture from Columbia, if she actually goes to Columbia. Now, you guys have to zip your lips. Keep me posted if anything happens. I gotta go, Laurie. I'll be putting a task force together including the NYPD organized-crime unit. This is serious, Laurie. This has organized crime written all over it. And it has to somehow involve the Russians. Jesus, Laurie, that polonium stuff is associated with nuclear weapons."

51.

Pia emerged from the subway at the same entrance she'd used on her way to the OCME, pausing near the MTA area map in the shadow of the Columbia Medical Center's art deco buildings. She'd raced out of the medical examiner's office with her head spinning. It was dark, the streets were wet and slick, and there seemed to be hundreds of people on the sidewalks. Pia couldn't face going all the way across town in the rain despite her umbrella so she took a different route, walking to Park Avenue South and the Twenty-eighth Street station on the 6 line, then traveling to Grand Central and taking the S train, the shuttle across town to Times Square. There she had taken the A express train up to Washington Heights.

Throughout the entire unpleasant train ride Pia had acted like a zombie, seemingly impervious to her environment. A few people, mostly men, tried to talk to her, but she didn't respond in the slightest. She was in a daze, going over and over the events since Rothman and Yamamoto had fallen ill. It was as if she were experiencing a living nightmare. Having her suspicions corroborated at the OCME afforded her no satisfaction in the slightest. All it had done was cement her fears and sense of dread. She didn't know specifically if the lethal agent that had been given to Rothman and Yamamoto was polonium, but her intuition told her it was. What to do now was the question for which she had no answer. Maybe she should just run and hide someplace until all the pieces fell wherever they were going to fall. The reality was that she had certainly opened the floodgates at the OCME. Whether she liked it or not or intended it or not, the police were now going to be involved, along with every other law enforcement agency. In her vernacular, the shit was about to hit the fan.

Pia's intention when she got out of the subway was to hurry back to the dorm. She felt her only resource was George. Even though she was under no illusion that George would know what to do, she hoped she could use him as a sounding board. The fact was, she had no one else. She'd thought briefly about involving the two other stalwarts in her life—Sheila Brown and the mother superior—to get their advice, but the story was much too long and complex and more important, Pia was reluctant to put either of them at risk. In the current situation, knowledge was dangerous.

Although Pia was desperate to get to the dorm, she was also terrified. The moment she'd emerged from the relative safety of the subway, she felt inordinately vulnerable. The men who had attacked her said they would be watching her, and she believed them. It meant that they were there, lurking somewhere in the darkness surrounding the medical center. Although where she was at that moment, near the corner of Broadway and 168th Street, was lit and crowded with commuters, looking west down 168th Street was neither.

Holding her umbrella in the crook of her neck, Pia got out her cell phone, which she'd turned off before going into the OCME. She switched it on. Immediately she saw she had more than ten missed calls and three voice mails. She called George, but he didn't answer. Instead she left a voice message of her own: "George, it's me. It's about six forty-five. I'm at the hospital entrance to the subway at 168th Street. Can you come get me so we can walk back to the dorm together? Okay, I'll be waiting here."

52.

George had not meant to fall asleep, but he had. It was a legacy from the soporific lecture. There was also the fact that he hadn't been sleeping as well as usual with everything that was going on. Not only was he asleep, he was in the deepest stages such that he didn't hear his cell phone emit its cricket chirping. The phone was on his desk not ten feet away. He didn't hear it again when it chirped fifteen minutes later. But that call brought him up from where he'd been such that when the phone chirped a third time, he got up and answered: "Hello."

"George, it's Grandma. I tried you before, but I missed you. How are you?"

George was suddenly wide awake. He didn't know how long he'd been asleep, and he fumbled for his watch, checking the time. It was almost seven, and he panicked. Where the hell was Pia?

"Grandma, I'm good, but I'll have to call you back, okay?"

"Oh, okay, George. Make sure you do now. We haven't talked in a while. Is everything good?"

"Everything's good. I'll call soon! Gotta go!"

George saw he'd missed two calls and listened to the message Pia left the first time. He checked his watch. Shit, she'd been waiting fourteen minutes. As he pulled on a pair of shoes, he tried calling her but got her voice mail. He then raced

out into the hall, heading for the elevators.

Prek and Genti sat in the front of the van
anxiously scanning passersby through the
windshield. Neri was perched uncomfort-
ably on the milk crate, just a little behind
and between them. What had been easy
earlier, checking out the students as they
passed, was now much more difficult.
There was a streetlamp at the corner of
Fort Washington and Haven, but it was far
enough away not to be of much help. It
was still raining and much darker. They
had been there long enough to be stiff and
sore, and in foul moods.

"Where the fuck is she?" Prek questioned morosely. He didn't expect an answer and didn't get one. "This is turning
into a bitch."

Neri, as the most inexperienced, was
suffering the most. He'd been so keyed up
with excitement, and now that he had had
to wait he felt let down, depressed. Although his role was going to be the easiest in that he was going to do the hit, he'd
never actually killed anyone before. He

had his right hand in his jacket pocket holding his military-issue Beretta M9 semi-automatic pistol with the thumb safety on. He'd fired the gun hundreds of times in practice and considered himself a good shot. But shooting a man in the head at point-blank range was a very different proposition from hitting static targets at twenty-five, fifty, or one hundred feet. Yet he knew he had to do it to rise within the crew. Like Prek and Genti, he had his wool balaclava in his lap, ready to pull it over his head and swing into action.

An NYPD cruiser drove by, and all three reflexively crouched down. Prek watched it disappear in his side mirror. Then another NYPD cruiser went past, and Prek tensed up further. He watched that one disappear as well.

"You see that?" he said.

"Of course," Genti said. "It's Friday night. I wouldn't give it much thought."

"I don't like to see cops in the area when we're doing a job. Where the hell is this bitch?"

"It's getting harder and harder to see these kids' faces until they're right on top of us," Genti said.

A group of three students in lab coats walked past the van, followed by a couple of people walking alone. One of them caught Genti's attention, and he leaned forward and picked up his balaclava. A minute later he slumped back in his seat. It was yet another false alarm.

Pia had been walking back and forth along the side of the subway stairs, waiting for a call from George, trying to figure out where he could be. They had definitely planned on getting together when she got back from the OCME. More than once, she had resolved to quit waiting for George and walk back to the dorm by herself, at least until she looked down 168th Street and saw that it was darker and more deserted than it had been fifteen minutes earlier. Pia had been about to call George for the third time when she'd been frightened by a hand on her shoulder. Spinning around, she had had to restrain herself from lashing out at her attacker. But it wasn't an attacker. It was Will McKinley, who'd come up from the subway and caught sight of her pacing back and forth. After initial small talk and mutual sympathies about

Rothman's and Yamamoto's passing, Pia had latched onto him for company back to the dorm. As an enticement, as if she needed it, she had offered to share her umbrella.

After reminding each other about the deaths, they'd each regressed into their own worlds. They walked in silence until beyond the 168th Street hospital entrance. Pia wondered what Will might say if she told him what she now knew. She thought he probably wouldn't believe her.

"I was surprised to see you," Will said. "Did you come out of the subway like I did?"

"I did," Pia admitted. She tried to think of what to tell him if he asked where she'd been, so she changed the subject. "Have you seen George at all today?"

"Wilson? No, but I haven't been around since lunch. Lesley and I still haven't found a home for our month's research elective. I took the opportunity to do a little shopping." He held up a shopping bag.

Pia spotted a police cruiser heading in their direction along 168th Street. She tilted down the edge of her umbrella to keep her face from being seen, which Will noticed immediately as it bumped into his forehead. She had reacted reflexively. She wouldn't have been surprised if the police were looking for her. Although being picked up by the police was surely not something she wanted to happen, at least not yet, she was the first to admit it would be far better than being confronted by her attackers again.

"What, are you a fugitive from justice?" Will quipped, unknowingly interpreting Pia's gesture correctly.

"Hardly," Pia said with a fake laugh. Another police car was coming, so she kept the edge of the umbrella angled down.

They reached Fort Washington Avenue and waited for the traffic light to change. There were only another couple of hundred yards to the dorm. Pia relaxed a degree. They had not seen any men in Columbia Medical Center security uniforms. She was looking forward to getting to the relative safety of George's room.

Genti was the first to spot Pia and Will coming around the corner heading right for them, backlit by the corner streetlight.

"There, in front, fifty yards."

"Both of them!" Prek voiced with delight. "Fantastic! D-day. Wait for my word. You okay, Neri?"

"Sure!" Neri said with more bravado than he felt. He slipped off the safety on his pistol and pulled on his balaclava as Prek and Genti did the same.

Neri looked out the van's rear window to see if anybody was coming in the opposite direction.

"Wait!" he said. "Who's this coming from the dorm? Is that him?"

"Who?" said Prek. He swung around to look at George. Then he flipped open his cell phone and studied the picture Buda had sent him. The only illumination in the van was from the dim streetlights and it was a small photo. He swung back around to look at the man walking with Pia. They could have been twins in the misty half-light. "It has to be the guy with Pia. What is this, the Swedish Olympic team? Everybody is blond."

Prek waited a couple of beats as the couple got closer. "It's him. Hell, he has his arm around her. How close is the guy coming from the back?"

Neri checked again. "About two hundred yards."

Prek picked up a rag from the dash and soaked it with a hefty slug of the Ultane anesthetic, which they were going to use to take down Pia. He shot a look at Genti, and Genti nodded back.

"Okay, go!"

Just as Pia and Will came alongside the van, the three masked men leaped out, Prek and Genti from either side of the front, Neri from the back. Neri stepped around from the back of the van as Will McKinley stood stock-still in front of him, his mouth open wide. Neri pointed the gun at Will's head and a fraction of a second later Will reacted by turning toward Pia, who'd let out a scream. Neri fired, sending a nine-millimeter bullet into the side of Will's head. Simultaneously Genti grabbed Pia in a crushing bear hug while Prek slapped the Ultane-soaked rag over her face. Almost immediately the fight went out of Pia, and she lost consciousness.

Neri ran around to the front of the van and got into the driver's seat while Genti dragged Pia to the back of the van and pulled her inside. As Prek ran to help Genti, he caught sight of Neri's spent casing. He picked it up from the sidewalk just before jumping into the van behind Genti and slamming the doors shut behind him. Neri already had the engine started, and the moment he heard Prek's "Go!" he accelerated from the curb, made a rapid U-turn, and headed north on Haven Avenue. The hit-and-snatch had taken about seven seconds.

There were three witnesses who saw everything and eight more who heard the gunshot and saw the van drive away. One of the witnesses had his own reasons for not wanting to talk to the police that evening so he kept right on walking as if nothing had happened. The second was a male med student who had been walking back to the dorm, twenty yards behind Pia and Will. He had watched in horror as the raid unfolded. At first he thought he might be watching a movie being filmed, but it was dark and there were no cameras. And the blood coming from the shooting victim's head was very real. He called 911 and tried desperately to remember what, if anything, he'd learned in the past two years about gunshot victims.

The third witness was George. He'd seen Will and Pia before the event and had stopped, waiting for them to come to him. He was relieved to see Pia, but his relief was short-lived. In the next second he saw the men leap from the van, shoot Will, and snatch Pia. It happened so quickly he didn't have a chance to move. He blinked, as if blinking would reset the scene back to when Pia and Will were walking toward him. But it didn't. It was only then that he ran forward to where the other student was kneeling over Will McKinley's body.

Inside the van, Prek used a prepared syringe to give the barely conscious Pia an injection of Valium, enough to knock her out completely.

"Don't drive too fast," he yelled ahead to Neri. "Keep it steady." Prek and Genti then struggled to roll Pia up in a threadbare carpet. It wasn't easy in the rocking and swaying van.

Neri's hands were shaking, and it was all he could do to stop himself from throwing up. The mark had looked right at him. Neri blinked rapidly and concentrated so he wouldn't drive right off the road.

"And, Neri," Prek said.

"What?"

"Good job."

On a quiet side street just north of the George Washington Bridge, Neri pulled over behind the waiting dark blue van, and the men quickly transferred their cargo. With that done, Prek returned to the driver's seat with Genti riding shotgun. Neri was told to keep a watch on Pia.

Abandoning the white van, Prek drove ahead to where he could get on the Henry Hudson Parkway to loop around and get onto the George Washington Bridge, heading over to New Jersey. As they expected, the bridge was chockablock with rush-hour traffic. But the crew didn't mind in the slightest. The hit-and-snatch had been flawless, and they were giddy with their success. It was, as Prek said, a tribute to the Albanian mob tradition.

"I even got this," Prek said proudly, as he pulled Neri's bullet casing from his pocket and held it up. "Are we good, or what?" He then handed his cell to Genti and told him to text Buda that the operation went smooth as silk.

53.

Aleksander Buda had been happy to get the text from Prek. He'd been mildly concerned about the operation even though it was a relatively simple job. But he knew from sore experience that "shit could happen." Be that as it may, the pesky girl was unconscious in the back of the van, and they were on their way to the agreed-upon location, Buda's summer home, and the boyfriend was dead. The white van they had used had been abandoned. Now the only suspense that remained was the fate of the girl.

Buda was confident Pia Grazdani wasn't connected with any of the prominent Albanian mafia crews in the immediate area; he would have heard the name, which he knew was undoubtedly Albanian. The problem was that if she was related to anyone in a crew, anywhere up and down the East Coast and as far west as Detroit, custom dictated that she be accorded a degree of protection. Even so, Buda had debated with himself whether or not he would have been justified in simply disposing of the girl at the same time as her friend. It would have been neat and efficient. She'd certainly become a serious pain in the ass, especially having somehow, on her own, figured out the polonium issue. But Albanian mob bloodbaths had been fought over even less of a provocation. Buda had decided he had to be sure.

A cautious man, Buda had made it a point to investigate Pia Grazdani in a discreet manner. He was known to the FBI, of course, and he knew how the FBI loved patterns and didn't believe in coincidences.

If the head of one Albanian crew, like himself, suddenly called all the other local heads in quick succession, Buda knew there was a good chance the feds would find out about it and come snooping around.

So Buda had sent live emissaries to crews in Queens and Staten Island and asked one associate to call a crew in Pennsylvania just in case. Manhattan and Brooklyn had also been dealt with, and since he controlled the Bronx, that was covered. He'd received negative reports all the way around, even from Detroit. There was no connected Grazdani. The future was not looking promising for the girl.

But there was one unit left unchecked: Berti Ristani's crew based in Weehawken, New Jersey. Ristani was a particularly nasty customer, willing to do just about anything to make a name for himself. Buda realized he hadn't seen the guy in a year. He thought it wouldn't be a bad idea to make the visit himself for political reasons in addition to providing an alibi for tonight, just in case. Buda grabbed his car keys and set out for Weehawken. He knew he didn't need to call ahead. Ristani could always be found in the same place.

54.

Detective Captain Lou Soldano was frustrated. He was standing inside the taped-off area of the street that marked the McKinley crime scene. A full crime-scene unit had combed the area for clues, but none were to be found. They hadn't even found the shell casing from the gun that was used to shoot the student. All they had was a shopping bag with a device one of the techs identified as a Geiger counter that the woman had been carrying when she was abducted.

Officers were taking statements from witnesses, hoping to get information on the perpetrators and on the van they had used. The reports he'd heard were wildly contradictory, from the men's heights to their clothing. One witness swore that only two men had been involved, while all the others claimed three. The one thing they agreed on was that all the men had been wearing ski masks. The van was described consistently as dirty white, but they had nothing on the make or license plate.

George Wilson had given the most detailed account, and even told Lou something important and most likely related. He said that Pia had been assaulted in her dorm room the previous night and threatened with violence, which now had come to pass. When asked why she didn't report the incident, George said she was afraid of the police because of her childhood experiences. He said that he had encouraged her to go to the police on multiple occasions. When asked why he didn't report it himself, George said because he respected her wishes and privacy, and she had asked him not to.

Lou's frustration was not only over the paucity of evidence at the scene. He was also frustrated that the local precinct of the NYPD hadn't blanketed the area with personnel after Lou had specifically sent out a message to do so. He had given them the description of Pia from Jack and Laurie with the added information that she was carrying an umbrella and a canvas shopping bag. He had hoped that the police or the Columbia hospital security would have been able to pick her up. He had wanted to detain Pia not just to learn exactly what she knew but also for her protection, and now the bad guys had beat him to the punch. If the local boys had done what he had asked, the snatch-and-killing might have been avoided.

The only part of the operation that seemed to be going right was the radiation angle. Lou knew that the ME's office had notified the relevant authorities about the possibility of alpha radiation at four sites in New York City: Columbia University Medical Center, the OCME itself, and the two funeral homes where the bodies of Dr. Rothman and Dr. Yamamoto were taken. But the ME wasn't able to mobilize law enforcement. Soldano had had to do that, and his task force was still more on paper than in the field.

One of the other things that had frustrated Lou was how long it had taken to get a photo of the Grazdani woman. Lou himself had called Columbia hospital security to confirm that Pia was indeed a medical student. Lou had also asked for Pia's details, as well as a recent photo, which the hospital security had trouble getting because it was locked up in the office of the dean of students, and the dean was unavailable. So it wasn't until after the abduction that the photo was sent out to law enforcement. That was akin to locking the barn door after the horses were stolen.

"God damn it," Lou said out loud for the umpteenth time. Nothing about the case seemed to be going well. The sole positive development was that a white van had been located that was believed to be the vehicle involved in the abduction. At that moment another team of forensic experts was going over it. Lou had no idea if it would lead to any clues, but he was hopeful.

Meanwhile an APB had been put out in New York, Connecticut, and New Jersey. Lou was hoping they'd get lucky. But he doubted that would be the case. Lou's intuition was telling him that organized crime was involved big-time. He knew for sure that this wasn't a kidnapping for money—meaning he feared for Pia's life.

All of a sudden several news vans showed up and parked just beyond the crime-scene tape. As their antennae rose, their doors burst open and a bevy of cameramen and journalists alighted.

Lou groaned. He knew this was going to be a media circus, and he wondered how long it was going to take before the mayor got involved.

First Will McKinley was unlucky—twice, in fact—and then he got lucky twice. Will was unlucky to have been involved in the Rothman case to begin with—to be found on the street with Pia and mistaken for George, resulting in his being dealt with as an annoying tagalong who knew too much. Will was also unlucky that Neri Krasnigi's gun had fired at all. When Neri had cleaned and loaded his gun earlier that day, he hadn't been as careful as he thought. A few sizable pieces of grit had been stuck to the first bullet he loaded and lodged inside the chamber. Under different circumstances, or if the pieces of grit had been just slightly bigger, perhaps the gun would have blown up in Neri's face rather than misfiring slightly and dispatching the bullet at perhaps fifty percent of usual velocity. That was lucky.

Will was lucky again, if someone shot in the head can be said to be lucky. Will had turned his head so that he was hit in the temple, not the forehead, meaning the bullet made a complete transit through his frontal lobe, a kind of injury that had seen miraculous recoveries in the past. It might also be considered fortuitous that he'd been shot a hundred yards from a major trauma center, where expert help was immediately available. A superb team of doctors had treated Will within minutes of his being shot and continued to monitor him closely. He was now in a medically induced coma, hooked up to an array of monitors and life-giving machinery. Everyone was hoping Will's luck would not run out.

55.

GREEN POND, NEW JERSEY
MARCH 25, 2011, 8:45 P.M.

Prek drove carefully into Green Pond, a private summer lake community in Morris County in northern New Jersey. What could have been an hour's drive had taken nearly two, partly because of traffic, partly because Prek kept the van well under the speed limit, even on the open stretches of road. Some of the items in the van would have taken a lot of explaining if the vehicle was involved in a traffic stop.

The Green Pond that lent its name to the town was actually a lake. This night its surface was dark as the moon had yet to rise. Prek navigated the twisting, hilly eastern shore road where the few homes, sitting at the end of long driveways, were mostly hidden by dense, leafless hardwood forest. There were just a handful of homes on the cliffs on the western side, which could be reached only by boat. The village itself lay to the north. After a mile or so the road wound closer to the lake and to the dwellings along the shore. Some of the homes belonged to year-round residents and their windows glowed with warm incandescent light and the occasional flash and flicker of the ubiquitous big-screen TVs. At the southern end of the lake were a number of summer cottages and they were dark, with their docks stacked in neat piles and their boats under tarps.

Prek pulled into the driveway of Aleksander's waterfront cottage, which was situated on a peninsula at the very southern end of the lake facing out onto a cove a couple of hundred yards in diameter. Aleksander had been drawn to the house by its private location on a spit of land. He had been delighted to find out that for seven or eight months of the year, the houses and cottages on either side of his on the eastern cove were dark and deserted with their heating systems off and pipes drained. There were only two houses on the western side of the peninsula, and they were also empty except during the summer months. Buda loved the place because of its serenity, particularly in the winter when the lake froze up solid.

Prek parked in back of the house facing the road, found his key and opened up, turning on the lights and the oil-fired heat.

"Honey, I'm home," Prek called out, laughing.

The closer they had got to this sanctuary, the brighter the mood in the van had become. Prek was positively gleeful that everything had gone so well. The boss was sure to be very pleased.

The three men unloaded the rolled-up carpet that contained Pia and brought it quickly inside. The front door opened directly into the living area, where there were two leather couches, one black, one brown, facing each other in the center of the room in front of a fieldstone fireplace. Prek moved a low coffee table scattered with automobile magazines to the side so that Genti and Neri could set down the carpet roll containing Pia. They then unrolled her until she lay sprawled, facedown, on the room's massive fake oriental.

Prek called Buda. He wanted to tell his boss that they'd arrived and all was well. He also hoped to get the okay to finish up with Pia. It was a perfect night, quiet and dark, to dump a body in the large swamp that extended for almost a mile from the southern end of the lake into a protected virgin forest surrounding a government arsenal called Picatinny. It was the kind of wilderness whose remoteness would come as a surprise to most residents of New York City. It had certainly proved useful to the Buda crew on more than one occasion.

To Prek's irritation, Buda didn't pick up. Prek didn't leave a message; Buda would see the missed call and know Prek was trying to reach him.

Prek's annoyance was exacerbated when it dawned on him that despite all their planning, they'd forgotten to bring any food. There was a store up the road about five miles north, but Prek didn't think it was a good idea for any of them to show their faces in a public spot, not when they were going to be disposing of a body. Prek went into the kitchen, such as it was, and looked in the fridge. There was one carton of milk with a past-due date. The cupboards were even more depressing. There was an open box of cold cereal, but one corner was chewed off and mouse droppings could be seen.

Discouraged, Prek reentered the living room. There was a sudden silence. Prek could tell Genti and Neri had been talking about something and had stopped abruptly.

"What is it?" Prek asked.

The two men were looking at Pia. There had been a disagreement.

"How long before she wakes up?" Neri said.

"She's got ten milligrams of Valium in her, so she's going to be sleeping it off awhile," Prek said. "She'll start to wake up, but she'll be very groggy. We can always give her another shot if need be. Buda didn't answer his phone."

"She's beautiful," said Neri.

"Our young friend here was just telling

me what he'd like to do to her," said Genti. "I suppose we could all take turns, maybe even be interesting to watch. What do you think, Prek? We should have done it when we were in her room last night."

"I like my girlfriends to participate," Prek said. "And anyway, we're not doing anything till I hear from Buda that she's safe to get rid of. Remember, she's got an Albanian name. We got to be sure we wouldn't be stepping on someone's honor, if you know what I'm saying."

"Oh, come on, Prek," Genti said, "what are the odds of that? There's two hundred fifty thousand Albanians in the area, and this is one girl. I've never seen anyone that good-looking related to any of us. She sure doesn't look like your sister."

Genti and Neri laughed. Prek didn't. He had a premonition there was going to be trouble after everything had been going so smoothly.

Neri and Genti were sitting on separate couches. Neri looked like a dog in heat, practically panting while adjusting himself. He was looking alternately at the supine Pia and at Genti, who he believed was in his corner as far as having sex with the woman was concerned. Genti Hajdini had come up through the crew's ranks at the same time as Prek, but Buda entrusted Prek with more responsibility and bigger jobs. As a consequence, Prek made more money than Genti, and when Buda wasn't around, Prek called the shots. He knew this was something Genti resented, but it rarely was an open problem between them. Prek knew that Genti was still miffed about not being allowed to have his way with Pia the previous night.

"The boy did good tonight," Genti said, pointing at Neri and making a shooting sound. Genti and Neri laughed again, then stopped and Genti looked at Prek. "Maybe we should reward him. Maybe we should reward all of us." There was a heavy silence in the air.

"Who made you the boss, anyway?" Neri said quietly.

Prek looked from Neri to Genti and back again. Neri was still wearing the black jacket he'd had on when he shot the boy in the street and Prek assumed he still had the gun in an inside pocket. Genti might be armed too, for all he knew. His own gun was in the glove compartment of the van.

Did he really think Neri and Genti would gang up on him and take him out? In this crew, as Prek and Genti both knew very well, stranger things had happened. Turning his attention back to Neri, Prek held his frankly impertinent gaze.

"Buda said I'm the boss when he's not around."

Pia let out a groan.

"Listen, you assholes! Buda told me we wait until he's sure there is no family connected with this woman. You go and mess with this woman and Buda finds out she's someone's daughter or niece and you two haven't been able to keep it in your pants? The uncle or father, whoever he is, is not going to be happy. He's going to be unhappy with Buda and that means Buda is going to be very unhappy with you."

"She's unconscious," Neri said. "Out of it. She won't even know, at least not for sure. It's such a waste. Like it's a crime."

"She'll know, you asshole."

"You not interested in girls anymore, Prek?"

Now it was time to stare down Genti. Prek knew that Genti's comment was meant to rile him, but he decided to ignore it. "She's a pretty girl, sure, but there are a lot of pretty girls."

"I don't see any others in the room," Neri said. He was looking at Genti, hoping for support.

"You don't want to be the reason for a blood feud. Trust me."

"Unfortunately, he's right," Genti said. He got up from the couch and stepped over to Prek. He draped an arm around Prek's shoulder and jostled him.

"We're just screwing with you. If we get the all-clear, Neri gets his, okay? I might take a turn, why not?"

Genti stepped over to Pia's body and with his forefinger lifted her skirt.

"Not bad, not bad at all. Whaddaya say?"

"I say we don't touch her until we get the green light to whack her. When that happens, you two can do what you like. For the time being, help me put her on the bed to get her out of sight. You two are like teenagers."

Prek went over to Pia and grabbed both ankles. "Come on! Give me a hand!"

With Genti and Neri taking an arm each, they carried Pia into the bedroom. There they tossed her onto the bed.

"Now leave her be," Prek said, motioning his two colleagues to precede him back into the living room. As Prek followed them he wondered what the hell was keeping Buda.

56.

So, Berti, what about this Grazdani girl?"
Buda asked. "Anybody in your organization might be related to her? I've been told
she's in her mid-to-late twenties and gorgeous. A real looker."

Berti Ristani was sitting behind a desk
in his office in a small industrial building in
Weehawken. Berti's office looked for all
the world like the workplace of a reputable
building contractor. Supply catalogs were

piled on the desk, the room was ringed with file cabinets, and a storage chest for architectural plans stood in the back of the room. Ristani was a contractor, Buda knew, but not all his contracts involved construction.

Berti leaned back in his office chair, his huge body causing the frame to complain bitterly. Berti's florid face, tracked with broken blood vessels, creased a little as he pondered Buda's question.

"Ah, yes, the business you came for. But I never see you, Aleksander, do we need to talk business? How about a drink?"

"It's a loose end, Berti. It's something I need to take care of soon and I'm trying to do the right thing. I can't leave the situation as it is for too long."

Berti Ristani had no business agenda he wanted to bring up with Buda, and he was mildly offended that Buda kept bringing up this Grazdani issue. He'd been enjoying talking to Buda about old times when they both first arrived from Albania. Back in those days it was no easy thing getting to America. Both had been lucky. On top of a common past, Aleksander Buda was one of the crew leaders Berti respected, and he'd been pleasantly surprised when Buda showed up unannounced.

"Okay, let's find out. I know no one by that name specifically, but I do have two of my best guys with a similar name. But it's not Albanian. It's Italian. Anyway, I might complain, but I appreciate your concern like this. There's been far too many blood feuds. Thanks for coming to talk to me."

"It's nothing, Berti. It would be foolish to act any other way."

Ristani shifted his weight forward and the chair complained again. He placed his fleshy arms on the table and punched a button on an intercom.

"Drilon, can you come in the office for a second?"

Ristani looked at Buda.

"Drilon, one of my most loyal guys. He and his brother, who's out on a job."

"Anything special?"

"Not really. He runs a bunch of books in South Jersey, down to Philly. Friday nights, he likes to collect. He's smarter than a whip, in contrast to Drilon, who, as the saying goes, is not the sharpest knife in the drawer. Oh, Drilon, come in here."

Drilon was used to being called into his

boss's office from his perch near the building entrance numerous times each evening he was on duty. Usually Ristani wanted something to eat, and this was what Drilon expected on this occasion. He walked into the office and saw the back of a figure seated in front of Ristani's desk.

"Drilon, Mr. Buda has a question."

Buda? Had Drilon heard correctly? The man twisted in his seat and Drilon saw the scar on his forehead. It was Aleksander Buda, a serious dude. What did he want?

"Simple question," Buda said without emotion. "Do you know anyone named Pia Grazdani?"

"Say that again," Drilon said. He thought he was hallucinating.

"Pia Grazdani."

He'd heard correctly. The name triggered a movie that played in fast-forward in Drilon's head. Twenty or so years ago, at least, Drilon had been drinking, drinking a lot. He goes home where he lives with his brother, Burim, and his brother's wife, Pia, and there's Pia looking as hot as you like almost without a stitch on, and Burim's out of the apartment running some errands like he was always doing trying to rise up in the Rudaj organization, one of the most notorious early Albanian mafias. But the bitch rebuffs his advances even though she was asking for it and digs her nails into his chest, like deep, and Drilon sees red. Goes berserk. What happens next, he certainly didn't plan. He grabs his gun in a rage and shoots her in the forehead. Blam. Story's over. But her kid's there—little Pia. He considers shooting her too except he can suddenly hear people next door, so instead he hits her in the head with his gun, trashes the apartment, and takes the $500 stash that the brothers had hidden in the stove. He goes back to the bar where he was drinking, drinks more, stays until it closes, sleeps an hour on a park bench, and goes home to raise the alarm that his sister-in-law was murdered by intruders.

The fallout turned out to be a breeze. Burim accepted the intruder story as he was happy enough to be done with his wife and had been thinking seriously of dumping her, and the Rudaj organization and crew took care of everything. There was no investigation, no nothing. As far as anyone was concerned, Pia had just disappeared, leaving her daughter behind.

Did Buda mean either of those Pias?

"So?" Buda said. He'd noticed Drilon's pause and blank expression. "Do you know a Pia Grazdani?"

Drilon felt the hair on the back of his neck stand up. His face flushed, he could feel it. Three questions immediately crossed his mind: One, was he talking about Afrodita, his little niece, or Pia his sister-in-law? Drilon hadn't given either of them a thought in more than twenty years, but one was dead and the other, who knows? Two, had Buda asked Burim the same question? And three, what the fuck was the correct answer?

"Er, I don't think so," Drilon said. "Why do you ask?"

Drilon had spoken to Buda, but it was Berti Ristani who spoke up.

"He's asking because he wants to know. I'm asking you too, Drilon. I haven't called your brother, because he's busy at the moment. I assume you'd know if either you or your brother is related to this girl. The surname is pretty similar."

"Let me think, we got a big family," Drilon said. So Burim didn't know—that was to his advantage. And perhaps it wasn't her at all. But Drilon feared it was the girl—whose mother he murdered, a secret he'd managed to keep all this time. But if Aleksander Buda was asking about her, she probably was halfway in the ground already. Drilon could see no reason to rock the boat. There surely couldn't be anything connecting him to the girl. "I don't think I've ever heard the name."

"You certain about that, Drilon? You took long enough thinking about it."

"You know me, boss, I'm not the brightest guy. Like I said, we got a real big family, but mostly back in the old country."

"So I've heard," Ristani said conversationally.

"That's right, boss."

"What's your family name?" Buda said. The expression on his face had changed not at all the whole time.

"Graziani," Drilon said. It had been Burim's idea to drop Grazdani after the Rudaj crew had been broken up and many of its members sent to jail. Graziani was the name Burim came up with when he asked Ristani for work years back. It was the surname of one of his favorite Italian soccer players, and he always liked the fact that it was close to his name too, off by only a single letter.

"It's close but different. Italian instead of Albanian," Berti said. "Close but no cigar. Thank you, Drilon."

Drilon left the room. He was sweating and the color had faded from his face. He wanted to hide as far away from Buda as possible until the man left.

"Anyone else you need to ask?" Buda said.

"No, I know all the other guys' families and have never heard of a Grazdani."

The men hugged briefly, Buda having difficulty getting his arms around Berti.

"Let's not be strangers," Berti said, waving.

Buda got in his car, but before he drove away, he called Fatos Toptani, his most trusted man back in the Bronx. In the Buda organization, Fatos was number two.

"It's me. I need to get hold of someone right now. Name is Burim Graziani, one of Ristani's crew. He's working down in South Jersey. . . . No, no, nothing heavy, I just need to ask him a question. Yeah . . . Something ain't right here."

From his office, Ristani waited a couple of minutes till he thought Buda had left the premises, then made a phone call of his own.

57.

Prek was pleased to leave the tense atmosphere of the house even to undertake the menial task of cleaning out the van, something Neri should be doing. Prek was going crazy just sitting around, waiting for Buda to call to give either a thumbs-up or a thumbs-down. The other two numskulls could not stop talking about sex and who was going to be first even though the woman was no longer in their sight.

In a closet in the house he found a mop and bucket and an inventory of cleaning supplies, including a battery-operated hand vacuum mounted on the wall. Prek filled the bucket with water and poured in a generous quantity of Pine-Sol, loaded up the gear, and walked out to the van. In the morning, they would take it to a car wash and take care of the outside of the vehicle; for now Prek wanted to make sure the interior was free of any trace of the girl. He vacuumed the cab and washed down all the surfaces with Windex. When he was finished he moved to the back to continue his work when his cell phone rang.

At last, he thought.

Neri Krasnigi got up from the couch in the living room, went to the window, and watched Prek get in the back of the van with his wet mop. *There's Prek doing women's work*, he thought to himself. It seemed appropriate. He hadn't been able to get Pia out of his mind, and he also felt slighted by Prek's attitude toward him. Through the whole job, Prek had ordered him around, throwing stuff at him in the van, giving him the toughest part of the mission but showing him no respect at all. Even when Prek told him he did a good job it was in the tone of voice you'd use with a puppy who was taking a piss outside.

Neri had forgotten the initial terror he'd felt after he shot the student. Now he was feeling bold, accomplished, entitled—feelings that had heightened when he chugged down the last of the Red Bull. Perhaps he had a chance to show up Prek and have some fun in the process, even if it would have to be a private triumph.

Neri went to check on Genti, who'd fallen asleep on one of the sofas. With Prek out of the house and busy and Genti asleep, Neri thought he could risk a quickie. After all, what could Prek do? Neri slipped a hand into his jacket to briefly fondle his gun. It gave him courage. He was his own boss.

Being careful not to make a sound that might wake Genti, Neri slipped into the master bedroom and went over to the bed, took a good look at Pia. She was again supine, clearly breathing, but she looked as dead to the world as she had when they'd first brought her into the house. Tip-toeing, he went back to see what Prek was doing and when he walked to the kitchen window, he could see the van's doors were open with someone inside. With Prek attending to his housekeeping duties, Neri thought he was safe for at least ten or fifteen minutes. With mounting excitement, Neri went to the front door and threw the dead bolt. Then he quickly tiptoed back into the master bedroom, literally shaking with excitement. He closed the door.

So what does that mean for us?" Prek asked Buda. He wasn't sure he understood what his boss was trying to tell him.

"It means we don't do anything with the girl till I figure out what's going on with this moron Drilon."

"You're sure he was lying?" Prek couldn't understand why someone might lie when asked a direct, simple question about whether someone was related to them or not.

"I'm pretty sure. Everything about his behavior told me he was lying. When I asked him a direct question, he hesitated and then started stammering that he didn't know if he was related or not. It was obvious to me he knows the name. And it's practically his name. If you're gonna change your name, change your name."

"And his boss didn't say anything?" Prek asked, meaning Berti Ristani.

"Nothing. Either he didn't notice or he didn't want to say anything with me sitting there. I bet it's the latter because he's not stupid. It's this Drilon guy who's stupid."

"Why would he lie about something like that? He must know what the implications are."

"I would assume as much," Buda said. This, of course, was the question that was nagging at him. If Drilon Graziani was lying, it meant whatever he was trying to conceal from his boss was more important to him than this girl's life, even if she was a relative. Paradoxically, that fact made the girl suddenly more valuable to Buda, even if he didn't know why. This was the reason it was so important for him to talk to Burim Graziani, if that was actually his name. Buda figured that Ristani had also realized Drilon was lying, which had an entirely separate set of consequences.

Buda himself didn't appreciate being lied to, especially by a subordinate, and he wouldn't want to be in Drilon's shoes if Buda was right about his supposition. It also put Buda in a tricky position. His visit was probably now the cause of a problem within the Ristani crew. He hoped Berti didn't blame him for that.

"I don't want to talk about it anymore," Buda said, meaning that he wasn't comfortable having even this guarded a conversation over a cell phone line. "I'm coming up there to the summer house. Just make sure our guest is treated as a guest until this is cleared up," Buda said.

"Will do," Prek said, ending the call. He'd left Genti in charge in the house, and he trusted him, for the most part. But he thought he'd better check.

Immediately after talking with Prek, Buda got another call on his headset.

"Aleksander, it's Berti. Sorry to bother you."

"No bother, Berti," Buda said.

"I talked with Burim," Berti said. "I asked him about Pia Grazdani, wondering if he'd ever heard the name. And you know what? He said he did. Can you believe that?"

"No," said Buda, but he could.

"Then Burim called back and said one of your guys tried to call him." Berti said nothing more and left the statement hanging in the air. Buda thought he'd better play it straight.

"I did have one of my guys call Burim," Buda admitted. "You know as well as I do, Berti, Drilon acted strangely to my question. My sense was that he was lying. I figure that's your business, him lying to you, but he lied to me too. If I could ask the brother, maybe I wouldn't have to bother you directly. But I have to find out so I can deal with the woman I'm holding without starting a blood feud."

"I appreciate that, Aleksander. Of course, none of us want another blood feud: Albanian brother against Albanian brother. Of course I noticed Drilon was lying, and I called him back after you left and asked him again. I said, 'No fucking around,' and he said yeah, well, maybe he did know a Pia Grazdani. He tried to say he'd forgotten because he hasn't heard the name or seen the girl for twenty-some-odd years."

Buda was relieved that Berti was seeing it his way.

"So what do we do, Berti?"

"You hold on, I can conference you through to Burim."

"I need to make another quick call first," Buda said.

"Okay. Do what you need to do, then call me right back."

Buda was navigating a complicated course but calmly made his call to Prek. When Prek picked up, Buda spoke and didn't give Prek a chance to respond. He told Prek that he had to talk to a man named Burim Graziani before he could say yea or nay about Pia Grazdani. He said he was about to talk with him, so he'd be getting back to Prek straightaway with a final answer. "Hold the course with our guest for another half-hour or so," Buda said. "I thought I'd also let you know I'm only about a half-hour away. I'm in Wayne, on Route 23. I'll be back to you shortly."

As soon as Prek hung up from Buda the second time, after being told to hold the course, he jumped out of the van. For a moment he stood and listened. He had expected to hear muffled conversation from his two sex-starved underlings, but he heard nothing, which was disturbing. A half-hour earlier the men had been unable to stop talking. With gathering urgency, Prek headed for the front door, hearing in his mind Buda telling him the woman was to be treated as a guest.

With his intuition setting off alarm bells, Prek reproached himself: He should not have left the two alone no matter how much he had wanted to get out of the house. He went to open the front door and found it locked.

"What the . . ." he said. He ran around the corner of the house directly to the window of the master bedroom. Neri hadn't even bothered to close the drapes. Prek banged twice on the window, then ran back to the van, grabbed his gun from the glove compartment, ran back to the window, and smashed it with the butt of the gun. He was furious. Reaching in awkwardly, he fired off a single round.

58.

TURNOFF ON ROUTE 23
WAYNE, NEW JERSEY
MARCH 25, 2011, 9:19 P.M.

I understand you're trying to reach me," Burim Graziani said.

"Berti, are you still on the line?" Buda questioned.

"I'm getting off. You two men talk." There was a click when Berti hung up.

"Yes, I need to talk to you," Buda said to Burim. "We haven't met each other, right?"

"No, I don't believe so. But I know who you are, of course."

In their line of work, everyone knew Aleksander Buda. This was going to be a complicated conversation, Buda could tell. He wanted to make sure it wasn't also too compromising. Cell phones could be hacked, even new cell phones like the one Buda was currently using.

"For that reason, we need to be careful."

"I understand."

Neither of them was willing to start. Burim had been shocked to get Ristani's call. He had been in his car, driving back to Weehawken from South Jersey where he'd concluded his business early. Ristani's question had shaken him so much he nearly rear-ended the truck in front of him. "Pia Grazdani?" he'd repeated out loud, and he thought of his wife, not his daughter. He remembered her fiery personality, the fights, how Pia stayed out all night to party, leaving him alone with the baby. His sudden fury meant he wasn't listening properly to what Berti was asking him.

"She's about twenty-five," Berti had said. "Apparently quite beautiful. Burim, shit, can you hear me?" The connection had not been good, going in and out. It was at that point that Burim realized Berti wasn't talking about his late wife, but rather about his daughter, Afrodita Pia Grazdani.

Buda cleared his throat. "Berti told me you recognize the name Pia Grazdani. Is there any relation?"

"I remember her by a different name," Burim said. "Afrodita, which is what I called her. Her middle name was Pia, like her mother. She was my daughter."

Afrodita. The kid had been a pain in the ass almost as much as the mother since she'd inherited her mother's personality. Drilon had been the only one who got along with her. A miserable little thing, very demanding at a time when Burim had been too busy trying to make the grade in the Rudaj organization. He'd had no time for a kid. After she'd been taken away by city services, Burim told himself that he'd go and get her back when he was legal in the country, but when he got his green card, he decided he was happier as a man without the burden of responsibility. Then he had to drop out of sight as Burim Graziani and he never got around to establishing his new identity beyond getting a driver's license in case there was ever a traffic stop. He imagined he'd now have to explain all this to Berti Ristani, something that was a bigger issue to him than the fate of his daughter.

"So you think this girl might be your daughter?" Buda asked, not wanting to believe this was happening.

"It's possible, for sure. It's hardly a common name, and the age is about right, mid-to-late twenties." Try as he might, Burim couldn't remember Afrodita's birthday—neither the day nor the year.

"What's the story with the change of the family name?"

Burim related that issue. Since Buda, like all Albanian mafia, knew the details of the Rudaj debacle, he understood. When the FBI came bursting in, lots of people had to go underground.

"So you lost touch with your daughter a long time ago?"

"Yes, you know how it is in this business."

Having been at the time a gofer in a neighborhood crew that was heavily involved in the drug business didn't make him ideal parent material. Buda and Burim both understood. Burim didn't think it was necessary to fill in the details. That the cops had come and taken the kid away and put her in foster care, that he hadn't bothered to stay in contact, was all understood. Burim went quiet again.

"You think she'd remember you?"

"She was six, I believe, when she went away, and I guess a kid can remember back that far."

Burim couldn't help wondering why a man like Buda cared about this woman who might possibly be his daughter. "So how did this Pia Grazdani show up? How did she get involved with you?"

"She's associated with a job I was asked to do," Buda said vaguely. "She's a medical student at Columbia University, doing work with some researcher who had an accident and died."

Burim was shocked once again. Could his daughter be a medical student? And at such a famous university? It seemed incredible. If pressed, he would have thought the girl would end up on a similar path as her mother, would have been with a guy like him or maybe even out on the street.

A medical student? He was surprised to feel something like pride.

"And is she pretty, like Berti said?"

"I haven't seen her, but I'm told she is quite beautiful. And, er, scrappy."

"You mean she likes a fight?"

"You could say that."

"That sounds right," Burim said ruefully. "Her mother was a tigress. So what is this about?"

"Where are you?" Buda asked. "With this development, we need to talk in person."

It turned out that Burim was only about fifteen miles from where Buda was parked, near the Lincoln Tunnel exit on the New Jersey Turnpike.

"Do you know the Swiss House Inn?" Burim asked, and Buda did. The restaurant was just off Route 80, convenient for Burim and Buda and not far, as it happened, from Green Pond either.

"I want my brother to come," Burim said.

"Okay," Buda said, curious. The two brothers seemed to be like night and day. Why he'd want his moron brother there, Buda couldn't imagine, but he didn't care. It was, after all, a family affair.

"I will have an associate with me as well," Buda said, thinking of Fatos Toptani. If he could get Fatos Toptani to get there in time, he thought.

"About thirty minutes," Buda said, and rang off. He wasn't happy that the call had taken so long, but his hand had been forced somewhat. What were the odds that Berti's guy Burim was this Pia's father? From that perspective, he was very glad he'd thought to look into the issue. Killing the daughter of a connected man, even a long-lost daughter, even a daughter the father was ambivalent about, would have been a serious matter, especially for a man associated with the Ristani crew. More than any other crew Buda knew, they were addicted to violence. For them it was like a sport.

Buda quickly phoned Berti back and gave him a synopsis of the conversation. "As strange as it may seem, this Pia Grazdani may be Burim's long-lost daughter." Berti was as surprised as anyone. "We're getting together in person," Buda added.

"Good," Berti replied. "I appreciate the care you are taking with this. I wouldn't want anything to come between our organizations."

"Nor would I," Buda responded, and meant it.

Buda then made one more call before heading off to the restaurant rendezvous with Burim. He called Prek. It was now more important than ever that Pia be treated with kid gloves. Her fate was going to have to be in Burim's hands.

59.

Prek's phone rang again. Again it was Buda, just as he expected. He took the news saying little until Buda had finished. He then reassured Buda that everything was fine at the cottage, and before he rang off, he asked Buda to bring them some takeout if it was convenient. Buda agreed, saying he'd bring it from the Swiss House.

"What is it?" Genti said after Prek had disconnected.

"The Buda is on his way with Fatos to a restaurant not far from here to meet with two of Berti Ristani's guys who are brothers. It appears likely that the girl is related to them—the daughter of one and niece of the other. If it turns out to be true, my guess is they're going to talk for a while and figure out how they will vouch for her silence just like we vouched for her safety. Then they're going to drive here and find out that our promise was worth nothing. Then they're going to shoot Neri in the head and you in the legs. If you're lucky."

Prek indicated first Neri and then Genti. Neri had crammed his body into the corner of the couch. His hands were thrust down between his knees and his body was slumped forward although his head was up and he was looking at Prek. His eye, where Prek had smashed him in the face with the pistol, was a livid red. It would turn into a big black shiner, if he lived that long. Genti was sitting at the other end of the couch. He wanted to be sitting up with Prek, who was perched on the back of the couch opposite with his feet on the seat cushion, but he understood the symbolism. He was in the doghouse almost as much as Neri was.

"You fucking idiot," Prek said to Genti.

"Hey, I trusted him too," Genti said.

"I trusted *you*! And you egged him on with all your sex talk."

"Well, you didn't say, 'I'm going out to the van now, Genti. You make sure that Neri keeps his pants on.' You said, 'The boss says he doesn't know yet, leave the girl alone,' and you said it to both of us. I figured he heard it as good as I did."

"So you went off and took a nap."

"You were right outside, Prek. If you were so worried about her, why didn't you stay in here? It's as much your fault as it is mine."

"My fault?"

"Okay, Prek, not your fault, but I didn't touch her. What about this little fucker?" Genti waved his hand in the direction of Neri.

"I never did nothing," Neri said very quietly.

"What did you say?" Prek said.

"He said he never did anything," Genti said. "He said you stopped him before he got anywhere. He said that already."

"Didn't look that way to me."

"Me, I tend to believe the guy. I would if someone near shot my head off like you did, then hit me in the face with a gun. This guy, I tell him the truth. Listen, Prek, the girl ain't gonna remember anything either way."

"That's not the point." Prek was yelling now. "He's saying he didn't do anything and I'm saying that is not what I saw."

"Which part, Prek?"

"Which part what?"

"What did you see?"

What Prek had seen through the window was Neri with his pants off lying on top of Pia—there was no other conclusion, he was raping her. When Prek smashed the window and fired the gun, it was with the intention of scaring Neri, but the shot had been too close, passing barely three inches above the young man's head and slamming through a cheap wardrobe into the brick wall behind. But it had the desired effect. The shot awoke Genti, who let the apoplectic Prek in the front door. Prek immediately went to Neri and hit him in the face as he stood there, his pants around his ankles.

Neri was thoroughly humiliated and more than a little scared. He was telling the truth, he didn't rape the girl, but it wasn't for lack of trying. He'd found he had the same issue with a sleeping beauty as he did with any hooker—he couldn't get an erection. He'd wanted to prove something to himself, but he'd failed. And right now, that wasn't the worst of it. The girl had squirmed pretty good underneath him. He was worried that she wasn't nearly as out of it as she looked.

Pia gradually felt more and more awake. Her head was pounding, but she remembered a few things. She remembered being at the subway station near the hospital and she remembered George was coming to get her. And Will was there. Something had happened to Will. She remembered that the street was wet, because it was raining. She'd hurt her knee a little when she'd fallen. Why had she fallen?

The room she was in was a mess of shapes she was having trouble deciphering. She was lying on a bed, she could feel that. She could hear voices from a room nearby. Who did the voices belong to? She shook her head. That's right, she was in a car. No, a van. And someone stuck a needle in her thigh. Ouch. She listened. The voices belonged to the men who had stuck her with a needle. They were the voices of the men who had attacked her in her dorm room. They were the men who had done something to Will. *And one of them was just doing something to me. I have to get out of here,* she thought to herself.

Pia could move her arms and legs. She was surprised to discover she wasn't tied up. She looked around the room and saw a closed door on one side and a broken window on the other. There had also been a really loud noise. *And a man on top of her.* Something in Pia's brain kicked in. She had to get out of that room, even if it was just to the other side of that door or out the window—either would be better than in there. The men's voices were loud again, and they were coming from the other side of the door. The window, then.

Pia swung her legs over the side of the bed and tried to stand but she flopped down onto her knees and then her hands. Avoiding shards of glass, she crawled to the window and pulled herself upright. The old-style window had a handle that Pia held on to. As she turned the handle, the empty sash flew open, and she fell halfway out of the frame. It took some effort to reach down until her hands were on the earth in front of the window and she walked herself forward, using them until she could lift one leg then the other out and over the sill. She collapsed on the ground. Pia assumed she'd made so much noise, whoever was shouting in the other room would have heard. But she could still hear the voices, fainter but still there, still raised in disagreement.

So what are you going to tell Buda?" Genti said. He was now scared.

"What do you think I should tell him?"

"Tell him nothing happened. Look him in the eye and tell him nothing happened."

"I don't want to lie to Buda. Why should I lie? It's you guys who are at fault."

Neri looked over at the door to the bedroom where Pia was sleeping. *She better not remember anything,* he thought, *or I'm dead.*

Now sitting on her haunches, Pia resisted the urge to close her eyes, lie down, and go back to sleep, although every bone in her body was telling her to do it. Not for the first time in her life, an adrenaline rush drove her on. She looked over at the van, but she realized it was probably directly in the line of sight of where the voices were coming from. And she was in no state to drive; she'd crash into the first tree she came across.

Pia had no idea where she was, so she tried to size up the situation. She was cold, she knew that. She had been in a house, and she couldn't see any other houses around, or any lights. She stared into the dark in front of the house. Was that water? Yes. A river? A lake? Was it the ocean? She had no idea. She saw the light of a midsize moon, mostly obscured by clouds, but she couldn't tell if it was rising or setting. Pia kept low but started to move to her right, away from the van. She could see better now, and on the other side of the body of water she saw a single house showing one light. There were other homes, but those that she could see both across the water and the immediate neighbors were just dark geometric shapes.

Leading away from the house in a curve was a pea stone driveway, and Pia walked unsteadily along its edge, trying to keep

off the stones. She felt like she was getting her legs beneath her now. Reaching a
stretch of pavement, she didn't know which
way to go, left or right. She noticed she
was somewhere out in the country, with
forest all around. Pia made an arbitrary decision and turned right. On the pavement,
she tried to up her speed to a jog, but she
staggered along like a drunk. Pia guessed
she'd been given some drug. Again she
remembered the stabbing pain in her thigh.

The road was flat and straight and Pia
passed driveways on her right but none on
the left. The trees kept the road dark; there
were no lights on in any of the houses she
passed. Pia listened intently for the sound
of the van back at the house starting up.
Suddenly, the road stopped and split into
a starburst of driveways leading off into the
darkness. Shafts of moonlight had broken
through the clouds and in a gap in the
trees, Pia could make out water to her left.
Water on her left, water on her right. She
got the uncomfortable feeling she was
heading down to the end of a peninsula.

Pia turned and retraced her steps, but
then, to her dismay, the quiet of the woods
was shattered by the raucous sound of an

automobile engine starting. It was coming from outside the house she'd escaped from. The light from the headlights bounced as the van made its way quickly down the driveway. If the van turned right, she was a sitting duck. Pia swung around and ran down a driveway to her left, trying to make as little noise as possible on the gravel. Reaching the house, Pia made a detour on flagstones set into grass around the house, quickly coming upon a small sandy beach. Now she could see she was at the edge of a circular two- or three-hundred-yard-long cove with its relatively narrow neck to her left leading out to a large lake. At this point, the opposite shore was just a couple of hundred feet away and along the shore was the house with the light on.

Pia weighed her options. If she yelled, Pia knew the men in the van were more likely to hear her than anyone else. She could hide, but she would have to move eventually, and when it got light, for all she knew, she'd be plainly visible to the men who had taken her. Noticing a pile of rocks breaching the water's surface in the middle of the narrow expanse between where she was standing and the opposite shore, Pia wondered if the water might be shallow all the way across. Although she knew the water would undoubtedly be freezing, she thought that crossing the cove represented her best chance.

Pia took off her shoes and her shirt and bunched them against her chest and stepped into the water. As she had expected, the water was numbingly cold, and Pia breathed in sharply. She looked behind her, but there was no sign of the van lights. There was sand on the bottom of the cove, then a slick mud and the occasional rock. As the water came up to her waist, there were mostly rocks and Pia slipped, exposing more of her skin to water. Regaining her balance, she continued forward. Suddenly, the headlights flashed across the water in front of her, then again, twenty feet to her right. Pia slowed as she reached the rock pile. Her legs and feet were totally numb and felt more like stilts than legs. Skirting the rocks, she had only fifty feet or so to go.

Without warning, the bottom dropped away and Pia's feet slid down an underwater slope covered with slimy silt. In the next instant, she was trying to tread water using one hand, holding her shoes and clothes over her head with the other. She tried to swim, holding her breath in the icy water. Almost immediately she felt her muscles begin to lose some of their function. She gasped for breath: now she was numb all over except for her face. Pia gave up holding her clothes over her head; she dropped her shoes and tried to swim a few strokes. She was able to move forward a little faster even though she felt like she was barely moving.

Eventually, her right foot touched a sandy bottom. She stood up with the water up to her neck and pushed toward the shore. She was shivering so much it was hard to hold her soaked clothes. Within a few feet, the water was back to waist-deep. The lighted house was about a hundred feet to her left. She tried to call out, but the loudest sound she could make was a whisper. She staggered; her legs weren't hers. Finally she was out of the water, on a kind of point with the shoreline falling off on both the lake side and the cove side. But the route to the lighted house along the edge of the lake was blocked by large boulders, underbrush, and numerous trees. She'd have to reach the house via the road.

Pia found a path of sorts through the uneven ground, and she saw there was a long dark driveway from the road down to the house. She made her way toward the driveway so she could reach the road. There were sharp stones under her still totally numb feet, and she was carrying her dripping wet clothes. What would these people think? She reached the pavement and turned left. Walking was difficult, but the house was getting closer.

Then, behind her, she heard an approaching vehicle. How far away, she couldn't tell. With mounting panic, she looked behind her into the darkness, and she could see the glow of approaching headlights. She had no time to hide, and she knew she wasn't able to run. She tried to call out, but the feeble noise was drowned out as she was bathed in bright light. Maybe it was someone else, part of her brain was telling her. Shielding her dark-adapted, squinting eyes with her free hand, Pia stared back. The vehicle braked and came to a halt within inches of her near-naked, shivering body.

Please, please, please.

Pia's heart sank. It was a van, a blue van.

60.

Aleksander Buda waited in the parking lot of the Swiss House Inn for Fatos to arrive. It was a standing joke among the crew that the thinnest guy they knew was Fatos, although no one ever said it to his face more than once. Fatos was slender and wiry as a greyhound, with quick hands that made him very proficient with a knife. He was rarely seen without his baseball hat, worn jauntily backward like a hip-hop devotee. When Buda wanted backup like he wanted that evening, he always called Fatos.

As dependable as ever, five minutes after Buda arrived, Fatos pulled his black Cadillac sedan into an empty space next to Buda's. Both cars were off by themselves at the back of the lot. Neither man got out. Buda barely acknowledged Fatos with a nod. They didn't need to talk a lot.

Buda's eyes swept around the half-full parking lot. A guy he thought might be Burim was sitting in a new Chevy Camaro in a slot facing out no more than twenty yards to his right. The driver sitting behind the wheel fastidiously ignored Buda. Then another car drove up, an Escalade, and Buda recognized Drilon riding high at the wheel. Drilon flashed his lights at the Camaro.

"Gang's all here," Buda said to himself.

Drilon parked, and first Burim, then Buda, then the other two men got out of their cars, met in the middle, and exchanged greetings.

"Let's get something to eat," Buda said. "I'm starved."

The restaurant and bar was situated in a rather ordinary-looking two-story wood-frame house painted a deep green with white trim. Except for the lighted sign announcing Swiss House Inn in front of the building next to the road, the structure didn't look much like a restaurant, more like another house along the road only in better shape. The parking lot was fairly full, so it was obviously a popular place on a Friday night. Burim walked in the door first and the lady at the door made a fuss of him, asking after his health and saying his table was ready. Buda guessed he'd called ahead and was a frequent patron. Other diners who had been waiting to be seated took one look at the group and to a man and woman decided not to make an issue with the men who jumped the line. They were all in oversized leather jackets, the accepted attire of the Albanian mafia.

In the back of the busy restaurant was a single booth situated partway between the kitchen and the main room. The only traffic was from staff coming out of the kitchen, several of whom made a point of saying hello to Burim.

"So they know you in here," Buda said.

He was mildly disappointed. If he'd known Burim was a regular, he wouldn't have agreed to the location.

"I'm a big tipper," Burim said, winking at Drilon across the table.

Buda studied the two men. Drilon was sweating and looked distinctly uncomfortable. Burim was relaxed and exuded calm confidence. Burim got the looks and the brains, Buda thought.

"What can I get you guys?"

It was the hostess doing double duty. They ordered four beers and the special, schnitzel, all around.

"So here's the deal, gentlemen," Buda said. He dove right in, dispensing with small talk. "I'm doing a job for someone and halfway through, there's a problem. The problem is this girl who is sticking her nose in, investigating a situation and making things very difficult for me. We tried to dissuade her, but it didn't work. The sensible course is to eliminate the problem, so I clear it with my client, who is willing to pay a hundred grand for the extra work, meaning to take care of the meddling bitch."

Buda paused to take a sip of water and he glanced at Fatos. Fatos knew the contract was for $250,000, but there was no reason these guys had to know.

"If, as might be the case, this girl is your daughter, then you have to take responsibility for her, and you and me, we'll share the money. But that means it's your responsibility to make absolutely sure she desists from investigating this case, from poking around, from talking to people, from thinking about it, from dreaming about it. And if she isn't your daughter, then we will fulfill the contract and you must promise not to mention anything about what we have done. In that case you get a quarter of the money for your inconvenience."

"Where is she right now?" Burim asked. At that point he was anticipating meeting her.

"Not far from here. She's perfectly safe."

"And what was she sticking her nose into, as you put it?"

"I'd rather not say. Ah, our food already."

The steaming plates of schnitzel and noodles arrived. Remembering Prek's request, Buda ordered four more to go.

"The key point is," Buda said, poised with a forkful of veal, "that she stops doing what she's doing. I have to tell you, she's making things very dangerous for me. It would be good if she went on a long vacation."

"I'm sure we can arrange that," Burim said. He had no reason to believe he could make that happen, but he liked the idea that there was to be a payday in this for him. "Right, Drilon?"

"Sure." Drilon was facing his own set of demons, but he had little choice but to play along. He pushed a noodle around the edge of his plate with his fork.

"We're happy to help you, Mr. Buda, but we are incurring some more expenses here," Burim said.

"Don't worry," Buda said, "we'll take care of dinner."

"No, really, your money is no good here. There will be other expenses, for the girl." Burim had already decided the girl had to be his missing daughter. The coincidences were too extraordinary. And if the girl's personality resembled that of his late wife, he was going to need some cash to even hope to control her.

"Of course," Buda said. He had been expecting this. "I think ten thousand is a fair amount for the girl."

"For her inconvenience," Burim said. Buda nodded at Fatos, who leaned back and shuffled some bills under the table and presented Burim with a thick wad folded in half.

"Either way," Buda said, "daughter or no daughter. If she is not your daughter, you can keep the cash for your expenses."

"You have been very thoughtful," Burim said.

"And you have been very cooperative," Buda said.

Buda and Burim shook hands across the table, and in turn all four men shook hands, making the agreement as binding as any legal document in Albanian tradition and logic. The men finished their meal quickly, and with the takeout in hand, they left. Burim, having left three twenties on the table as a tip, was detailed to follow Buda, who would lead the way in a motorcade of sorts.

As Burim walked out of the restaurant, he patted his pocket with the fresh bulge of cash and smiled, thinking it was going to be an interesting and profitable evening.

61.

There was nothing the occupants of the summer house could do but wait. Prek sat next to Neri on one couch with Genti and Pia sitting opposite. He had thought about tying her up, as he should have done before, but he didn't want to make a worse impression than he had to. Besides, the girl wasn't going anywhere. Prek had found an old T-shirt in a closet and gave it to Pia to wear along with one of his own

New York Jets sweatshirts he kept at the house. The jersey came halfway down her thighs. She also wore a pair of soccer socks pulled up to her knees. She had draped a towel over her shoulders, but she was still shivering.

Pia sat and glared at Neri. That was the guy who had touched her, she was sure of it. She stole glances at the other guys too—the one who seemed to be in charge with the thick scar on his upper lip, and the guy with the dominating nose. She wasn't entirely certain but believed they were the men who had attacked her the night before. She recognized their voices.

Prek cradled a gun in his hand. He wondered if he would have to use it that night, and if so, who would be the target. He could make a case for any of them: Neri for brazenly disobeying an order, and Genti for failing to stop him. The only person Prek wasn't mad at was Pia. He admired her for trying to escape and for getting as far as she had. If he had to shoot her, it would not be emotional. It would just be business.

At least the fiasco was going to have a conclusion soon, thought Prek, as he heard a group of cars pull into the driveway one after the other. A moment later they heard car doors opening and then slamming shut in quick succession.

"Go wait in the bedroom," Prek said to Pia.

As soon as Buda, Fatos, Burim, and Drilon walked into the house, they could all tell that something was wrong. The atmosphere among the three men inside was clearly strained. Neri was sitting on the couch, staring at the floor and didn't stand up. Genti wouldn't make eye contact, and Prek acted fit to be tied. Buda had to find out what had happened and fast.

"Gentlemen," he said, turning to Burim and Drilon. "I left the food we picked up in the back of my car. Would you mind? I'd just like to have a quick word with my guys."

Burim and Drilon left the room and closed the door. Buda lit into Prek.

"What the fuck is going on here? Stand up, Neri! Genti, look at me when I'm talking! Where's the girl?"

"She's in the bedroom," Prek said. "She got out the window, jumped in the lake, and swam off."

"What? Are you serious?"

"Yes, but we found her right away."

"Did anyone see her?"

"No, I'm certain. There's no one here but us."

"You quite sure about that?"

"Yes."

Buda's three men were standing like guilty schoolboys in front of the principal.

"What happened to you?" Buda asked Neri, whose eye was closing rapidly. Neri didn't speak but looked across at Prek.

"Did she do that?"

"No," Prek said. "I did."

"What for?" Buda leaned forward, his hands on his hips. Fatos was standing by the door with his arms crossed. The message was clear: No one out or in.

"Prek," Buda said, "you better tell me what happened right now, or we're going to have a major problem."

"He attacked the girl," Prek said. Neri's face fell. He'd hoped Prek would make up some story on his behalf.

"Was that before or after she escaped?"

"Before."

"And where were you?" he asked Genti. Silence.

"All right, I'll deal with this later. It all depends on whether or not this girl is the daughter. Let's hope for you she isn't. Fatos, let 'em in."

"Burim, Drilon," said Buda in as friendly a tone as he could manage. "What happened here is that the girl tried to escape, but she didn't succeed. My men are very embarrassed, as they should be."

Burim looked at Neri but no explanation was forthcoming regarding his injury.

"My wife was certainly a tigress," he said. "Perhaps this woman is too. Mr. Buda, I am ready to meet her."

Buda showed Burim into the bedroom and left. Pia was sitting on the bed, facing the window, shivering.

"Afrodita. Pia," Burim said. "Is it really you? I am Burim. Burim Grazdani. I think I'm your father. Pia, look at me, please."

Pia sat for a second and then turned, glowering at the man, her face clouded with unadulterated fury and loathing. Burim's expression went from disbelief to pure amazement.

"Oh, God," he said. "You're exactly your mother's image." Burim knew the look she had on her face, from the first Pia, a beautiful woman full of hatred. Burim had feelings he'd never experienced and couldn't come close to articulating.

"I'm told you're a student at Columbia Medical School. That's amazing. You must be very intelligent."

Pia had turned around again, and Burim continued talking to her back.

"You look like your mother, you know that? Probably you don't. The same hair, the same eyes, it's amazing."

Pia said nothing. Could it possibly be him?

"I feel this is a miracle, our meeting. Pia, please say something."

Silence.

"Your uncle Drilon is here."

Now Pia reacted. She hacked up some spittle and spat loudly on the floor by the bed. Burim was disconsolate.

"Pia, I'm sorry I never came for you. I was young and stupid. I meant to come, so many times, but I knew that if I came forward they would find out I was illegal in this country and send me home, and then I would never have a chance of seeing you. I was working with these guys, the

Rudaj group, you know, and the organization fell apart, and Drilon and I had to go underground. Then when we started working for Ristani, we had to change our names and leave our pasts behind. I wish we didn't have to do it, but we did. Pia, please."

As soon as Pia saw Burim's face, she knew who he was. This was the man she had waited years for, the man who put her through torments while she fervently hoped that he'd come back to save her. He never did. Now he was showing up, and for what? And he had brought that monster with him? What were they going to do, kill her? At this point, Pia barely cared.

"Listen, I know I abandoned you, but suddenly, now that I see you, it's important to me that you are my daughter and that you're safe."

"Safe? Do you have any idea what it was like for me in foster care?" Pia snarled. Burim was startled by the sound of her voice.

"Do you?"

"But you're going to be a doctor, look how it all ended up!"

"*This* is how it ended up, you moron.

Guns, gangsters, *murderers*. That's what I remember from being a kid. And my mom was there, and then she wasn't. What happened to her?"

"I don't know."

"You're a liar!" Pia turned and screamed the words. Buda opened the door—he must have been standing right outside.

"Everything okay?"

"Leave us, please," Burim said. Silent tears were tracking down Pia's face. She turned back around and faced the wall. Pia couldn't make sense of what was happening. How was her father involved with the people who murdered Rothman, Yamamoto, and Will McKinley? They had been waiting for him to show up, which meant that he might be able to stop them killing her too. When she spoke again, Pia's voice was quieter.

"That's all I know about you. That you're a liar."

"I'm here now."

"Are you here to finish the job they started?"

"I understand why you say these things, but you have to believe me, I am here to save you."

"You and your white horse."

"What?"

"Whatever."

"What I am telling you is no lie. Those guys in the other room, they have been paid money to stop you because you were looking into some deaths. And they want you to stop looking."

Pia said nothing.

"They know you have an Albanian name and they asked around if anyone knows you, and I said, 'Yes, maybe.' It's the case that Albanian cannot kill Albanian: not in our business unless the killer wants to die too. If you weren't Albanian, if you weren't my daughter, you would be dead already. Do you understand?"

"That's very nice of them."

"Actually, it is, yes."

"They murdered my teacher and another doctor by giving them typhoid fever and a massive dose of polonium. Tonight they murdered my friend by shooting him in the head because he was helping me. I should be grateful to them because they're sparing me?"

"I can't do anything about the other people. What I can do is save you."

"And how will you do that?"

"I guarantee them that you will give up your investigation. And that you won't mention their involvement to the authorities. Take a vacation. Something. We can work it out."

"You? You haven't seen me since I was six. They'll take your word?"

"If I give it, yes. I have shaken their hand, and my family honor is at stake."

"Or they'll kill me."

"Or they'll kill you."

"And you'll take my word that I'll give up?"

"If you give me your word, yes."

Pia snorted. It seemed that the only person who could save her was her father, the least likely person on the planet, the person she trusted the least and hated the most, the man who was the cause of all her travails. In a situation that defied comprehension, Pia tried to think dispassionately. The drug wasn't completely out of her system, she could tell; she was more fatigued than she could ever remember being, and frightened and upset and angry. Yet she had to think.

In order to live, Pia would have to promise

to stop investigating, but could she do that? There was very little left to investigate. At the OCME, she had proved that polonium was involved in Rothman's and Yamamoto's deaths and she was certain the MEs would be looking into what she had found. The police would surely be all over Columbia, searching for Will's killers and her kidnappers. There was nothing more she could contribute to the investigation, other than providing evidence, and he hadn't mentioned anything about that. Her work was finished.

"As if you care about family honor," she said.

"I do. But if you don't believe it, take my word that I care about my honor."

"And that's all I have to do, stop investigating?"

"But you really have to stop—maybe go away for a while. You have to believe me, they will kill you otherwise. Whatever you think of me, you have to look at the alternative. You have to stay as quiet as you can. If you lead the police to Buda, there's no chance that you would ever testify against him."

Pia realized she had no choice. But

perhaps there was something her father could do for her and right some of the wrongs she had suffered. Pia turned to face him.

"Okay. But you should know, not all these men have been exactly honorable with me."

"I'm glad you agree, Pia. But what do you mean?"

"When I got here I was drugged. But I remember one of them at least forced himself on me, the young one for sure. Maybe all of them."

Burim reacted the way Pia had hoped. He looked at her for a beat, with his face empurpling, then leaped up and threw open the door.

"Mr. Buda! I need to talk to you."

Buda could see Burim was spoiling for a fight, flashing angry looks at Neri. The girl must have told him what had happened in the house. Everyone in the room stood and the tension was immediate. Buda took Burim by the arm into the kitchen. The packages of takeout sat unopened on the stovetop. Burim spoke quietly but with suppressed fury.

"She is indeed my daughter. And she

says she was raped. By the youngest one for certain, maybe more of them. Did you know about this?"

"Listen, I was told that one man did lose control of himself briefly but there was no sex—"

"But—"

"I understand this is shocking to you, all of this, but there was so little chance she was your daughter—"

"That is no excuse. Perhaps it is better if she was killed rather than be shamed like this. I gave my handshake, but perhaps I have to take it back."

Buda looked Burim in the eye. Was he serious or was he just shaking him down for more money? Ten minutes ago the guy didn't even know he had a daughter, and now he was concerned about her honor? Some of these guys really were peasants.

"I will punish the men, you can be assured of that."

Burim shook his head and pulled back his jacket, exposing his shoulder holster.

"It can only be put right if I get to do the punishing. Do you want me to call Berti?"

"No, of course not. The reason I called you was to avoid this kind of situation. A killing will only lead to more killing—that is always the way. Punishment, yes. Killing, no. I will apologize to her myself."

"I doubt she is going to accept any apology. That's how I knew it was her, she has the same temper as her mother."

"Listen, I will apologize. I will pay money to her and to you, money I will take from the three men in there. But I will not have a blood feud over this. It shouldn't have happened. I regret the situation. Ultimately, I am to blame. But I need you, Burim, to live up to your handshake and for her to give up her investigation."

Burim paused to think. Buda wouldn't allow a man from another crew to punish his own men. A blood feud was in no one's best interests, and he didn't want to be the cause of a dispute between Aleksander Buda and Berti Ristani.

"Okay. Let me talk to her."

Burim went back to the bedroom. Pia knew she had to accept Burim's help, however distasteful it was to her. Now she wanted more than anything to get out of there, to go and find George. Burim closed the door and relayed what Buda had said. Would she be willing to forgo the revenge she was entitled to? Pia knew justice was being twice denied—she was being prevented from implicating Rothman's killers and also from seeing some street retribution brought down on the person who attacked her.

"If that's the way it has to be, I want to talk to those men outside," Pia said.

"Okay," Burim said. "But I want to shake on our agreement: an Albanian shake."

Burim thrust out his hand. Pia eyed it. She didn't care. She shook hands, and her skin crawled when she touched his.

They walked into the living room where everyone was still standing, although in slightly more relaxed poses.

"I am going to accept the offer," she said to Buda. "I will do what you ask and drop the investigation. But I have a couple of things to say." Pia walked over to Neri and stood right in front of him. Neri started to shake, looking first at Prek, then at Buda, then at Burim.

"You are a piece of trash."

"I swear I didn't do anything. I can't, it's impossible—"

Pia jabbed Neri hard in the sternum with her forefinger.

"You're not so tough when the girl is awake, are you, huh? You know what my father is going to do with you? He's going to cut off your tiny little prick and shove it up your ass."

"No, no, I didn't—"

"I'm sorry?" Pia jabbed Neri again. He was crying now, great shuddering torrents of tears pouring out of his eyes. He held his hands together, pleading with Pia.

"You see how much stronger than you I am? You're a pathetic little boy." Pia poked him once more, and Neri collapsed backward onto the couch where he sat whimpering.

"And you," Pia addressed Drilon. "You will never speak to me or ever come near me again."

Drilon looked at Burim and raised his hands as if to say, "I don't understand." Quickly Pia went on.

"Now I have a question for you." Pia looked at Buda, who raised his eyebrows.

"Me?"

"Some men paid you money to frighten me?"

"Yes."

"Some men paid you money to kill me?"

"Yes."

"Are these the same men who asked you to kill Dr. Rothman and Dr. Yamamoto?"

Buda paused.

"Yes."

"Why did they do it? When I realized the deaths weren't accidental, I couldn't figure out why anyone would want to go to such lengths to kill two medical researchers. The work they were doing—they were about to change the world."

Buda looked at Burim. Was it possible to control this woman at all?

"Some people had investments that were threatened by the research."

"Investments? You mean they did this for *money*?"

"I guess," Buda said. Why does anyone do anything? he thought.

Pia was incredulous. She thought back to her heart-to-heart talk with Rothman and how it had seemed to be the start of something meaningful in her life: the father she never had. She recalled Yamamoto's kindnesses, small and large. And Will, his life snuffed out too. Then she remembered standing in the blue-lit room looking at the pulsating baths of artificial organs and the enormous excitement she had felt. And the even greater joy she experienced at the awe-inspiring sight of the artificial pancreas. Now, it was very likely those two rooms were being closed up and put in mothballs. The research would continue, but not at Columbia and not with her. Pia felt empty and bereft.

It was likely that Rothman and Yamamoto's killers were in this room. Pia couldn't touch them, she knew that; her life depended on their getting away with murder. But she wasn't completely powerless.

"In that case, there's something I want you to do. And then I promise I will stay off the trail and hold my tongue."

Pia told the men her idea. Buda liked it—this job had far too many loose ends. Burim agreed that it would satisfy his daughter's honor. The men shook hands again, and then each in turn shook hands with Pia.

Buda was happy with the resolution, although he was left with more work to do and he'd have to decide what to do with his men, especially Neri, who seemed to have fallen to pieces completely. Prek and

Genti were eating the lukewarm takeout, but Neri was still cowering on the couch.

Buda found an old pair of his wife's sneakers, which were too large for Pia but would work for now. He took them into the bedroom where she was resting.

"What will you do now?"

"You think I'm going to tell you?" she said.

"Listen, I'm sorry it happened this way."

"It's a bit late for that. Please, leave me alone."

When Pia came back into the room, it was filled with cigarette smoke. The men were standing around talking and a couple of them were laughing. Pia went over to Buda.

"Where's my cell phone?"

Buda looked at Prek, who shrugged.

"May as well let her have it. Just don't turn it on till we're done here."

"I won't."

Prek took Pia's cell phone, student ID, and wallet she used for her credit card and cash out of his jacket and gave them back to her.

"I'll be outside," Pia said. "It stinks in

here." Without another word, she went outside, slamming the door behind her hard enough to shake the house.

Burim shook his head. "She is her mother, exactly."

"We should go out there—she might call someone," Prek said.

"She won't," Buda said. "She's Albanian, she promised."

"She's half Albanian," Burim said. "And half Italian. I better go."

The men laughed.

Standing on the other side of the van, Pia had turned on the phone and it flooded with messages and e-mails and texts. She saw there was a text from Lesley Wong.

"God bless you," it read. "Praying for Will's recovery."

"Pia?"

It was Burim. She shut off the phone and emerged from behind the van.

"We're leaving," Burim said.

Pia had but one thought. Recovery? Could Will possibly be alive?

62.

GREEN POND, NEW JERSEY
MARCH 26, 2011, 12:03 A.M.

Buda gave his men their marching orders. He would drive back to the Bronx with Prek and Genti, while Neri would remain at the house and clean it and the van thoroughly to erase all traces of Pia's stay. Buda was quite specific about what products Neri would use and how long he should spend on each part of the task. Buda empha-sized what a good job he wanted Neri to do and that it would take him the entire weekend to complete. That would give Buda time to figure out what to do with Neri. Before he left the house, he put the van's keys in his pocket. Fatos had to drive Drilon back to the parking lot at the restaurant to pick up his car because Pia flatly refused to get into a car with Drilon. She wasn't about to explain why.

Pia sat in the front seat of Burim's vehicle and stared straight ahead as the men said their goodbyes in the driveway. Burim and Pia set off, heading for Weehawken. Burim turned up the heat for Pia's benefit.

"What's your problem with Drilon?"

"I'm not going to talk about it," Pia said.

"I hope you will later. So, tonight we'll go to my house."

Is he kidding? thought Pia. She was desperate to get away from this man.

"No, I want to go back to the hospital."

"I can't let you do that," Burim said.

"Sure you can," Pia said. "I promised not to meddle any more and I'm not going to. You'll have to trust me. It's the same tonight as it will be in a week, in a month. I have to check on something."

"The place will be swarming with cops."

"I'll have to talk to them eventually. Or

do you think I'll move in with you and live in New Jersey and play happy family? Because that's not happening. You can't just walk back into my life, don't you understand that? We have an arrangement, that's all. You have to trust me, I have to trust you. We shook hands, remember?"

"You can't tell the cops anything, obviously, you know that. Anything about Buda or his men or about seeing me and Drilon."

"Don't worry, it won't be difficult to forget you."

Burim ignored the barb.

"So we have to come up with a story for what happened to you," he said.

"The police will know as much as I do, about the polonium. But I don't know who did the killing, I just know the why."

"The less I know the better too."

"They'll find my system was full of drugs, I imagine," Pia said. "So I'll say I was drugged, then I was held in a house outside the city, but I escaped."

"So how did you get back to New York?"

"Okay, I woke up in New York, and I don't know where I've been."

"Where did you get the clothes?"

"I don't remember where I got the clothes and that's the truth."

"So it's this: You were out of it, drugged. Some guys drove you around, but you never saw their faces. Then they stopped in a house somewhere, and you were given different clothes. Then they drove again and let you off in Manhattan. I can't drive to the hospital myself, I can't risk being seen. You better get in the back, stay out of sight of the cameras on the bridge. I'll drop you at the top of Manhattan, on Broadway somewhere. You can take a cab from there."

"All right." Pia climbed into the backseat and curled up. She was exhausted and still shivering.

"Pia, we have to stay in touch. What's your cell phone number?"

Pia figured he could find out if he wanted to so she told him, and Burim said he would remember it. He didn't bother telling Pia his number.

Burim continued to talk, telling her little anecdotes about times he remembered from when Pia was a child. Burim convinced himself that his memory was correct, that these things had happened the way he remembered them. He concentrated on the road, and he knew Pia probably wasn't listening. He would try to reach out to her, but he wasn't confident she'd respond. After a while he stopped talking, and they rode in silence.

After forty minutes, Burim reached Broadway at the very tip of Manhattan. In the middle of a quiet block, he slowed down and Pia hopped out of the car without saying a word and didn't look back. Burim stopped the car and watched as Pia walked to an intersection and held out her hand to hail a taxi. A gypsy cab pulled over, and Pia leaned toward the window and told the driver something. Before she got in the car, Burim thought she looked small and vulnerable in her crazy mismatched outfit. But he had a feeling she'd be okay.

63.

COLUMBIA UNIVERSITY MEDICAL CENTER
NEW YORK CITY
MARCH 26, 2011, 1:00 A.M.

Pia asked the car to drop her off as close as he could get to her dorm building on Haven Avenue. There was still a police presence with artificial lighting at this location of the abduction and shooting. The fare was $12, and she gave the driver the twenty Burim had given her and didn't stop for change. On the ride down, Pia had concentrated her thoughts on Will, ignoring her father, who was jabbering away in the front seat. She tried not to think about her ordeal; at least she was safe now. Pia had no thought about whether or not she was going to try to establish a connection with her father, but she did know she'd have nothing at all to do with Drilon. The few things she remembered about him were all painful.

Pia focused. She wasn't worried about talking to the police—after all, it wouldn't be the first time. She'd build a wall around what happened at the house and not recount any of it; in all other aspects, she could be truthful. And there were some truths she was still determined that everyone know. There would be no possibility of a cover-up.

Pia walked up to the front desk in the dorm. There were two uniformed cops by the elevator, but Pia hoped that her strange garb and the fact that she'd bunched her hair up under a baseball cap would throw off a casual onlooker. Despite the late hour, students were coming in from studying at the Health Science Center or from a night out. A few others were on their way out, having been called to the hospital for emergencies.

Pia knew the person staffing the front desk and asked him about Will McKinley.

"Pia, is that you?" the young man said. "Cops are looking for you. They said you got *kidnapped* or something crazy."

"No, I'm fine. Will—tell me about Will." Pia gestured with her index finger over her lips to silence the man from calling attention to her presence.

"Oh, man, I heard he got shot in the head, but he survived. He was taken over to the Neurological Institute, and he had surgery. One of the other fourth-years said he's in Intensive Care."

Without another word, Pia turned and walked away from the desk and made her way over to Neurosurgical Intensive Care. She saw plenty of cops and security guards, but they were on the lookout for a woman with long black hair, not someone wearing a New York Jets sweatshirt to mid-thigh, soccer socks, and a baseball cap. She looked like a cheerleader.

At the doors of Intensive Care, there were more police. Pia was stopped by the nurses, who eyed her less than appropriate clothes and the bruise on her jawline. Pia explained she was a medical student and flashed her student identification with her finger over her name. She hoped that everyone there had been on duty the whole night and hadn't seen or heard the news. The head nurse said she wouldn't let Pia into the intensive care unit, but she paged the resident.

When the resident arrived he looked quizzically at Pia. Still, he was considerate after hearing that she was a medical student interested in the case. He assumed she was a girlfriend of the young man.

"Mr. McKinley is being maintained in an induced coma post-surgery," the resident, Dr. Hill, said. "He received a gunshot to the head, but the bullet made a complete transit through the frontal lobe. It's an injury that people have recovered from in the past. But I would emphasize that anyone suffering this kind of injury may not be exactly the same person he was before being shot and having brain surgery."

"He's a friend of mine," Pia said. "I was there when he was shot."

"So it's very important that you understand he will be different even if there is a seemingly complete recovery."

"Different how?"

"It would take too long to go into now. Look up the case of Phineas Gage, from 1848, which involved much more severe trauma to the frontal lobe. It was the first recorded case about how penetrating head trauma can affect personality."

"Can I see him?"

"I don't see why not. His family is on the way. You have to wear a gown and so on."

"Of course."

Pia went off to don her protective garb.

Only then did Dr. Hill remember something about being on the lookout for a young woman.

In Will McKinley's room, Pia found George standing by Will's bed.

"Pia, my God!" George said, and grasped her in an embrace. "Are you okay? What happened to you?"

"I'm fine. I'll tell you later. Will . . . how is he doing?"

"No one knows. I have to go back and talk to some more cops, but I wanted to see him. I saw the whole thing. I saw him get shot and you taken. I can't believe he's alive. And you too. Thank God. What happened?"

George stared at Pia as if she were an apparition, but she turned to look at Will. His breathing was being handled by a machine, there were tangles of wires and tubes enveloping him, and he was surrounded by banks of devices with illuminated readouts. Will's face looked calm and peaceful and his color was normal. Except for all the medical equipment and the beeping and clicking, he might have simply been sleeping. A nurse hovered nearby. Pia looked around the room and caught her reflection in the unit's large window. She looked terrible, like something the cat dragged in. She turned her attention back to George.

"George, I'm so sorry I got you into this. Please forgive me," she said. "If I had listened to you, then this would have turned out differently, I know that."

"Pia, I feel as terrible as you do about this. I was sleeping while you were waiting for me at the station. I slept through your calls. I should have come to you. It should be me lying there."

"That doesn't make me feel any better. Will had no idea what was going on and I didn't say anything. I don't know what's going to happen to me so there's a couple of things I want to say while I have the chance.

"I want to say thank you for going out of your way to help me. I don't really understand why you'd do that for someone without her asking, and without her appreciating what you're doing. But there are a lot of things I don't understand.

"I guess the main thing I don't understand is myself. I think you do know yourself, which is why you're able to say you love someone, like you did to me. And I'm sorry for not listening then either. I'm jealous that you can do that, and I wonder why I can't. I think there's something broken in me or something that was never there, and it's taken until now for me to see that. For a lot of reasons, I find it very difficult to trust people. As if I need to tell you that. . . . But I don't know how to love someone either, or how to accept their love. It's a big responsibility, being loved, and you should think hard before rejecting someone's love.

"But you've made me want to learn more about myself, to see if I can't fix that broken part. I think we studied that course together, in first-year psych, the part about people with personality issues who never accept that they're the ones who are different. So if they're marching, if they lead with their right foot while everyone else uses their left, they say with unshakable belief that it's everyone else who's out of step, not them. I think I'm like that."

Pia looked around. She hadn't realized the nurse had left, nor had she seen or heard the man enter the room. He was stocky, in a cap and gown, just like she and George were wearing, over his street-clothes. He was standing at the back of the room as she stood with George by Will's bed. The man waved his hand as if to say, "Don't mind me! Go on!"

"I never understood people's feelings, George. I sneered at people who said they were in love because I never knew what that meant. I don't know if I can change, and I don't know if someone can be taught how to love. But I do know I want to try to change."

Pia reached out and touched George's cheek with one fingertip.

"Please try to forgive me."

George closed his eyes.

"Pia, there's nothing to forgive. I'm just so happy you're safe."

Pia stepped back and studied Will's peaceful face, then turned toward the visitor. She sensed he was there to talk to her.

"Miss, I'm Detective Captain Lou Soldano. You're Pia Grazdani, I assume?"

"Yes."

"You have to come with me now."

"I understand. Do you mind if I use the bathroom first?"

"Of course not," Lou said.

After Pia told George she'd see him later, she and Lou walked out of the intensive care unit.

"I'm glad to see you," Lou said. "Are you okay?"

"I'm fine," Pia said, before disappearing into the women's room near the elevators. After locking the door, she took out her smartphone. Quickly she tapped out an e-mail, forwarding a sizable message she'd already written. After making certain it had gone, she used the toilet. She then looked at herself in the mirror over the sink and said: "Now the shit hits the fan." Taking a deep breath, she composed herself to go out and meet Detective Lou Soldano who represented her old nemesis, the City of New York.

64.

The man was aware of the buzzing of a phone right next to his ear. He went immediately from deep sleep to partial consciousness but it took him a few beats to realize where he was. He picked up the phone, saw his device, didn't recognize the number but accepted the call just to stop the noise.

"McGovern. This better be good, who- ever you are."

"Is this Chet McGovern?" a female voice said.

"I believe so, ask me tomorrow. What time is it anyway?"

"About two-fifteen, sorry about that."

"Do I know you?"

"My name is Jemima Meads. I'm calling from the *New York Post*."

"The *Post*?"

The mention of the paper made McGov- ern sit up. He looked across at the red- head lying fast asleep on the other side of the bed. Her bed, he remembered, some- where in the Village. What was *her* name?

"Dr. McGovern, we're looking at a story that has two researchers at Columbia being killed by the radioactive agent polonium-210, just like the KGB colonel in London. Do you have a comment?"

"It's two-fifteen in the morning," McGov- ern said groggily.

"And I do apologize, but we want to be first and make sure we have the story right."

"But I thought we weren't releasing the cause of death," said McGovern.

"So you can confirm it?"

"That's not what I said."

"It kind of is."

"Look, speak to my colleague, Jack, he did the autopsies. But I recommend it be tomorrow during normal business hours."

"Jack Stapleton, the ME?"

"Yes, him."

"Okay, thanks. And sorry for disturbing you."

The woman ended the call, and Chet lay back in bed. What was that about?

EPILOGUE

GREENWICH, CONNECTICUT
MARCH 26, 2011, 6:05 A.M.

Even though it was Saturday, Russell Lefevre had set his alarm for 5:45. He clamped down on the buzzer, before it woke his wife. Lefevre padded into the bathroom and then downstairs to make coffee and to check on events on the Internet. As the coffee was brewing, Lefevre scanned the online headlines of *The New York Times*, *The Wall Street Journal*, and *The Washington Post*. Russell had always been fastidious about keeping up with the news, but in the past few weeks he'd become obsessed, especially since Edmund had become less and less communicative.

Even though Russell had asked him numerous times, Edmund had never told him what he and Jerry Trotter had talked about at Edmund's house a few weeks before, even though Edmund had looked thoroughly shaken afterward. A week or so later, Jerry Trotter disappeared. When Russell called Max Higgins, Max said Jerry had gone on a fact-finding trip to Asia, and he had no idea when he'd be back. Edmund had nothing to say about that. Then Russell read about Gloria Croft being attacked while out running one morning in Central Park, and Edmund told Russell he had no idea what had happened then, either.

Two days earlier, all the newspapers carried the story about Rothman and Yamamoto, first about their being sick. Then they reported that the pair had died in a tragic accident in the lab. Russell didn't know what to feel or what to think. First Jerry disappeared, then Gloria was attacked, then Rothman and Yamamoto died.

On its own, each of the latter two events was a piece of good fortune, but together, they were surely more than a coincidence. Did Edmund have anything to do with it? Could these events have been what he and Jerry talked about? It seemed impossible to comprehend that Edmund was involved, but Russell couldn't bring himself to confront his partner.

Russell made coffee and looked for the *New York Post*. When he saw the newly updated headline on the home page he nearly choked:

COLUMBIA MEDS IN KGB COPYCAT SLAY?

Under Jemima Meads's byline was an exclusive about Rothman and Yamamoto. Hedged with "allegedly" and "reportedly," the story said that acting on an anonymous tip, the reporter had contacted members of the New York Office of the Chief Medical Examiner who were working on the theory that the exotic radioactive agent polonium-210 was involved in the deaths of the two prominent Columbia University researchers. The find was made by the husband-and-wife team of Drs. Jack Stapleton and Laurie Montgomery, who, having been reached by the reporter at their

Upper West Side town house, refused to confirm or deny the story, referring the reporter to the OCME's public relations department.

The discovery was immediately reported to the FBI, the CIA, Homeland Security, and the NYPD Joint Organized Crime Task Force because of its significant implications and similarities to the 2006 murder in London of a defected Russian FBS agent by the Russian FBS, the current incarnation of the Soviet KGB.

Polonium-210, the article said, is a remarkably poisonous compound millions of times more deadly than cyanide if swallowed or respired. It's also extraordinarily difficult to come by because of its association with triggering nuclear weapons and is thought to be available only in Russia, Pakistan, and North Korea.

At this time it wasn't known if the deaths were connected to a shooting reported outside the Columbia Medical Center that evening.

Russell dashed to the phone and fumbled to call Edmund. He knew he was waking him as the phone rang for the sixth time.

"Russell, what the hell?" His voice was thick with sleep.

"Edmund, go online, look at the *Post*. It says the researchers were murdered, with some nuclear poison. Oh my God, Edmund."

"All right, Russell, calm down. You better get over here." Edmund hung up. Russell wanted to throw up, but he composed himself, went back upstairs, and got dressed.

He started driving toward Edmund's house, his mind racing, trying to make connections, thinking about the coincidences and how they now looked like something so much more. Like murder. As he drove, Russell failed to see that a beat-up old Toyota Corolla had pulled out and was following him through the twisty Greenwich back roads.

Edmund had opened his gates and Russell drove directly into the walled courtyard in front of the waterfront mansion. He leaped from the car and bounded up the front steps and impatiently leaned on the doorbell, whose muffled chords he could just make out coming through the massive door. Where was Edmund? He rang the bell again. The only other sound he could hear was the gentle cacophony of songbirds.

At last, Russell heard a bolt being drawn back on the heavy door, then another sound, of a car coming quickly up the drive. He turned and watched bemused as a tan sedan skidded to a halt inches from his own vehicle and two figures jumped out and ran toward him. They were wearing hoods and holding guns. The door opened and Russell twisted his head back and said one word. "Edmund."

"They sold us out," Edmund said.

Then the men opened fire, both with pistols muffled with silencers. Russell fell forward the way he was facing, across the threshold of Edmund's house. Edmund had no time to process what he was seeing, that there were two men firing weapons at him, that he'd gambled on this venture and this was how he lost. He fell backward, propelled by three bullets in the chest. He fell straight back, only the soles of his most comfortable pair of slippers visible.

The first man walked up the stairs, looked at Edmund, leveled his gun, and shot him once more in the forehead. The second man kicked over Russell's body and did the same to him. The men looked at each other and nodded. They found the spent cartridge cases and picked them up, then walked back to the car, got in, and removed their balaclavas before driving off.

At the wheel, Prek Vllasi navigated the drive out of the gate and turned onto the road. Prek turned to Genti Hajdini and banged once on the steering wheel. Both men smiled.